17478 F1
B2

THE NOVELS OF
SIGRID UNDSET
Winner of the Nobel Prize in Literature for 1928

❧❧

"She writes slowly but incessantly. She lives with her characters until they become a part of herself; that is why they are so vitally real to her readers, in their hours of simple joys and, more often, their days and nights of mental and spiritual conflicts. In her earlier stories she is observer and narrator; in her later novels of medieval Norway, she has formulated a definite plan and theory of life. The general trend is towards tragedy, when a character has violated racial ties and moral laws; the dénouement is as inevitable as in Greek drama, from scenes of remorse and retribution. In her later novels she has found a solution for spiritual distress in the peaceful cloisters and practical, self-sacrificing service of the Church. Her fiction reflects her deep interest in humanity." Reprinted from Annie Marble Russell's *The Nobel Prize Winners in Literature* 1901–1931, through the courtesy of D. Appleton & Co.

❖

An Early Novel
JENNY

Her Great Medieval Romances

KRISTIN LAVRANSDATTER	THE MASTER OF HESTVIKEN
A Trilogy	*A Tetralogy*
THE BRIDAL WREATH	THE AXE
THE MISTRESS OF HUSABY	THE SNAKE PIT
THE CROSS	IN THE WILDERNESS
	THE SON AVENGER

Her Latest Work
THE WILD ORCHID

THE BURNING BUSH

❖

THESE ARE BORZOI BOOKS PUBLISHED BY ALFRED · A · KNOPF

The Burning Bush

UNIVERSITY OF VICTORIA
LIBRARY
Victoria, B. C.

OXFORD PUBLIC
LIBRARY
Victoria

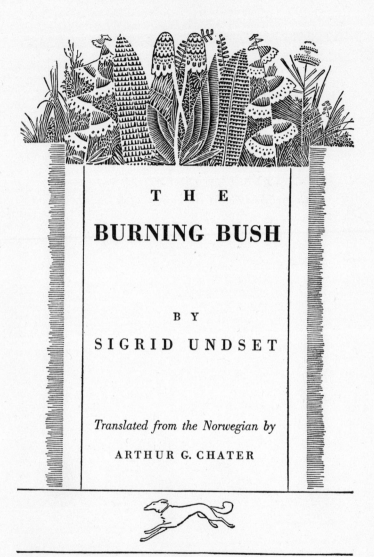

THE
BURNING BUSH

BY

SIGRID UNDSET

Translated from the Norwegian by

ARTHUR G. CHATER

1932
ALFRED · A · KNOPF · NEW YORK

COPYRIGHT 1932 BY ALFRED A. KNOPF, INC.

All rights reserved
No part of this book may be reprinted in any form
without permission in writing from the publisher

FIRST EDITION

Originally published as
DEN BRÆNDENDE BUSK
Copyright 1930 by H. Aschehoug & Co., Oslo

MANUFACTURED IN THE UNITED STATES OF
AMERICA

BOOK ONE

IN THE AUTUMN OF 1916 PAUL SELMER AND HENRIK ALSTER begAN seriously to discuss a rearrangement of their business relations. Both Alster and Jens Mortensen had speculated, the former on a fairly large scale; he had been lucky and was able to add considerably to the firm's capital. Paul Selmer had kept outside speculation. But the result was to disturb the relations between the partners.

They had gone through many strange experiences in these last years.

First a practically complete stagnation in their business until late in the spring of 1915. Then they too began to feel the effects of the high prices in the freight and fish markets. And before long they were caught up in the new movement.

Their direct foreign connections had been with Germany and Sweden; sanitary appliances and the like which were of English origin had been obtained through Norwegian representatives. Then in 1916 their firm was put on the British Black List. Henrik Alster had been in the fishery line in former days, when he was with his uncle in Christiansund, and now he had acted as intermediary in some German purchases of oil and fish.

There was a certain irony of fate in this. Paul had never had much sympathy with German ways. Grossmann's long epistles at the beginning of the war had made him furious—precisely because he had always liked Grossmann personally. There was something so incongruous in the fact that all these tirades about the Will to Power and the saving mission of the German arms

3

among the other utterly rotten peoples emanated from that quiet, rather childish old gentleman; Grossmann impressed one as the kindest and most straightforward of men, with a somewhat naïve enthusiasm for everything he thought beautiful and grand in this country and for all that he imagined to be genuine Norwegian. It was precisely this voluble enthusiasm which was the only thing Paul had had difficulty in swallowing when he had the Grossmanns up here—especially when it came from madame. Whenever "die Mama" said "wunderbar," he replied with "ganz nett"—even if he agreed with her in his heart.

Now he read Grossmann's letters with a different feeling: Junior had fallen as early as October 1914, Kurt in the spring of 1916—he was the one Paul and Henrik had known best; he had twice gone shooting with them during his visit to Norway. Werner was a prisoner of war in Russia; Paul had tried to find out where he was, but without success. And if the war should last another year, no doubt the twins, Egon and "Liebling," would also have to go to the front: two little youngsters with fair curls falling over velvet blouses, so they had been when they were here with their parents. But the father did not complain.

Paul was nevertheless aware that if his feelings towards Germany had changed, it was not merely the result of old Grossmann's letters having given him an inkling of what the Germans had to endure, and of the way in which many of them, at any rate, were bearing the endless sacrifices for that Fatherland of which they had made the whole world sick of hearing. It was not merely the reversal of feeling which was bound to result quite naturally from the gradual encircling of the Central Powers as one State after another joined the side of the Entente. It was due more or less—he could not say how much—to the intrusion of the commercial war upon Norwegian territory, and to its being brought before his eyes every day; both groups of Powers were equally determined to carry it on with all the means at their disposal. And in dealing with Norway the Entente disposed of means which were just as effective as mines and torpedoes—and

4

the public knew a great deal less about the pressure thus exerted. Nor did they have any very clear idea of its implications, from what was said about it in the press and in private conversation.

Paul had been obliged to make a trip to Christiania in connection with this black-listing affair; their firm could not get on without Allied goods more than any other. His mother had then reproached him with being tinged with pro-Germanism. She herself was incapable of seeing that any comparison whatever could be drawn between the Norwegian-British commercial agreements and the U-boat war. It was a matter of course that England should guard against the enemy's deriving any profit from the goods she delivered to Norway; it was a matter of course that the Entente should use the means at its disposal to prevent Germany obtaining pyrites from Norway.—Yes, that was quite natural, Paul admitted.—And the U-boat war against neutral seamen was being carried on with such revolting, cold-blooded brutality that it was unparalleled in history. Yes, to be sure, the U-boat war was revolting and brutal—but whether it was conducted altogether in so cold-blooded a way, Paul didn't know—and "history, mother, is an ugly book, you know."

"And of course you are yourself directly interested in the export of pyrites, aren't you?"

"No, I'm not." He gave a little laugh. "But I can't deny that it's frightfully inconvenient our not being able to get the new machinery for our soapstone works that we had ordered from that firm in Cardiff—"

"Well, there you see!"

"You've made money in shipping shares yourself, mother," Paul reminded her.

"Yes, I have. And I can't see that there's anything reprehensible in that. Our mercantile marine is about our only chance of asserting ourselves a trifle even in these times. The more we can add to it, the better. And it means *everything* to the country that we maintain our imports to the greatest possible extent. Do you think our seamen themselves would hear of our laying up?

On the contrary—they prefer to sail in the ships that ply in the danger zone."

That of course was perfectly true.

"And you yourself—aren't you making money out of the war too?"

That also was perfectly true.

Then he had to go. He was going to the clinic to see his father. Erik Selmer was now a dying man.

It was a metabolic disorder, and the doctors really did not know much about it, Hans said. It was the first case he himself had had an opportunity of following. And in general it had scarcely been observed except in younger people.

"You'll see," said Erik Selmer with a chuckle. "I'm lying here to provide material for your brother's doctor's thesis."

It was late in the evening, and only the little lamp on the bedside table was alight. All the light fell upon the scanty, white hospital bed and on his father's pasty and puffed up face—its decorative frame of well-trimmed silvery hair and beard seemed shattered; the hair had become stiff and bristly in the swollen flesh.

All about the dimly lighted room one had glimpses of flowers; the scent of roses mingled with the indefinable clinic smell of rubber and disinfectants. The darkness and the warmth and the stillness put Paul in mind of soft, thick carpets and curtains which deadened sound and shut out light—such rooms had always framed in his father's life. There had been something stagnant in the very air, wherever he lived. Well, now he lay here, the last place he was to occupy.

He had been a conscientious worker, Paul knew—but his Department and all belonging to it formed a world of which he had never spoken to those nearest to him. For that matter, Paul had never been inside the doors of a Government department until now, when he had been obliged to call there again and again about these war-time arrangements. In his younger days his father had been a keen sportsman, fisherman and climber—but that had been the holiday side of his life. His home could hardly have been more than the place where he lived, as a lamp burns that is turned low. As their home is to most men. If it came to that, how many men *were* there who were fond of their homes—if they were forced to tell the truth?—But thank God, one doesn't have to tell that kind of truth.

"You look as if you didn't like my saying that?" said his father, and there was a touch of banter in his tone.

"Like—"

"Fru Ingstad looks in on me now and then," the sick man went on. "You know, their little boy has suffered from convulsions from infancy and has grown more and more imbecile as he gets older. He's here under observation—of course the doctors can neither say nor do anything. But Fru Ingstad consoles herself with the idea that after the war they will have gained a better understanding of diseases of this kind, since a lot of the children born during the war are of course like that.—So she hopes that science will surely be equal to doing something for her little Goggeman too."

"Yes—" said Paul in a low voice.

"She's a very charming and warm-hearted little person, Fru Ingstad," said his father.

"Yes, she is."

"People *are* like that, Paul—it's no use our thinking it's sad.—Oh, would you mind opening the window a little—"

Paul crossed the room and opened the window. Outside the fog was dense, coloured by the glare from lighted windows and distant street lamps. The little garden in front of the clinic seemed deep and dark as a forest under the groups of trees which dripped moisture and shed their leaves with a subdued rustling sound. The clinic was situated in a quiet, rather secluded part of the town.

"But that's what makes it so hopeless, father. All this talk about this being the last of all wars and the war against war—"

7

"Not a bit. Do you mean, because people will never be any different? Better they won't be, I'm with you there—it won't be for *that* reason that they will abolish war, and I for one don't believe it will make them any better if war is abolished. But they may come to see that they can't afford to express themselves in so expensive a fashion. And of course it's possible that they may actually acquire a sense for more polished forms, even for national hatred. Good heavens, Paul—you yourself have seen, for instance, how your mother and I have learnt to associate in all friendliness, like cultured people. But you don't imagine, do you, that this means I have ever forgiven her?"

Paul turned half round, as he stood at the window. But he said nothing.

"Oh no," his father went on. "War—it's nothing else but an outbreak of a disease which is endemic among us Europeans. But that need not prevent us from hoping that the common sense of humanity may finally succeed in gaining such control over the disease that it may be kept within normal peace-time bounds—in such a way that it will still be a private amusement among individuals to fight for places in the sun and to asseverate one's own ideal aims and the boundless injustice and cruelty of one's opponent. No, for I do hope that at least men will succeed in prolonging the peace intervals if nothing else. Just as you know medical science has succeeded in raising the average duration of life here in Europe. It's proved by statistics, Paul, and it's a sign that the health of the people has improved. Heh, I ought to be the last to doubt it—we saw how it was in your uncle Alarik's case. Everyone knows that the doctors succeeded in prolonging his life by six years, from the date of his first operation till he died. Oh yes—there we can really talk about progress—from the medicine men with their magic bags and sharks' teeth and owls' hearts to serum institutes and operating rooms. Yes, medicine has advanced almost as superbly as has the science of war since the days of flint flakes and hand-stones. So I should really be glad, Paul, if the observations which my son Hans is making here by my death-bed can serve to prolong the lives of some of my fellow-sufferers."

"People are like that too, father," said Paul warmly; "that's another thing they can't be cured of—trying to find out more, when once they have begun to find out something."

His father laughed quietly.

"Must you go?" he asked. "I see you're going out this evening. Are you going to Julie's?"

"No, we're going to the theatre. Björg was so keen on it.— You see," he said apologetically, "she'll soon be obliged to keep pretty quiet. So it's not surprising that she wants to get about as much as she can while she's in town.—I'll come in tomorrow, father, before I leave."

"Are you going to meet your mother tomorrow?"

"No, I'm engaged all the morning. And we're going to dine with Lillian. No, we lunched with mother yesterday, in the Mirror Room—Ruth and Uncle Halfdan were there—he's in town just now, did you know that?"

"Yes, Hans mentioned that he'd come up."

"By the way, Uncle Halfdan said he would come and see you. He spoke of some new injections that he thought you ought to try. Mother seemed to think you ought at any rate to talk to him about it."

"Not if I know it! Oh, by all means, if he'd like to pay me a call, let him do so. But as a doctor I won't have anything to do with him. You know I've never had any confidence in woman doctors."

PAUL had hoped he could have come up to Christiania once more to see his father. But Herr Selmer died in the first week of November, so when he came south again it was to the cremation.

When his little son was born on New Year's Day, Paul would have liked to call him Ole Erik after his two grandfathers. But Björg had taken it into her head that if it was a boy this time, his name was to be Helge. And Paul gave in, knowing that

9

if he did not, he would hear of it for years to come.

PAUL himself thought it strange that he should feel the death of his father as a loss. But he had discovered, when he went to live so far from all his own people, that the bond between relatives and affection between relatives are not quite the same thing. The bond consists of all the other things which force people to accommodate themselves and their interests to those of the others with whom they have to live, to make allowance for their habits, the daily temptation or opportunity of talking in the family circle of all that interests oneself. Affection is like a fluid that fills the home and causes the bonds to feel supple, like something which holds a man together, but not shackled. Even the recollection of moments when one was far too confidential with another person can be transformed by affection into pleasant memories instead of intolerable ones.—

All bonds between him and his father had been severed while he was a boy, but nothing had been able to sweep away the affection between them. He now saw that the feeling of unrest that had tormented him in his adolescence had been due to his missing his father—to his feeling the want of a man to whom he could attach himself by bonds which he found endurable. He had lacked a relation of this sort with one of whom he could be fond, a calmer relation, less liable to tension and to alternations of exuberant affection and sharp irritation—the sort of feeling which a man cannot entertain for any woman, even for his mother or his daughter. The effort of subduing this craving for calm friendship had made him indignant, so long as he believed it was his father who had cheated his sons of the friend they had a right to look for in him. Of course he had pretended to himself that it was on his mother's behalf he was indignant. He now knew perfectly well, after the event, that if he had seen his parents living happily together, it was quite possible he would have felt a kind of jealousy of both of them. His mother would certainly have been capable of occupying her husband entirely. And she

10

would have had less to give her boys of what after all had made their life at Linlökka varied and bright—when she visited all the warmth and agitation of her nature and all her inexorable robustness upon her sons and demanded their admiration in return.

When he had got over the first shock of being told, cynically enough, by his mother that it was she who had seized the first available pretext to escape from a husband who worried her, he had actually been grateful to her for telling him this. If the worst came to the worst, it was easier to forgive a proud and hasty, handsome woman for being brutal to a man she no longer loved —that is, so long as she did not take to herself any stranger and bring him into the children's lives. If it had really been the case, as he had believed in his boyhood, that his father had been capable of failing in his duty towards those to whom he had bound himself—why, that would indeed have been unforgivable, in a man like his father. He had been grateful to his mother for restoring his father to him. They had not chanced to see each other very often, his father and he; he really knew very little *about* his father; but at the same time he was certain he knew all that was of any significance. Oh yes, he had known his father well.

One result of all that he had experienced in his relations with his parents was this: he would always instinctively regard women as slightly less responsible than men, when it was a question of right and justice. No matter how capable and independent they might be in practical affairs, he would always feel that in passing judgment on them they had a claim to extenuating circumstances.

ONE evening shortly after Björg had entered the clinic, when Paul came up to say good-night to Sunlife, he asked her: "Tell me, Sunnie, doesn't mamma hear you say your prayers, before you go to sleep?"

"No!" said Sunnie, intensely interested. "Prayers, what's that?"

"Why—don't you ask God to bless you before you sleep—and thank him for all the good things you have been given in the day?"

"God—that's somebody who lives far up in the sky, isn't it—right up in the air?"

"Yes, but he's here too, he is everywhere. So he's where you are too, always, looking at you and hearing all that you and I say to him. Like the sun, you understand—that too is high up in the sky, and yet it's in our rooms and out in the garden and in the wood-shed and everywhere—"

"The sun's in the tram-car too," said Sunnie in corroboration; "and it's at the hospital, with mamma and Baby."

"Quite right." Paul felt quite proud; his explanation of the elements of religion was going splendidly.

"Oh—then God is the sun." Sunnie too was evidently not a little proud.

"No—it was God who created the sun and the moon and all the stars—the whole world and all the people in it—you and me and mamma and Baby too."

"Did he? Then how does he do it, when he creates us and all the other things?"

"Why, you see, Sunnie—when I'm going to make something—when I make birds for you, for instance, I must have paper to cut them from, and coloured pencils to colour them with. And when mamma is going to make you a frock, she must first get hold of some stuff to make it of. When we men and women have to make anything, we always have to have something that we can make it of. But once, a long, long time ago, there was nothing at all but only God. But he had thought that there should be a world some day—there should be a lot of suns and stars, and this sun we have, and the moon, and the earth we live on, with mountains and the fiord here and trees and animals and people and children. And it was so, because God willed it."

Sunnie sat staring at him, and Paul had a strong suspicion that he had gone out of his depth here.

12

"You see, God is like this, when he wishes a thing, it is so."

"But then he's just like mamma!" said Sunnie triumphantly.

Paul hurriedly took her up in his arms. Her hair was still damp and dark from the bath—her curls had got into ropes. The whole child in her pink flannel night-dress smelt sweet and fresh and clean. She threw her arms round her father's neck and began to rub her nose against his cheek.—This little youngster was the only being in the world that he loved so that life would seem utterly desolate and of no account without her. Well, of course, he had the boy too now. But he was so new, he had not yet penetrated his father's consciousness, as it were—though naturally it was jolly to have a son.—

"Come on, Sunnie, you and I are going to say our prayers."

He took a cushion from the couch, sat her down on it and knelt by the child's side, took her hand and made the sign of the cross with it over her face and breast: "In the name of the Father and of the Son and of the Holy Ghost. Amen."

Sunnie looked up at him. Then she burst into a little rippling laugh:

"Do that again, papa!"

Paul bit his lip so as not to laugh too openly—then he repeated the signing as seriously as he could: "and then you're to say after me: Our Father, which art in heaven—"

Sunnie repeated the words, and now she was quite absorbed in this new game, eager and earnest as she could be:

"buddeliverusfrevil—amen—I say, papa, can God stick his finger on the stove without burning himself?"

Paul ignored the question, lifted Sunnie up and put her back in bed. He had kissed her good-night—when she suddenly crossed herself again: "Papa—why are prayers like that?"

"I'll tell you next time—now you must lie down and go to sleep." And then he fled.

On entering the dark drawing-room he checked himself—he had such a queer feeling, just as if he had come well out of a risky enterprise. He laughed at himself, happy and bashful—

yes, that was exactly how he had been, bashful of talking about God to his own little child. But it was the first time he had admitted to another human being that he really believed.

Paul stood at the veranda door looking out—it was pitch-dark, a darkness full of the flickering and whispering of snow driving against the glass, so that the lights of the town below were scarcely perceptible.

So it was then—in the midst of his own hesitation and uncertainty, in spite of his incessant occupation with the question, do I really believe, or do I only imagine I believe, in the desire that it may be true?—so it was, that not only had he dared to teach his little child to believe, but he had dared do nothing else. Nothing in the world that he could give his children or do for them was worth a scrap, if they were to grow up without knowing God.

The question therefore was not as he had hitherto put it to himself: can you really say, if you are to be entirely honest with yourself: I believe in *one* God, Father, Son and Holy Ghost—the God whom the Christian Church has preached for nearly two thousand years? The question was: dare you take your own child in your arms and say, I do *not* believe?

No. If I could thereby procure for my children all the glories that this world has to give—I dare not look them in the face and deny.

There was another thing, but he only glimpsed it as a fleeting thought—this was the first step he had taken on the road by which he knew he must go—when he confessed to the little mite upstairs, I believe in God. A miserable, uncertain little step, but one which it was impossible to retrace.

"I am the Way, the Truth and the Life." He believed that this was true, and what he himself had called his doubts were—something else.

Oh yes, I believe; Lord, help thou mine unbelief.—By the way, the man in the Gospel who said that was also a father.

14

PAUL had to dine in town next day, so he did not see Sunnie till he came up in the evening to say good-night to her. She started up in bed the moment he opened the door, and climbed out on to the floor:

"Papa—shall we play the same game we did yesterday?"— she had already got hold of the sofa cushion, thrown it on the floor and flopped on her knees upon it: "Come on, let's do it— prayers—"

For an instant Paul was troubled by a reminiscence of his Fossbakke days: children mustn't play at or make fun of religion. But then he checked himself, said nothing, but knelt by the side of the little girl. "Suffer little children to come unto me—" so they must surely be allowed to come and play to begin with.

WHEN the boy was a fortnight old Björg came home from the clinic. She went to bed immediately after dinner, and in the evening, when Paul came back from the office, he found her there. She had evidently been waiting for him and was a good deal upset:

"—but Paul, may I ask what you've been doing with Baby? The child's utterly off her head, she talks of nothing but God— you've been stuffing her up with religion, of course. I can't imagine what makes you do such a thing—putting a lot of ideas into the child's head that she doesn't understand an atom about—"

"It seems to me she understands quite a lot," said Paul meekly.

"And you go and do this behind my back too, while I'm lying away at a clinic having your little baby! I should have thought it was the mother's place to teach her children their prayers and that—I'm sure they ought to learn that in their mother's lap—"

"Well but, Björg, it happened quite of its own accord," he protested tamely. "I asked her if she said her prayers every evening—and as she hadn't learnt any yet, I taught her one—"

15

"Ah, yes! The Lord's Prayer too! I never heard anything like it—a little tot that's not yet four. She doesn't understand a word, as you can well imagine. And I'd been looking forward so much to teaching her 'Now I close my eyes in slumber—' "

"But, dear me, why don't you teach her that then? The more prayers she knows the better."

THE affair ended in a compromise. Sunnie was to perform her evening prayer, sitting up in bed, but she was not allowed to do "that sort of thing"—the sign of the cross. But she could have her Lord's Prayer—she always forgot one or two of the sentences, but Paul thought in his heart that didn't matter—and afterwards she repeated: "Now I close my eyes—." Her father could not understand why *that* should be easier of comprehension. Finally she prayed: "God incline my young heart to true piety. Amen." She had learnt that from Sister Hjördis, who was looking after her little brother, and Sunnie and papa agreed that *that* was a really nice prayer.

She positively collected prayers. One day she had been to a children's party at Uncle Jens and Aunt Else's, and on coming home declared exultantly that she had learnt a new prayer:

> "Some have food and cannot eat,
> Some can eat and have no food—"

"But I say, Sunnie, what nonsense is that you've got hold of?" Paul asked with a laugh.

"Oh, but it *is* a prayer, Uncle Jens says so."

"Don't you know any more prayers, papa?" she asked sometimes. But Paul dared not teach her any more.—

One afternoon she came into his study, as he sat there writing letters. She stopped just inside the door; slowly and solemnly she made the sign of the cross—and then she broke into a little laugh of delight, dashed up to him and climbed on to his knees. After a moment she peeped up at him with an extremely roguish look: "you do that too, papa," she whispered and crossed her-

16

self again.

She evidently regarded it as the symbol of a secret under-standing between them—something like the little conspiracies they had entered into, when her father helped to conceal some of Sunnie's little transgressions from mamma.—But it wouldn't do—for her to get the idea that there was anything in religion which she and her father practised furtively behind her mother's back.

But it had been quite clear to him for a long time that his domestic relations might turn out fairly disagreeable in the future.

Chapter Two

NATURALLY HE WAS AMONG THOSE WHO HAD MADE MONEY out of the war.

Alster and he had always tried to work in Norwegian goods wherever they could be regarded as at all capable of competing. And as time went on and people began seriously to believe in the unbelievable—that the war might last for years yet—they had been forced to interest themselves in one or two industrial enterprises. Imports from abroad were becoming more and more difficult and uncertain. The only question was, whether these war-time industries were laid out in such a way that they would be able to survive when normal conditions were reestablished.

No doubt one could count on a heavy demand for goods from the belligerent countries for a shorter or longer period after the peace. It might also be regarded as probable that as soon as they could set their industrial life going again, they would try to stop the flow of imports from neutral countries. But there ought to be grounds for supposing, not only that Norwegian industry would acquire a larger share of the home market, but that, at any rate in certain branches, a permanent connection might be established with foreign consumers.

In the spring of 1917, therefore, Paul retired from the Trondhjem firm and took over the stone works in the Gudbrandsdal for his own account. Henrik Alster had never taken an active part in its management; it had been Paul Selmer's special concern all along, and at this time in any case it was quite a good business.

One of the first important orders they received was from Hans Selmer; he was building himself a tip-top modern villa on the Holm. Besides building stone and facing stone and stoves and fireplaces the order included a quantity of stone-cutter's work for the garden—which was to have terraces and stone bowls for flowers and a sort of stone lanterns in a sort of Japanese style and God knows what there was not to be: all this was no doubt Evi's taste, and the money came from her. After that they had an even bigger order from Hans's father-in-law, the ship-owner, who was erecting a fairly palatial residence at Sköyen—on a site which was far too small for such a house. Herr Hansen was to have not only gargoyles outside, but even caryatids in-doors in the billiard-room and the music-room. For the execu-tion of the sculpture Paul had got hold of a young sculptor named Jo Braastadlykkjen. Paul had made his acquaintance in Trondhjem, where he was working for a time on the Cathedral: but he came from a little farm near the stone works. He and Paul had taken it into their heads to make some tombstones to-gether. They based them partly on the baroque headstones which one sees in churchyards in the Gudbrandsdal, and partly on the flat mediæval trapeziform gravestones. Of course it could never develop into anything big, but it amused them both to keep on with it.

They were still without electrical power. The parish had a contract with the new generating station in a lateral valley, but they could not get the cables. And the new machinery from Eng-land did not arrive. So for the present Paul had to work in a small way on the old lines. Meanwhile he had the refuse dumps of the old working cleared and experimented with one thing and another—such as the manufacture of French chalk and various articles of applied art. Braastadlykkjen was so talented that it was a pleasure to watch him.

The houses of the old farmstead, which lay below the principal quarry, were converted into offices and a studio for

Braastadlykkjen, and some of the workmen lived there. Paul and Alster had kept a couple of rooms for themselves in the pensioner's building, but it was far too small and primitive for him to live there with his family. So when Björg consented to accompany him to Gudbrandsdal in the summer, they had to quarter themselves on a farm some distance away, where they took in lodgers.

It was just as if there were no war.

As early as eight in the morning, when Paul walked up the old road through the forest, the day was sunny and warm, full summer.

At the gate of the big field he would generally stop for a while, light his pipe and look at the view. The valley was already brimfull of heat-haze, although a chilly breath came from the wooded slopes after the night. To the northward the mountains met, dark with forest, with little light green patches of pasture around a solitary croft; farther off rose the bare crags with grey mossy ledges, still flecked here and there with snow, and beyond them again there was a bright gleam of glaciers. Towards the south the valley spread out, and along the slopes on the sunny side lay a row of big farms; above them the green forest extended to the grey screes of the mountainside, and below the farms were dark pine-woods, but at the bottom of the valley broad water-meadows followed the line of the river. In the boggy tracts, where it ran quietly in great curves, the water shone with a brownish reflection, but where it formed little rapids the river was dark green streaked with white.

Along the light ribbon of the main road lay the small holdings. A motor-car was crawling along there, raising a little cloud of dust.—There were a good many cars to be seen now. And motoring was marvellously good fun, no doubt about that. It looked now as if gasolene would be harder to get—Henrik talked of selling his car and buying an electric coupé. Well, in ways like that one did feel the war—even in this country.

Paul struck across the field by the path leading to the three new little quarries. The houses shone with their bright new timber. It was jolly to see what good carpenter's work they could still do in this part. Most of the new buildings on the big farms were horrid—but they would have it so.

Hans Skaare's old mother stood outside her door washing clothes. Paul stopped and chatted with her a moment. He liked both her and her son—they reminded him of his father-in-law, a good deal.

Hans Skaare, the engineer, had come into the office one day to show Paul some photograph frames which he had been carving out in his spare time—terrible things in the shape of letters. There was a big B which he thought Paul must be able to use, for the portrait of his lady. Paul had suggested his making some larger objects—ordered some bookshelves and a hanging cupboard for his rooms in the pensioner's house.

He was well aware that it had its comic side, but here he was carrying on missionary work for things like arts and crafts and cottage industry. For it was not at all certain that one could succeed in infusing new life into such things in the country-side. Even though it was surely nonsense to say that mechanical civilization must necessarily fill the world with nothing but ugly things, at any rate for a long time to come. People could not be forced to turn out nothing but ugly things, just because they had easier processes of manufacture. More probably it was a kind of cheapjack humour that was abroad— the world was like a fair, with every booth shouting its wares, and the buyers jostled one another, dazed at hearing they could get such a lot of frippery for so little money. The fun consisted in buying it, not in owning it; nor was it worth owning for the most part, it might just as well get smashed, and then one could buy something new.

Perhaps it was the feeling that this is a period of transition which made people yield so cheerfully to all such publicity-fostered needs—they had an idea that this is the last day of the

21

fair. Perhaps it was the war itself which gave them a suspicion that the great business of Progress had hitherto only been occupied with dumping, and now the exploitation of poor, confiding modern man was about to begin in deadly earnest—if it is true that civilization has run over itself with its own motor-car, and we are like the beggar Ruth described, sitting at the gates of the Vatican. He had lost both legs, but was said to be a rich man who owned a villa, and an automobile, and kept servants. In that case our whole culture is like that maimed man's villa—there we sit looking down from our cripple's point of view upon the naked, shapely savages who hunt and dance and fashion their slender spears and their three or four earthen pots as handsomely as they can and who sow and reap and live and die in a succession of rites and festivals.—

Haugen, the little mountain farm, was powdered all over with grey stone-dust. Even Berte's calf, standing on the flagstone outside the old storehouse, had powder on its coat. A short line of rails crossed the meadow below the cattle-sheds. Blocks of light stone stood stacked up in the porch of the old main building where the workshop was.

Paul took a turn round the place. On the level behind the outhouses the new sheds extended in the direction of the old red engine-house below a little waterfall on the hillside.

Knut Moen and a boy were engaged in packing the stoves for Frikstad hotel. Some of the slabs were uncommonly handsome, scaled with magnesian spar and very rich in chloride, so that the stone had a fine greenish tone. It came from a little ledge below the main seam, which was of purer stone, more valuable for that reason, but not so showy.

Saws and polishing machines shrieked and hummed; a chipping and hammering and banging went all over the works. Now and again there was the tinkling of a horse-bell from the wood above, where the cable-way was stretched over the tree-tops up towards the white mass of refuse dumps round the quarry.

The light blocks of stone and the white dust were dazzling

in the sunshine. The office was bathed in sunshine, when Paul came down again. He hung up his jacket, sat down in his shirt-sleeves and set to work opening the letters. Vinsvold, the cashier, came to the door—would Selmer ring up the station-master at once? Deuce take it! of course the man would say he couldn't provide freight-cars before Friday—

Paul only wished he could have moved up here for good. But poor Björg would be bored to death; and then she said that all the noise and blasting would make her so nervous. He himself had made up his mind to go into this concern up to his neck and get out of all other businesses in which he had a part-interest: it would be amusing to see what he could make of this!

He was well aware that what had interested him in the Trondhjem business was that it was new. It was fun to take part in working up a thing from a comparatively small beginning. But when the work became routine, and still more, when there were too many people in it, it ceased to be so amusing. Here they had not even a lady clerk, he himself and Vinsvold did all the office work between them. Henrik got all the excitement he required through his speculations, and Jens Mortensen had no use for excitement, rather the other way. Paul himself could hardly be called a *born* business man. When he had seen a thing succeed, he had a fancy to try something else—to see if *that* would go.—Meanwhile he must not forget that he had a wife and children for whom he was responsible. Paul sighed at the thought.

He dined up at the farm with Vinsvold and Braastadlykkjen; the tenant's wife cooked for them. After dinner he went into his own room for an hour's rest and reading. Here at any rate he could be left in peace with such books as Björg looked on with disfavour, if he left them lying about at home. French books she specially disliked. If it was nothing more than the *Voyage autour de ma chambre*, she was sure it was "some of that Catholic stuff."

When he went down to their lodgings in the evening, Björg would generally come to meet him on the heath. As a rule

Sunnie was with her—there was no sense in putting the child to bed so early these summer evenings.

Paul was in good humour after a whole day up at the works, and in a kind of surplus of well-being he was once more rather in love with his wife. Down here on the heath the scent of the firs was so good and strong towards evening; the sinking sun gilded and reddened the stems and made the pine-needles glow with a golden green. Just below them the river roared as it foamed over the rocks in the gully. Björg walked bareheaded, in a light summer dress—she had got a little podgy since her last confinement, but more radiantly pink and white than ever under her golden hair. Sunnie's resemblance to her mother was quite astonishing—no doubt that was what had made Paul gradually drop the habit of criticizing Björg: she was not particularly intelligent, there was not a trace of refinement about her blond and exuberant youthfulness. But bless her, he was well pleased with his wife, taking her as she was—and she was a sweet little mother to the two youngsters she had borne him.

So he gave her a rapid kiss on her fresh lips and fastened some flowers he had found in the thin dress over her warm, round bosom.

"Oh, what a lovely scent they have," she said, or something of the sort—of the little bunch of pyrola or linnæa. He knew Björg didn't care very much for flowers—except as things one could smarten up a room with. But he himself could not help picking some, when he saw a cluster of fine, full-blown flowers of one kind or another. And Sunnie wanted to know the names of the flowers; she stood still and looked at them:

"Why are they called linnæa, papa?"

Paul took it for granted that Sunnie would hardly think it fun to be told about Linnæus. So he invented something: "Because there was once a little girl named Lina, and she had a pink and white frock just like that."

"Was she as sweet as I am?" asked Sunnie.

"Oh, much sweeter," and he laughed at her little air of displeasure. "Nobody says you're sweet, do they?"

"You—" The child thrust out her underlip.

"I? That's only something I said in play." He took her hand. "You know very well I don't think you're sweet. It's Little Brother who's sweet—"

"Ugh, Paul, you ought not to say such things to the child. One ought never to say anything to little children if one doesn't mean it; it unsettles them and breaks down their confidence in their parents," said Björg. Now and again she took to studying some book or other on the bringing-up of children, and then she put it in practice for a time. But fortunately, it was never a long time.

"Just so—only why should the child have confidence in me? I'm not the sort of person to have confidence in—" he laughed.

"Oh, how you talk!" She hung on to him in childish fondness. "A nasty papa we have, haven't we, Sunnie?"

Paul listened with half an ear while Björg related what the other guests "at the pension" had said and done and thought. Colonel Dahldorff had driven up today in his car to visit his wife and daughters—he brought a friend with him. Björg wondered if there wasn't something between this friend and their daughter Ingrid, and the colonel's wife was so keen on bringing off the match, she had seen that all right.—Phew, then I suppose I'll have to sit there the whole evening playing bridge with that terrible blitherer, thought Paul.

When they entered the courtyard the nurse came to fetch Sunnie, who protested with all her force against being carried off and put to bed. Björg gave a demonstration of calm decision, till she was red as fire, poor little thing—the whole of the colonel's family were sitting in the veranda, and there were ladies singly or in groups on all the little balconies which stuck out promiscuously like opened drawers all over the walls of the hotel. This huge lumbering pale-green house, with its zinc tower and chaotic gables and projections and its meaningless red and

25

blue paint on the verandas, had taken the place of the fine old
main building which Paul remembered, as he had once passed
the night here in his student days. He had made one or two
sketches of it at that time.—And what made this new monster
look doubly idiotic was that the buildings round the grass-
grown yard, with its trodden paths between the houses, were
really old. There were two handsome storehouses and a stable
which faced the yard with a bold gable of choice timber. The
Selmers had been given a room in what had been the pensioner's house—a fine building of the early nineteenth century,
without balconies and with a steep slated roof. The two entrance doors were uncommonly elegant in their lines.

Björg's little display of maternal dignity ended in a smack,
and Sunnie set up a loud squall—was ready to fly at her mother.

"There, there, my girl!" Paul stepped in. "We don't care
to have you here any more now. Off with you to bed—no, be
good and go with Margit." Sunnie stole off behind her nurse,
much subdued.

"Papa, you'll come up and hear me say my prayers, won't
you?" she cried from the steps, looking very pathetic.

"Ugh, yes, it's you who spoil her so terribly.—Yes, my
husband does spoil her so terribly," said Björg to the ladies
on the balconies—she blushed and looked foolish and was obviously angry, and Paul put his arm round her shoulders and
laughed:

"Come in then and keep me company while I have something to eat. There's a dear!" Clasping each other lightly they
walked towards the main building, for Paul knew it was Björg's
pride that their marriage was such a happy one that all the
other visitors in the hotel talked about it. He granted her that
pleasure with all his heart.—For they actually were happily
married—and at the bottom of his mind Paul knew that the
happiness *he* had found in his life with her was not exactly up-
lifting.

In the empty dining-room there were still a few flies awake

26

and buzzing. The long table was already set out for next morning's breakfast. The room was now cool and the air seemed exhausted with the stale smell of food. Against one wall stood a magnificent old press and by the other a sideboard painted like oak which was overloaded with objects in nickel and copper; round about it were hung framed views of the Jubilee Exhibition at Frogner and plates bearing portraits of the King and Queen.

The pretty, sandy-haired maid in country costume came in and handed him fricassee. Björg's face puckered in a terribly sly little smile:

"Tell me, Anne—what's become of Guttorm's old goat that was always about—it's not been seen for some days?"

"Us've sent him to the sæter, you see," said Anne, with the ghost of a smile on the corners of her mouth.

Björg nodded mysteriously as the girl went out:

"Sunk without trace! And tomorrow we shall have roast mutton, I'll bet you what you like!"

"It tastes all right anyhow," said Paul as he ate.

"And then I can't see the sense of our never getting anything but plum-porridge and canned fruit and puddings that taste like scouring powder—when the hills are positively red with strawberries everywhere. Such masses of them!"

"But you had strawberries yesterday, didn't you say?"

"Yes, but they could so very well get us strawberries every day of the week—"

Margit, the nurse, came and announced that Sunnie was in bed.

"Very well, I'm coming."

HE stood outside on the steps and finished his cigarette before going up to the children. From under the eaves came the sweet sound of subdued gurgling from swallows' nests full of young. The sun had long ago disappeared behind the mountain, coolness and darkness issued forth from the steep, black wooded slope north of the house. Over the tree-tops the sky was white, but higher up it darkened into the blue of the boundless depths of space. In the clear, pale light the river twinkled brightly and the roads shone white and the lean, dry slopes were dimly grey. But hidden in the lush grass of the meadows and in the grey-green cornfields and gathering in every copse lay the darkness, ready to well out—only the fleeting semi-darkness of a summer night at present, but it would grow denser and darker with every evening it came pouring out of its hiding-places.

When he went upstairs Sunnie was already asleep. In the basket cot by the side of Björg's bed the boy slept—he was a mighty sleeper, that fellow.

It was a big room with windows on three sides and unpainted timber walls which reflected the evening light. The air was very close. Paul opened another window. A little draught couldn't possibly do the children any harm. He must remember to run up and shut one side before Björg came up to bed.

Paul stood for a moment at the open window. A few little clouds had drifted across, high up—glittering and golden in the afterglow.

There came Björg running across the yard. No luck; he guessed what it meant, and he ran down to meet her. Quite right; it was an invitation from the colonel. And it included a whisky and soda.

"I'm sorry, dear"—Paul kissed her rather irrelevantly— "I must go and see the station-master. No, I'm sorry, I'm obliged to go, it's something I must see about myself. Yes, I'll look in when I come back—"

THE white road stretched before him in the twilight; the dust smelt so good, as it were innocent, and was so silent to walk on. Huge old birches hung their branches over the road, darkening it and shedding a bitter, cool scent; a little breath of wind rustled them feebly. Farther off, where the wood closed in, were bright spots of women's summer dresses—some of the people

28

from the pension were out taking an evening stroll. Paul jumped the stone fence and crossed a meadow where the grass had been cut—the hay lay in fragrant swaths which slipped under his feet as he ran down the field. It ended in a marsh, with bright pools of water and dark clumps of osiers. Then he came out on to the road which followed the stream from Gröndalen; the river ran rapidly here over a bed of large, flat rocks, and divided into many little arms among the pale banks of gravel. The lights of the station glowed red against the woolly darkness of the mountain.

The station-master was still up; he came out in his shirt-sleeves and Paul confirmed the arrangement he had made with him on the telephone that morning. To satisfy his conscience he even went across to the siding, pottering about among half-loaded trucks and chatting with the station-master about the shooting prospects.

Over on the other side of the valley stood the hotel, a pale grey patch in the summer night. All the windows of the drawing-room were lighted up.—Paul had no inclination to play cards, nor to drink whiskies with the colonel and listen to the man's elucidations of how the operations on the various fronts would develop.—

He struck into the side road which led the other way, towards Gröndalen. Here under its high rocky banks the river was like black glass; it only gurgled and crooned faintly under the peat. After a while the road passed between the houses of an old farm. All was closed and still, with a pale reflection of the night sky in the upper windows. But a warm smell breathed from byre and stable, and behind a manure heap a pig was rooting.

In the little overgrown garden by the corner of the house the dark grass stood high under the great wild cherry-trees— for an instant he felt with all his senses what it would be like to be standing there now. To start at the snapping of a twig under one's foot, to go quietly forward to meet someone who was waiting in the blackest shadow of the trees. Tall and slender and dark-haired she ought to be, and dressed in some thin, washed-out blue cotton gown which bore a gentle, human scent of her working day and clung, a little damp with the evening air, about her warm and healthy body—

Begone, tempter.—He laughed quietly at himself. For a smart and energetic business man with a wife and two children it is bad taste to embark on summer adventures of that sort, and ridiculous to dream about them. For heaven's sake then let such trysts be the privilege of the young who have something to stake on the game: "the heart too has its virginity which can only be lost once"—something like that Ewald said in his *Life and Opinions*. He remembered the passage, because he had read it at *that* time—. No, at any rate on a night like tonight everything of that sort ought to be forbidden except to those who still had their heart's virginity to gamble with. "Pledge one's troth—" a pretty phrase; it entirely covered the notion of something venturesome.

Oh no, my boy, you're not yet such an old fogy that you can be allowed to grow sentimental by the fence of an old farmhouse garden.

But the night *was* so beautiful that there was—there was no sense in anything. That light from the dark sky—so that every tone that detached itself from the darkness down here on earth was merely the light of heaven absorbed by the ground. Even the grey tinsel of the moths that hovered and flickered their wings over the heather by the roadside.

The corncrake was chirping somewhere in the field. And from within the fir copse came a dull thudding and the rattle of gravel scattered by a horse's shoes. The horse came out of the wood on to the road and stood for a moment, a heavy, dark mass, before it jogged off again and was lost among the trees.

It was impossible to imagine—that there was war going on in the world tonight. But equally unthinkable were all the indications of war one saw at home—the feverish hunt for all this money which was floating about and seemed only to be there in make-believe, till grown-up men became like children playing at keeping shop with bits of paper. And it would be—yes, by God, it would be still worse if it really was profit, solid, actual profit, this money we made out of other people's fight for their lives.

But that's exactly what I'm trying to do—to build up something lasting and real out of the chance that has come my way, because other people want to build themselves castles and villas and business palaces. So after all I suppose I'm no better than the others who spend their time speculating and buying and selling everything between heaven and earth on paper. I help five or six men to set up their own houses, I provide work for fifteen hands, where formerly four men quarried stone, two by two.—And here I am, regretting the old days, when folks worked in a small way and were their own masters, and what they turned out was fine, handsome work, done by men who brought to the materials they worked in a whole world of knowledge.

But a man must do something, whatever the times may be like. And one can't, for instance, go and buy a picturesque old farmstead in a beautiful spot in Norway—and give one more demonstration at the cost of oneself and one's family that a farmer's calling in Norway is not a thing one can take up like amateur theatricals. It is no more than justice if this country gives such a man a rough lesson—it has not suffered itself to be brought under cultivation in play by people who did not know their trade.

O God, it's so beautiful here that we can never realize to the full how beautiful it is. *Nobody* knows it. Nobody knows what it actually means for a man to be a part of his nation and his country. Those who are in the war have never been able to know and feel it, except in flashes—we only guess at it in flashes, once in a way, and in time of profound peace. In the ordinary way we toil on each at his own job, never realizing that we are like flying specks of dust, ground from the same huge block of stone.—

31

Oh, it's unbearable— A night like this, and the honest old road under one's feet, with its stones and holes and deep-worn ruts and grass sprouting here and there and the light shoots of golden rod on the sloping side.—

As though there were nothing real and true and changeless except that happiness is there waiting for us. But human beings cannot wake up and see it; they lie on with closed eyes spinning their dreams—nightmares of horrors, ridiculous dream-triumphs, improper dream-farces—and imagine there is sound sense in the most idiotic tissue of their visions, just as we do when we lie dozing, half-asleep. That feeling one sometimes has at the moment of waking, when one remembers the fancies one has conjured up—may that not be a kind of foreshadowing of the moment after death, when the soul awakens and sees what rubbish one's life has been—?

And all the time the real reality has been at our side, glorious and terrible. All men have known and believed this in all times, clearly or vaguely—excepting us post-Christian heathens. Is it because our incredulity is something we have chosen deliberately—rejecting the reality, the Word which commanded that all the things we see should have being, when the Word was made flesh to dwell among men? To scare away reality, to bury ourselves well down in our dreams, to kill him who tries to wake us, no doubt we are all tempted to do this. Is this what is meant by all that is said in the gospel about our being the children of darkness, abhorring the light?

O God—to think that one must not only pray God to preserve one's children from misfortune, from all the terrible things one does not know; but just as much that they may be saved from the happiness one does know.

ALL the ladies in the pension complained bitterly that they had never once been given cream porridge since Midsummer Eve. So Paul once more showed himself an angel; he promised the ladies cream porridge if they would make a trip up to the Hauga sæter; the tenant's wife should make it for them herself.

In return for this Björg displayed a sympathetic understanding and declared that Paul should be let off taking part
in the expedition, one man among six women. So he was left in
peace at the pension on the Sunday when the cream porridge trip
came off.

After breakfast he put a book in his pocket, took Sunnie
with him and went on to the heath.

As he walked her father looked down at the little round
head; the sun was baking the fair, silky hair, and the neck was
so pathetically tender, nut-brown but growing whiter where
it was lost in the frills of white lace on her frock; "But oughtn't
you to have put on a hat, Sunnie?"

"Oo, no, the string cuts my neck so—"

She was laboriously wheeling a doll's perambulator and
gave a little angry scream every time a stone or a root nearly
took it out of her hands.

They crossed a little field of short, sun-burnt grass that
gave off a spicy smell in the heat. Eyebright grew here as thick
as a carpet, and the little plants were quite russet, but the flowers
were violet in the full heat of the sun.

The roar of the river from the ravine grew louder and
louder as they went along. The fir-trees around the little meadow
stood far apart, their needles already scorched to a yellowish
green—it was so dry here on the rocks by the stream. The
ground underneath them was covered with light grey lichen in-
terspersed with tufts of heather.

Paul flung himself on the grass by the stone fence and tried
to read. But the trees exhaled so warm a scent, the sky was so
infinitely blue and deep—and his little white-frocked girl
stirred continually in the outskirts of the father's consciousness.
Paul let his book drop and took to watching all the minute life
that swarmed in the grass around him. A little farther off were
some plants of wild strawberry; the straight, slight stalks bore
so gracefully their little round berries, red or bright green, with

33

a last snow-white flower at the tip. He would show them to Sunnie and let her pick them herself.

Sunnie had taken her doll out of the perambulator and pulled down its drawers; she was prodding it behind with a stick. Paul grew attentive, frowning involuntarily: how is it that all children are so fond of doing things that they know are not nice?

Sunnie held the stick up to the light:

"Ah yes! You see, it's just what I said!" Paul couldn't help smiling: the querulous little tone mimicked another voice with such comical accuracy: "So now you've got a temperature again—ugh, what a terrible temperature you've got! You must open your mouth when I tell you, so I can see if you've got a temperature in your throat too—" she shoved the stick against the doll's china teeth.

Then she discovered that her father was looking at her:

"Papa—oh, can't you come here and be doctor, Julie's so terribly ill—she's got her tonsils full of temperature—"

Paul got up lazily and strolled over. With furious zest Sunnie pulled down the doll's linen, and Paul knocked at its back and chest with his finger till the sawdust dribbled out of the seams. Stiff with seriousness Sunnie handed him the stick.

"Thank you, I don't think we need take her temperature again. She has got a chill, and she has a touch of pneumonia and scarlet fever and rheumatic fever with it—but I don't think it's anything serious. You must keep her in bed for a couple of days and be careful of her diet—no sweets on any account!—You want a prescription, do you say?—all right"—he took a scrap of paper out of his pocket-book and scribbled on it: "You can give her half of one of these powders three times a day. But the main thing is that you must make her lie quietly in bed and do all she's told"—he glanced at Sunnie to see if this would go home and damp her spirits. But Sunnie stared up at him with round eyes, swallowing every word he said.

"And now you must pretend to be the druggist—"

Paul acted druggist; with profound gravity he served her with sand in a little flat packet and gave change for two crowns fifty in sorrel-leaves.

He lay with his hat over his eyes listening as he dozed to Sunnie scolding her doll for not lying still in her perambulator.

Once more he was overwhelmed with the beauty of the day. He remembered that when he was quite young he had thought the world must always have been beautiful, throughout all its cataclysms and upheavals it must have had a wild beauty and been full of charming little things and overpowering sights in air and sea and mountain. He had examined the fossils in a piece of limestone and felt an impossible desire to be contemporary with the life of these creatures—a word like "tundra" filled him with migratory longings. It was terrible that men should always have had before their eyes the earth's evidence of beauty, power, the perfection of all living organisms— and of destruction; and men only imitated this last, destroying wherever they went, and destroying one another. It is not surprising if millions of them have arrived at the belief that the very beauty of the world is a deceit and a delusion which must be broken down. Manichæism oozes out of life itself as a kind of black subterranean fluid.

It *is* a reasonable explanation. The other reasonable explanation is that which calls us the exiled children of Eve. And who could tell whether in his heart he had not been assured that the latter explanation was the right one? Ever since a certain day of blue skies and summer like this—a long time ago. True enough, he had been able to laugh at himself for it afterwards: the greenest of green students who took it prodigiously seriously when his lady-love was so silly and prudish that she was ashamed to bathe with him. But every time he had chanced to call it to mind—the cliff that rose steeply from the brown waters of the forest lake, the sun-drenched woods and the glistening osier-boughs that waited for his milk-white mistress to emerge from her leafy hiding-place—he had always thought that at that

35

moment the conviction had come to him that their race was descended from an estate called Paradise. But they had had to leave the manor, and he was to learn that it was vain for a boy to attempt to recover the fee-simple.

Ah well—how might *she* be getting on now? He had seen a glimpse of her last winter, in the Mirror Room at the Grand, a mass of ermine and diamonds. Her husband had made a pile at the beginning of the war, someone had told him. Funny that she should end as a profiteer's wife. Dear, dear, he remembered that ring he had bought her with a little chip of a diamond in it. She had sent it back with his letters. He had given it to Tua's eldest little girl for a Christmas present one year.—

Sunnie came and crammed a dirty, sweaty little hand over his mouth, daubing his lips with strawberries: "Those are for you. I'm fond of you, papa—"

"Thank you, my dear, that was nice of you—"

She plumped herself down on his chest. "No, leave me alone, child—now I shall have to change my shirt before dinner.—Oh, what a pig you are"—but he put his arm round her and held her fast.

Anything so perfect as a little childish frame like this. The dear round little knees—but the brown calf above the sock was rough and covered with scabs, where she had scratched her midge-bites.

WHEN they came back to the house at dinner-time Paul discovered that the mail-cart with Helge in it was standing against the wall, right in the blazing sun. The poor little boy was hanging half out, asleep, with a soaking linen hat across his face.

Paul picked up the child—he was dripping wet and started crying bitterly on waking. The nurse came tearing out of the shady garden round the corner; she had been helping Kari pick currants, was her excuse: "Fancy now, the sun's come right round this way; it was in the shadow when I put him there—"

However, the boy seemed none the worse—amazing what

a little thing like that can stand. "But now you'll have to take him upstairs and change his things, Margit, and will you please give Sunnie a clean frock."

Margit trailed up the steps with the children, scolding at Sunnie for having got green stains on her best frock: "Won't you catch it when your ma sees you!"

So Paul had to wait outside while his offspring completed their toilet—and here came the colonel puffing along, heavy and perspiring, with his wife in tow:

"Hullo—been out for a walk with the young lady, what?"

"Well, I *must* say it's quite touching," his wife chimed in; "the way you sacrifice yourself to that child.—Oh, but she *is* such a good little thing—"

Phew!

AT last Margit had got Sunnie to bed and Paul had performed the whole evening ritual with her, said prayers and given her a glass of water and been unable to guess what it is that is as round as an egg and as smooth as a church-wall, or what is neither in nor out and cold as a dog's snout.

And again it was a summer evening, dusky and cool, with a white gleam from the sky and a loud roar from the river in the stillness. Paul stood by the wall of the old house, smoking and chatting with the ladies who had arrived that afternoon, after a prodigious mountaineering tour in the Jotunheim. All of a sudden Sunnie called from the window just above his head:

"Papa—do come up—I've got something to talk to you about!"

"No, no, Sunnie, get back to bed at once."

"Oh but, papa, I *must* talk to you. It's about the Holy Ghost."

The three ladies showed surprise, and Paul was annoyed and felt rather foolish. The Holy Ghost continued to be one of Sunnie's favourite topics of conversation, even after Paul with great difficulty had induced her to withdraw her assertion that

37

the Holy Ghost had eaten peas from her hand one day in the Cathedral Close. With great reluctance she had finally accepted the view that perhaps it was only an ordinary dove, but it was *like* the Holy Ghost—perfectly white and awfully pretty—

Soon after she was back at the window:

"Papa! It's so hot in my bed. Mayn't I get into yours?"

"Yes, yes, do." It was true, the room upstairs was stifling hot.

After a while the little white figure appeared again at the window:

"Papa—Baby's so queer—he's been screaming so horribly again—"

"Rubbish. I haven't heard a sound from Baby."

"Oh yes, papa. Just now—a great big ugly cat came in at the other window and we were so frightened. I'm so afraid he's bitten Baby, because he jumped up into his cot—"

Paul dashed up to the bedroom. The little boy lay sleeping like an angel, sucking in air from his empty bottle. Paul took it away—and Sunnie, who was standing at the foot of his bed, forestalled him before he had time to say anything:

"Papa—why is it so frightfully hot up here?"

"Because the sun's been baking the walls all day long.— But what put it into your head to tell such stories?"

"Oh, but it was true, papa, there *was* a cat in here. It was one of Pisi's kittens too, that they couldn't get hold of, because she's hidden them in the heap of stones down in the field— don't you remember, we saw them there the day we went to the village shop and I got my coat in such a mess with flour?"

Paul stood for a moment looking at his little son. There was nothing in the world the matter with the boy, thank God.

"There, Sunnie, now your bed's got nice and cool. Crawl back into it now—"

"Don't go, papa!" She made a grab at him, as he was trying to put his down bed straight—of course she had tossed sheets and blankets anyhow. "Papa, I'm so afraid that cat'll come back—"

"No, look here, Sunnie, you know it's not true, that about the cat."

She looked up at her father in boundless astonishment:

"*Isn't* it true, papa?" Then she lay down with a little sigh and closed her eyes.

But scarcely was he out in the yard again when he had her back at the window. She called out—and this time she had a reason to which he was bound to yield. So he rushed up again.

"You ought to be ashamed of yourself—a big girl like you —can't you really manage that for yourself yet?"

"Oh yes," said Sunnie composedly. "I've managed it already. I only wanted to tell you.—Besides"— she saw that her father was getting angry—"I must go *outside* too—"

Paul put some clothes on her. And then he had to walk with her right across the yard, past the ladies who were smiling with amused sympathy, over to the little house behind the cattle-shed.

So now that was done. And he took her back to the bedroom and helped her to get out of her clothes.

"No, you oughtn't to have unbuttoned all the buttons!" She shrieked with rage, pulled on her vest again; "I can quite well unbutton the bottom button myself—you ought only to have unbuttoned the top ones," she howled, struggling to button up the garment again at the back.

Paul tore it off her rather roughly, picked her up and plumped her into bed; he assured her harshly that "now we're not to have any more bother with you tonight, do you hear? I'm angry with you now."

As soon as he was outside again, Sunnie peeped out of the window:

"Beg pardon, papa—can't you come up so I can say beg pardon properly—"

"No, thanks, that'll do. Good-night to you—"

"Perhaps she *is* rather a difficult child, your little girl?"

39

the ladies said smiling, as they walked up and down enjoying the fine evening. "A little spoilt by her papa maybe?"

"I *won't* even beg pardon then," howled Sunnie from the window. "If you're so horrid you won't come up to me—"

Paul ignored her completely. She continued to show herself at the window, expressing her sense of injury at her father's refusing to take notice of her. Till screams from the infant within the room were mingled with Sunnie's howls.

Paul ran in and upstairs.

"There, there. Now you're to be quiet—do you understand?" She was smacked and put back to bed with emphasis. —Paul turned the baby over on his other side—the little chap curled up and went to sleep at once.

And no sooner was Paul down in the yard again, standing against the wall to light his pipe, when Sunnie put her head out of the window just above him—pt, pt, she spat and cried triumphantly:

"I can spit down at you, papa, but you can't spit up at me!"

He gave up and ran, so that the youngster shouldn't see that he was laughing.

"WELL, but I've never known anybody so foolish as you," said Björg with a laugh, next day. The other ladies had given a description of Sunnie's evening performance. "What can you expect—when you're so silly as to stand sentry just under the window—"

40

Chapter Three

THE NEW PLANT FOR THE QUARRY ARRIVED BIT BY BIT IN the course of the autumn. Then there was some timber to be felled in the Hauga forest during the winter months. Paul Selmer had several reasons for spending a good deal of time at Haugen that winter.

He had left the Trondhjem firm as long ago as May, but then he and Alster had been obliged to take over some brickworks down in Romerike, and Paul agreed to Alster's proposal that he should undertake the management of the concern, at any rate for the present. He was not an expert—but where the devil did one find anything managed by experts nowadays? That is to say, in private businesses it might still be the case, but the custom was evidently on the decrease.

Anyhow, it was feasible to live there with his family, though it still meant living in the country and Björg was only moderately enthusiastic about it, in spite of Paul's assurance that with the car it was only a short run in to Christiania. But she could quite well stay at Trondhjem through the winter—the house at Berven required pretty thorough repairs. Paul had sold the villa at Trondhjem on fairly favourable terms; they were to be out of it by October. But by a lucky chance a man they knew, a mining engineer, had to go over to America for six months and wanted to take his wife with him—it was another man's wife whom he had lately married, and the former husband was making things unpleasant for them. Paul had an offer to take their flat furnished and accepted it.

41

As a matter of fact he had no objection to letting his family
stay in the North till the spring. He would be on the move for
some time to come. Strangely enough—during his first years
at Trondhjem a journey to Christiania was still reckoned as
something. Now it seemed nothing worth talking about—
though of course it was not *every* month he could pay a visit
to his home. He travelled between the quarry, the brick-works
and Christiania. It had become a matter of course—when it
was a question of a big order the customer rang up and wanted
a conference. Business men rushed all over the country by car
or by rail. And in a way Paul liked having it so. All this unrest in commercial life, where all old limitations were being shattered and one was constantly compelled to readjust one's ideas
of figures—the ceaseless innovations about which it was as
yet impossible to say whether they really contained the germ of
something lasting, or whether they merely meant the breaking-up
of old forms—naturally he could not help being influenced
by the spirit of the times. Even if he tried to listen to reason and
not let himself be infected by this fascination for the huge sums
with which people had to deal. It was a fact that old, experienced men who for years had borne the responsibility of large
undertakings were now made giddy by the new scale of figures
to which one had to habituate oneself in every sphere. The vast
masses of troops which were put into the field on every front,
the fabulous consumption of munitions, the incredible inventive-
ness of mankind, the technical triumphs—they felt positively
edified by all this. They consoled themselves for all that the
war involved in the way of—well, unedifying phenomena, not
to call it downright misery: this was after all only the beginning, a bloody and brutal beginning of course, but the beginning of a new age. They were so accustomed to imagine that
technical development in some mysterious manner meant progress towards better times, that they assumed almost unconsciously that good must finally result in some way or other from
a thing like the perfecting of the technique of war. Never more

42

would mankind have to return to its little flesh-pots—from now on its cooking would be done in big steam boilers.

He could try, of course, to keep in mind what goods and labour might be worth in reality, after allowing for the inflations and fluctuations of war-time prices. But like other people he had to aim at covering the cost, while high prices lasted, of introducing more rational methods at the quarry, and he had to try to make the brick-works pay—he too was bound to hope for a boom in the building trade, when at last peace came.

Nevertheless, it got on one's nerves, this ferment of speculation everywhere, these random reconstructions and attempts to found something stable in the midst of all the unreality. And it gave a kind of illusion of activity to be caught up in the stream of travellers. Besides, he could not avoid being continually on the move.

BUT it was strange having to leave Trondhjem. Particularly strange that he did not feel it more, it seemed to him. As diplomats are in the habit of saying to journalists: it is with a feeling of sadness—here where we have taken root, etc. He could not say that.

He had been fond of the town from the first day he saw it, and of the country round, the fiord, the mountains—he would always think this the finest part of Norway. He had made many friends there whom he liked. And it was there he had been given a taste of independence, of a life of individual work. Even when the original reason for it no longer existed, he had never regretted having abandoned the studies on which he had been engaged ever since his boyhood. But in those plans his people at home had always had too much share. And it had been an inconceivable relief to be free of all that—fond as he was of his parents and his brothers and sister.

He said good-bye to his little villa up on Mill Hill without regret. There he had passed his whole married life, his children had been born there—at least, not actually born—but it was

43

there he had seen them grow up from queer red crawlers wrapped in white wool into little human beings. The garden he had taken such a lot of trouble with all these years—of course the new owner would tear up the slopes of alpine plants and put in something else; he looked just that sort. But Paul felt he had done with all that.

No doubt this was due in the first instance to the change in his position in the business. And in particular—to the change in his relations with Henrik.

Luckily it had taken the course of a gradual cessation of visits between their families. Their wives could not stand each other. Of late years they had only entered each other's houses on the occasion of dinner-parties.

But actually Henrik and he had found it a comfort to resume their friendship more or less on the terms of their bachelor days. They were together at the office, they went shooting together, and when their wives were away they went home together and sat, now at Paul's, now at Henrik's, smoked and had a drink or two, played cards and talked till well on in the small hours about everything between heaven and earth—except their wives.

Then the incredible happened. It was in August 1916. Paul had been obliged to go to Stockholm, and he went by road —he had just got his car. Coming back he took it into his head to drive through Värmland. And there, at the hotel on the far-famed lake Fryken, he came upon Henrik's car in the garage. So it was no more than natural that he should enquire at the office, and there he was told that the lady and gentleman had arrived the day before and no doubt would be going on next day. It did not occur to Paul to send up a message—though he was rather surprised that Henrik should also be in Sweden just at this time. But then Henrik had so many irons in the fire. So probably he had picked up Berit in Christiania; she had motored there a week or so earlier; he knew that from Björg, who had lately been pestering him to let her learn to drive a car.

Then, just as he was surveying the side-table for an appe-
tiser, Berit came into the dining-room followed by a somewhat
mysterious fellow who had been hanging about Trondhjem for
the last six months. And it was hard to say which of the three
had been most painfully surprised. Well, not the fellow anyway.
He had the devil's own cheek.

Afterwards Berit came storming into his room after him,
all wound up for a scene. "Unless you swear, by the God you
believe in, by the head of your little child, that you won't
tell Henrik, you may be quite sure there's no chance of my
ever going back to Trondhjem! Then there'll only be one thing
for me to do—make away with myself—or throw in my lot
with Aage Halvorsen and follow wherever our path may
lead us!"

"I don't think you're quite right in the head! You surely
don't suppose I should say anything to Henrik. But I can tell
you one thing, that if you don't break off your acquaintance
with Herr Halvorsen straight away, you can bet your life somebody or other will soon say something to Henrik—or write it.
You don't imagine an affair of this sort can go on very long
without being discovered."

"Will you swear that you won't—"

"No, I'm hanged if I will. I've told you—one doesn't
do such things, that's all about it. But I'm going to propose
that you go on with *me* tomorrow morning—go straight home
with me. Then you must decide for yourself how much of the
truth you think you ought to tell your husband."

All the same, it was a piece of luck she did not accept his
rather ill-considered offer. Heaven alone knew how the couple
had managed about passports on this trip—and then there
was the other car, Alster's. And whatever explanation Berit
might choose to impose upon Henrik, it would certainly have
been pretty painful for him to meet his partner after this. All
the more as Berit before withdrawing found occasion to declare

theatrically that it was he who had first disturbed her peace of mind and taught her to feel dissatisfied in her marriage with Henrik Alster. Presumably that was the form his idiotic flirtation with her before his own marriage had now assumed in her memory.

Berit came home to Trondhjem three weeks later. She had sung at a charity concert in Christiania and the papers had said some nice things about her; she was in high spirits and altogether awful. Her behaviour to him was so unconcerned that Paul thought everyone, Henrik included, was bound to suspect all kinds of things.—And shortly afterwards this individual, Halvorsen, turned up again in the town.

By chance—as one might call it—Arnt Hauan happened to mention the fellow, one evening when Paul was up at his house. And it appeared that Hauan knew of some pretty dirty affairs that Halvorsen had been mixed up in. Then Paul Selmer took upon himself what he felt to be a disgusting piece of work —he said to Hauan that he thought it might be just as well if Trondhjem were spared Halvorsen's presence. They summoned Halvorsen by telephone, and when he came they gave him to understand that he would do well to take himself off voluntarily.

He had not told Hauan why he wanted to get rid of Halvorsen; Hauan was pretty sure to know anyhow. Afterwards his conscience troubled him for not setting the police on the rascal—but probably it wouldn't be long before he fell into their clutches in any case. Amongst other things he was more than suspected of having supplied information to foreigners about the sailings of Norwegian ships. But he didn't feel that he could be a party to involving Henrik's wife in matters which might cause her relations with the swine to become common talk all over the town.

Berit was sure to meet him on her trips to Christiania. But at any rate she wouldn't be doing it under Henrik's roof and before the faces of her own children. But if Berit had dared

46

throw vitriol in Paul's face, she would certainly have done so.

And after this miserable business it pained him to be in Henrik's company day in, day out. He believed he could not have felt more ashamed if it had been himself who had deceived his friend. And God alone knew what Henrik knew and thought. They never spoke of Berit.

But Henrik Alster had changed a great deal in the last few years. They were about the same age, in the middle thirties both of them—no age worth talking about. But Henrik was no longer a young man, far from it; he had become a person of indeterminate age—unhealthily fat, especially about the shoulders, where he had developed a shocking hump. He stooped a good deal in his walk too.

He had given up all interests outside his business—at least, that depends on what one calls interests. He still went shooting, he motored, they gave a great many parties at the villa on the island, and he bought pictures galore. But business and speculation and the gamble for money were the only things that really made up his life. All the rest was only a means of spending the money he made. But he had lost his interest in the many things of which he used to be fond—he had given up his interest in the reality of existence. At times Paul caught himself looking at him with a kind of shudder—what about myself, am I too expelled already—?

ALL through the autumn Paul was chiefly at Haugen, had no time to visit his family before Christmas. Then he went home for the holidays and circled round the Christmas-tree with Björg and Sunnie in a room belonging to perfect strangers, among huge pieces of furniture in highly polished mahogany and curtains and portières of plum-coloured silk and mouse-grey velvet. Björg spent the whole of his first day at home showing him all the glories of this modern house: this and that she wanted to copy, when they came to furnish their new home at Berven. Paul hum'd and ha'd; fortunately the matter was not urgent just at present. He shrank from telling his wife that he could not spare very much money for their personal expenditure just now; the works required all he could make—and perhaps a little more.

He had always let Björg have everything she asked for; she had wanted a good deal, but mostly trifles. Her ideas of comfort had been determined by her home above the little draper's shop in Storgate, and she had prided herself on being capable and economical, in the way her mother thought a young housewife ought to be. She had no real sense of economy, as Paul had discovered long ago, and he knew very well that on their scale of living, with constant demonstrations of saving and not much more entertaining than was involved in Björg's everlasting tea parties, their housekeeping cost more than many of their acquaintance spent on running a roomy, restful and attractive house. But he bore it with tolerable composure—he could bear the expense because Björg's extravagances were kept within the bounds of a kind of lower middle-class orthodoxy, and he discharged his duties in the way of business entertaining at hotels and in motor trips as far as he could.

But these months that Björg had spent surrounded by the Holms' elegance had evidently given her a taste for a more fashionable mode of life. Paul retired to rest by his wife's side in the Holms' French double bed—a huge, low-lying monster in gilt rococo style with plaited cane at its foot. And Björg whispered, before they settled themselves to sleep under the hangings of apple-green brocade which were held up by a cluster of cupids above the head of their couch, that, gee, wouldn't she like to have a bedroom like this.—

Helge had grown into a stout little chap who was crawling about the floor wherever Paul might go. He yelled with all the force of his lungs if his father attempted the slightest advances. "He's just at the age when they're most afraid of strangers," said Björg.

Sunnie followed her father about from morning to night,

48

insisted on his showing her all the picture-books they used to
look at, cutting out the same animals and singing the same
songs, taking their old walks—and every evening he had to
say her prayers with her and give her a glass of water and hear
the same riddles that papa never could guess.

"Shan't we soon go home again, papa?" she was always
asking.

"We'll soon be going to another house, Sunnie, and we'll
all live there together. So that will be home, you understand.
In the South—where your grandfather and both your grand-
mothers live," said Paul.

Sunnie did not seem to find that very attractive. She remembered one grandmother, curiously enough—it was two years
since she had seen her, when Julie Selmer took that trip to the
North Cape. But she and Sunnie had shown remarkably little
enthusiasm for one another. Nor did Sunnie seem to care so
tremendously for her other grandmother, and it was so long
since she had seen her grandfather that she didn't remember
him.

On the morning after Christmas Day, when Paul had finished
dressing, he ventured to ask Björg—she lay in the gilded bed
of state drinking coffee out of one of Fru Holm's grandest cups
and looking perfectly happy:

"Have you any objection to my looking in at the church
with Sunnie—I've promised to take her for a walk this morning?"

"You know very well I don't like it," said Björg reprov-
ingly. "But for once in a way you can—"

So Paul breakfasted alone with Sunnie, and that put the
child in a radiant humour. And then she had got a new cloak
and hood of gold-coloured velvet, which her father had not yet
seen.

"It goes so well with the colour of my curls, mamma says."

That was true enough; she looked awfully sweet in it.

49

Paul had not had many chances of attending High Mass up here at Trondhjem. Björg thought their late Sunday breakfasts the happiest time of the whole week; for on week-days they could never breakfast together. And to be quite honest Paul had to admit that he himself preferred going to church on week-day mornings to low Mass. There were not many people, and there was no sermon.

People talked about it, he knew. And it had sometimes happened that his acquaintances talked to him about Catholicism. He could see they assumed that he *was* a Catholic—after his own fashion; not in such a way, of course, that he would consider himself obliged to join this or that sect because he found something in its services which corresponded with his religious feeling. They agreed that the Catholic service was more inspiring than the Protestant; especially while the French priests were officiating at Ila it had been fairly common for Protestants to attend their church now and then, at Christmas, for instance. At that time the new Catholic church up at Elgesæter bridge was a rather poor affair.

Paul usually gave an evasive answer. He felt it would be impossible to get these friends to grasp his meaning if he said that the very word "inspiring" was repugnant to him, when it was a question of religion. He had never been drawn to the Catholic Church by anything except a presentiment, which sometimes took the form of a dazzling hope, and sometimes, to put it bluntly, that of a chilling fear: could it be that its teaching was absolute, revealed, supernatural truth?

He could not help thinking it uncanny in a way, this feeling of having run his head against a wall of truth. Much the same as when one runs up against a house in a thick, damp, woolly fog, but has not so much as a glimpse of its outlines, can only guess it to be something big. But if it was so that the very truth dwelt within, a truth which would bear being handled firmly, nay, roughly, without going to pieces—a truth which a man could take upon his tongue and swallow—why, then he was compelled to feel his way to the door, knock and ask to be admitted. Or run away and have it on his mind for the rest of his life: I would rather be left off making the acquaintance of the truth.

It was considered very compromising for a man to be afraid of the truth—and of course, if it were so that an absolute truth existed in this world, he would have to pluck up courage and give himself over to it. But—

Most people were agreed that decent people ought to be truthful. But—what is truth? Maybe old Pilate's celebrated aphorism was not so fatuous after all.

He had always had a rather sceptical eye for the popular enthusiasm for general notions such as its being good form to "love" truth, liberty, justice, knowledge, and so forth. He remembered one prize day at school—he had had his eyes fixed on their school banner with the motto "Knowledge is power." And all at once it had struck his schoolboy's brain: What kind of knowledge is power—for what?

For it had always been served out to them as the sum and substance of all their historical studies that those in power had always without exception been a rotten lot. No sooner did a man or a nation or a church or a class of society or anything of that sort become powerful—than they grew corrupt beyond measure. But then what was the sense of schoolmasters sweating away at stuffing children full of knowledge, so that they might one day have power and become corrupted? In a flare-up of boyish impatience he had thought: this headmaster of ours, who is always pitching into all dead and deposed potentates and yet goes on keeping school because he believes that knowledge is power, he must be either a scoundrel or a fool.

It had then dawned on him that the convictions people believe themselves to hold and those according to which they act—are often glaringly different. It is positively indecent to doubt that freedom is a good thing. Although, for instance, in the last days of the Roman Empire a lot of people voluntarily

51

became slaves, to be rid of the burdens which the State had heaped on the shoulders of freemen. And every day of our lives we see men binding themselves to one party or another and becoming the slaves of its policy—in order to gain what they understand by a position in society and to "get on." But more often than not it is slaves of this kind who languish platonically for freedom.

It is the same with the truth which people assure us they love. If they are forced to explain what they have in mind when they use the phrase, it will appear more often than not that they mean certain mummified old truths as harmless as sofa cushions or stuffed birds of prey. Or they declare it gives them pleasure to utter truths—though it may often be disagreeable enough to be forced to do so. He knew very well that he himself very often preferred to keep his mouth shut; a man should have too much respect for himself to tell untruths, but that is an entirely different matter. One learns that more from love for oneself than from love for virtue at large. But Björg, for example, felt morally obliged to utter a heap of tactless things —for she had learnt from her mother that by so doing she was "keeping to the truth."

To meet unflinchingly the savage and bloodthirsty truths of life—why yes, one had to keep a stiff upper lip and do so, but he for one would not feel convinced of a man's veracity who said he loved them. Love to be told the truth about one's little child who is backward—the reason is that it's an idiot. Love to be told the truth when one has lain for months in hospital after a motor accident and been cut about and put in plaster of Paris and hung up and twisted this way and that—at any rate Leif Hauan shot himself when he was told the truth that he would be paralysed after all. The full truth as to what other people think of one's appearance, when there is nothing left of one's face but scars of wounds and burns—is there anyone who loves that? And to hear one's first love—"the lily of the valley, the flower of flowers," "my white swan, tranquil and

mute" and all the rest of it—give a truthful account of the
fellows who had had her before one came on the scene—he
could not pretend that he had loved the truth in that case either—

A man must be able to *bear* the truth—that's the thing.
But that he shall love the truth is too much to ask. If the truth
is anything but a person. And that person is such that he is worth
loving more than all a man can lose here on earth, more than
the mortal life of every single man. So that the man who has
discovered him runs after the scent of his garment, as King
David expresses it—and makes straight for the herd of this
world's truths as if they were no more than Our Lord's private
royal tigers.

"Papa—why can't you answer me?" said Sunnie, tugging
at his hand. "You look so fierce—"

Paul gave a start:

"Do I, Sunnie? I didn't hear what you asked—"

But it was only about Vinsvold's little elk-hound, whose
eyes had got bad when they took him reindeer stalking last
autumn. Paul remembered now—he had told Sunnie something about that trip in a little letter he had written her. "But
now he's quite well again, isn't he, papa?"

The dog had not recovered from his snow-blindness, and
Vinsvold had asked Paul to shoot him, as he didn't feel like doing it himself.

"Yes, now he's all right."

"Do you think he'll know me when I come to Haugen
again? he was *so* fond of me—"

"No, I'm afraid he won't.—Now you must remember to
make a nice curtsy, Sunnie," he said, rather superfluously, as
Sunnie had already begun to drop a low curtsy to Fru Hansen,
who was coming towards them far up the street.

There was a rust-red gleam of sunshine through the frost-
fog as he and the child walked under the rime-covered young
trees up to the little church. Paul had said nothing to Sunnie
except that she was to sit still while the people were singing

and the priest was talking to them. Afterwards everybody knelt down and prayed to God, and the priest went up to the altar and stood there praying—but Sunnie must only pray quietly, to herself. Otherwise she could do what she saw all the others doing.

So Sunnie knelt when he knelt, after they had entered the bare little church. Paul found a place on one of the last benches, and Sunnie got up and stood nice and still during the *Asperges*—only peeped up with a smile to see if she was meant to laugh when the priest came past them sprinkling holy water. On the bench in front sat some little girls who had books which they were reading—with great presence of mind Sunnie picked up a book lying in their pew and held it before her face. Her behaviour was quite exemplary, she scarcely looked about her and did not utter a sound. Till everybody stood up and the priest began to read the gospel.

The little girls in front had coloured cards for markers in their books. Sunnie craned her neck and peeped:

"Oh look, papa, what lovely pictures they've got," she whispered delightedly.

As the priest ascended the pulpit and the congregation settled themselves one of the little girls chanced to knock her missal on to the floor. A mass of picture cards fell out and scattered between the benches.

"Oh, papa, look what a *lot* she's got," said Sunnie, so overwhelmed that she spoke quite loud.

The little girls had picked up all the cards, and the one they belonged to turned round and handed one to Sunnie, with a smile and a nod.

"May I *keep* it?" Sunnie asked her father, and Paul nodded. "Thank you," said Sunnie, bobbing to the strange little girl.

During Mass Paul saw that the child was kneeling with her hands pressed against her face—and now and again she peeped through her fingers at the card.

A Christmas manger had been set up by the chancel arch, and when Mass was over Paul took her to see it. He had expected to find her in raptures over the stable and the beasts and the Virgin Mary with the Child Jesus and Joseph and the shepherds and the kings and angels. But Sunnie said nothing, and kept looking at the card she held in her hand.

She shook her head energetically when her father offered to take care of it for her. She had pockets in her smart new coat, and as they walked down Munke-gate the little picture was in and out of her pocket continually.

When they were sitting in Erichsen's, the confectioner's, and Sunnie had got her chocolate and cakes, she handed the card to her father: "You may look at it too—"

It was very fine, with a mass of gilt and bright colours, rose-pink and sky-blue; it represented Christ standing before an altar with the ciborium in his hand, giving the host to a kneeling child in white. Other children dressed in white were coming down from the altar rails with bowed heads and nicely folded hands, and on the other side some lanky and ungainly angels were driving forward a fresh group of little children. Underneath the picture was printed, in English: "Jesu, our only joy be Thou. As Thou our prize wilt be."

But Sunnie did not ask any questions. She put out her hand and took back the card. All at once she said, aloud and eagerly:

"I say, papa—I got all my prayers said such a lot of times—a hundred, I believe. You know—it's much more fun praying to yourself, because then it goes so quick—it's just as if I wasn't praying myself, but it was praying inside me—

"—Papa, did you get a lot of prayers said too?"

"Eat your cake, child," said Paul, laughing. "It's time we were going home—"

So they walked by Kjöbmands-gate along the river and past the quays and looked at the red winter sun which cast a long streak of coppery reflection in the waters of the fiord. The weather was calm with a slight frost-fog; the brightly painted wooden houses looked dull and dimmed against the snow on

55

their roofs and in the streets, and all the trees were furry with hoar-frost.

THEY came home to dinner, and Paul cut up Sunnie's helping of venison, while mamma was mashing potatoes in gravy for Helge, who was allowed to sit at table in his baby chair, because it was Christmas and papa was at home. Helge was almost reconciled to his father's presence now, so long as Paul did not attempt any advances.

Then it came. Björg asked with angelic meekness:

"Well, Baby—was it fun going to church with papa?"

Paul saw Sunnie slowly turning red; her little face put on such a queer, closed look. She gave a couple of decided nods, but said nothing.

"Now then, Baby—can't you tell mamma something about what you saw in church? Let's hear now—?"

"They sang."

"Oh, they sang, did they? But didn't they do anything more? You can guess mamma would like to hear about what her little girl has been doing!"

"The priest told us a story about a man—what *was* his name, papa?—Ste—Stefanus, wasn't that a queer name, mamma? And then there were some people who were so naughty to him; they began to throw stones at him."

"Yes, but didn't the priest say anything about God? Weren't you told anything about Jesus, for instance?"

"Oh yes. This man Stefanus saw Jesus standing at his gate, and then he called to him. And then Jesus went and fetched the policeman. But then Stefanus said they'd begged his pardon already, so the policeman was not to take them up. And then Stefanus went home with Jesus to heaven, and then they went to bed."

Björg laughed loudly:

"There, you can just hear, Paul! A lot *she* has understood. Well, I must say, it's some use taking her to church!"

Sunnie looked up, red as fire:

"It's not at all—isn't it true, papa? That's just what the priest told us—didn't he, papa?"

"Almost." Paul bit his lip.

"Oh, deary me." Björg shook her head. "Well, you're a nice lot, both of you.—But weren't there any more strange things, Sunnie, in that church—can't you tell mamma a little more?"

Sunnie shook her head energetically.

Paul looked thoughtfully at the little girl. It would have been grand to know just what was going on inside that little head of hers—

"Papa, when are we going to church again?" Sunnie asked that evening, when Paul had gone through the whole good-night ritual with her.

"I'm not quite sure, my child." He had an inkling that, when once he had been received into the Church, it would be more difficult to get Björg's leave to take the child there.

As it happened, Björg told him so that very evening; they were sitting in the Holms' smoking-room.

"But I will say this, Paul—I *don't* care for such goings-on —you're positively getting Baby into the way of making fun of religion, you are. I was brought up to reverence all that kind of thing, let me tell you!"

Paul replied from the depths of the chesterfield on which he was lying:

"Poor child, she has no idea of making fun of it, Björg— she kept so quiet and good. And you could hear how she paid attention—"

"Well, anyhow, I can't bear that kind of thing. I think anything to do with religion and such like, *must* be treated solemnly."

"I think," said Paul quietly, "that a little child amusing herself is one of the most solemn sights on earth."

However, it was no use entering on an argument with her, he knew that of old. So he lay where he was and smoked in silence, till Björg had to come to a pause. Paul sat up hastily:

"By the way, Björg, that letter from your mother that you wanted me to read—have you got it down here?"

ON the third day of the new year Paul left for Christiania. He had made a vow during Mass on the day he took Sunnie with him to church, that when he came south he would go to Harald Tangen and ask for instruction. This was the last evasion he had practised with himself: no doubt the parish priest at Trond-hjem was an excellent old priest. But Paul imagined that perhaps he would not be able to appreciate so well the difficulties confronting a man who had never believed in anything. He considered it would be easier to talk to Harald Tangen.

Chapter Four

PAUL WAS AT A MEETING WITH OTHER MEMBERS OF THE stone industry when a page boy came and told him he was wanted on the telephone.

He had himself rung up the Catholic presbytery every day while he had been in town, but each time the answer had been that Father Tangen was still at Fredrikstad. So he had asked to be informed if the priest should come home today, as he had to leave for the north that evening; he was taking with him a man from the firm of contractors.

It was Harald Tangen himself who was on the telephone; Paul recognized his voice at once. It had impressed him at the time, many years ago, that Harald Tangen spoke exactly like any other ordinary educated Christiania man—doctor or lawyer or business man. In talking to other theologians Paul had always had the feeling that they were accustomed to address a flock which was not expected to answer back, and that their manner of speaking bore the stamp of this, even when they were talking to a single individual. But of course this might have resulted from the fact that at that time all of them—Uncle Abraham and his colleagues, Halstein and the whole crowd—counted him a greenhorn, and a fairly brazen and abandoned fellow into the bargain.

There was nothing to prevent Paul's meeting Father Tangen in his study in an hour's time. With that message he returned to the other men in the hotel writing-room.

Paul resumed his seat in the window. The rain streamed

in torrents against the great sheet of plate-glass. Outside in the street the motor-cars, with big gas-bags on their roofs, jolted over holes in the road, splashing the snow-slush all around. People crouched along under their umbrellas at the bottom of a grey world dissolved in moisture.

The meeting was important enough, for that matter. They were discussing the prospects of an export prohibition; all of them had received large or small orders from abroad.

But now he only felt impatient to be finished and to be able to see these gentlemen well outside the door. It was half an hour over the time he had appointed to be at Tangen's, before they went. Then he had to go up to his room, lock up his papers and tidy himself—and then the telephone rang. It was Ruth; they arranged that he should come up to her studio about five.

He was a whole hour too late, he saw, as he came out into the street and put up his umbrella. What filthy weather! Now he couldn't be sure of finding the priest at home. He was not certain he wouldn't be a trifle relieved at another little postponement for which he was not to blame.

But Harald Tangen opened the door himself. And to Paul's excuses, as he got rid of umbrella, galoshes and mackintosh in the dark passage, the priest returned a "don't mention it—it makes no difference to me—"

It was the same big, dark study, but today the lamp was lighted on the writing-table, although it was the middle of the day. Bookshelves from floor to ceiling, with here and there cheap Catholic pictures and statuettes and faded photographs. Paul recalled the last time he had sat in this room—wondering whether the other was thinking of it too.

He suddenly saw, clearly and sharply, what had been the inmost reason for his shrinking so long from this step—why he had entrenched himself behind doubt after doubt, even though his doubts were all honest enough. It had now come to this, that he was to talk to another person about himself. Not about this or that of the external circumstances of his existence; he had not come here to chat about anything, no matter how much it interested him, or to detail relations in which he had become involved—he had done that once before, to the same man who was sitting opposite him at the writing-table in a long black soutane, and he had found it difficult enough then.

But the thing was that the other sat there believing that he, Paul Selmer, had an immortal soul which Harald Tangen's lord and master had created. And as his soul had done the same as all other souls, run away from its home and lost itself in trackless wastes, its creator had followed it down upon earth in order to save it, had redeemed it from captivity at a price which human thought is utterly unable to grasp.

And he himself sat here in order to confess—I believe this is true. That very word, soul, he had regarded with extreme suspicion from his earliest youth—and now he had ended in admitting: yes, I believe that that within me which feels and thinks is a soul which longs for its origin. And if it is true that my origin will acknowledge me, longs for me, cares for me and surrounds me with its love—then that gives a meaning to life itself. In that case one may get to understand even what seems most hopelessly meaningless and fortuitous—

All other explanations of life but the Christian end in self-contradictions and mists or in downright nonsense. At any rate I think so. There is only one thing that I'm not sure about—can it not just as well be true that life *is* meaningless?

Aloud he replied to Father Tangen's question:

"No, it's already nearly a year since I left my old firm at Trondhjem. No, we had to take over some brick-works at Berven —that's where I'm living now. The idea is that my family shall join me there in the spring."—

But as a fact he had never before confided in another human being—not verbally in any case. He had always *felt* as if he was on confidential terms with his mother—but not so much when they talked together, and least of all when they talked of serious subjects. He thought he had confided in his mistress—

with his body and all his being, but not in words. This was just what had given him a profound feeling of happiness in his relations with her—his belief that they understood one another so intimately and deeply and without the use of words. In this he had presumably been totally mistaken, as the issue of the affair showed.

In a way, of course, he had also talked confidentially to Henrik Alster and to Arnt Hauan, about many things. Religion among them. But compared with what he was now to go through this was like sitting in one's shirt-sleeves against stripping to the skin.

Paul was reminded of the medical examination when he was a recruit. There had been a lad there, not exactly hunch-backed, but at any rate badly deformed. And he had seen how the poor fellow dreaded coming forward, so that he himself felt humiliated in sympathy. His own feelings at this moment were something like those of that lad.—

But he might just as well take the bull by the horns:

"Well, Father Tangen—my real business with you today was to ask if you will give me the instruction which is required before one can be received into the Church—"

"Very well." Harald Tangen nodded. "May I ask—is it your intention to begin the instruction at once?"

"Yes, please, I should prefer it. As perhaps you know, I have been thinking about this for years. I have tried to read as much as I could—"

As Father Tangen only nodded again, Paul began counting up as many of the authors he had read as he could think of at the moment: Newman and Ward, Gasquet, Veuillot, La-cordaire, Léon Bloy, Battifol, Joseph de Maistre—

"Just so. But the New Testament—haven't you read that?" For the first time the priest smiled—and at once Paul saw that Harald Tangen had aged in the last few years.

"Yes, of course. I believe I know it almost by heart."

"Well, that's excellent." Now he was laughing. "And what

62

about the Catholic catechism—have you that?"

"No." Now Paul was laughing too. "I must confess—I hadn't thought of that."

"Then I'd better give it you at once." The priest got up and fetched from the shelf a little book in a brown binding— it looked extremely like a school-book. And God help us, if the man didn't mark it with a pencil—from there to there!

He laughed again on seeing Paul's face:

"Yes, we shall have to go through this. The best way will be for you to read up at home each section that we are to take— write down the questions you wish to put—any difficulties you come across. And then we must arrange—when will it suit you to come here and take your lesson—?"

They arranged for the present every other Friday afternoon. And Paul stood with the little book in his hand, feeling strangely foolish and definitely a little disappointed. It was obviously not Harald Tangen's intention to demand any such spiritual stripping for examination as he had dreaded. More than anything else this reminded him of making appointments with the dentist.—

Paul was out in the passage again, putting on his wet things.

"Possibly we may find it necessary," said the priest, with another little laugh, "to spend a little more time than usual over this. At any rate that's my experience—with people who have been in touch with the Church for so long, and who have shown a preference for those Catholic writers who are at the same time artists—orthodox as they may be. We shall have to go very thoroughly and soberly through the doctrine of the Church, so that you may know what it is in itself—not merely how it appears when seen through the temperament of various very temperamental Catholic authors."

"Very well—I understand."

"Well, I shall put it all before you as dryly as can be managed." They both laughed. "And then you must take part in

the Mass as often as you have an opportunity. And pray a great
deal. Then I hope you won't find it too dry after all."

So now that interview was over and done with, thought Paul as
he walked down Akers-gate. He felt a trifle flat.

But when he met Hans Selmer on the stairs of the tailor
they both went to, a mad, boyish humour suddenly bubbled up
in him. What on earth would his brother say, if he were to tell
him what he had just been doing?—

"So you're not coming out to see us, this time?" asked the
doctor.

"No, thanks—I must go home tonight—I'm taking a fellow
with me who's going to look at the new drying-shed. Is Evi quite
well again?—well, give her my love—good-morning."

He arrived at Ruth's a little late and it annoyed him, for it was
one of his ambitions always to be punctual. But Ruth met him
with her usual calm and pleasant smile.

There was no other light in the room but the standard lamp
in the corner by the sofa, where an open book lay among the
crumpled cushions. The lamplight was reflected on the mahogany table close by; on which stood a green earthenware dish
of apples and an old copper bowl full of many-coloured tulips.
Ruth's slender figure took on a golden outline: she had on a
reddish brown dress which looked warm and soft to him, coming from the dirty weather outside.

The night lay black against the great studio window and
the rain dripped down the glass with a quiet, monotonous sound.
The room seemed bigger than it was, losing itself in the darkness, with pictures and empty frames showing dimly along the
walls.

Paul always felt rather touched on first coming in here.
Everything bore a stamp of rather cheap and naïve æstheticism,
of a womanly affection for little things and of loneliness and
quiet. Nobody lived in this office building except the painters

who had the four studios at the top. There was something honestly workmanlike in the smell of oil-colours and turpentine,
and the big table on trestles, crowded with her painting things,
reminded him of a similar one he had had in his student days, of
which he had been mighty proud. Ruth gave him the idea of a
young anchorite, serious and industrious.—Not but what he
knew very well that she had plenty of society.—

"But you must have something to warm you, Paul; I suppose you've been trotting round all day, poor man—tea with
claret and lemon, do you like that?"

He didn't, but said yes, please, seated himself comfortably
in the corner of the sofa and helped himself from the cigarette-
box which she pushed towards him. That too was a specimen
of the kind of art handicraft that one buys in the little shops on
the left bank of the Seine, and the tea service she brought out
was made of thick, brightly coloured earthenware—horrid to
drink out of, as he knew from experience.

The lamp-shade was composed of sheets of parchment, in-
scribed with monkish characters—not a very good imitation.
And on the ledge under the studio window stood some of those
long-necked stoneware cats, yellow and green, that they had at
the Chat Noir. Again Paul felt a warm gust of tenderness for
her—poor thing, she didn't paint at all badly, there was just
something that was wanting always in her pictures—

"Shall we get rid of our business first?" he asked, as she
was busy with the gas-ring. He took out his pocket-book:
"Would you mind counting—there ought to be twelve hundred—"

"It's really splendid"—her voice showed how glad she
was. "Having you for a dealer. No commission to pay even.
You'd like to have a receipt, wouldn't you?"

"He was awfully keen on your pictures too." Ruth had
seated herself at her writing-table and lighted the lamp there.
Paul went across and handed her the card of the man to whom
he had sold the pictures for her. Her hair had just the same

warm mahogany tint as his mother's when she was young. And it was pretty, the way she did it now, with the little old-fashioned curls hanging against her cheeks and the dark twisted knot low down on the white curve of her neck.

"And he really does know something about painting—I was quite astonished to see what good things he's got together. You ought to go and call on him with me one day—he said he'd like you to see how he's hung your pictures."

Ruth put out the writing-table lamp, got up and fetched the teapot.

"That over there is Lisieux with the cathedral," she said as she poured out; "that *is* a good picture, I may tell you. About the best I've done—though that's not saying much."

"No, look here, Ruth!" exclaimed Paul in alarm, for it so happened that he had just been thinking rather compassionately of her artistic ability. "Good—that's just the word for everything you do, in my opinion. That's what's wrong with it, I was going to say—you understand what I mean. But there's no doubt the best of your things have personality enough too—and they're delicate—tender almost in their colouring—like the one I have with the reflection of the pale blue sky in the running water—"

"Oh yes, I dare say." She was sitting in the arm-chair facing him. It was charming, the effect of that necklace she wore just under the soft curve of her throat—little beads of a kind of turquoise blue with a metallic sheen.

"No, Ruth—I don't think you have any reason to be so dissatisfied with what you have achieved—"

"Oh no. In view of the fact that my powers are not sufficient to let me do anything which is really art. And that's what you meant just now, isn't it?"

"Well, there are so many kinds of art, you know—"

"I used always to draw, ever since I was a child, and I was good at drawing. But so were you, Paul. You wrote well too, you remember, as a young man. I'm sure you could have been just as much of an artist as I am. And yet I've never heard of your having any such ideas?"

He shook his head:

"No, for I've always known that that wasn't the main thing, even though, as you say, I had an aptitude for drawing correctly and writing clearly. But that's only a necessary means, the essential is something different."

"Precisely." Ruth smiled rather mischievously. "But what do you mean by the essential? Do you know that?"

"I suppose I fancy I know it. That when one has mastered reality, so as to be able to reproduce it, one extracts from it what one requires to create an image of what appears most real to oneself—what one has at heart, isn't that the phrase?"

"And you've never felt drawn to that?"

"No, decidedly not. It never occurred to me to attempt more than reproducing things as they are in themselves—drawing a plant, for instance, so that it could be used in a book on botany, if necessary. Or a landscape so as to make the geological structure clear, or a house so that one can see how it is built. But I've never felt any impulse to make pictures of them, *my* pictures.—Sometimes I think it will be amusing to show my children those old portfolios and sketch-books of mine. But only in the same way as I think it will be amusing to teach them a little geology and botany and so on. Get them to *see* things. How they may choose to transform them must be their own affair. That is, if they wish to transform anything at all—"

Ruth said quietly:

"You see, Paul, that's exactly what I ought to have said to father.—But I was so young at the time, and you know, the prospect of going abroad—and then the artist's life, of course I had such a lot of childish ideas about how rich and fine it was and how it enlarged the mind. Well, you know what father is like, terribly naïve and emancipated and all that, and rather mad about artists. So when he had got it into his head that I had talents as an artist, because I drew nicely and correctly, he

67

would hear of nothing else but that I must devote myself entirely to art. Literally devote myself—

"Actually, you know, grandmother Randall for instance got a great deal more out of her accomplishments, when she made drawings of the houses they lived in and did water-colours of grandfather and their children or of baskets of flowers. She could afford to be an amateur—literally an amateur of all that she thought pretty, for she played and sang too, and wrote the most enchanting letters. Not to mention their financial difficulties and that grandfather was not an easy man to live with and she had his parents in the house and had seven children and lost five of them while they were young. But she had the chance of using all her powers in the order which seemed natural to her, so no doubt she always felt free. So that both your mother and mine were able to grow up to maturity with sunshine all about them.—

"The most nonsensical thing of all, in my opinion, is that nowadays if a girl has ever so little talent, it must be commercialized. Either she's fond of dancing or she sings nicely while she's washing up, or she can do pretty little water-colours of the house at home and the veranda with father reading the paper —then she must be trained. But if I'd been in the same position as grandmother Randall or as old Berret Andersstuen, I'm sure I should have turned out an amateur like them—and drawn and painted when I had an hour to spare, or sung while I was at work, and I would have sat and told stories while I was sewing and weaving, just like Berret—"

Paul nodded.

"No—but you mustn't forget that grandfather Randall was a domestic tyrant, and there were a good many more like him—they can't have made life too pleasant always for the women they had to provide for. And there's no doubt the bulk of the male sex did something to hasten the movement—glad if they could get off having to provide for their unmarried daughters and sisters. So they haven't worried about who is to per-

form the work of culture properly so called which we men are
incapable of taking a hand in. I have often thought of that,
when I look at my own lady clerks and others like them—they
certainly possess treasures of humanity sufficient to have charge
of a whole flock of children and to be allowed to form them
during the years which are of most importance. And there are
thousands and thousands of men who might be put in a subordinate position without any loss to the world."

Ruth laughed quietly:

"Aunt Julie would call that taking part in the work of culture—the great work of culture which consists in putting as
many people as possible into situations subject to short notice,
or making them irremovable State functionaries."

"Yes." Paul gave a little laugh. "But you know, she didn't
get that out of her own head. We had an old postman at Trondhjem, and he's the only State functionary I've ever met who
wasn't convinced that the functionaries keep the State going,
and the State keeps us all. So I suppose mother's idea comes
to this, that if some day we have female postmen, that will be
another sign of female emancipation—"

"To Aunt Julie it would certainly mean emancipation if
she could be a postman. As it meant emancipation to her when
she worried Uncle Erik till he let her go her own way and do
as she pleased. But it would have tickled me to death, you
know, to see Aunt Julie kept under! My goodness, how I should
like to see the society that could manage to keep her sort
under!"

Paul said nothing, feeling rather embarrassed.

"And the rest of us are so ungrateful as not to appreciate
our emancipation. Instead of giving thanks for being able to
sell our amateur productions to profiteers and not having to
hang them up in our own rooms and nurseries. We don't see
where our freedom comes in, if we can't break out of our own
ego and forget ourselves in others whom we can help and make
happy—"

"Well but, Ruth," asked Paul in a low tone; "there's always somebody who needs one, isn't there? You especially—you make so many people happy—"

"Oh yes! By sending parcels to prisoners of war and refugees with the money I beg from you—and getting you to hoard butter for me for a few old servants and sewing-women—"

"It isn't only that you get from me," he interrupted.

"You know very well that's not what I mean. You understand quite well what it is. And yet you don't understand—"

Paul looked down into the ash-tray and took to breaking matches. It was fairly easy to guess that he understood what she was driving at.

"Well, I'm not ashamed of wishing I had children and a home that needed *me* to keep going, a world which would cease to be what it was if I wasn't there. Or that I had *really* been a painter—so that my pictures stood there and lived their own life, when I had let them out of my hands—full of secrets even from me, their creator. But it's not enough, it's not enough—"

"Aren't you pretty exacting?"

"What about you—aren't you rather exacting too?"

"My dear girl—I *am* married, and I have two children of whom I at any rate am very fond. And the businesses I'm in give me so much to do that I'm always kept at it, and I never liked having no work to do. I remember when I was quite young I always looked forward to the summer holidays, because it was then I worked best; then I was working on my own account. And at any rate it means something to the welfare of a whole lot of people, their economic welfare at least, if I can put the enterprises I have in hand on a sound footing—"

"You say 'at any rate' after every other word," laughed Ruth. "It sounds rather non-committal, Paul? I believe you do think you haven't got enough out of life?"

He joined in her laugh:

"If there *is* any more—why shouldn't I wish to get that as well? Especially if what we're cheated of—when we feel

70

ourselves cheated—is reality itself?"

Ruth was silent a few moments.

"At Lisieux, where I was painting," she said slowly, "they have a little saint who is being tremendously boomed just now—a brand-new one, you understand; she died some time in the nineties. I wonder now—if you had seen something of all the fuss they made and the pilgrims that came there and so on —if it wouldn't have done a good deal to cure you of your Catholic sympathies?"

"It's quite likely that much of it would have shocked me. And much, of course, I shouldn't understand. Up here in the North we're specially trained to be shocked by anything we don't understand. And if this saint of Lisieux that you're talking about is really a saint, then we should expect to find every possible and impossible sort of person coming there to be given a hand and led upward."

"No, look here, Paul—you surely don't imagine that you would be able to join in that kind of thing—hagiolatry?"

"Yes—that is, I can't imagine anything else, if I'm to become a Christian. The same rule must apply to the Kingdom of Heaven as to other kingdoms—when a people forgets its heroes or tries to depreciate them, instead of showing them honour and gratitude, it condemns itself to insignificance and cowardice and loses the instinct to defend itself against all that is inimical and alien to its nature. Besides—I *can* take it into my head to believe it to be simply autosuggestion, when I feel that I am placed in connection with something and receive something, as often as I pray to God. But nobody will get me to believe that autosuggestion can make people what the saints have been. On the contrary—those open to suggestion are usually natures that have begun to crumble and are liable to go on crumbling, and the moral cohesion that you can induce in them by suggestion is a bare minimum—my brother admits that too; you know Hans went in for all that at one time. Suggestion won't turn people all at once into organizing geniuses and ecstatics or get

71

people who are chronic invalids and suffer from severe nervous symptoms to think of everything and everybody except themselves. I at any rate can't believe in any other explanation of this—holiness—except that there is a reality which the saints have got hold of and live in communion with—a personality outside their own, which literally nourishes them with its substance and its blood—"

"Well, I must admit I know very little about it," said Ruth reflectively. "I've always thought really that the saints must be terrible bores. But probably it's like this, that religious feeling is a source of power, whether it is to be found in our own subconsciousness, or comes from a power-station outside in space. It doesn't matter which—so long as it gives us the feeling that we are growing and being charged and steeled to hold fast to what is best in ourselves."

"Ugh no, Ruth!" He laughed. "There may be just a few people who can find the source of such an uplift within themselves and come well out of it. The great majority of those I've seen are turned into frightful pedants by it—they stalk about as if they had a kind of idealistic stiffness of the joints. They always make me think of old Hagen, my father's colleague. He used to tip me whenever I met him, but in spite of that I always cut into a side street if I saw him in the offing—to escape having to walk home from school with him."

"Then I don't understand what you mean by religion," said Ruth; "if you don't think it's a feeling in the first place—?"

Paul dropped his voice: "Ruth—a boy's eroticism, before it has found any personal object, or before he has courage enough to make love to any woman—I say nothing about his having moral or immoral intentions in his advances, all I mean to say is that, so long as it is only an impulse within himself to which he resorts in solitude, in a bestial way or more delicately and subtly—you know what that leads to very often. Or a man's eroticism, when he's in solitary confinement. I'm not talking about what moral judgment one would pass on it—

72

all I mean is, at any rate it is not love. But if a man makes his religious feeling into his religion—that is self-abuse just as much."

"Yes, but *they* know that women actually exist. They have that fact to go upon, and they dwell on it pretty often in fairly realistic terms," said Ruth rather sarcastically.

"Precisely. The question is whether a feeling which in many ways is analogous to eroticism is barren and purposeless—or whether there exists something extraneous—a spiritual foreign substance to which we can find our way and which we can embrace and get to know. But we shall not find anyone we can love by shutting ourselves up in our room and feeling erotic, nor shall we find the divine by burrowing down into ourselves and feeling religious.—

"I remember a walking tour we took on the Hardanger moors, Haagen Nikolaysen and I, the year we were freshmen. We had stayed the night at a lonely little sæter and made an early start next morning, though the woman at the sæter advised us not to—it was nasty weather.

"Naturally the fog came down as thick as soup—we were walking on a scree of big stones—and we found that it was getting steeper both above the path we were on and below it. So in the end we had to sit down. All at once it came on to blow —and the mist was swept away and the rain came tearing down. We saw that we were sitting half-way up the side of a peak, and just below us was a little fold of the moors, shaped like a bowl and cleft by a black gully full of rolling clouds and mist. The little tarns on the level began to show blue, when they were not ruffled steel-grey by the wind—and then the sun came out and sparkled on the water and all the wet tufts of grass and clumps of bushes, and there was a gleam of smooth wet rocks far away, and then the gusts caught the birches on the slopes, showing the white side of their leaves and scattering raindrops in the sunlight as we went down.

"But then, you see, then we came upon it, underneath a

73

ledge of rock that jutted out over a little patch of swamp—there the tufts of high grass were perfectly grey with dew, dripping with moisture as on the calmest of mornings, while the wind rampaged all around. I don't believe I could *feel* much more if I witnessed an actual miracle—awe, rapture and —well, downright humility—than I did on catching sight of that little patch of undisturbed morning underneath the rock. It *was* like a miracle. But if I were to meet with a miracle which was not anonymous—that would mean an increase, not of feeling, but of acknowledgment. I should know to *whom* I could address my devotion and who it was that made me feel humility, because I should see not merely a sign, but him who gave the sign—"

Ruth smiled faintly:

"I think that was very nice, Paul. But I don't really see why you can't be content with *seeing* signs like that—in nature too. Perhaps in your children as well? Why are you so set on getting hold of the miracle-worker?"

"I'll tell you. Because it has always seemed to me, when I got up to the top of a mountain for instance—that it would really be much more natural to erect an altar there and offer some sort of sacrifice—than to add a few stones to the cairn or leave an empty bottle with one's cards. But if I were to take the butter out of my butter-box and smear it over the cairn and offer it to the sun—that, you know, might give me some personal gratification; it would be an expression of my religious feeling. If only I did not know that I was doing the sun no pleasure by sacrificing my butter to it as a sign of my gratitude. My religious feeling tells me that sun-worship and offerings to the sun are natural—so long as men have not discovered that the sun itself is not conscious of us and the good it does us. It is the same with all natural religion—we are bound to regard it as a matter of course, until we discover that nature has neither thought nor feeling for us. After that it can be religion no longer—in the sense of a relation between two different personalities—a great one which gives everything and a small one which receives so much that it longs to give a little in return. After that we know that what we want from nature we must take from it ourselves—whether it be peace of mind or agricultural produce or coal and iron—but however much we love nature, it has no knowledge of us who know it, and if we wish to give thanks for its gifts, nature itself does not know what it has given or that there is anyone thanking it. When we say that a field is grateful for some artificial manure, we know very well that we are not offering a sacrifice which the earth is to consume; we know simply what influence certain substances will have on the crop we want to raise—"

Ruth took, as though absently, a great yellow apple from the green dish, smelt it and continued to turn it between her long and slender fingers. Then she looked up at him and burst into a laugh:

"Good heavens, boy—are your manners so good that you feel you simply must find the giver of all good gifts to take him by the hand and make a nice bow—or kneel I suppose it is—and say thank you kindly?"

At that he laughed too.

"Well, anyhow I must say thank you for the tea and be going. I've got to meet this engineer fellow, Eker—won't you come and join us at supper? He's quite a good sort and amusing to meet—has spent a long time in Africa—"

"Thanks, but it's Bibbi's birthday and she's giving a little studio party. But at any rate we can go downstairs together—"

"Well, but I shall have to take a taxi, so we'll drive out to Skillebæk first and put you down—it's filthy weather."

"I should be rather glad to get away to the mountains for a bit, by the way," said Ruth, as they were putting on their outdoor things. "What did you tell me, isn't there a sæter belonging to that farm of yours by the quarries? Are you going to use it this winter?"

"No, you're welcome to borrow it—but you'll have to take

somebody with you. Nobody spends the winter up there—there's nothing but little sæters. But it's a fine situation—good ski-ing—"

Ruth said quietly:

"Of course you know, it's the same with me too. Among the mountains I expect we Norwegians all have a kind of re-ligious feeling."

"That day I was talking about," replied Paul, "towards evening Nikko and I came upon two little mountain farms which stood just on the edge of the valley, so that we saw their roofs against the sky. About the finest Hallingdal cottages I've seen, they were—and with the evening sun warming their sunburnt timbers and their tall, whitewashed chimneys—in-conceivably beautiful, with flowery meadows and patches of corn and potatoes round about—

"We were given beds at the first farm we came to, and we had curds and cream and bannocks for supper. While we were eating the woman showed us photographs of their three chil-dren: one son was a school-teacher in Christiania and the daugh-ter was a teacher at Sarpsborg and the other son was in America; the picture showed him standing outside his store—

"I happened to hear the other day that the farm where we spent the night has been bought by Borgersen, the banker; they say the shooting is good. And the other place is given up too."

"Who do you think was dining with me today?" said Ruth, when they were being jolted this way and that as the taxi bumped and splashed through the puddles. "Why, Braastadlyk-kjen. He hadn't been gone long when you came."

"Yes, his exhibition opens next week, doesn't it? It's good, I expect?"

"He's written a novel, did you know that?"

"Yes, I know he was writing something last winter."

"He read one or two chapters aloud to me. And I must say I think it sounds promising. The beginning, where he tells you about Gjest's earliest impressions—when it dawns on him that he's illegitimate, and he guesses the meaning of these visits that the men pay to his mother at the sæter on Saturday nights. And then his feelings, when his mother has married the worthy, quiet-spoken cottar—Paal Vassplassen he's called in the book —and he finds that his mother neglects him for her new children, and his step-father distrusts him. And then he begins to spin romances about his real father, the gipsy lad who decoyed his mother one Midsummer Night on the mountain. There were first-rate things in it, I thought. But then of course, in this book he's had the impressions of his own childhood to fall back on all the time. Whether he can do it as well when he tries his hand at something that is not so directly autobiographical, time will show—"

Paul burst out laughing:

"Jo? As a matter of fact, he was born in lawful wedlock of Hans Braastadlykkjen and Marit his wife, as far as I know. There are at least three children of the marriage older than Jo —the one who has the farm now and a brother who has a draper's shop at Lillehammer and a sister who's a nurse—and Marit Braastadlykkjen's reputation is as spotless as it can be, and the farm of Braastadlykkjen has been in possession of the family for sixty years. But if he has succeeded in making something good out of those old country life topics, so much the better. The lad has talents as a sculptor anyway. Ah, we're there already!"

He helped his cousin out of the taxi: "Well, good-bye, Ruth—"

Paul was feeling rather flat as he drove back into town. There was a whole lot of what he had got ready to say to Harald Tangen—and now he'd said it to Ruth instead. And evidently Jo had been there just before him and poured out his confidences to her. It was the very devil—. But there was something about Ruth which invited confidences. Presumably it was her being so calm and ladylike, although she frankly admitted that she

77

was sure of nothing but the limitations of her own ability. And she bore her anxiety and her sense of shortcoming in a composed and dignified way—without any of the flutterings that you generally see in women who have not found their proper sphere in life. She was a charming little person, always ready to help and take an interest in others—

Then he found himself at the hotel.

Chapter Five

P AUL NEVER HAD A CHANCE OF TALKING TO HARALD TANGEN
about what he was now forced to call "his inner life"—in
spite of his rooted distrust of such expressions. The priest
gave him not the slightest encouragement to make confidences
of that kind.

He did ask several times in the course of their lessons
whether this or that point raised any difficulties. These were
especially matters to which Paul knew that Protestants in general raised objections. But Paul could honestly reply that
neither the doctrine of Mary's exceptional position among all
created beings nor that of purgatory and indulgences caused
him special difficulty. If one once accepted the view that the
origin of all things was a personal God and that he himself
had given a revelation to men, then all the rest followed in
logical sequence, right down to holy water and the blest medal
with an image of St. Hubert, which Father Tangen had given
him one day when they happened to be talking about hunting.

The priest laughed as he gave it him, and Paul laughed
and put it on his key-chain, as he wore a wristlet watch.

HE was well aware that it was emotional factors which had
delayed his decision so long. When he felt as though God were
actually and invisibly near him, his doubts immediately announced themselves—this *may* be autosuggestion. *One* at least
of the elements of faith must be an acknowledgment which is
not affected by my own feelings at the moment, warm or cold.

But when he thought that it was precisely that—a conviction of realities which was felt to be oppressive, tiresome even, when he himself was in a dull humour, it made him uncertain—for it was unnatural that a man should regard the idea of a living God as troublesome, a thing which did not kindle the slightest emotion—

Of course he had always had a religious feeling, however reluctant he might have been to confess it. He had heard people appeal to their religious feeling as a kind of proof that what they believed was true—for themselves in any case. "My God is thus and thus." "My faith is thus and thus." He thought it rather ridiculous and rather shabby that they could not be content to say: "Thus am *I*."

But he must have been aware that he too was seeking with a kind of spiritual sense for something real which was at work within the reality of sensation, like a body inside a garment.

For that matter, this was the first thing he remembered. He had been sitting on the bare ground in nothing but his little shirt on a flower-bed warmed by the sun, and the mould was grey and loose on the surface, but dark and moist when he dug his fingers into it. He could feel that the earth was tepid a long way down, and that filled him with an indescribable contentment. When he put his head back and looked up from the good mould, he saw some big dark-green leaves high above his face and above them the blue sky, and it was as though the warmth and the light were creeping in on him from every side. A tiny little animal came and crawled over his leg—a beetle, grey like the earth. And it was just as if a mass of new feelings sprang out everywhere inside him—surprise, rapture, benevolence, deep gratitude to this little living thing which had come here to crawl over him—

His ecstasy was broken into by somebody picking him up roughly and giving him a spanking—he had a vague idea that this somebody had been his grandmother Selmer or her old maid. Whether his transgression had been running out of doors without his breeches or sitting down on a flower-bed.

But all through his childhood this feeling kept recurring every now and again—that something sprang out within himself, or that a light from without sank into him, as sunlight sinks down into sea-water. When he plunged into a thicket, so that the bushes rustled as they closed around him, or amused himself by shuffling his feet in the thick, white dust of a road —or when on a frosty day in autumn he could suddenly tell that it was going to snow.

Of course it was different as he grew bigger—he began to take country walks and ski-runs, and then they moved out to Linlökka. He was now living in the country all the year round, and his mother had a garden, and he himself kept rabbits and pigeons, and one year he had a tame magpie. The more he became an intentional observer, the rarer were the moments when he felt he was taken by surprise and shown something of an invisible being; but they did come, from time to time—in the forest in spring, just as the snow is gone and the ground still shows a white gleam in the shadows and there is a cold smell from the rocks. Then there comes a moment when one suddenly stands still, as though alarmed or afraid of alarming all the fresh shoots that are about to break through the surface. Most children probably have heard the grass grow now and then.—Or when one checks oneself in a ski-run and all at once the murmur of the woods becomes audible and one looks around and sees that the daylight is about to vanish—then it comes upon one, a feeling that time is like a moving pavement, and one seems to recall one's own sensation at the moment when one stepped upon it from the timeless beyond—

It might come indirectly—when he was arranging his herbarium and *one* particular pressed flower caused him to fall into a reverie. Or when he was looking at his collection of minerals—taking up one specimen after another to feel the consistency and weight and coldness of the various ores and rocks.

81

He might perhaps have been able to work up a sort of pantheism out of this, if he had not had companions who did so and talked about it. "I must go out into nature," said Aaser, "if I am to find my God. He doesn't submit to be shut up in a low, narrow church built by men."

Paul thought it was rather nauseating to hear such things said. Besides, he had a vague suspicion that a God who submitted to be confined in anything created, might just as well let himself be shut up in a church as in a universe. That he should prefer a big house to a little one was too human an idea. For this reason it was the thought of God in the sacrament that had first led him to surmise—maybe the Faith is not so impossible. If the Almighty voluntarily submits to be confined, then the Church's explanation is the most reasonable one—he does it from love. But if God really cares for men so much that he desires to gain their love, he must make himself shockingly small—into an infant that a little girl can carry about on her arm, or a piece of bread that a man can swallow.

Besides—nature had another face to show. He remembered a little pond up country, some three miles from Linlökka. It was actually two ponds, connected with one another. First you came to one which lay on the outskirts of a big field. In summer the vegetation was tremendously thick around this pond, tall, red-flowered wound-wort and golden-topped loosestrife rose high above the rushes, and his stockings got covered with burs when he broke through in search of aquatic plants and insects. In warm weather the level of the water sank rapidly, exposing a broad edge of shiny grey mud which broke into cracks, and the pool exhaled a stale and sickly smell. It was not a good place. But if he forced his way through the osiers on the swamp that separated this pond from the other, he came to a black, round piece of water below a smooth, dark cliff —here the forest began, but the firs were black and scraggy with dead branches a long way from the ground. It was impossible to say why this place should have such an uncanny effect, but it had, and part of its spell consisted precisely in standing there and feeling this unreasonable dread.

He could well imagine that in old days people would have believed that all the ills which befell the country-side— epidemics and foot-and-mouth disease and sudden madness— were sent by something which had its abode in these two evil ponds. And if one would propitiate it or seek to win its friendship, it would have to be done by some action one knew to be evil. If this place had its genius loci, it must be worshipped in ugly deeds.

He had never heard any story connected with these ponds —never even known if they had a name. But he remembered another spot, on the way from the Aune sæter down to Rise, taking the short cut. Underneath some small ridges of rock he had felt, passing there at dusk, and once or twice in broad daylight even, that he was afraid, without the slightest reason; it was simply a physical sensation which gave him a sudden palpitation and sent a cold shiver down his back—and his dog was so frightened that he had to drag him past the spot. He had mentioned it at Rise one evening, and he saw they didn't like it; Elen said that folk didn't go past that rock if they could help it, not after dark, no, it wasn't safe.—Afterwards he was told by Martin Aune that some fifty years ago they had found there the body of a girl who had been in service at Rise, and the brother of Anton Rise's grandfather had been suspected of having made away with her; he was afraid of his mother, if she should find out that the girl had been his sweetheart.— So as far as that place was concerned there might easily be something which brought fear to the living.

But apart from that it seemed as though nature itself might suddenly show a threatening and hostile aspect. Not in the violence of storms or what were known as wild landscapes— on the contrary. There was a little copse a mile or so north of the station at home, between the railway line and the highroad to Christiania. There he and some others had found the corpse of a man; it must have lain there three months at least. Not exactly a comfortable experience. But the most gruesome thing about it was that such a miserable little remnant of undergrowth could preserve all the forest's silent and impenetrable indifference to mankind. A few brambles, barberries and elderbushes underneath the thin-stemmed and unhealthy fir-trees were enough to hide a secret like this.

It is not without reason that there are so many cruel features in all nature-religions—so long as they remain religion.

It had never occurred to him that the religion they learnt at school and that Uncle Abraham talked about could be based upon any objective reality. This could hardly have had any direct connection with his mother's freethinking—her convictions had been just as far from striking him as peculiarly convincing. On the contrary, it had always appeared to him that the others' belief and her disbelief were at bottom the same—other people's subjective convictions, or personal opinions as they called them. But he could not discover any reason for their holding these opinions, except that they gave them the right to be and act and pass judgment according to the dictates of their own nature. So that, long before he was grown up, he had already accustomed himself to judge people by what he saw of their natures and actions; but he took very little interest in the excuses or explanations of themselves which they called their convictions.

Indirectly, no doubt, it had meant a good deal that never in his childhood had he had any ideas about God. His friends had told him of the faith of their childhood. In the last few years, since it had become known in his circle that he was "interested in religion," as they said, Henrik, for one, and Kristvik too, had told him one or two things. They had believed in God and imagined God in the likeness of an old, white-bearded, mighty man to whom they said their prayers; they had confidingly prayed for fine weather for the Seventeenth of

May and that they might get the Christmas presents they wanted. As they grew up and had to change their ideas about this all-too-human God who could find it in his heart to let it rain on the Seventeenth of May though all the little boys in town had prayed for sunshine, God had become, to many of them at any rate, a concept that was in a continual state of trans-formation, "was subject to the law of change," as the phrase went in their grandparents' jargon. But reverence for this con-cept was ingrained in their whole mentality—as was respect for the figure of Jesus, even after they had ceased to believe him to be God. It had never struck them, as it struck him, when he read the gospels for the first time, unembarrassed by any kind of religious complexes from earlier periods of his life —that, if he was not God, then the crucifixion was nothing but justice pure and simple according to the law of his country, even though his judges were compelled to put pressure on the alien official in order to obtain his concurrence. But the others who had been accustomed from childhood to feel reverence for Jesus preferred to imagine an entirely different story about everlasting reformers who were eternally being crucified one after the other by the hatred of gouty and uncomprehending old fogeys. That a good many of the reformers came to grief, not because they met with hatred, but because they achieved success, and that there were traitors and brigands among the crucified, did not seem to have occurred to them—though it is one of the points of the story.

Then folk were supposed to have spun legends around the memory of a preacher who bluffed about his father's twelve legions of angels and assured people that their sins were for-given them, though he maintained that no one could convict him of sin—a man, that is, who was talking about something he didn't understand. That explanation satisfied Halstein's re-ligious feeling, for example. And for the sake of this fable the preacher's former companions—who did not give the im-pression of having been particularly heroic while they were

85

wandering about in his company—suddenly became willing to
let themselves be dragged from one torment to another; men
had to kill them to stop their mouths. And their madness had
infected generation after generation, was infectious to this day.
There never was a time since the crucifixion of Christ when
men, women and children had not been willing to face martyrdom. But they believed in a Jesus who was God and had voluntarily laid aside the insignia of his omnipotence to put on the
garment of poverty, vulnerability and mortality. Therefore
they had bound themselves by vows and set limits to their own
poor human powers—they had embraced poverty and humiliation and torments and death in order to be more like a
God who reigns from a cross. And they had believed that their
Christ had real power to forgive their sins, because it was
against him they had sinned, in any evil they had done to
themselves or to anything else of his creation.

Of course, life might be such a diabolical thing that men's
utmost achievements in the way of heroism and passion and
self-sacrifice have been wasted on a misunderstanding. Until
the misunderstanding is cleared up, and men must find something else to misunderstand in order to provide themselves
with a new faith. For instance, that there is a mysterious connection between genetic evolution and what decent people regard as progress in human morality or technics or the like.
Though it is hard to see how notions of this kind can take the
form of religion with those who have seen something of the
world outside their own little corner of existence.

Every single illiterate person in a Catholic country, if he
do but know what it means when the priest celebrates in red
vestments, possesses in any case the key to a more tenable outlook.

As far as that went Paul ought to find it easier to believe—he
had no home-made notions about God's goodness and God's
economy which had to be revised to keep pace with his ex-

perience.

Nor had he felt the want of God, consciously at any rate. True, he had always felt a kind of unconscious want—but that had been his normal state of mind, as far back as he could remember. Or, to be quite truthful—since the time when his parents separated he had always known that there was something lacking. But he had done his best not to notice it, to avoid thinking of it, because he had a feeling that it would be disloyal to life to mope over something he lacked instead of keeping before his eyes what he had. That is to say, disloyal to his mother.

Now, after the event, he thought it might be more than a mere chance that it was precisely when he had re-established relations with his father that he had set out on this blindfold search after God. At that very time it had begun to dawn on him that what he felt the want of was something different and greater.

Of course, he had then been at the age when a man ought to be able to mate—if the world were reasonably ordered. But then he had got himself a woman. And he had not considered himself bound to account to anybody for his relations with her. He had never thought of anything but living up to what his parents meant by honourable and upright conduct; that was his duty, and it was in accord with his own instincts. Then he suddenly discovered—here was a sphere in which he would never admit their right to an opinion, for here his own opinions were different from those on which his parents had acted.

Nor had he known of any others to whose judgment he attached importance. It had been no revulsion of remorse or fear, after all, of conventional morality which had impelled him to ask Harald Tangen's advice. The fact was, he had never been able to see what there was wrong in his relations with that girl. Sin, that must mean using another person purely for one's own pleasure—but he had never thought of anything but paying Lucy honourably with his whole self as long as he lived. It had really come upon him as a new discovery that something, some

kind of natural moral laws, might underlie the laws of conventional morality—though the latter had changed almost as
fast as the fashions, even in the few years that made up his lifetime. That notion that the wedding ceremony had such a remarkable value in itself that it could render even temporary
connections moral—perhaps it was based on the memory of
some kind of consecration which had really been able to sanctify
the cohabitation of two human beings into something higher
than nature?

Till now he had had nothing but his own conscience to go
by. Though in a way he had always felt it was something like
treason to claim autonomy for it—only he could not tell against
whom it might be treason.

It was true he had seen that the people who declared that
the judgment of a person's own conscience was all that mattered
were as a rule decent folk who kept to current moral ideals—
except that they might find it rather hard to keep strictly to
them when a threat of bankruptcy or a new love affair tempted
them to turn into a side track for once. They were still talking
about the authority of their conscience, in the fourth year of the
War. Did they dare to say that the freebooters of the stock
exchange, the speculators in war material and food, the fabri-
cators of lying propaganda, must have guidance enough in their
own consciences—or did they venture to assert that people of
that kind had no conscience, and that it was the peculiar property of those who condemned occasional sins? But if wife-
tormentors and bread-and-butter politicians and weak-minded
individuals and toadies stand in need of an authority to give
some slight direction to their consciences, what sort of damned
Pharisees are those who dare to say they can get on without?

One can of course abstain from condemning wife-tor-
mentors and food-speculators—admit that I am not like that,
but others are different. In other words, give mankind a sort of
general absolution without hope of salvation and rebirth.

But naturally the judgment of his own conscience was

determined more or less by the traditions of two thousand years of Christianity. And the same was true of the consciences of all so-called decent people. Their conscience would no longer approve of parents selling their daughters to yoshivaras or killing superfluous female infants, or of the slaughter of prisoners of war or of the sale of their subjects by princes, though all these things had been good morality in other traditions.

So no doubt it was an authority he had sought for in the first place. But he had not been able to discover any legitimate authority in the world outside—only various kinds of "authorities" with a relative right to direct the traffic on man's road between the cradle and the grave; and he had suspected the various moral authorities to whom he had been introduced of being Köpenick captains every one. Till at last he stole into a church to ask: "Are you here, God?" For it had become clear to him that there can be no absolute authority but that of authorship. *Jesu, auctor vitæ*, the Litany calls him.

It had been as when, one fine day, an unaccustomed light falls upon an old picture on the wall. Suddenly one discovers that there is a unity in it—the two or three details which were all one had hitherto noticed fall into their places as parts of a composition. Things which had happened to him, and thoughts which had passed through his mind years before, recurred to his memory and acquired significance in a new association. It was just the same as with the poems he had had to learn by heart at school—at the time he hadn't even attempted to get at the meaning of them, for of course they were only stuff to be crammed. But it sometimes happened, when one of these poems flashed across his memory after he was grown up, that it came back to him illuminated by one meaning behind another upon a background of unutterable things.

When once he had come to see existence in the way one discovers the picture in a painting, he could not forget it again.

Though he had tried—and at other times he had tried to follow up the lines of the hidden drawing which the light had once shown him.—In both attempts he had allowed himself to be influenced by the ups and downs of his little private life.

When he thought that life had a fuller flavour, when there was something which seemed to him worth longing for and desiring, he had instinctively longed for God. When he was so fond of another person that he simply wished he could love that person much more deeply and affectionately, he had looked for the source of all love in order to enrich his own love. But when he tried to persuade himself that he was satisfied with what he had got out of life, then it was that he was so profoundly dissatisfied that he felt sick of the whole thing. He had no use at all for letting himself be filled with more life—on the contrary, it would be extremely inconvenient.

This was childish and pitiable. And besides, it was probably what was called in theological phraseology sinning against the light and playing with the grace of God.

He had begun to think of his first confession. And he discovered with a kind of calm dismay how little qualified he was to judge of his own life. Actually he had never transgressed to any extent against the moral law he had imposed on himself, and he had kept pretty well the commandments he had himself set up. He had always tried to be a good comrade, he had never refused to help a fellow-creature when he could do so, he was not in the habit of lying—for he did not let people come to such close quarters that they had a chance of asking him questions which he did not care to answer truthfully. He was not given to gossip, for he had never regarded gossiping as anything but a kind of unseemly mental habit; and he had never taken offence at tale-bearing in others, for he had assumed that those who practised it were born that way, just as imbeciles can't help being uncleanly in their habits; he had never paid attention to any scandal that came to his ears—naturally those who spread it never had hold of the rights of the story. He had never had any immoral connections with women beyond his marriage—*that* of course was somewhat dubious, but at any rate he had tried to keep it as decorous as possible and to be what Björg understood by a good husband.

And the result had been that he thought life was hardly worth the trouble of living. It might be good enough to be an honourable man, but it was unendurable to have nothing but purely human aims and ideas. *He* had never been satisfied with it—he found that it must lead sooner or later to encystation. If the most that a man could work for here on earth was to create happiness for men on earth—and men who felt satisfied were as a rule so appalling. If any human beings could actually be content with that—with living on earth like trichinæ in meat, in order to attain to their full development, encystation.

He had heard his uncle Abraham lay down the law that in reality it was much better for a man to yield to the power of sin now and again, so that he might experience his own impotence; those who succeeded in living blameless lives were actually in a much worse way. At the time he had been shocked by these views of the old clergyman—had thought them crude. Though even then he ought to have been old enough to know that many truths *are* crude. Now he saw that after all there was something in what his uncle had said. He thought of his own children. To be sure, he would wish them to find out their own impotence by measuring themselves against God's perfection and not by discovering what it meant to yield to temptation. Though one may easily discover that too, if one puts a rather more rigorous interpretation on the world's modest demands in the way of uprightness and human solidarity—he knew that and it must be known to all grown-up people who have thought a little about war-time housekeeping. But if the worst came to the worst it was better that they should be taught their own shortcomings according to the method approved by Uncle Abraham, than that they should become so easily satisfied that they were content to be simply themselves.

PAUL happened to mention his children to the priest, one day when he had had his lesson. As he was putting on his overcoat he showed Father Tangen some snap-shots of them which had come that morning.

"What is your wife's attitude," asked Father Tangen, "with regard to the bringing-up of the children?"

"That's what I don't know. I'm afraid it won't be easy to get her consent to bring them up as Catholics."

He had never before spoken to Harald Tangen about his family affairs—had scarcely mentioned his wife in all these months.

"Has she any objection to *your* wishing to be received into the Church?"

"I haven't told her yet."

There was a pause. Paul asked:

"Do you consider that I ought to talk to her beforehand?"

"Yes, of course you must talk to your wife about it."

So Paul knew that too. To what extent he shrank from talking to Björg about this.

Presumably what people would say was that he was under petticoat government, he knew that. He had humoured Björg, whenever it was in any way possible to do so—and fortunately he had not often been compelled to insist in spite of her protests. As in the first days of the War, when she was full of absurd notions; poor little thing, she was not the only one. But as a rule he had been able with an easy conscience to give in at the first word and let Björg arrange as she pleased. For a man *can't* descend to scenes, and disagreements between him and Björg could never end in anything else. An exchange of opinions was out of the question, as Björg never had an opinion for which she could give rational grounds, he had discovered that long ago. She had simply taken over a set of opinions from her home and her surroundings—though no doubt there was some sort of system about it, which permitted her to choose or

reject according as it suited the needs of her soul. And what she
needed was to be entertained—and kept. She had preferred her
mother to her father, because she had instinctively divined that
her mother was the one who would see that all her little ambitions were gratified—pretty clothes, a "smart" school, all the
things which in the eyes of his mother-in-law stood for her
daughter's social advancement. Mother Andora was the one
who had kept father-in-law in order, so that he slaved away at
his shop and didn't indulge his inclination to go out with gun
and fishing-rod more often than his wife gave him leave.

Paul knew very well that Björg was fond of him for having provided her with a comfortable home and presentable connections and for being himself a gentleman who always remembered to show her little attentions about which she could tell
her female friends. He had heard her at the telephone: "Oh, I
say! do you know what my husband's given me—oh! what do
you think Paul's promised me—" And if it so happened that he
came home one afternoon while her friends were there, and
he accepted his cup of tea as if he liked it and made nice conversation with the ladies—then Björg was happy for days after
and assured him that he was her boy. And sometimes she took
it into her head to be spoony when it was getting on for bed-
time—in a way that was really rather touching: she was so
certain of the value of the reward she bestowed on him.

But she was not consciously designing; her calculations
even were unconscious. She clung to those who could entertain
her—the husband who provided for her and the women friends
who amused her. She was a little egoist, but Paul thought she
had a right to be that, as children and poorly equipped persons
have a right to be egoists in so far as they know themselves
to be dependent on the support of others and incapable of supporting anyone.

But what made his married life with her a little wearisome
at times was precisely the fact that she was *not* a child; she was a
person of full age without the charm that a child's childishness

93

possesses—the ceaseless development, the everlasting and spring-like surprises of growth. She had simply stopped growing at a certain early stage, and she was no more amusing than any little girl would be who was kept back in a school class below her age. A man would pretty soon grow tired even of the sweetest flapper in the world, if he did not know all the time—as she is today she will never be again, she'll turn into something new almost while you're looking at her.

He saw now that his relation to her was among the things which would have to be changed—in one way or another; how, he did not know. To talk to her of God would be useless; he at any rate could not do it in such a way as to be of use. It was through his life that he must try if he could make it clear to Björg that she herself was something infinitely more and of greater worth than he had previously been able to see in her —or than she had seen in herself, for that matter. She had always assured him that she kept the faith of her childhood and she was sure she would go to Heaven when she died. But he had never seen that she thought there was anything remarkable in that. That she had a soul that was worth God's dying to save it—he was indeed compelled to admit to himself that he found that remarkable. That God might be willing to suffer and die in order to save thorough-going, notorious sinners—well, one can understand that in a way, since with the very notion of sin one associates such ideas as suffering, spiritual crippling, some kind of fracture of the spiritual skull. And whether or not it was presumptuous to think so, he imagined he understood in a way how God had been able to wait for *him,* till he was tired of trying if he could gag his own soul.

But people of that kind, who are so cheerful and contented precisely with their own limitations, who curl up snugly in their own ego like a cat in a basket—well, well, if God created people like that, then he knows all about them that passes the wit of man, and then they must be just as precious in his sight as any other souls. It is *de fide* to believe that.

She was in any case very fond of her children. *They* might perhaps be able to awake a generosity in her fussy little soul which nothing previously had called forth.

IT was arranged that Björg should come south at Easter to look at the new house.

It stood in a fold of the great clay banks facing the river, which here widened into a little lake. The big old garden ran right down to the water. As soon as Paul saw the situation of the house, he began of course to picture to himself the accidents that might happen to the children.

Otherwise he liked the place uncommonly well. The villa was built of wood and painted white, with verandas in the Swiss style which reminded him of the old houses behind Hegde-haugen, where his father's family had lived. And there was plenty of space indoors, large rooms without too many windows and doors. For the present he had taken up his quarters in a bedroom on the first floor. It had a window which looked north, towards the high clay bank with a clump of old aspens on its crest, and another window looking west. On that side he had a view of the pool beyond the bare trees of the garden, and on the other side of the water there were steep banks with a thick growth of spruces and bushes in the hollows, but above them the cultivated land extended in an endless white surface at this time of year. Dotted with groups of farm buildings it stretched away towards distant, low wooded ridges which changed their colour every hour of the day with the variations in the weather and the light.

Paul found a continual joy of recognition in looking at this stretch of east-country scenery; Romerike—nothing over-whelming to people who travel through it as tourists, but charming to one who has been familiar with such country from childhood. There were now signs of spring hereabouts, and the snow that covered the pool was getting soppy—a soft greyish green with puddles of brownish water; when the sky was blue it was reflected in them.

The snow had begun to thaw on the level ground, dark brown plough and pale, withered pasture were gradually appearing above the white surface. As the sun declined towards the hills in the west the colours began to blaze and glow in the red farm buildings and yellow houses. But in the sunset light the distant wall of wooded heights beyond the plain became a series of ridges, the nearest olive-green from the forest, behind them others which were dark blue, and still farther off a pale blue ridge of mountain with glistening streaks of snow on its summits.

The roads round the brick-works were deep in mud in the middle of the day, when Paul walked down to the station; he took dinner and supper there at a little hotel. It was half an hour's walk, unless he could get a lift on a freight car; there was a siding up to the brick-yard. As he walked home in the evening there was a crackling of thin ice under his feet in the ruts of the road, and the tops of the spruces stood out black against the golden sunset sky, but above the slope on the north the air was white and pale green and a light still shone on the bare tops of the aspens. The birds had begun to sing long ago, and his puppy pointed some sparrows that were sitting on horse dung in the road—then they flew up, and the puppy dashed after them into the field and sank in the snow, as the thin crust broke under it.

Paul strolled about the garden and watched the stars coming out above the intricate trellis-work of the apple-trees' branches. The huge old lilac shrubs were thick with black seed-capsules from the year before. In summer the roof of foliage over the garden must be altogether impenetrable. He turned over the dead leaves, where the ground was bare of snow, to find out what grew here: little whitish shoots of snowdrop were just breaking through the surface, and up by the veranda steps the first shoots of day-lilies had come up where the sun shone during the day.

When he entered his bedroom it was full of cold, pure air, the bed shone white in the twilight, tempting as a cold bath. The woman who did the work of the house had laid wood in the stove, but as a rule he did not care either to put a match to it or to turn on the light.

Kneeling at the open window he said his evening prayer. The country was now like nothing but a dark, undulating coast against the closely-packed clusters of twinkling stars. He took out his rosary, and as he silently recited the mysteries of Christianity one by one, he felt that the string of wooden beads became as it were a staircase up which his thoughts could go—after a while his fingers grew cold and numb, but his thoughts took shape as images.

He lay awake for a while reading some pages of Juliana of Norwich's *Revelations*. He was immensely impressed with the universality of that young girl's thoughts; they belonged to no period—it was five hundred years since the anchorite of Norwich had asked these questions and received answers to them, and they were the same questions as applied in every age.— Well, of course, the beauty of her language had something to do with his finding this almost the richest of the religious writings he had come across.

The feeling of being quite alone in the house gave him boundless gratification. In the whole house there was only himself, and the puppy asleep over there in his basket.

Inconceivable that that young forester hadn't more sense —they had been talking today at the hotel dinner-table. The forester held that the working classes ought to be contented, seeing the splendid wages they earned now. Certainly they made good wages at present. But what about the uncertainty under which they had lived for several generations? It must lead to the formation of a new and different human type, when a whole class is forced into migration, following its changing centres of employment, and family circles are constantly threatened with disruption, and people are continually being packed

97

together with strangers. The tie of blood is no myth, but a stubborn biological fact. Men cannot be contented when they are not allowed to live according to the laws of nature, even if they know nothing about the law they are breaking. And it is a law of nature that men must be formed in close companionship with those to whom they owe the very type of their being, and when they are grown up, their conditions must be such that they can be left alone as much as they need—

IN the morning as he went across to the works his steps rang on the road, where ruts and footprints were as hard as if cast in iron. The whole country-side shone with a gleam like silver and quicksilver on the frozen snow.

PAUL had a secret and devout hope that Björg would now agree to let him keep his own bedroom. He had given the big veranda room next to it such a pronounced feminine character with little rococo chairs and spindle-legged tables; he had even found a bed which faintly recalled the Holms' bed of state. Not that it was gilt or anything of that sort; it was of English make in carved walnut, but it had panels of plaited cane at its foot. He half counted on her coming to the conclusion of her own accord that a great big man would be out of place among all these knick-knacks.

He sincerely wished she might like her new home. There were a great many more things to be got, and she could have her fling with those as much as she liked. The dining-room furniture was all he had permitted himself to bring in, so as not to risk any proposals she might make in the matter. He had inherited it from his uncle Paul, who had inherited it from the grandparents; his great-uncle, the first architect Paul Selmer, had designed it, in early nineteenth-century Gothic with finials and ball-flower ornaments on the chair-backs and flamboyant tracery in the pointed arches of the sideboard doors. It was quaint, and the rosewood had toned to a fine, warm brown with age.

He had had a garage built in continuation of the old outhouse. Paul smiled—wouldn't Björg enjoy being able to talk
about "our garage."

UNIVERSITY OF ....
LIBRARY
Victoria, B. C.

Chapter Six

AT EASTER PAUL WENT UP TO CHRISTIANIA AND STAYED at an hotel. His mother had gone to Finse, Hans and Evi to Copenhagen, so he did not have to go out at all, except on the evening of Good Friday, when he was invited to supper with Tua and Halstein.

They had been living in town a couple of months, and Pastor Garnaas was in the best of spirits about the move. Tua had never been really well since her operation five years ago, and the work of a country parsonage was now too much for her. Halstein hoped her health would improve now they had a modern labour-saving flat and the children were off her hands the whole morning; the two eldest went to school and the two youngest to the kindergarten.

Paul thought his sister looked a good deal pulled down; her face was old and drawn, but otherwise she had grown stout; her hands had a swollen look. His brother-in-law was evidently very solicitous about her. Perhaps he rather overdid it—at any rate Tua replied in a fairly peevish and weary tone to her husband's constant: won't you sit here and can't I do this and shan't I fetch that, Sif dear—

The two eldest little girls were nice-looking, in their father's pale, blond style; all four children had his fair, curly hair. There was a curious lost or neglected air about them— no doubt their mother had not been strong enough to give them much attention of late years, and probably their father hadn't time.

100

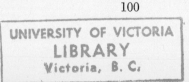

UNIVERSITY OF VICTORIA
LIBRARY
Victoria, B. C.

To his brother-in-law's question Paul replied that he had been to church both morning and afternoon on both these holy days. Halstein said something about their having also had a good congregation; he sat down to the piano and sang a couple of the hymns they had sung in church. He would obviously have liked to start a conversation with Paul on the subject of Catholicism.

Paul was himself surprised at his positive disinclination to talk about it. But he now felt an absolute repugnance to engaging in the kind of religious discussions into which he would have plunged in old days if his brother-in-law gave him but the shadow of a pretext. It could not be simply that he had grown older. But at that time he had not known himself what he was to believe; he had merely been trying to find out what was worthy of belief.

Just now at any rate he did not feel equal to talking about his faith, precisely because he believed, and was still overwhelmed by what he saw ahead of him—the consequences which must result from his belief. The services of these two days had as it were compressed him inwardly. The close network of rites, the endless succession of readings from the scriptures and prayers and hymns which hammered into people one single message —with words and with symbols, music and gestures, so that not *one* of the senses of soul and body might be allowed to leave the church uninfluenced—that men always ill-treat God upon earth; this is the tragedy of the Godhead and the tragedy of mankind; there is no other Saviour than this God who leaves his grave again in order to meet his persecutors anew. That is the explanation of all problems—from shabby little squabbles between two and two, to the great world-wars between races and classes. And whether we know it or not, we are all involved in it—in slaying God and in begging him to come back and in driving him away again.

Finally he had followed the stream that moved slowly up the nave to kiss the crucifix—it was placed on a cushion on the

101

steps of the choir. The gruesome distinctness of the symbol, that in itself was almost enough to explain the eternal revolt of the nations against the Church; and as he himself knelt and kissed the feet of the emblem he felt that now for the first time he really understood why he had tried to put off this decision so endlessly. That expression, to creep to the cross, was no doubt due to this custom. It was barbaric—like a revelation of the Church's indomitable realism, almost intolerable to people who had grown up with the unreal phantoms of materialism. "They shall look on him whom they have pierced." "And by his stripes we are healed."

They had had supper, and Halstein followed Tua out to the kitchen; he would help her with the washing up, in spite of her protests. It was the maid's evening out, and Guro went to put the two little boys to bed. Only Ambjör was left in the drawing-room and she strummed the piano unceasingly.

Halstein's Good Friday sermon was printed in the local paper of his former parish. Paul read it through—it was well written in its own way, bright and cheerful in spite of everything. At least one was bound to admit that Halstein Garnaas's bright and cheerful view of life had been capable of withstanding a good deal of wear and tear. Halstein also had that quotation: "by his stripes we are healed," but it did not appear, in this context at any rate, on what reasoning a liberal theologian based that assertion.

It had struck him during the ceremony of stripping the altar—as he looked at the bare high altar, the overturned candlesticks and the empty tabernacle with its door standing open—what if this had been the end? A world which had really got rid of God—which God had abandoned for good— How is it I have never thought of that before: what the world would have looked like without the faith which, though I did not know it, had a share in me? I should have been different—

Whether it was that he was getting old enough to be interested in his own childhood's memories, or was now instinctively trying to discover what impressions had moulded him at the outset—it was in any case a scene of his childhood that he chanced to recall.

One summer morning long ago, in a garden flooded with sunlight. The Persian lilacs were sinking under the weight of their clusters of bloom. He plucked some and took them to Tua, who was sitting on the steps of the veranda—she pulled off the flowers and threaded them together into little wreaths. It was in grandmother Selmer's garden, and they had been staying with her a long time—he had no idea how long—while their mother was ill. From their father's looks when he came up to see them, from words exchanged by the grown-ups, he had guessed that it was terribly serious. His parents had taken him with them to Hvitsten one day when they were looking for rooms for the summer, and then he had sat on a beach and watched the storm come up from behind the hills on the other side of the fiord and swallow up the daylight, and the water went a leaden colour; then the wind came upon him and big turbid waves broke quite close to him, foaming and roaring. That night he woke up, and there was his father moving about in his night-shirt with a lighted candle in his hand, and he heard his mother groaning, as if she were clenching her teeth hard, but the whole house groaned and the windows rattled and the wind roared and crashed everywhere about. Next morning when he woke his mother was gone; he had not seen her since—and he was getting more and more afraid she would never come back. He dared not ask anybody any questions, and it hurt him when the two little ones played and made a noise; but it felt much worse when he too forgot about it for a while and played and made a noise himself—and then remembered—

But that morning she had driven up in a cab, and she had a white dress on. When she had taken him in her arms and kissed him he had to run away and hide; for she had always said that a big boy like him mustn't cry. Afterwards he had a violent attack of kindness. Tua was sitting on the veranda steps, and so he made up his mind to be kind to her.

All of a sudden Tua set up a howl.—A boy who often came into the garden to play with them was standing by the steps; he had pulled his sister's lilac wreaths to pieces and trampled on them. Paul dashed up and flew at the sinner.

He had got the other boy down and was belabouring him for all he was worth—when somebody took hold of him and pulled him up. His mother stood there, in white—she held him by the shoulders looking down at him with her shining yellow eyes:

"But Paul! Are you *hitting* one who is smaller than yourself?"

Nobody had needed to tell him that again, that a boy doesn't do such things.—

By nature his mother was just as pitiless a foe as she was a faithful friend. Who had taught her that there are limits within which a self-willed person must confine himself, both in anger and in affection? Had she been as much of a heathen as she imagined, it could never have entered her head that one must spare the weak, even when they behave meanly.

Nor would it ever have entered his own head.—

It annoyed him too that he could not help being irritated by Ambjör's incessant strumming. He had set himself to live according to his new faith—so he must begin by trying to teach himself a little patience. It occurred to him that perhaps he ought to go in and remind his niece of the meaning of the signatures, but maybe it would only make her sulky—

So tomorrow Björg was coming. The service on Holy Saturday morning was the longest in the whole year, he knew; after it there would be just time to go and meet her. They were invited to lunch at his father-in-law's.

JACOBSEN had sold his property in Storgate; a five-storied office building was now being erected on the site. He had retired from business and bought a nice little villa up by the Ullevaal hos-

pital. Ole Jacobsen pottered about all day long with carpentry
and painting, and he was going to keep bees and chickens and
breed rabbits for fur. He had been given permission to bring
home his sporting dog—until now it had been boarded out in
the country—and this made him touchingly happy.

Björg looked beaming as she stood at the carriage window—
the musquash coat and black fur hat suited her golden hair and
fresh complexion splendidly.

No sooner were they seated in the taxi to drive to the hotel
than Björg burst out with her great piece of news:

"I can *tell* you there's been an awful time at the Alsters'
—the most terrible scenes. Just imagine, Henrik has found
out that Berit has been unfaithful to him—to any extent!

"—I dare say you knew about it?" she asked, almost offended when her husband said nothing.

"I? How in the world do you imagine *I* should have heard
about anything of that sort? I'm surely the last person Berit
would honour with her confidence."

"Oh.—You gentlemen generally know everything of that
sort about a lady."

Paul shook his head.

While Björg was tidying herself in the hotel room she gave
him additional information. In the previous week Henrik had
come across a letter to Berit from her friend, arranging to meet
at a mountain hotel for Easter, while Henrik was at the Syrstad
sæter. Then he had searched Berit's desk and found a heap of
other letters.

I wish to God I knew what was in *them*, thought Paul
anxiously.

At first Henrik had been quite determined to apply for a
divorce. But for the sake of the children—. And then that fellow, Halvorsen, was not the sort who would be likely to marry
Berit, and so it was hard to say what would become of her.
So Henrik had restored her to favour. And of course that was

splendid of him. But there had been some scenes that would frighten you.

"I say, Björg. Be good enough not to say anything about this at your parents'. Not a word—do you understand? I beg you as earnestly as I can."

"But, dear me—the whole town knows it. They're talking about it all over Trondhjem."

"Yes, yes, but that doesn't make it certain that anybody here— At any rate *we* mustn't say anything about it. Not a word to *anyone*. I beg you as earnestly as I can," he repeated.

He took her in his arms and kissed her between the eyebrows:

"Björg! Henrik and I have been friends since we were boys. You must surely see—this thing, it's so—tragic that I can't tell you—oh! can't you understand? If other folk don't know any better than to gossip and cackle about it— From *our* side at any rate not a single word must be said about the business. Promise me that!"

"Yes but, Paul!" She looked up into his face. "You may be sure mamma will ask after the Alsters. You can't want me to tell mamma a *lie?*"

"If they've made it up," said Paul harshly, "then you're not telling a lie if you say they're getting on well."

"It doesn't sound quite honest to me," replied Björg, rather disheartened.

THEY went out to look at the house together on Easter Day, and Björg was beside herself with delight at the new furniture and stood quite awestruck at the door of their own garage. No sooner were the holidays over than Paul let her simply wallow in her shopping.

She was radiantly pleased with her trip to Christiania and looked forward joyously to their all coming together again at the new house.

Paul was conscious of a hope that now he would reap the

fruits of his bribery, when at last he pulled himself together to tell his wife what he intended to do.

They had dined late at the hotel, by themselves, the day she was to go back to Trondhjem, and he had asked to have coffee served upstairs in their room.

He was standing at the window, looking down at the street, till Björg called to him:

"I've poured out your coffee long ago—come and get it before it's cold."

She was cuddled up in the big arm-chair with her feet under her, smoking and sipping the liqueur that Paul had succeeded in procuring in honour of the day. When he came up and stood behind her chair with his arms resting on the back of it, she turned her face to him. She raised one hand and slipped her fingers under his cuff, scratched his wrist and smiled coquettishly:

"Sorry I'm going to leave you, old boy?"

"I should say I was! But, Björg, there's a matter I should like to talk to you about before you leave—"

"How solemn you're looking!—It isn't anything horrid, is it?" she asked in some alarm.

"I've been fancying that perhaps you'd think so. It's this, Björg, that I'm going to be received into the Catholic Church quite soon."

So now it was said.—Björg turned half round in her chair and stared at him round-eyed:

"Received? What does that mean? Does it mean that you want to join the Catholics?"

Paul nodded.

"But what in the world do you want to do that for?—you've been going to their church anyhow for ever so long. Why can't you be content with that?"

Then he shirked the explanation.

"I can't receive the sacrament there, for one thing, unless I belong to the congregation," was all he said.

107

She looked at him in surprise:

"Dear me—! Well, you know, if *that* means so much to you, I won't say no. I don't suppose they're as bad everywhere. In this country of course they're bound to behave more or less decently—

"You'll regret this, Paul, I can tell you that beforehand; they all do, I know that—

"When you come to think of it, Paul," she said reflectively, "it's queer that you should be taken like that as you're getting on in years—religious, I mean. For I'm sure you were a pretty loose fish in your young days, what? But maybe that's the reason," she wondered.

"I expect it is," said Paul as seriously as he could.

"You just see that they don't trick you out of too much money—for I *know* they're awful that way—"

Then he burst out laughing, took her face in his hands and kissed her:

"Bless my heart, child—you are sweet all the same!"

"Ugh!" She rubbed her cheek caressingly against his sleeve. "Can't you ever be serious?—But I tell you this—you're not going to be allowed to drag priests and such like into the house—so that they turn the children's heads with any fanciful stuff.—Ugh. Now of course you'll be stuffing Sunnie worse than ever with all that kind of thing.—Oh, that child—I assure you she says such a lot of queer things that I'm often quite ashamed at her. Else says the same, she's quite hysterical with all her prayers and all her talk about God and Jesus and the Holy Ghost—"

"Does she still keep that up?" asked her father.

"Yes—but don't imagine it makes her anything out of the way—more pious or anything of that. I think all children would be the same, if they were given encouragement.

"Gee, I remember my brother and I when we were small. We were living then in Trondhjems-vei in an old wooden house that stood in a garden. And when the moon was right behind the

108

trees we used to sit in the window and talk about how one day
we would crawl up into the tree where the moon was shining
behind, for we thought we could get into heaven through the
moon, for we thought the moon was a hole in heaven, and then
we'd walk in and pay our respects to God,"—she laughed
quietly.

Again he took her face in his hands and kissed it gently.
Of course it was only because he was so nervous this evening—
but he was surprised to feel tears in his eyes. It was that glimpse
he had seen of her for an instant—from the time when she really
was a child that was growing and feeling its way towards the
world and life. Before she came to a standstill. These eyes of
hers that he was kissing now, perhaps they had really been the
starry eyes that he saw in her confirmation photograph—as
Sunnie's eyes were now.

"Paul, what is it?" she whispered in alarm.

"Nothing. Except what I've always said—that you *are*
sweet."

But afterwards he was well aware that he had skipped over
all the things which were bound to make their relations more
awkward in future. He had not felt up to going further into
it now.

Well it was that he had not given her a chance of discussing
the matter with her mother.

HE told Father Tangen that he had now informed his wife of
what he had in mind. And when the priest asked him what she
had said to it, he answered:

"Why, her attitude was really more sympathetic and understanding than I had expected."

THEY finished going through the catechism. And then it came
—Harald Tangen asked him when he would be received.

Paul had no other feeling but a desperate sense of his own
coldness and insensibility. He *was* convinced—believed it to be

109

the absolute truth that had chosen to express itself to the world in these configurations of dogmas. But just at this moment they seemed to him more of a Chinese puzzle and harder to get at than ever before. He thought he *saw* that they were true, but he hadn't the ghost of an appetite for them. He was not at all happy, but he knew he could not live without them. So the only thing to do was to get it over.

Afterwards it would have to be God's affair to thaw him and put fresh vital sap into the dried up mass of tissue that composed his soul. And that was what the sacraments were there for—

So he mentioned a day, and Harald Tangen made a note of it.

The priest said:

"You know there must be two sponsors present at your reception. Do you know any Catholics whom you would wish to apply to?"

"Herr Eberhard I used sometimes to meet in former days, perhaps one could ask him?"—Paul had been to see the Eberhards once, in 1914, when he came home from Paris. It was one of their little girls who was to have had Randi Alme's rosary, so he had bought another fine rosary of malachite for her. He had had the impression that they were not at all well off; there were many children. Since then he had often seen them in church, Wilfrid Gotaas too, had bowed to them, but never got into conversation.

"I am quite sure he would appreciate being asked.

"You know," said the priest, "that you have to lay your hand on the gospels while you recite the profession of faith. We usually open the book at the first chapter of St. John. But if my converts desire it to be opened at any other passage of Scripture, I usually comply with their wishes."

Paul thought for a moment:

"Then I should like it to be the sixteenth chapter of Matthew: 'But you, whom do you say that I am?' "

"Very well," said Harald Tangen. "If there should be anything else you wish to know, you'll be good enough to ask, won't you?—"

Chapter Seven

I T RAINED STEADILY FROM EARLY MORNING ON THE DAY AP-
pointed for his being received. As he was dressing Paul
sensed the whole concord of various sounds as something intensely sweet and comforting: the trickling on the window, the
gurgling in the gutter, the rain falling fast with a subdued murmur on the thick foliage of the garden.

From the window he looked out over the tops of lilacs in
bloom; they spread like a continuous surface around the house,
and there was a constant twinkling of the leaves as they were
struck by the rain-drops. The dull brown water of the pool was
lustreless and ruffled by the rain, and the country beyond was
lost in the light grey mist.

It was pouring when he left the office at midday. He dined
at the little hotel by the station with the usual two, the dentist
and the forester. The dentist proposed that they ought to get
up a little dinner for Selmer, before he relapsed into the bosom
of his family. Paul said yes, that would be very pleasant.—All
the time he knew that he felt nothing beyond the humdrum nature of the day and its dreary wetness, but on a much deeper or
higher plane of his being he had the certainty that he had made
a decision, and that it involved far more than he could survey
at the moment. Meanwhile he was neither happy nor sad; he
was doing what he had to do.

"Oh, are you going to take the train?" asked the forester;
they were standing outside the hotel putting up their umbrellas.
"Otherwise I'd have offered you a lift—I'm driving in directly."

112

"Thanks, but I've got some business to do in town."

HE felt a kind of shock of repugnance the moment he entered the vestibule of the church and saw the assemblage of umbrellas that stood there dribbling streams of water far across the floor. He had not imagined that there would be any strangers present at his reception.

As he entered the church he saw a number of St. Joseph's Sisters kneeling on the back benches, and farther on there was a crowd of Gotaases and Eberhards, big and little. He walked up the nave, subdued and a little bewildered—then Karl Eberhard and a sacristan appeared simultaneously beside him and piloted him into a seat in one of the front rows. Paul knelt down, hid his face in his hands and made a desperate effort to collect his thoughts.

I am tired, tired, tired, God, of all the devious paths I have sought out for myself. And now I am come here to ask Thee to open to me—to open Thyself to me.—But at the same time he knew that what he saw in his own soul was only a reflection—in a tiny and uneven mirror—of reality. In reality it was God who had pursued *him*, tracked him down and hunted him from one hiding-place to another. It was God whom he could no longer escape. God stood before *him* and bade him open. "Behold, I stand at the gate and knock. If any man shall hear my voice and open to me the door, I will come in to him and will sup with him, and he with me."

That then would come tomorrow. And he admitted with his whole heart that he was incapable of imagining what communion might be in reality. Only that thereby in some way or other he placed his old self in the hands of another. But that was precisely what he wished to do.

When he came into this church for the first time he had prayed: Jesus, have patience with me! Vain to reflect after the event that it would have been better if he had prayed God to deal quickly with him. Somebody had said to him once that

113

one ought to be very careful about what one prays for, for it very often happens that one gets it. It must have been Randi, presumably.—Where could she be now—? He had never ventured to ask Father Tangen about her. Though he really didn't know why he hadn't done so.

My Lord and my God. I will all that Thou wilt. I will, because Thou wilt. I will that which Thou wilt. I will so long as Thou wilt.—By Thy grace I will try to be equal to it.

At the same time he could not help noticing, with another part of his consciousness, that Eberhard, who was kneeling by his side, had taken off his overcoat and was in a frock-coat— and looked rather odd in it. And he felt uncomfortable because he himself had kept on his wet rain-coat and had come in a grey suit. Maybe it was utterly incorrect and irreverent.

Then somebody made a sign to him. Soon after he found himself kneeling again by the side of Eberhard inside the communion rail. A lighted candle had been placed in his hand. And before the altar, with his back to them, knelt Father Tangen in rochet and violet stole reciting the *Veni Creator Spiritus*.

Paul looked up at the door of the gilded tabernacle and for an instant felt dizzy, weak and light—as an empty shell that is sucked in towards the vortex of a living whirlpool. He saw that his left hand, which held the candle, was shaking.

But when he began to recite the profession of faith, he was perfectly calm. It only suggested a sheet of music—it was like reading music without having an instrument on which to play it.

Then he laid the three fingers on the open book of the gospels:

"This I, Paul Alarik Selmer, do declare, promise and swear. So help me God and these His holy Gospels."—And meanwhile he saw beneath his hand the clear, spaced type of the great red-covered book:

Respondens Simon Petrus dixit ei: Tu es Christus, Filius Dei vivi.

Respondens autem Jesus, dixit ei: Beatus es Simon Bar

Jona: quia caro, et sanguis non revelavit tibi, sed Pater meus qui in cœlis est.

Et ego dico tibi, quia es Petrus, et super hanc petram œdificabo ecclesiam meam, et portœ inferi non prœvalebunt adversus eam.

Et tibi dabo claves regni cœlorum—there the page ended. And then the book was taken away.

So now I have done it, he thought. He tried to grasp it during the remainder of the ceremony. The priest and his acolyte repeated the penitential psalm and the prayers together: now that boy was answering—it was evidently one of the Eberhards —now he is answering on my behalf, so now I too have given him authority to answer for me: *Deus meus, sperantem in te* . . . *Et clamor meus ad te veniat* . . . *Et cum spiritu tuo* . . .

WHEN he drew aside the green curtain, let it fall behind him and knelt down in the dark confessional, he felt once more like the little dry shell that was being whirled into the centre of a maelstrom. And suddenly he was unable to remember a word of all he had prepared himself to say—. Now that he was called upon for the first time to perform an *action* within the Church, it seemed to him that he was making a very poor show of it—

He could just make out that there was someone on the other side of the close grating and began: "I, poor sinful man, confess to Almighty God and to you, father, in God's stead—"

When he had finished he began to wonder what he had forgotten—

The voice from behind the grating was as it were quite impersonal—he had no thought of its belonging to Harald Tangen:

"You may now make Saint Augustine's words your own: 'I call upon Thee, my God, my compassion; upon Thee who didst create me and hast not forgotten me, as I have forgotten Thee. I invite Thee into my soul, which Thou dost now prepare to receive Thee, through the longing with which Thou hast

115

inspired it. Forsake me not now, when I call upon Thee, Thou who didst prevent me before I called upon Thee. Earnestly didst Thou call upon me in many ways, that I might hear Thee from afar and turn about and call at last upon Thee who wert calling me—' "

CERTAINLY he was glad all the same that it was done, he thought, as he rose from the bench after the final thanksgiving.

He had the impression of blundering into the middle of a street row when he came out into the vestibule—Eberhard made a dash for him, shook him by the hand and congratulated him and handed him a little flat parcel: "just a little souvenir of the day—"

After him Margrethe-Marie came up and did exactly the same.

"And Lisa wanted so much to be allowed to make you a little present—it was her you gave that beautiful rosary to," her father explained as he brought her forward. Lisa was a little object with black curls and wild, dark eyes—about the same age as Sunnie, no doubt—and Paul felt a kind of stray current of tenderness pass through him as he took her little hand and thanked Lisa for her parcel. Lisa curtsied, and they curtsied and bowed all down the line of children. The Gotaases' eldest son, whose name Paul couldn't remember, was there too with his wife and what were presumably their children. Every one of them shook hands with him and wished him joy.

Wilfrid Gotaas stepped forward and handed him a huge parcel in brown paper:

"Well, it's really from my mother, this. My mother prayed a great deal for your conversion, I must tell you. Well, we've all done that, but—. But my mother always said: 'Now if Selmer becomes a Catholic, you're to give him that crucifix that used to be in his room when he lived with us.' She reminded us of it before she died too—"

Paul was a trifle overwhelmed. It was quite right, of course;

116

indeed, it was noble and fine and all that, their having prayed for him; and now it would be his duty to pray for others. And it was only an old bad habit of his to feel jarred at hearing that so many strangers had been concerning themselves with his most intimate affairs. A bad habit and nothing else. But now he longed to make his escape—

"My wife"—Wilfrid Gotaas introduced a pale, fair little lady. "She was received into the Church four months ago. A month before our wedding—"

He had had no idea that he was going to be faced with anything like this distribution of presents and all the rest—

Finally Harald Tangen came out, congratulated him and gave him yet another parcel—evidently a thick book.

At last he got away. He had an uneasy feeling that he had begun his new Christian life by being annoyed with his fellow-Christians, and it was awkward to have to drag about all these parcels when he had an umbrella—even though he had stowed away the smaller ones in various pockets.

And when he had finished unpacking all his new possessions in his room at the hotel he stood and looked at them with something like a smile: they called it practising Catholicism. Well, here he had something to begin on—

Nevertheless, if only he had been able to grasp it, it must be an infinite mercy that had led him blindfold all the way he had gone since he last saw that little crucifix of light wood, with a corpus of white metal and a death's-head and cross-bones at its base. Now at any rate he would always hold it in reverence —and never forget old Fru Gotaas and what she had done for him.

There was only this, that not a single one of his own people knew about today. He had told nobody when it was to take place. Only to Henrik had he mentioned it in a letter.

And when all these strangers came swarming round—he had been overpowered for an instant by a feeling that now he had severed himself from all that was homelike and familiar.

—But it was touching about that little girl. Her gift, a little picture of the Heart of Jesus in a tin frame, should be hung up in his own room.

Father Tangen had presented him with Augustine's *Confessions* in Latin—a fine old edition in two volumes, charmingly bound. Paul was somewhat reassured to find that the French translation was printed below.

There was a knock at the door—the page boy came in with a telegram.

"Dear friend, accept my warmest greetings. May the step you have taken today bring you happiness, peace, every blessing. Your Henrik."

Hm. Old Henrik—yes, he had always been a faithful friend. What Björg had told him—that was a dirty business. And even now he could not help reflecting—if he telegraphed to him in those terms today, Henrik could never have found out about his being privy to Berit's villainies—

Paul sighed, desperately impatient with himself.

Tomorrow, tomorrow. But Thou knowest, God, I *am* in earnest, I will try to let Thee do with me as Thou wilt—not struggle against it. I am in earnest, I will try tomorrow, when the priest offers the bread and wine, to offer myself also with my soul and my heart, that Thou mayst transform me—

All the rest he would dismiss from his mind for the present —let the difficulties come when their time came.

A WEEK later Björg and the children arrived, and then they were busy with the move from morning till night. Early in the morning, before he went to the works, in the middle of the day when he was at home, and in the evening till late at night, he was waltzing round in his shirt-sleeves, hanging pictures and shifting furniture.

The youngster was no longer afraid of him. Far from it; Helge had now reached that stage of his development when he definitely preferred big, strong men to his mother and the maids.

118

He ran after the workmen, got between their legs and wedged himself in everywhere to see what they were doing. He insisted perpetually on papa's attending to him. And Paul was immensely flattered and touched by his little son's overtures.

It was Sunnie who had now deserted her father. She was extremely distant and reserved and could get on entirely alone —she didn't require his help even at her prayers, she declared. "I'm big enough now, I can do *everything* for myself almost." She had shot up into a lanky creature; not much more than a year and she would have to start school. It was a pity, her father thought.

Until late one summer evening.

It had been broiling hot during the day. Paul was sitting in the veranda; he had been reading, but now it was too dark for that. Björg was in town; it was a whole hour before he need drive down to meet the train.

Looking out into the garden he caught sight of a little brownish grey ball creeping over the lawn in front of the veranda. A hedgehog. He went up to it, and it stopped a little way from him, but without curling itself up. He saw its head with the coal-black, pointed snout; the prickly body went in and out as it breathed.

Only a moment before he had heard Sunnie pattering about with bare feet in the nursery. The heat must be keeping her awake.

"Sunnie," he called up to the window; "are you awake?— get on your slippers and come down quickly, I'll show you something!"

Next moment she appeared under the creepers of the veranda—so small and so bright in her white nightgown, under the pale sky of the summer evening.

"What is it, papa?—oh—oh!" She took him by the hand, and he felt how her delicate little frame trembled with excitement when she caught sight of the wonder: "papa—what *is* it?"

"A hedgehog. Have you never seen a hedgehog before?"

"Will it be all right if I pat it—"

"Yes, but look out you don't prick your fingers."

Cautiously, cautiously she bent down and touched it with the tips of her fingers—the hedgehog rolled itself up into a ball.

"Why does it do that—was it afraid of me—oh, but why? I only want to be fond of you, hedgehog—oh, isn't it *sweet*, papa!"

"Wait, stay here and you'll see. I'm going to fetch it a saucer of milk."

He came back with the milk, poured a little on the grass in front of the animal and put down the saucer. But the hedgehog refused to move, in spite of all Sunnie's coaxing and assurances of her affection.

"No, you'll get cold, child. We must go in, then it'll take the milk. It won't as long as we're standing here."

She asked question after question, full of eagerness, as her father went with her up to the nursery: "Now you must go to bed, Sunnie. The hedgehog's sure to come out another evening."

"Papa—mayn't I say my prayers over again—you can help me if you like—"

He stood and looked at the little white figure kneeling down. Till she jumped up: "inthenameofthefatherandthesonand-theholyghostamen—papa, now I'm *sure* the hedgehog has begun to drink its milk—come, let's look—" and she flew like the wind out into the passage.

Paul followed. Sunnie was crouching on the top of the old chest which stood in one of the little windows under the eaves. Paul peeped out over her head:

"Yes, you're right—can you see it, Sunnie?"

The saucer showed up as a pale round on the dark lawn, and in it the little pointed black head could be seen busily engaged. The child was on her hands and knees on the chest, and as her father sat down beside her he heard how she was panting with excitement. The hedgehog was not quick at drinking.

120

"Papa, does it drink with its tongue like a kitten or does it do the same as Ran?"

"Oh, look—papa—oh, look, now it's trotting off, so quickly!" The little ashen grey animal hurried away through the grass and disappeared under the dark lilac-bushes. "Oh, how sweet, how sweet it was—"

Paul took her up in his arms, carried her back and put her to bed. She threw her arms round his neck and hugged him delightedly: "Oh, papa, I do love that dear little hedgehog—"

BOOK TWO

Chapter One

I N THE FLOOD SEASON IT SOMETIMES HAPPENED THAT THE
road leading from the brick-works to the villa was under
water, so that Paul had to walk some way along the parish
road and take a path across the fields when he went home.

This evening was grey and light, the clouds were high; in
the north-west they were streaked with gold from the sunset.
The country was at its best in weather like this. All over the
plain groups of trees surrounded the farms with swelling clumps
of cool green, above meadows and cornfields which still showed
grey, weighed down after the rain, and the distant line of wooded
hills was dark blue.

The path brought him out on the bank below which stood
the house. On its crest was a grove of great aspens whose
leaves shivered and rustled. Paul was reminded of Helge, who
had asked the other day: "Papa, why do the trees that have all
that yellow moss on their trunks go differently with their leaves
to the birches? The birches do like this"—the boy swayed his
arms gently backwards and forwards in the air—"but *they* do
like this"—and Helge shook from head to foot. So he had
noticed that.

Beneath the clay bank lay the house, buried in dark summer
foliage. The river had fallen a little; you could get out to the
landing-stage now.

Down the slope on the north side he had laid out a road
which wound through his plantation of fruit-trees. Many of the
trees were doing well—the sun came full on them, and he had

taken great pains to get the soil right. He passed the seat and saw there was a big teddy bear lying on it, drenched with the rain —it must be the one he had bought for Little Erik last Christmas. Paul picked it up. Well, well—it was natural enough that the other children should have taken over the toys he left.

He laid the bear on the couch in the hall and hung up his hat and coat. Susanna, the parlour-maid, came to the door and asked if she should bring in the tea: "Fröken Wangen hasn't had tea yet—she said she'd wait for you, and now she's upstairs putting the children to bed—"

"Thanks, but you needn't bring it in till Fröken Wangen comes down."

The smell of paint penetrated the whole house. Paul went through the empty, darkening rooms—got rid of some papers and reviews that had been sent to him at the office. In the little room stood Ruth's easel with the picture of Sunnie and Helge.—She ought not to do any more to it now. It was very like and quite good as a picture. She had done pretty well with portrait commissions the last few years—was clever at bringing out the likeness. And it might often be the fault of the sitters if her pictures turned out rather uninteresting in their posing and colouring.

He was hungry; it was after half-past eleven. There had been so much to clear up at the works before he left for the north. Better to go up and say good-night to the children straight away.

Upstairs the smell of paint was even worse. The door of Björg's room stood open and the evening light was reflected brightly on the newly polished floor. The whole of the big first-floor landing was lumbered with its furniture. And over in the corner lay Sunnie, in nothing but her chemise—she had unrolled a corner of the carpet and made a bed of it, with her mother's sofa cushions stacked around her.

"Hullo, are you lying like that—spoiling your eyes—you can't see to read there. Why aren't you in bed yet?"

"Why, because Aunt Ruth's going to give me a bath—she's bathing Helge now. And then, you see, Helge and I have made a sort of play-room here. This where I live, sort of, don't you see?"

Her legs were horribly dirty, and her linen had an acrid smell. His perpetual, galling antipathy to his wife became acute —he had spoken about it to the nurse too, but she replied that the mistress would not allow her to give the children clean things any oftener.

Sunnie pulled off her chemise and came running up to him, to show her hip, where there was a big yellowish green mark: "You see, it still shows," she said proudly; "papa, I might easily have been killed—wouldn't it have been sad if I'd been dead too?"

"Yes, yes, Sunnie—but thank God, it was all right," he replied, dismissing the subject.

To her it was nothing but an exciting experience, now that it was all over. But he remembered very clearly that Sunday early in the spring. He had been to communion, and afterwards had gone with Father Tangen to the presbytery to have something to eat before going to High Mass. Then the telephone rang —it was a message for him, that Sunnie had fallen down in the shed with the stack of wood on top of her; they had found her insensible and terribly bruised. What despair he had been in as he dashed home in the car: perhaps another sorrow, and then to know in advance that in *his* home no sorrow was allowed to be merely sorrow, unsoiled by bitterness, distrust, mutual re-criminations. Even if he held his peace—in his heart he would still reproach her, and she knew it; she would say to him: "of course you imagine—," "I know what you're thinking—" Much uglier and more brutal thoughts than were really in his mind—but if he should try to tell her his opinion as forbear-ingly as possible, he knew that, translated into her train of reasoning, it would sound far too blunt and harsh.

However, it had not been so bad as it looked at first sight:

127

"it doesn't hurt there any more, does it, Sunnie?" He put his finger on the spot and pressed against the edge of the hip-joint.

"A little bit. I *can* feel it," she said, with satisfaction. Her eyes seemed even bigger and more sparkling, now that her face had grown narrower and her chin firmer—she was now shedding her teeth. Sunnie had shot up beyond the childish age, was now a girl—lanky, slight of limb, quick in all her movements. Her long and slender arms and legs with their rather large joints made her father think of the stalks of growing plants. A little eight-year-old girlish body like that was charming in the same way as young animals are charming— foals and setter puppies and young kids. Her cinder-blond hair fell over back and breast in long, smoothish curls.

"Papa—I'm looking forward so *much* to tomorrow!" She jumped for joy.

"Yes, but how are we going to get you two up in anything like time?—we must start at nine—"

Sunnie swung round and made a dash for Ruth, who appeared at the door with Helge riding on her back.

"Good-evening, Paul," Ruth nodded, as she unloaded the little bundle of woolly combinations into his bed. The long white apron she had on was soaking wet and her hair was curly and damp with steam and perspiration. "But I say, can't you go down and begin, you must be so hungry? It was about impossible to get these youngsters in this evening," she said with a smile. "They were perfectly wild."

It was getting on for midnight and fairly dark before the two could at last sit down to table in the dining-room. But they would not light the lamp because of the midges; they were a pest down here by the water.

Only the little electric toaster was aglow, shedding a faint red gleam over her hands and part of her face, as she attended to it. In some way or other it reminded him of her voice, Paul thought—that warm, dark glow.

128

"I had told Susanna to go to bed," said Ruth, when the maid had brought in the tea. "There's no sense in her sitting up just for this."

Paul felt a vague wish that the girl had done as Ruth said. Of late years he had got into the habit of sitting up till far into the night; it was not merely the stillness of the house that he liked, but the consciousness that he was the only one awake.

It did not occur to him that he made an exception of Ruth. He liked having her here—one of his own people. He had rather lost sight of the others, in a way, of late years. Since he became a Catholic.—Or perhaps that was not the only reason; he had been living in another part of the country for a long time, and had married one who decidedly did not harmonize with his family. So he took his ease in the society of Ruth, who let him feel perfectly free and unconstrained.

THEY went out for a stroll in the garden after supper.

"I should be glad if we had fine weather for the drive to-morrow. It's no fun if we have to put up the hood."

"It looks like clearing up. I dare say we'll get a shower or two on the way."

They had come as far as the pool. The railing Paul had put up to keep the children away from the edge was now far out in the water, but the stone landing-stage showed above the surface.

"It's too late for a row this evening again—"

"If you're not too tired—" said Ruth. "I should like so much to go out. Only a little row."

"Oughtn't you to have put on something?" He opened the little gate and they went along the pier. The night was spacious and light about them, coming from the thick leafy darkness of the garden; a pale gleam came from the pool.

Paul rowed out. The leaves of the water-lilies were beginning to float up to the surface.

"No, there are only the yellow ones here," he replied to her question. "Are you so fond of the white? You ought to have seen them, in a lake over by Ronglan—I've never seen so many water-lilies—"

Farther out the current ran strong. It felt refreshing to row against stream. The alders lining the bank were far out in the water.

He was grateful to Ruth for sitting perfectly silent—huddled up, with her hands inside the sleeves of her golf jacket.

Daylight was appearing already. The sky had cleared, as though the veil of cloud had been imperceptibly sucked up and had melted away into the pale blue vault. Now they had come out into the big upper pool and had a view of the country to the northward. All the farms were still asleep; there was no light to be seen anywhere and not a sound, but the white farmhouses were beginning to show up against the grey dawn. Then a fiery eye appeared far away under a belt of forest, hovered and came nearer, and the roar of the motor-car became audible. It swept over the bridge at Narum, projecting huge cones of light before it along the road.

The birds were awakening when they returned to the landing-stage.

"Is it really impossible for you to take a few days' holiday?" Ruth asked, as he held out his hand to help her out of the boat. "Well—now of course you've stayed up far too long, and it's my fault. But you *have* been looking rather tired lately, I think."

"I can't *now*. I hope I'll be able to manage it in the autumn. But you know I shall look you up at the sæter, every time I'm at Haugen."

NEXT day Paul drove off in glorious weather. Ruth sat in front by his side and the nurse behind with the children. They cheered loudly as the car dashed through water on the road by the river, and every time they came to a bad piece of surface Paul heard their shouts of joy as the wheels gave a jump or splashed up water from the puddles.

130

HE had seen Ruth properly installed at the Hauga sæter with Gladys and the children, and on the following day he had had enough to do at the steatite works; so it was fairly late before he could drive on. But he liked motoring at night.

These trips by road between Berven and Haugen were really the only rest he had known during the last few years. Driving a car—and driving alone—was rest. And even that meant a good deal.

Now again as he drove up through Dovre this feeling of well-being settled upon him. The amount of external attention he was compelled to give was sufficient to keep his own thoughts comparatively passive—though they were stirring the whole time.

Now and again he saw patches of sky among the hills which were still red and golden from the evening sun. The river at the bottom of the valley ran swiftly, grey-green and streaked with white in the rapids. Here and there a yellow-foaming brook came tumbling down the hill-side and darted under the road—for an instant its roar could be heard above that of the car. The sides of the valley with the old brown farms were in shadow; herds of goats and lines of cows strayed along tinkling their bells or stood in a clump lowing and bleating outside a gate; there seemed to be many places hereabouts where they had not yet moved the cattle up to the sæters. Often and often he had to slow down and hoot at beasts in the road.

Who can tell whether *this* won't be a thing that people will dream about, some day in another age—if they take the trouble to dream about our times—the romance of the automobile? If by that time traffic has been transferred to the air. All the changes in the external forms of life which we have witnessed, the inventions and the names of the inventors—all these they will simply jumble up together, and they will judge of our social conflicts and wars and the rest from the standpoint of their own sympathies and political system, just as people always have done.

But no doubt they will weave fancies about cars rushing along on the old high-roads, through the depths of forests, between banks covered with flowers, under cliffs and fir-clad slopes. About folks who drove through the spring night— splashing their way through pools of water every moment, while the gleam of their lamps went before them lighting up stretches of fencing and spruces, the outposts of dark, mysterious woods beyond.—They will look upon us as men who still lived in close association with living nature.

He had ordered supper at Hjerkin, and went out to stretch his legs while it was being got ready. The night was cold up here among the mountains, but it was wonderfully still, with a babbling of water and a murmur of wind over the waste. Grey snow was lying far down the slopes, a white gleam shone from the snowfields above, where they rose against the bright sky. He had not met a car since passing Fokkstuen, had had the road entirely to himself.

Undoubtedly he would do better to employ this time in telling his beads. That he felt no desire to do so was only a reason the more—he ought to take himself by the scruff of the neck, force himself to think of other things than his own affairs.

The humiliating and disheartening part of it was that he *could* not look forward to being with Björg, even for so short a time as this would be, without positive dread.

Of course he was well aware of its tragi-comic aspect. But the first result of his new Christian life, at any rate as regarded his relations with his neighbour, was to make him a stranger to those nearest him. And his married happiness—such as it had been—was a thing of the past.

The first six months or so had gone smoothly. Mrs. Anderson came on a visit to Norway early in the summer, and this time she behaved as a model Catholic. She may have been that when she was here before, for all he knew—she had no idea that he had ever been interested in the Church, and as for her

132

own circle, she knew well enough that prejudices against Catholicism formed an integral part of their very mentality. So why should she waste her time in idle demonstrations?—Now at any rate she was very "devout," and during the six weeks she stayed with them at Berven she collected all the children every evening—Sunnie and Helge and Etta and Sid and Bridget and little Peter Pan—for very long-winded evening prayers. Sometimes Björg too came into the nursery while this was going on, sat on a chair with her hands clasped in her lap and wore a devotional look.

But when Aunt Selma had retired for the night, Björg was apt to throw her arms round his neck and burst out laughing:

"Goodness, Paul—but isn't it frightfully comic—that *you* should be taken this way!"

"Comic, yes—" he laughed too.

"What do you think your mother would say if she could see you all kneeling like that, the whole roomful of you!—But seriously, Paul, I can't make out how you can like it."

"Are you sure I do like it?"

"Well, but if you don't like it, it's hypocrisy, isn't it? No, thanks, let me worship God in private if you please!"

"But one can do that *too*, Björg. I can worship God as much as I like when I'm alone. But I'm not sure that what I *most* need to learn at present isn't this—that God is everyone's God, and that what I wish God to be for me, God Himself wishes to be for *all*. Without respect of persons. So I *ought* to rejoice in every human being who pays Him adoration, and I ought to be grateful to anyone who may say to me, come, let us worship—"

"Are you that though? Does it really make you so frightfully glad on God's behalf when Aunt Selma gets up and announces that 'now it's time for evening devotions'?"

"You mustn't be so sharp at cross-examining one," he laughed.

But she acquiesced in Aunt Selma's presenting the children

133

with handsome rosaries and crucifixes and pictures of the Holy
Family and St. Patrick and "The little Flower." And Aunt
Selma was deeply moved one evening, when she came in and
found Helge standing up in bed, licking away with all his might
at the picture she had hung over his head and pretending he was
eating the grapes that the Child Jesus held in His hand.

Björg went to High Mass with them on one or two Sun-
days and let him take Sunnie. They filled a whole bench.—
Paul began to hope she might soon follow him into the Church.
And then surely their marriage would acquire the human quality
it had lacked. Perhaps she had unconsciously felt this want as
much as himself, perhaps she had felt how undernourished her
soul and heart had remained, in which case she would be grateful—would be much more pious, gentler and better than it had
made him. She said nothing either one way or the other, when
he ventured to hint at anything of this sort to her.

Even his mother-in-law was surprisingly amenable. But
he knew very well that this was due to her respect for Mrs.
Anderson's affluence. Mr. Anderson evidently occupied a certain position where they lived. The convent where Etta went to
school looked like a country seat with parks and playing-fields
on a grand scale.

He was fully aware that he himself would not have liked
Mrs. Anderson, had she not been a Catholic. But what then—?
That her religion was the best thing about her was quite as it
should be. It was splendid that it should stimulate in her a
certain spiritual enterprise and supply the motive power for
benevolence and generosity—she helped a great deal in the
congregation of St. Olav's while she was in Norway. Had she
not had a religion which demanded of her a continual effort on
her part to keep the road clear between herself and God, she
would probably have been pretty close-fisted like her cousin.
She got him to subscribe to a few American Catholic magazines,
and he had got a good deal of pleasure out of them; they often
had good and interesting articles, particularly about topics of

the day.

His mother thought Mrs. Anderson simply awful, and she made no scruple of showing how she pitied him. Her son! who had now learnt to put up with the most second-rate society and had ended by feeling at home in his wife's circle. His mother laid the blame for everything, his conversion included, upon Björg.

As usual her intuition had put her on the track of the truth, whereupon she had formed for herself entirely erroneous opinions regarding the semblance of the truth.

For naturally, now that he had to judge of his life as something for which he must answer to God, one of the first things he discovered was his wife.

He had never denied to himself that he had acted foolishly in becoming involved with Björg. But he had tried to make the best of their relations, so far as his understanding went. Regrets after the event would be shabby. No more miserable creatures existed than such men who tried to rid themselves of wife and children because it dawned on them later that their marriage had been a blunder, or who excused their extra-connubial adventures by saying that they didn't know what they were about when they married, and that their wives only cared for them as breadwinners and fathers of their children, so they were not robbing anyone in giving to a mistress what the woman at home cared not a rap for. To be sure, this was true enough— he too could easily imagine relations with other women which would not lessen Björg's share in him in the slightest degree.—But if ever, in his callow youth, he had imagined marriage to be something like the perfect mutual devotion of two personalities, a kind of wordless and profound interdependence, he had been cured of such ideas so effactually that the feeling remained with him. Not two human beings who were merged in one another, but two who charged themselves with duties and tasks in common, that was what it was. And should it turn out that one was not equal to performing one's tasks and duties so well that it was not easy to imagine how they could have been done better—then one had to go on doing one's best. And even if in one's heart one thought the other partner had not succeeded according to one's expectation—that did not excuse one's contributing less than one's full capacity in the circumstances, or actually turning one's back on the whole thing. Regrets for a stupid act were out of place.

That he had really done something which he *ought* to regret—had wronged another, Björg—had not occurred to him.

Now he understood that it was so. He had married as one accepts a conventional present, something one has no use for and would never have thought of buying for oneself—but it would not be polite to refuse it, and it does give one a sort of agreeable surprise at the moment, to be given an unexpected present. But it was another human being that he had accepted with this levity, a young girl—and at any rate she was innocent and inviolate, whether significant or insignificant. To a certain extent at least her whole life was bound to depend on the sort of man who took away her virginity. He had taken Björg as one opens a box of sweets. And he had continued to live with her as one might nibble at a box of chocolates, not because one is particularly fond of them, but when they're lying so handy—

And now, after being married to her so many years, he had come to realize that he had sinned against her—and he was forced to admit that he could not discover how he was to make amends.

Do not attempt to influence your wife with *words*, said Father Tangen; but by *living* your faith. Do the holy will of Christ, lay up His words in your heart after the example of Mary, lend a quick ear to every impulse of God's spirit, learn from the saints' way of life—and have patience, also with yourself. Gradually, as the change comes about in you and she understands it, your wife too will feel impelled to adapt herself, so that the harmony between you may be re-established. Even if this may take time.

But is it not conceivable that she will not do so? he had asked. It was in his first year as a Catholic that he had had this conversation with the priest; at that time he still had some kind of notion that a confessor ought to be able to do some prophesying about the affairs of this world.

"Yes, unfortunately. That is not a very rare case. That one partner in a marriage after his conversion continues to have difficulties with the other. It may be years before the other begins to grasp the implications of conversion. Sometimes it does not occur in this life. In that case it is the duty of the Catholic to hold out loyally and patiently."

That did not seem to be asking so very much—just after a confession and a communion. He felt quite safe—how should he not be patient when he had been given glimpses of what was meant by the patience of God? He who had tried to ignore his own soul—could he not learn to be mindful, in reverence and tenderness, of his wife's neglected little soul? For more than eight years he had lived with a woman and had children by her without ever reflecting that she had a soul which must one day stand naked before eternal decisions.

BUT no sooner had Mrs. Anderson gone back to America than Björg began to show her distaste for all his new "notions" as she called them. Why should he want to go to church every blessed Sunday? He had his own bedroom now; he stole out and took the early train to town, attended early Mass and was home again for their late Sunday breakfast; but Björg was annoyed for all that, and it made her angry when Sunnie fidgeted to be allowed to go with her father.

"The children belong to the State Church, and you'll be doing a dirty trick if you try to lure them over to your side in that way. Do you think it's acting like a Christian to bring them up to despise their mother's religion?"

It seemed to Paul that he was really innocent of anything

137

like that. Björg had decided to take Sunnie to the parish
church one Sunday; it was four miles away and Björg drove the
car herself. Sunnie was delighted as they drove off, but expressed great disappointment when she came back:

"The parson preached the whole time and then they kept
on singing, so there wasn't a chance of praying to God the least
little bit. They're not allowed to do anything themselves in
that church."

On the whole it was unfortunate that the children had got
that impression—that religion was a thing about which papa
and mamma disagreed. Björg was vexed at all the devotional
objects with which her aunt had crowded the nursery. Paul took
most of them away and hid them in his own room: "you'll like
them better when you can have them all brought out at once."
But when their mother was out for the evening, Sunnie and
Helge came and asked him to get out all the pictures and rosaries and medals. They never did that when Björg was at home.
And one evening, while they were looking at the things, Sunnie
caught sight of her mother coming along the road; they had not
expected her before the last train: "Hurry up and hide them,
papa; mamma's coming.—We must run down and meet her,
you know," she corrected herself, turning red.

He had invited all the Gotaases and Eberhards to dinner
one Sunday, the first summer. Doubtless Paul had always been
aware that within what he lumped together as a unity, the lower
middle class, there existed class distinctions as sharp as those
dividing Indian castes. But personally he had not realized it.
Björg considered that such people as the Gotaases and the Eberhards were certainly no society for them, and she greatly disliked their children mixing with her own.

Yes—she was also afraid these people might ask him for
help, and that altogether his new faith might prove a costly
business. When maximum prices for building materials were
fixed that summer, Björg seemed to think that too was in some
way a result of his conversion. But it was all so sickening that

he scarcely cared to think of it.

His attempts to be a better husband for Björg had turned out miserable and ridiculous failures. What could he do for her beyond what he had always done—give her presents, provide her with amusements? He went to town with her and took her to the theatre, they dined at restaurants, took lessons in the new dances. She was bored out here in the country. He went with her to the cinema in town, when she had no one else to go with her. That was the most depressing thing he knew, sitting in the cinema. It always reminded him of those fans of picture post-cards that Lucy had had on the wall of her first little room. It was as though a nightmare had endowed those cards with a kind of caricature of life—they grimaced with their crudely made-up faces and parodied human passions and actions. Even if the films were not improper it had an uncomfortably improper effect to see this pictorial matter in motion, weeping and kissing —a kind of slandering of life; everything essential, everything explanatory, all the multiplicity, light, air, colour, tempo, was suppressed. And ridiculous it was that the only thing he could do, now that he was trying to make amends for the wrong he had done to Björg, was to follow her about to the kind of amuse-ments which forced him to exercise patience.

All she demanded of him was that he should humour her, as he had done hitherto, since nothing but trifles had been involved. And she became indignant because there were now points on which he could not yield.

He had been forced to board out the two Viennese children that he had agreed to take into his house the summer before. On the other hand, he had refused to give Frans notice. This was a Catholic lad for whom Father Tangen had asked him to find work if he could; the priest said plainly that he was not a pattern of virtue, and it would be a good thing if he were got away from Christiania. Frans had a driving licence, but it was agreed that he was to work in the garden as well. He was fear-fully lazy and discontented because he was so seldom required in his capacity of chauffeur; otherwise he was obliging and peaceable enough, though not exactly a good advertisement for the Catholic Church. Björg had some reason for being annoyed about him; but Paul thought, if Father Tangen once in a way had asked him to do something for one of his own faith, why then—

AND then, suddenly, the ill humour between him and his wife changed—from petty nagging irritation and skirmishes over trifles—to earnest.

Björg discovered that she was going to have a child again. She was in utter despair and beside herself with rage. This was about the New Year, 1920.

Of course he had always known that this was one of the points on which he and she differed fundamentally. *He* had tried to silence his own conscience by arguments and quotations of other people's opinions. In this, as in so many other things, it seemed to him that what the Church taught in clear and concise dogma was nothing else than what he himself had divined, in a vague fashion, confused by fear of the consequences, if he put his most hidden instincts into definite thoughts. That was all.

But if a man tells a woman that, he naturally receives the answer to which no rejoinder is possible: that it is not he who is to run any risk, to bear the burdens and suffer the pains, and it is so easy to insist that another shall sacrifice herself to one's instincts and ideals and principles. And a man is forced to hold his tongue—even if he knows that he too is willing to make sacrifices for the sake of his principles, that he too is willing to take the full consequences of what he did in choosing to found a home for himself. But his knowledge of men's shabby and stupid irresponsibility as regards women in general and of husbands' brutality in particular is sufficient to keep him silent, for shame's sake alone. And he is conscious that he too of course has given pain to his wife a number of times without knowing it, has worried her through thoughtlessness and want of imagi-

140

nation and because she is the one who is always there when he
is out of temper or tired or has his head full of worries—

Björg had let him know three years before, after Helge
was born, that now she considered she had done her duty as a
citizen: a boy and a girl, that was what one could wish for. She
referred to them on occasion as "the two children I have given
you."

Now the fact was that she regarded the relationship between them, man and wife, as though she bestowed on him
something of immense value to a man—even if she could not
quite make out why men should be so dependent on this, and
she felt that she was considerably superior to him and his whole
sex, because she was not dependent in this way.—This last consideration however was not entirely in accordance with the
truth—in any case she demanded his advances as a homage
and an acknowledgment that he could not do without her. But
of course, erotic she was not—though she was pretty spoony
and could be downright clinging in a flapperish and immature
way which was often tiresome enough.—Another man might
perhaps have been better able to strike erotic sparks from her,
one who had not discovered how retarded she was in her growth,
but had met her as an equal, with a different kind of egoism
from his own—more exacting and imperious. But he was not
the man for that.

Nevertheless he had always believed that when she talked
of their children as though they were two prodigious prizes she
had bestowed on him as a reward for good behaviour, this was
merely a figure of speech she had picked up from books and
ladies' papers. He had been certain that in reality she was just
as fond of the children in her own way as he was. To her as to
him they were two little marvels, riches and responsibility, life's
earnest and jesting, God's precious works of art which had been
entrusted to their care. Damn it, of course she was an anæmic
little soul, healthy and sound as her body might be; no one
could expect her to supply any surplus of vital warmth to

another. But suppose her life had been that of an old maid, working for strangers—that certainly would not have suited her.
Now she simply took it as a matter of course that she had a husband and children, because she was incapable of imagining anything outside her actual circumstances.

That is what he had believed. And in reality he believed
it still. And it had been due to a kind of childish obstinacy that
she would not submit to be mollified even after the boy had been
born. The possibility of their losing Little Erik could not have
occurred to her, any more than to himself. He had been so well
and hearty at first, just like the two elder children. For them
they had never been seriously alarmed, and this little one was
thriving and developing all the time, in the same way.

Then, in February, when he was five months old, he died
of meningitis.

It had been terrible, to see the little child suffer like that;
sometimes he had screamed as though in extreme torment and
terror. Hans said the boy was unconscious, scarcely felt what
was going on in his own little body. It was unbearable all the
same—when one was so utterly powerless. Then he died. It
was better so, said Hans; there was no knowing how the child
would have turned out, if he had got over it.

And then Björg's face, paralysed with horror, her eyes staring, black and terrified. She fled from the sick-room when Erik
screamed, sat huddled up downstairs, winced when he came in.

"Can't you pray that we may be allowed to keep him?" she
whispered in a scared voice. She dared not look at him when he
was dead—not before the next day.

Afterwards she turned upon Paul in her despair: "Of course
you think this is a punishment on me for not wanting to have
him—"

"No, Björg, I don't think that."

"Oh yes, you do, don't deny it; I *know* you do. I'm *sure*
you believe it's a punishment for my not wanting to have any
more children. Why else do you think God should take Little

Erik from us? How much good did it do, your praying that we might keep him?—can you see now how much God cares for your flying off to church every blessed Sunday and saying your prayers morning and evening and crossing yourself at table and all that— Ho no, that's not what's wanted. Oh—why couldn't he be spared all that suffering at least—when he was so small—"

But they had always known that there were little children who suffered and little children who died. She too had known it, she too had lived through the whole war—and it had not disturbed her belief that God was kind and accommodating to all decent people. So long as it was not their children who were called upon to pay their share of the debt of the whole race. Erik had paid, before he was old enough to contract any debts of his own. But it would have been vain to attempt to put before her the explanation he himself had accepted. He tried to hold fast to it now, when his own child had been chosen to suffer innocently and to leave the world to receive his wages with Christ. But to Helge and Sunnie he said that they had now a little saint who was their own, and when they said their prayers they must also pray for Little Brother's intercession.

Björg went about in fear and silence, but met his every attempt to break the ice between them with distrust and hostility. The children noticed that something was wrong in their home; they were quiet and dispirited when they had to be in the room with their parents. When they were out of doors, thank God, there was nothing the matter with them.

He got Ruth to come, so that she might begin on the portrait of the children that he had promised Björg for a birthday present. This put Björg in rather better spirits; Ruth had always made herself very pleasant to her, and she admired Ruth and would have been extremely glad to meet the "amusing people" who formed Ruth's circle. But when Henrik Alster wrote to Björg proposing that she should accompany Lillian up to his new sanatorium and stay there some time as their guest, she eagerly snatched at his invitation. And now she had been away from home some five weeks.

PAUL drove on in the light summer night. That the road over the mountains was practicable was just barely true; there was still a good deal of snow on it. Twice he was held up by drifts and had to dig himself out. At sunrise he swung into the yard of the sanatorium, and Henrik himself came out to receive him in a dressing-gown: "Cold driving over the mountains, wasn't it?—Oh no, don't worry about its being a bit late—early rather. I've got some food and a drink for you in the office—"

Yes, he thought Björg had picked up very well, he said. Berit was here with Lillemor. They had had a number of visitors—not many just now, but more were coming for the holidays.

Then he took Paul over to the new building: "Tomorrow you shall have a room in the main building next to Björg's. But for tonight—I thought you would prefer not to wake her and to have a long sleep in the morning." He himself was yawning.

ALSTER had bought Syrstad towards the end of the war, and when rationing was being given up he had had the idea of building a big modern tourist hotel or sanatorium on the place. When the Dovre railway line was opened it would certainly have a future before it. He got Lillian Selmer to join him in the undertaking. She had speculated with and without success since she had been a widow; besides which she considered herself far too young to have nothing to do, so she was to have the business management.

Paul had had some misgivings and mentioned them to his step-mother: Alster had bought Syrstad at the top war-time price and had built on to it and fitted it up regardless of expense. He disliked saying anything against Henrik's proposal, but his father before he died had made his sons promise to look after Lillian to the best of their power. Hans however advised

144

acceptance; he himself was gambling pretty freely with the money his wife had brought him. So Paul did not insist very firmly on Lillian's following his advice.

BJÖRG came and knocked at his door next morning while he was shaving. And he had already lost the laboriously acquired habit of his early married years—of patiently acquiescing in the presence of a stranger while he was dressing.

"You can guess I'm *terribly* anxious to hear all about the children and how they are." She seated herself in the rocking-chair; she looked well in a thin silk dress with a black and white pattern. When he had finished washing she called to him from her chair: "Aren't you going to say good-morning to me properly, Paul?" Her voice sounded sprung, as though she were a little anxious. Afterwards he had an uncomfortable feeling that he might not have succeeded in putting very much cordiality into the kiss he greeted her with.

"Won't you go across and start breakfast, Björg?—I'll be there in a moment." He did *not* want to have her sitting there while he said his morning prayer.

As he crossed the yard to the main building a few moments later, Paul felt that Sunnie might have good reason to find fault with him today, as she sometimes did with Helge: "I don't believe *you* were really thinking about God while you were saying your prayers—"

HE had to drive back the very next day, and glad he was to get away. He was not in the mood for society of any sort. And those people he had spoken to at the sanatorium were at any rate not of a kind to alter his inclination. There was a business man named Schjistad and his wife, to whom Björg had evidently attached herself. Paul was only moderately pleased to hear that the Schjistads were also leaving tomorrow and that Björg had arranged that they were to drive in company across the mountains, so that they might have supper together at Dombaas before separating. But he could not think of any pretext for avoiding this. Well, after all it was only a trifle—

The Schjistads were going abroad at once, they would only stay in Christiania a day or two. And in the afternoon, when all four were sitting together in the veranda, Schjistad proposed that Fru Selmer should join them; it was an invitation, they were taking their car, and they would be so glad to have Fru Selmer with them. Berlin—"just think of all the things you can buy there, Björg," said Fru Schjistad. "You were saying you wanted a new fur coat so badly—even with the duty it'll be frightfully cheap.—Or you might wait till we get to Paris." They had planned a trip to the front in Flanders and Northern France as well—that would be so interesting.

Paul declared it could not be done. "It would be far too fatiguing for my wife, who has just been ill and suffering from her nerves. What you want now is to come up to the sæter for a while—and the children are looking forward so much to seeing you."

"Dear me, it's only for three weeks, Paul. I'm sure Ruth will look after them very well, that little time—"

"We can't ask Ruth to stay and look after the children. She has taken a house at Vasser with Marie Aaser. Besides, you know it will take some time to get your passport in order. You would be delaying Herr Schjistad."

He could not give her the money for a trip abroad at the moment; as usual he had big payments to make in his businesses. And he thought these tourist trips to the war countries a disgusting thing.

In the course of years he had accustomed himself to her little linguistic solecisms. When they were first married he had tried to correct her now and then, but he soon found that she was hurt by this. This afternoon these slips of speech began all at once to irritate him past bearing, and he found that Fru Schjistad spoke the same dialect.

No sooner had they gone up to their rooms that night than

she began:

"Paul—do you know, I think, when the Schjistads are so sweet and want to have me go this trip— You never have time for anything, you haven't; I shall never get abroad again with you! And then, when one's offered such a frightfully interesting foreign trip perfectly free gratis—"

"Yes, but one can't accept an invitation like that from perfect strangers, Björg. You've known the lady a fortnight, and I haven't set eyes on them before today."

"Well, I never! Anybody can see with half an eye that the Schjistads are tip-top people. And just let me tell you, I've got to know them thoroughly, I have. I count Hjördis Schjistad as a real *friend*!"

"Well, well, I'm sure they're amiable people. But all the same you can't accept anything of this sort from them. Besides, I can't afford to stand you a trip like this just now— that's the truth, Björg! For you know, you couldn't anyhow have accepted more than just the journey—"

"Pooh! I shall simply be saving money, old thing! For I shall buy a whole lot of things we must have, for myself and the children—just think of the exchange!"

"Do you really want to let them call you an exchange-hog down there?"

"Pooh! That only shows their foolishness. They ought to be thankful, I should think, to have foreigners coming and spending money in their country.—Paul," she said beseechingly, "don't you really think I need a little cheering up? Before I have to go back to Berven and all its sad memories?"

Because her saying that jarred so unpleasantly, he took pains to give her a gentle answer:

"Yes, yes, Puss, I quite understand that. But listen—I shall do my best in any case, and it's quite likely I may be able to arrange things so that you and I can go abroad together—a little trip in the autumn."

"Oh yes! I fancy I see it! You'll come and tell me you

147

haven't time after all—except to go away for the shooting,
you always find time for *that*. Besides, you've got everything
arranged with papa for the shooting, I know—do you mean to
let him down perhaps?"

"I can always put it right with your father, Björg."

"Or else you won't be able to afford it! It seems funny to
me how little you're able to afford since you turned Catholic."

Paul made no reply. Then she came up to him:

"I'm sorry, Paul—I didn't mean to be horrid! But *can't*
you let me go—I want to so terribly!"

"I've told you, no. One doesn't accept invitations of that
sort from people one knows so little."

Björg let go of him, stood still a moment. Then she
stamped her foot, ran into her own room and slammed the door,
turned the key in the lock.

Paul fervently wished she might not take it into her head
to unlock it again.

Next day he and Alster had a long talk about the brick-works.
But after that Paul had nothing to do but hang about and long
to get away. They were to leave as soon as they had had coffee.

Berit's being here did not make things any more comfortable for Paul. He had never got over his feeling of awkward-
ness, whenever he had to be in the room with her and
Henrik now.

It was simply and solely his being in such a wretched
temper that made him behave like a brute to Lillemor. But it
did annoy him to see how the child had got herself up—in
short skirts, with cropped hair, powdered, blacked round the
eyes and with reddened lips. It suited her very badly; she was
like her mother, tall and powerfully built, with rather coarse
features and a pronounced brunette. All the same he had thought
Lillemor had grown pretty, when she visited them a year ago
on her way to the continent. She had had a lovely dark complexion, fresh lips and splendid dark eyes. They had always

been such good friends, he and Lillemor.

She sat next to him at the dinner-table and told him about her meeting his brother in Paris:

"Terribly sweet he was to me! Was on the go with him all the time! I suggested that he'd better come home with me—promised to take *such* good care of him. But oh, no. Not even that would tempt him. *I* think it's such a pity that Uncle Sigmund has never made anything of it really. But he'll never get away from Paris, you know. And I can quite understand that. What I *don't* understand so well is that he can't get away from that lady of his! Goodness, how wild she was with me! But I was Siggen's chum, you see—my word, what times we had together! He thought bobbed hair suited me so toppingly. Do you think so, Uncle Paul?"

"No, I think it's a sin."

"Sin? Oh! Well, of course *you* would. Though I must say I can't see why it should be sinful to cut one's hair off—"

"Oh, that way—" Paul laughed. "No, no, Lillemor—I meant it's a sin against your pretty hair."

"Ouf, that! Horsehair—just like mother's. And such a bore too. Well, then you don't think it's a sign of profound moral corruption if I smarten up my façade with a little powder and lip-stick and so on—?"

"Bless you, no, child. I'm sure you're just as sweet and good as you were when you were a little girl—and sometimes forgot to use your table-napkin after a meal."

"Goodness, what *do* you mean?"

"I mean that it comes to about the same thing if little girls forget to wipe their mouths after they've been gnawing chicken bones, or if they go smearing their faces with a lot of flour and red grease—"

"Well, I must say! Are you *really* so old-fashioned, Uncle Paul?—For you needn't think the men of our day agree with you. I assure you they don't think a little embellishment of that kind makes a face any *less* inviting—to kiss, for instance."

149

"Well, but, Lillemor—you weren't always so frightfully clean and nice in old days either, when you came and wanted to kiss me—and yet I thought you were quite inviting!"

"Oh, you may be sure you'll be let off now!—But I suppose this is the old drivel about us women being less cleanly than the men-folk—"

"Ssh, my child. *I* have never asserted that cleanliness was a virtue; it's a luxury. And if you refuse to take the consequences, after enjoying the luxury of a bath, but make haste to smear yourselves again with flour and other food products, I'm not going to be scandalized by it—"

"I never heard anything like it! You say straight out that it's piggish of us to use cosmetics.—Well, well, it's a good thing everybody doesn't agree with you. Then we should be obliged to go about looking like dowdies and scarecrows before you would condescend to bestow a few squeezes and hugs on us—"

"Oh no, it's not so bad as all that. We're really not half so particular when it comes to that sort of thing—"

"Goodness, how nasty you've grown in your old age," said Lillemor indignantly.

As they went out to get into the car Björg declared that she wanted to drive.

"Oh no, Björg, don't. The road's so bad in lots of places."

"But why mayn't I drive, when I want to so much—"

Paul went forward and started the engine, as Björg jumped up into the driving seat.

Paul said good-bye again all round—to Henrik and Berit and Lillemor and Lillian: "Now, Björg, you must make room for me, please."

Björg flung out her hand, indicating the seat by her side: "There you are, my lord and husband!" Her eyes glistened and she was very red in the face. Not that in any way she had drunk too much. But she showed it at once when she had taken anything. And the Swedish punch that Henrik had produced in these days of prohibition had been a huge success with the ladies. Well, not only with them—

"Now then, Björg, please move over. I don't want you to drive. Not now at any rate—if you like to take a turn later on—"

She gave an angry scornful laugh: "I'm going to drive now—"

He bent down close to her and whispered:

"Björg—you *know* I never touch a drop when I'm going to drive. And I won't *have* you drive just after a good dinner—"

She gave him a flabbergasted look—went scarlet and moved without saying a word.

PAUL's speed for the first twenty miles was the most law-abiding he had ever driven in his life. He hadn't the slightest desire to overhaul Schjistad's car.

Björg sat looking straight before her and answered in monosyllables each time he said anything to her. Once, when a car that had not hooted came suddenly upon them on a steep bend where the road was covered with ice, Paul congratulated himself from the bottom of his heart. Björg was on the whole not a good driver—got nervous at the slightest thing—and yet she would never slow down at the bends. He was always afraid when she had charge of the car and could not stand it when she had the children with her.

They drove through Opdal and a country store came in sight.

"Would you like me to stop? Is there anything you want? You seem to be coughing a little—would you like some sweet-stuff for it?"

"No, thanks." She was wild. Presently she said scoffingly: "You know very well it's only drink that's made me hoarse!"

"Oh, drop it! It's nothing to be offended about. That you took a little wine at dinner and a glass of punch with your coffee —why shouldn't you? *I* didn't because, as you know, I don't

151

think anybody ought to if he's going to drive—"

Björg began to cry.

"Oh no, don't, Björg. Do you really think it's worth wasting tears on such a trifle!"

"Oh, then you think it's only a trifle to have a drunken wife!"

Paul laughed. Then he said more seriously: "You know perfectly well that you're misunderstanding me on purpose."

"Right in front of all their faces you say to me that I mustn't drive because I'm drunk! And you—you make yourself out to be the fine gentleman who can teach me what's good behaviour and what isn't! And you sit there and tell Lillemor you think it's dirty to powder oneself and put on rouge—with Lillian sitting opposite you and hearing every word! Yes, it was a sight to see Lillian's face!"

Paul turned red as fire. It was perfectly true. But he really hadn't thought of Lillian—he had never seen her without paint since he was quite a little boy. So Lillian's make-up had become as it were Lillian's natural complexion in his eyes.

After that they did not exchange a word as they drove through Drivdal.

At Kongsvold they found Schjistad's car, and they went in and had coffee. Björg seemed rather excited. And when they came out into the yard again she made a sudden dash for the other car: "Schjistad, Schjistad! May I come with you?—there's something I *must* talk over with Hjördis!"

Herr Schjistad looked only tolerably pleased, as he shifted the baggage in the back of the car to make room for the ladies. Paul remained perfectly passive. Björg shouted "na-na" and "ta-ta, see you later" and waved the ends of her white motor veil spasmodically as they drove away.

WHEN he came to the hotel at Dombaas the others were not there. Paul ordered supper for himself and then began ringing up all the places along the valley where he thought it possible they might have stopped. In many places the telephone was closed, so he couldn't get through. But at long last there was a call from one of the hotels at Otta: the party he had inquired about was now having supper there.

"Thank you. Will you be kind enough to ask Fru Selmer to come to the telephone?"

He could hear by Björg's voice that she was in a very excited state:

"Ah—you're there. Well, I only wanted to find out where you had stopped. Will you please order a room for me too. I'm having supper here before going on. Thanks very much."

When he got down to Otta the Schjistads had left half an hour before, he was told. There was a note for him in his room.

"I'm going on to Christiania with the Schjistads. And then it's settled that I'm going abroad with them. You needn't think I'm going to put up with anything you please!

Björg."

Paul gave up the pursuit and settled down at the hotel for the night.

Chapter Two

HE DROVE UP TO THE STEATITE WORKS NEXT MORNING. To put a good face on it was the only thing to be done now, he thought. So he rang up his bank in Christiania and arranged about a letter of credit for his wife. After that he wrote to Björg, telling her what he had done about money. He was seriously angry, for which reason he only added a few lines:

"I assume that at heart you think the same as I do—that you have behaved like a naughty little girl." Then he tore that up and wrote instead: "that you have behaved rather childishly. But as you *have* started on this trip, I hope it won't turn out a disappointment for you. You know yourself it has happened before now that you've come to me and complained about strangers whom you have taken up too confidingly. For all I know the Schjistads may be excellent people. But should it turn out on closer acquaintance that you don't harmonize after all, you must part company with them in a friendly way and come home. If you go through Paris you know that Sigmund will help you in any way you wish.

"As I said, I wish you a pleasant trip. I'm going up to the sæter on Saturday evening, and by the end of next week I expect to be at Berven again. Best wishes,

Your Paul."

He addressed the letter to his parents-in-law and rang them up to give them some idea of the situation. For once in a way luck was with him; Jacobsen himself came to the telephone and explained that Andora had gone to market. Paul told him

154

that Björg would probably arrive in town that day and was
going abroad, on a motoring tour with some friends: "To tell
you the truth I didn't like her going with them at all. But you
see, she'd taken it into her head that she wanted to get away—"

"I see. I see. It's very awkward, that is—very awkward,"
came Jacobsen's old man's voice, weak and mournful in the
distance.

"Oh well, father-in-law—it's no use talking about it now.
—Yes, thanks, the youngsters are first-rate—"

"There's something I'm wondering about," said the old
man, and then he went on to explain at great length how a
friend of his had to deliver a motor-lorry to a dairy up the valley, and if he liked he could get a lift on it: "Well, if it isn't
inconvenient to you—it would be jolly to have a look at the
children—"

"Yes, come along," said Paul gladly. "You may be sure
you're welcome!"

That in all probability Björg had more than once handed
him over in his capacity of husband to the tender mercies of all
and sundry—that he had known before today. But he had never
worried himself about it—so much as he did now. The fact
was he had shed a husk which previously had protected all that
was sensitive in his mind, when he accepted a religion which
forbade him to look on his fellow-creatures as a herd of "all
and sundry." He was aware, of course, that now he ought to
worry even less than before about what other people thought
and said of him. But previously he had been indifferent to
people's opinion from a sort of arrogance—and now he ought
to be so from a sort of humility. At that time it had been due
to his stressing the points of difference between himself and
the rest—now it was due to his acknowledgment of a fundamental resemblance. So he felt rather as if he had shed his
old skin, and his new skin had not yet begun to harden.

He *could* not help wincing when he thought of the confidences which Björg was certain to impart to Fru Schjistad,

and all the conferences that the women—and the man—no
doubt would hold in the course of the trip as to how his wife
ought to "take him" in future.

RARELY had Paul been so glad of a visitor as when he came
down from the upper quarry on the Friday evening and saw his
father-in-law sitting on the door-step outside the office building.

Jacobsen got up and toddled across to meet him. His thin
and angular little face was furrowed with anxiety, and from
below his pomaded reddish forelock his blue eyes looked up
mournfully at his son-in-law.

Paul squeezed the other's hand:

"It was fine, father. That you were able to come."

"I only hope I'm not in the way," replied Jacobsen in a
worried tone. "I didn't know you had this cousin of yours up
here. The artist." He pronounced the word as though greatly
impressed by anything to do with art.

"Ruth? She'll be very glad to see you."

In the course of the evening Paul could plainly see that
his father-in-law had something on his mind. Up to now he
had only mentioned that Björg did not stay with them this
time and they had seen little of her. But no more was said about
that.

Paul talked about the works. They were still working short
time, as during the war, and he would have to extend the grinding mills. Their best sale was for ground stone. Unfortunately
the times would not allow him to keep a tame sculptor here
any longer. The contract with the electric power station was
also very unprofitable, so long as he could only make a limited
use of the current. But of course he was not the only one who
suffered in that way—

"Is it true," asked Jacobsen anxiously, "that you have
gone surety for all those of your people who have bought their
houses?"

"Oh no. Not for all.—And I hope it won't be long before

I can take on all those who were employed here before—

"By the way, who told you that?" asked Paul.

"Björg talked about it—"

All the same, Paul could not guess where Björg had got it from. He never talked to her about his business.

"I'm real sorry, I am," said Jacobsen with a sigh. "Over this about Björg. I think she's behaved real bad, I do. And her mother takes her part, no matter what she does—"

"Well, well, father, that's nothing new."

"Yes, but it isn't *right*, Paul!"

"Oh, right, right— I expect she'll come to her senses again during the trip, enough to keep her from doing it another time."

"Ah, but it isn't right, this—you ought to have talked to her *severely*, said you wouldn't hear of it!"

"Have you ever tried to talk severely to Björg?" Paul laughed.

"Oh yes, I have that. When she was small. And it was some use then. For at that time Björg was fond of me. She hadn't learnt yet that I wasn't a gentleman."

Paul said nothing, humiliated and unhappy on the other's —or on her—behalf, he did not know which—

On Saturday afternoon they walked up to the sæter together.

The children came rushing to meet them down the steep grass slope, and when they saw it was their grandfather who was with their father they went simply wild with joy—they jumped up all over him like puppies and poured out a stream of chatter. They could tell "whose cattle that was" as each string of cows moved up to the sæter pastures, for they knew them all by the bell-cow—and Sunnie showed the new gap in her teeth; this time she had pulled out the loose tooth herself, and they had been with the dairymaid and had coffee and waffles at the Ledum sæter on Wednesday, Ruth had come too, and Sunnie was to put on her peasant's dress tomorrow—

It was not till Paul and Jacobsen had been down and got

157

rid of their rucksacks and fishing-rods in the old hut that Sunnie remembered her mother: "But hasn't mamma come with you —is she driving up?"

"Mamma won't be here just yet. She's gone for a little trip abroad with some friends. But next month—"

"Oh, I say! What do you think she'll bring us when she comes home?" asked Sunnie.

After that the children said no more about their mother.

Next day they all went up to the top of Torsgar hill— even Helge managed it, if he was carried on somebody's back now and again. Then it was decided that their grandfather should stay with the children when Ruth left. Fru Andora was going to Skodsborg in a week, so it suited uncommonly well.

THE children had picture post-cards from their mother now and then, and Paul too had had a card—from Berlin; one of those with greetings and signatures from a whole party, but it was easy to guess that she had sent it because she had chanced to meet some acquaintances down there. She had evidently made up her mind to be offended with him for the present. Well, let her be.

Six weeks passed. Paul had been up at the steatite works again for a week; he had intended to bring the children back with him this time, but they were enjoying themselves so much where they were, and Jacobsen was still a free man. So he would let them stay there a fortnight longer, perhaps over the shooting. It was not worth while taking Sunnie's schooling too seriously just yet.

On his return he found a letter from Björg at his office in Christiania. From The Skaw—she had turned up there now, and her mother was there too. It was a real unmannerly little missive—would he send her some money, "that is, if you can find any for *me*, otherwise of course you know I can get what is necessary from my parents."

Paul swore a very unchristian oath and sent a telegraphic

158

order.

When he came home to Berven that evening the parlour-maid told him she had had a letter from the mistress asking her to send the children in to Fru Hans Selmer, as soon as she rang up to say it would suit her; the mistress had written and asked their aunt to see about getting the children's clothes for the autumn.

This was carrying the nonsense a little too far.

Paul had not been to see his brother and sister-in-law for many months, so as he had to go to town again a couple of days later, he went over there in the evening.

Paul had never been able to get up any real enthusiasm for his brother's house. It proclaimed far too plainly that Hans and Evi had let the architect have his own way in everything. By so doing they had got a home which was both elegant and original and resembled a whole lot of other elegant and original villas belonging to the war boom period.

In the yellow warmth of the evening sun the big front garden lay perfectly bare of trees and strangely deserted. By the side of the flagged paths great autumnal perennials shone with their red and yellow and purple flowers; the square lawns were neat and newly mown. Along the terrace and on the broad steps leading to the garden-room crimson pelargoniums and russet brown Indian cress overflowed their great stone vases. There was not a spot in all this wealth of flowers where a person could walk or sit without being seen from the road.

The quiet whitewashed façade of the house with its framed windows and the elaborate portal of the garden-room, of blue-green soapstone carved in renaissance style, were very handsome and remarkably well proportioned. It had once occurred to Paul that if this building had served as the museum in a small town, the architect would have accomplished his task to perfection.

But he had to confess that this frame suited Evi. As he entered the cool garden-room she rose from one of the high-backed renaissance chairs. She was as handsome as ever: that

159

was just the word for her lithe and supple figure and the pale cameo profile under the hood of smooth black hair. She looked almost too remote and mysterious; when she talked she was very ordinary, but sweet and pleasant. She had a bright little south-country voice. Altogether she reminded one a little of an actress who has all the looks for an interesting part, but is incapable of playing it.

Yes, thanks, Little Erik had got quite well and strong this summer, she replied to Paul's question. They had had a boy— the first child—about the same time as his own little Erik who died came into the world. It had nearly cost Evi her life, and she had not been really well since.

"And yourself, Evi—how are you now?"

She smiled rather sadly and raised her great grey eyes— looked into his with her wide and unfathomable gaze: "Thanks, I think I got pretty well again at home at Veiholmen," said her commonplace little voice.

"You'll stay the evening, won't you?" she asked cheerily. It was Hans's bridge evening, and Herr Waaler had just rung up to say he couldn't come: "fancy, he stumbled over the carpet and seems to have broken something in his foot! Isn't it awful that an accident like that may happen in one's own drawing-room!" Again she looked into her brother-in-law's eyes with a deep, momentous gaze.

Paul had no desire to sit up playing bridge till all hours, as he had thought of going to communion next morning. But he was obliged to accept.

Evi took up her embroidery again, and Paul sat feeling bored as he chatted with her.

It was a large, handsome room with whitewashed walls and a parquet floor, furnished in the modern style with a few old renaissance cabinets and gothic oak chests along the walls. The few pictures that hung here were good and showed to advantage against the great creamy surfaces. In some way or other this room contributed to increase his feeling of dejection

—what strangers he and his brother had become—

"You've had a letter from Björg, haven't you?"

"Yes," said Evi. "What a long trip she's making."

"Yes. I hope it will do her a lot of good, poor girl. She was badly pulled down in the spring; she wanted a change.

"We needn't bother you now about what she asked you to do for the children. I'm letting them stay at the Hauga sæter till after the shooting, and then I expect Björg will be back and can look after it herself."

At last Hans came—in riding clothes; he barely gave himself time to say how d'ye do to his brother before he went up to change. He rode every day, for the exercise—the rest of his time was taken up by the clinic and his big practice, and they were out nearly every evening.

HANS had always been keen on cards, and the other two men, Doctor Krog and Captain Tangen, were also very serious bridge-players. Paul had always thought it pleasant to get an occasional game of cards, but that was as far as it went with him. So his game was far from being on a level with the others'. It was amusing enough—but all the time he was secretly longing for the evening to come to an end.

Captain Tangen had noticed that Paul drank nothing after twelve o'clock: "but tell me—are you all obliged to fast from midnight on? My brother does so, I know, but I thought it was an obligation which only concerned priests?"

"If one intends to go to communion next morning, one must have fasted since midnight," said Paul.

"Well, but you're not obliged to go, are you—both priests and laymen?"

"No, not obliged." Paul laughed. "But one likes to go as often as one has an opportunity. Many of us anyhow."

The other men looked rather embarrassed. And Paul himself felt embarrassed at having to talk about it.

It was nearly two o'clock before he could get away. His

161

brother saw him out through the garden. The lights from the house fell on the thick flowerbeds, and the vivid colours of the phlox blazed out in patches from the sultry darkness of the August night. The sky was black and full of stars. Their footsteps on the stones of the path rang harshly in the stillness of the quiet villa quarter.

"Tua's in a very bad way now," said Hans Selmer.

"Oh? Is she any worse?"

"Yes. I'm afraid it can't be avoided; she'll have to have another operation. I would rather Krog did it, only Halstein has such a strong objection to him."

"That's very sad. Will it do for me to go up there tomorrow afternoon, or is she not supposed to have visitors?"

"Yes, you ought to go.—Mother feels it very much too," said Hans. "She's aged a great deal in the last few years, mother."

Paul kept waking up—each time he heard that the street was quieter; at last it was so quiet that the steps of a single pedestrian sounded plainly, and there were long intervals between the cars that dashed by sending a gleam of light across the white ceiling of his hotel room.

He had not reserved a room in advance, and so they had given him one in a sort of annexe, on the first floor overlooking the street. His first impulse had been to get angry—they could surely find something else for him when he had been a regular visitor for years. As it was always his first impulse to be angry over trifles: if his room was not done when he came home from church in the morning—if he had to wait and wait for a long-distance telephone call—if he had to fill up in his own hand any of those official forms, such as dispatch notes or postal orders, which it is impossible to write on without the nib digging into the paper and making blots. Now that he was to get out of the habit of swearing he discovered how often he must have said "damn" and "hell" in former days.

Old Father Kindrich said with his bland, rather stereotyped smile: "Oh, but your holy angel makes a note in his book every time you suppress one of these ugly oaths out of love for Our Lord."

"Then I hope my guardian angel's a good stenographer."

This was one evening in the St. Joseph's Society; Eberhard and one or two other men had laughed when he said it. Then, one Sunday after High Mass, Eberhard came up and handed him a little card. On it was drawn a quite clever caricature of himself: he was telephoning, and on the other side of the writing-table sat an angel with note-book and pencil, looking at him attentively.

Eberhard laughed: "I was to give you this from Sister Marie-Halvard."

And again his temper was ruffled. Was it Eberhard who had told her, or had he talked about it at home and one of his innumerable youngsters had then carried it round? He could not bear having his bad jokes retailed.

He had just bowed once or twice to Sister Marie-Halvard at church, no more than that. The first time he saw her in her nun's habit he had quite failed to recognize Randi Alme—the freckled little face with scarcely any eyebrows looked utterly different when framed in a stiff white coif and a long black veil. It was her lovely red hair that had made her so pretty. She retained her bearing, though, and her easy, graceful gestures. But it annoyed him that he could not help paying attention to her altered appearance. Besides, he did not know how he was to address her —whether it was proper to address a nun familiarly, on the strength of their having been fellow-students.—

It was fairly light already—five o'clock. Two hours before he need get up. Paul turned over in bed with a sigh. If only he didn't oversleep himself. It had happened twice before that they had forgotten to call him.—

A heart and a soul that were filled to overflowing with impatience over trifles—that was what he had found within himself,

in these last years. And it filled him with bitter impatience that
he continued to be the same. What then would he have been
like, if he had been forced to put up with greater troubles and
real dependence—with poverty and a subordinate position—
if he had been obliged to accept unintelligent orders, outbursts
of other people's ill humour, undeserved reprimands—?

At any rate he had been satisfied with himself in so far as
he had believed industry and a love of work to be part of his
very nature. He had always been glad to have work to do—but
he had always been able to work on his own account, at things
of his own choice. But presumably all work would have been
equally repulsive if he had been obliged to work under someone else. Therefore his love of work was essentially a mani-
festation of his desire to be independent and to have his own
way. For this reason he was not so impatient when faced by
real difficulties—he could do something to overcome them.
And he liked that.

Of course there was nothing wrong in this. But there was
nothing good in it either. Naturally it is very moral to be industrious. And morality is an indispensable aid to the development of virtues in a metaphysical sense—power to desire ab-
sorption into God's universal scheme, courage to exalt oneself
towards one's origin. If morality is reduced to being an end in
itself—a system of convenience for this life merely—it very
soon falls into corruption. Utilitarian morality always has a
corpse-like smell.

He chafed, inwardly at any rate, even if he could control
himself outwardly, at anything that happened to him independently of his own will. This applied to small things and to things
that had made the deepest impression on him.

He had not revolted at what had really been sorrow. In a
purely intuitive way he must always have guessed that in the
presence of real sorrow man is powerless. He who has courage
and patience enough to bear his sorrow, instead of trying to
crawl away from it, will always end by discovering it to be a

powerful and mysterious domain of life. If he succeeds in working his way through it, he himself will undergo so great a change
that he will have grown out of his old notions of what is good
and happy. He will be strengthened and emboldened to seek
what, in his new state, he considers goodness and happiness.

A man need not be a Christian in order to see as far as that.
He in any case had had a kind of intuitive feeling that it was
so, long before he dared to give a name to that external influence which ordered him to go on and prevail. Simultaneously
with the destruction of all his own illusions—or fancies—about
her he loved, it had become clear to him that now he *must* love
her, in a more real and mature and prudent way than before.
Her misfortune was a part of the punishment for a sin for which
he himself and all men shared the guilt, and at the same time
it was a price that she had paid for her life; it gave her the
right to demand something more of him than his semi-egoistic
worship of a self-made image—a more manly and a more human
affection.

He had seen it then, and he had tried to treat her according
to the understanding he had gained. It was the thought of those
two fellows who had had her before that soiled all his feelings
with bitterness and humiliation—that he would never be able to
get them in his clutches and eliminate them most emphatically.
Two strangers who did not concern him in the least, but who
nevertheless had had the power to penetrate into his mind, to
force themselves intimately upon him. Unconsciously no doubt
it had always been his foremost desire to protect himself against
people encroaching on him farther than he gave them leave.

And *that* had been the unbearable thing about the conclusion of his affair with Lucy. If at that time he had lost her
through death—well, then he would have sorrowed for her, no
doubt as long as he lived, in a way. For he would never have felt
that he had lost her entirely—even if he had not arrived at the
belief that life is without end, he would at any rate have been certain that her life in his did not end so long as he himself was

alive. But she had chosen to disappear in such a way that he did not know to that day whether the only human being to whom he had endeavoured to surrender himself completely was not a perfect stranger to him.

It is one of those time-honoured banalities that religion is a kind of substitute for erotics. He was certain that the very reverse is the truth. Probably all men know in their hearts that they are only created in order to let themselves be flooded by the love of God and to give back the little drop of it which they can take into themselves. But men are afraid of a love that passes all understanding and afraid of a lover who gives all—but the little He asks in return is all we can give. We try to flee from so unequal a conflict of love as that between the Creator and His creature, and still to preserve an illusion that we have realized the end for which we were created—in loving something which is created, even if it be only ourselves. Only to find out how small is the range of our power of loving and how slight the strain it can bear, when severed from its connection with God.

Oh—if even he had loved Björg. Then of course he would still have been just as angry at this latest prank of hers. But not in so miserable and humiliating a way.

For it was not that he missed her, as he was obliged to acknowledge to himself. On the contrary. Ever since their newly-married days he had always felt as if he had been given a holiday when she left him for a time. Then he was let off listening to her chatter, let off having her sham childishness always about him—so at any rate he would have said, now that he really was seriously angry with her for once. If, that is, he had not come to recognize that no one may despise a fellow-creature in that arrogant and scornful way.

It made no difference if *he* could discover no positive good in her—and no positive evil either. Even her little pink and white doll's face was only a mask that concealed the image of God in her. Buried under a whole mountain of ideas which she

166

had received as presents from her mother and her relations and friends lay a soul which was to live its life when all the stars are burnt out. Like a costly pearl at the bottom of a trunk of old clothes—though perhaps she herself could not see that the pearl was any more than a smart button on her old cast-off confirmation frock.

And he was no doubt the last person in the world who could teach her anything else. For what had he really done in marrying Björg Berge? Seduced a little girl who was under the age of consent. That the child offered herself to the best of her ability did not free him from an atom of his responsibility. He had known very well that it was only her body which was that of a grown-up woman—was ripening and even getting a little over-ripe. But at that time it had seemed to him in a sort of way convenient to have a wife to whom he *could* not abandon himself, even if now and then he should feel tempted to commit such a folly a second time. He was not going to have any repetition of his foolishness with Lucy.

So things had turned out exactly as he wanted them—in the days when he took no account of God. Or at all events did not believe that God could mean to him both the beginning and the end, could give everything else in his life a meaning and significance, a daily bread which he could not dispense with, a love which made torments and fetters of all that hindered its growth: old bad habits from his former life, inclinations which broke up his aspiration towards the invisible beloved, distractions which made him cold and dull—and short-sighted and deaf and disinclined to concern himself with God.

It was becoming clear to him how Protestants—and other decent folk as well—had got the idea that he so often heard them express: that converts always regret it, after they've gone and turned Catholic. There was *something* in it—though regret is a very misleading word.

But it was true of him and probably of a good many other converts, in any case: that there comes a hard time when one discovers how difficult it is to shake off old habits, how lazy one's soul is whenever it is called upon to do a little for itself. Like a child that wants to be carried all the time and howls and frets whenever its mother puts it down and tries to teach it to walk. But God knows whether the disciples themselves, who walked with Christ and could look on His face and hear His voice, did not have their attacks of ill humour, when the straps of their sandals chafed them—

"Jesus, gentle and meek of heart, fashion my heart after Thy heart." He prayed thus every day, of course, and meant it too.

But evidently that was still a long way off. Especially as a man has first to learn what those two words, gentle and meek, really mean. For at any rate they do not mean anything passive, anything sanctimonious, but something electric, a dynamic force—otherwise they could not be said of the heart of Jesus—

The time had dragged on to past six; so he might just as well get up and dress.

Although he went to communion as often as he possibly could, he almost always passed a restless night before it, even now, after three years. And he could not tell whether it was due chiefly to a kind of fear or to longing that he woke so many times during the night. The strange thing was that he was never the least tired next day, when he had had a sleepless night from this cause.

Chapter Three

JULIE SELMER HAD BOUGHT THE HOUSE NEXT DOOR TO THE old printing works and made one big office building of the two. So when Paul had to have an office in Christiania he had rented two rooms of his mother.

He generally looked in on his mother the days he came to his town office, but as a rule the visit was only a short one. They seldom had much to talk about. Well, that is, they chatted about business and motoring—

Of the other things that concerned them both there was really not much to be said. That Tua was always ill and seemed to have little happiness in her life. That Hans constantly looked overtaxed—overburdened with work, and rushing about with his wife whenever he could steal a moment from it—and he was reckless in money matters. He had lost heavily in his speculations of late and continued to speculate in foreign markets; in reality he had very little turn for finance, but it had become a hobby with him. From Sigmund they seldom heard, but what they did hear was not encouraging; it looked as if he would never make anything more of his music, and then he was more or less living with a middle-aged English lady whose acquaintance he had made during the war, when they had both been engaged in some kind of work for assisting refugees. Naturally none of Sigmund Selmer's relations had tried to get at the real ins and outs of the story—but amiable outsiders took care that they should hear a good deal of what people said.

And yet Paul knew that of her four children he was the one

169

who had disappointed his mother most deeply. With her nature it did not mean so very much in her eyes that he had been outwardly successful, in his various undertakings. Though it would have meant a great deal to her if he had *not* been so. But that he had crept to the cross and become one of these Christians on whom she had always looked down with a certain good-natured pity—a Christian, moreover, of the most reactionary and obscurantist kind, had become a Catholic and abjured all intellectual freedom, confessed and fasted and went to church like any other sheep of the flock on every single holy day, besides going voluntarily on ordinary days—that was bound to appear to her as an admission of failure. Just as if his unfortunate weakness for blonde and stupid girls of the people had not been a sufficient admission of the same kind. Now he attended the meetings of something that called itself the Society of St. Joseph and indulged in semi-pious chat and smoked his pipe in the company of a lot of Catholic men-folk, mostly of the lower class, and he was the father of two children who took after their mother and her set—so hopelessly that Julie Selmer could not conceal her feeling that it was almost as bad as being the grandmother of two little mulattos. No doubt it had been harder for his mother to bear all this than he would ever know.

How intimate was the bond between him and his mother Paul had never fully understood until now, when they could no longer exchange ideas. The jargon of old days, with its limited and careless vocabulary, which was the expression of a world of affection and cheerful confidence, was no longer of any use, since it would have expressed nothing. And the rude figures of speech they had made use of, when they disagreed about everything between heaven and earth, would have had a different meaning now. In those days they had both known that such relative trifles as conflicting subjective opinions did not touch the secret bond between mother and son—the obscure consciousness that he had grown out of her, that he must accept or reject all the impressions of life through organs which had come into being in her womb.

JULIE came in to see him one evening at the end of September, while Paul was in the outer office copying the letters. He was rather unpleasantly surprised on hearing her knock—botheration take it, hadn't she gone yet?—

She always regarded his Catholic staff with distrust. He had engaged Fröken Alsaker because Father Kindrich asked him to; and for that matter she was admirably industrious and reliable, but undeniably rather slow. The errand boy, or "volunteer," as he styled himself, had been found and offered the place by Paul himself; he was wide-awake enough and to spare. But Julie evidently considered the boy as a freak, and she regarded him with a mixture of ironic gaiety and frank astonishment.

She had entered her son's office one morning when the boy was taking physical and spiritual refreshment with a piece of dry bread and a Dutch New Testament. He then gave Fru Selmer the unsolicited information that he ate dry bread and read the gospels in Dutch because it was his firm intention to enter the Franciscan Order in Holland, as soon as he had reached the age.

Julie's notion of cloister folk was probably something to the effect that they were fugitives from life and its problems, usually people who had suffered defeat, in love affairs for choice. But no doubt at the same time she imagined that monks were equipped with a certain external dignity in appearance and manner. So she was rather flabbergasted at this aspirant to the cowl and sandals—he was a little pale-faced freckled fellow with a pronouncedly vulgar physiognomy and huge projecting ears. Thin and childish he looked in his grown-up, ready-made clothes, and then his name was Anton Todderud.

Another of Julie's opinions was that folk went into convents purely out of egoistic solicitude for their own souls—but now Anton explained to her that the saving of souls was all he meant to live and die for, and by way of a beginning he made an assault

171

on Fru Selmer's soul, as often as she got into conversation with him. Till Paul himself had to suggest to Anton that for the present they should confine themselves to praying for his mother's conversion—he did not believe the time was yet ripe for influencing her more directly.

Anton had lost his parents and had been in an orphanage as a child. There he had heard so many strange and dreadful stories about the Catholic Church that they had roused his curiosity and he had begun to go to St. Olav's as often as he got a chance. After that he could not rest till he had got to the bottom of it all, so he had asked for instruction and had been received a few days after his fifteenth birthday.

His zeal was apt to be rather embarrassing.—One day when Paul was attending a meeting in town he had to ring up his office and ask for a file of papers to be brought to him. Anton arrived, came straight to the door of the private office where the conference was taking place, knocked and delivered the file into his chief's hands with a loud-voiced greeting:

"Praised be Jesus Christ!"

"For ever and ever, amen," replied Paul devoutly. But afterwards he told Anton nevertheless that he did not think it necessary that they should use the Catholic greeting every time they met. The boy protested warmly—he at any rate, as he was to be a Franciscan, must confess his faith wherever he went; he was sure that Our Lord and Father Franciscus expected that much of him.

But Paul had grown fond of the lad, and since Anton was so anxious to learn Latin and German—he had already been reading Dutch for some time—Paul saw to his having lessons. And he lent him books. One day when he had received a fresh parcel Anton took up one of the volumes, a new novel, and regarded it thoughtfully:

"Well, I expect I'll have to ask my confessor's leave before I can read this one. Not but what—I can tell you, I've seen and heard some things in my time, as far as that goes—-pooh, not that I think I'd come to any harm reading it. No, but just to train myself, in the virtue of obedience—"

Paul modestly suggested that perhaps he too might assist Anton to train himself in the virtue of obedience.

The boy looked at him a moment—then grinned from ear to ear: "Queer I didn't think of that before—"

From that day he had been a good deal less troublesome.

JULIE made no remark about Paul having once more let his whole staff go, presumably to some kind of service or other, while he himself dispatched the mail in Todderud's place.

His mother had just come from the clinic: "I thought Tua was going on quite well this evening."

"Yes, I had that impression too, when I was there yesterday. If only it may lead to her getting quite well again, this time."

Julie shook her head:

"I'm afraid Sif will never be really well. Not as long as she's forced to go on living with that man. And I suppose it's not so easy for a clergyman's wife to get a separation."

"I've never heard anything like your talk—" Paul frowned. "Halstein has always been an excellent husband, at any rate as far as we know. I can't say I've ever felt very sympathetic towards him. But with Tua he's patient and attentive and affectionate—"

"Oh yes, he's all that. But what good does it do, if he only worries and torments her with all his care and attention? Have you really so little imagination, Paul, that you can't realize—for a woman at any rate it only makes it so much the worse to be married to a man, if he goes on showing her affection—?"

Paul turned red. He did not venture to say anything.

Julie shrugged her shoulders, impatiently:

"Of course the child was so young and inexperienced when she married him. I suppose it was partly that confounded spirit of opposition which possessed you all—thanks, I know why you're smiling, my boy. But poor little Sif never had much

173

brains—so her little opposition meant that she wanted to be
confirmed and then she toddled off into that Christian students'
movement and all the rest—got engaged to a theological student so as to be a parson's wife and helpmate. Without a notion
of what she was letting herself in for. Good Lord, what does a
little girl like that know about marriage and married life—however much she may have studied it all in theory—"

"Well, you can't very well expect young girls to gather
practical experience of married life before they get married—?
I don't believe you'd have liked it for all that, if your own
daughter had done so."

"Perhaps not. At that time," said Julie. "But I tell you
straight out, Paul, after what I've seen of Tua's life in the last
few years I believe it would have been better if she had— In
short, if she had found out that she could not be happy in an
intimate married life with Halstein, before she went and bound
herself to him for good. And this I know, that if I believed there
was a God to whom it was worth while praying, I should give
him no peace till he had found some way of releasing Tua from
this miserable marriage—"

"There is nobody who believes it to be worth while praying
in that way," said Paul shortly. "If things are as bad with them
as you seem to think, I can't see that anything more than a
change of place is called for. There's Halstein, for one thing—"

"Perhaps you believe *he's* happy in his marriage?"

"Yes. It's my decided impression that he is, in a way—in
spite of everything. He puts it down to her illness that she has
adopted this tone towards him. He is fond of her and glad to
be able to do anything for her. And no doubt a divorce would
be absolutely ruinous to his position as a clergyman. Then there
are all the children—"

—But if Tua had been allowed to grow up with a father
who idolized her and was only fonder of her because she was not
particularly pretty or clever and was rather naïve and not very
brilliantly endowed to make a success of life. Then surely Tua

would never have taken it into her head to make such an experiment as she had done. To be sure, we were all fond of her. But specially kind to her we were not. We always let her see that we thought she hadn't very much sense. So perhaps it was not so strange that she should look for a road which she could have to herself—and chose it blindly, so long as it ran in the opposite direction to ours.—But this was not the kind of thing to say to his mother *now*.

Paul had finished with his mail. Julie asked:

"Won't you come home with me this evening? I see you have your hand-bag here, so you could manage, couldn't you?—Do you know that you haven't been out there since that time you went north to join Alster?" she added, seeing Paul hesitate.

"All right. If you can wait while I ring them up at home. Helge was not quite well when I left yesterday."

"Very well. I'll slip out and find something really nice for supper meanwhile. Give me your letters, I'll drive round and post them for you—" His mother smiled radiantly, waving her hand to him from the door.

How handsome she has grown again, thought her son. Now that her hair was quite white it made her eyes and complexion look even darker and warmer than before. It was as though he could never accustom himself to think of his mother as an old lady. Or remember that some day he would lose her too.—It was wrong, of course, that he so seldom came out to see her. But as he was obliged to travel about so much, he was very unwilling to be away from home—especially now that the children had not their mother with them.

His poor mother must be suffering painfully now. Tua had always been left out of things at home. They all had qualms of conscience about her, now that she was ill and unhappy. They would never be able to make up for what they had left undone, whatever turn things might take. And when she left the clinic her husband and children would close in on her again.

Certainly he understood well enough that his mother was

right—for a woman it was even worse to have to live with one she did not like. But although in his heart he could not imagine that any wife could possibly like Halstein Garnaas as a husband, his feeling was always instinctively on the man's side when he was together with them both. Could it be a kind of *esprit de sexe* which made him feel irritated when his sister constantly gave her husband a cross answer and thanked him for all his anxious little attentions in such a way that she might just as well have said straight out: "don't worry me"?—

It was Sunnie who came to the telephone, when at last he got the connection. Oh no, Helge had only been a little poorly, and she had been reading fairy-tales to him this afternoon, and now he was asleep. Poor child, how disappointedly she said oh—oh —when he told her he should not be home before tomorrow. But she showed her good manners: hope you'll enjoy yourself, and give my love to grandmamma.

He had not yet had a reply from Björg to his last letter, though it was over a week since he sent it. He had taken pains to write as nicely and earnestly as he could—that now she must come home, the children were longing so to see her.

He had not noticed that they did so, by the way. But they were so young—with them it was out of sight, out of mind. When she did come back of course they would be delighted.

WHEN they came out to Linlökka it was already so dark that Paul could see nothing of the garden. But the great bed of white tobacco-flowers on the lawn in front of the veranda shone through the dusk, sending out its strong, sweet perfume. His mother had always had white tobacco plants in her garden, as far back as Paul could remember. And this scent which recalled all the summers he had spent here made him feel strangely sad and cut off from his mother. They sat out on the veranda after supper. The light from the room within poured out, shining upon the curtain of Virginia creeper, which had begun to turn red.

176

Now he thought that this light from the house spreading over a dark garden had a mournful effect. But he remembered that in old days he had strolled outside on autumn evenings like this and loved the light that swept over dark lawns so that a patch stood out, mysteriously green, and touched a fringe of the bushes and late-flowering perennials.

Julie's thoughts were centred on Tua the whole time, he could see—she returned unceasingly to her daughter and son-in-law.

Paul was not sure that she did not exaggerate Tua's dislike of her husband. God knows whether she herself, without thinking of what she did, had not helped to aggravate the misunderstanding between them by showing so plainly that she entertained a real antipathy against Halstein.

And poor Tua—that time she was trying to find her own way out of her mother's world of ideas, which gave her nothing she could live on. There was not a single one of them who saw at that time what could have driven her in that particular direction —towards Christianity, in the form which lay nearest to her. And then she had met Halstein Garnaas; with him she had been able to talk about all that was in her mind and that nobody at home took a scrap of interest in, least of all when it was Tua who tried to talk about it in her uncritical and naïvely enthusiastic way. And then she had fallen in love with him, or imagined it to be love—

Only once during the last month had it happened that he and his sister had spoken of such things—it was little enough they had said even then. But one afternoon when he was sitting with her at the clinic she had asked him:

"Paul—has it made you happy, do you think, your turning Catholic?"

He had not been able to answer at once, because "happiness" seemed to him so narrow a conception that he did not quite know how he was to apply it—in connection with so infinite and complicated a subject as was raised by his sister's question.

"Happy—" he said at length. "Well, it depends on what you mean by that."

"Have you found peace, I mean?"

He tried to explain to her—and to himself:

"If you mean—whether I have found out what is the meaning of peace—yes, I have. That there is only one who can give us peace—and that God's peace is beyond all understanding. And it is not peace in the sense of the world's peace. But you remember, Jesus said once to the apostles that they were those who had remained with Him in all His temptations, and they should sit at table with Him in His kingdom."

"Well—?" his sister asked, a little bewildered.

"Well, then you can see"—he gave a little laugh—"that about peace—and a whole lot of other things—there's a great deal that I can't possibly know in any proper sense until it is put to the proof—"

Tua had looked at him in silence for a while—then she sighed and began to talk of something else.

Paul was thinking of this when his mother came out with:

"She'll never be equal to it—if she's to be forced to live with that husband of hers year in, year out—"

"If you say anything like that to her, you'll only make bad worse," said Paul with impatience.

Julie lit a cigarette—the match flared up in front of her face:

"Well but, Paul—?"

"Yes, what is it?" he asked, as his mother said no more.

"Oh no, it doesn't matter—

"Well, yes. In certain circumstances—I don't know how you formulate it exactly—but actually you can get a divorce too, can't you, even if it may be a good deal more difficult in the Catholic Church?"

Paul merely shook his head.

Julie said quietly:

"But—what is going to happen about you and Björg then?"

178

"Me and Björg! Things will go on just the same as they always have been, no doubt. Now that she's coming home very soon—"

"Then she *is* coming back?"

"Why, of course—you haven't imagined anything else, have you?"

"That friend of hers—Fru Schjistad—has gone about saying you're going to be divorced—"

"Oh, what rot!" In reality he was a good deal scared. And made up his mind on the spot—he would have to go to Copenhagen and fetch her, and that immediately. "She was offended with me when she left," he said, with a careless air that was rather overdone. "Because I didn't particularly care for her travelling with those people. And as I expected they quarrelled on the way. Then she took it into her head that she would meet her mother at The Skaw and go with her to Skodsborg. But now Fru Jacobsen has nearly finished her cure—"

His anger boiled up in him. That female—Fru Schjistad! His angel stenographer could have some work to do now— And that idiotic baby Björg—heaven only knew what she had said to that friend of hers—and what kind of a story she was now carrying round. He would have to see if he could get away on Saturday—

Julie said quietly:

"Well but, Paul—the Catholic Church doesn't recognize marriages that are celebrated in Protestant churches, you know. It doesn't hold your marriage with Björg to be a real, lawful marriage—"

"Oh yes, you may be very sure it does."

"But that's exactly one of the things the Protestant clergy are most furious with them about. I read an article on it only the other day by a parish clergyman in *Aftenposten*. He writes in so many words—"

"Yes, there's no limit to the nonsense they can write," said Paul resignedly.

179

But this was indeed something new—his mother reading articles that parish clergymen wrote in *Aftenposten*! After that she might imagine all sorts of things about him and Björg—!

THEY had not much to talk about next morning when Julie drove him into town in her car.

He had not finished reading his morning mail when the telephone rang.

"—you, Paul?" It was Halstein. How odd his voice sounded. "It has come. Sif has passed away. This morning at half-past seven."

"Oh!"

"Yes, it's terrible.—It was the heart that failed. Quite suddenly—"

"I can't understand. We thought she was over the worst—"

"Yes," said Garnaas's voice. "So did I. But it was not to be. I can't say more now. But you'll be coming here— But will you please tell your mother—"

Anton Todderud had been standing on the other side of the writing-table.

"There's nothing wrong, is there?" he asked, wide-eyed.

"My sister is dead." Paul felt he would like to shake the boy, when Anton slowly and solemnly crossed himself and clasped his hands. Though of course it was the lad who did the right thing—

Paul went along the corridor, knocked at the farthest door —his mother's private office.

Julie stood erect and straight in her black lasting apron; under the wavy white hair her eyes looked out from her distorted face in a great wild stare. Paul never forgot it—she had guessed what he came to tell her before he opened the door.

She clasped her head in both hands when she saw her son standing there: "Oh-oh, oh-oh, oh—" and she sprang forward and flung herself into his arms:

"Oh, Paul!"

180

She writhed in his arms, moaning, as he held her fast: "Mother. Mother. Mother dear!"

"Oh, Tulla, my Tulla. Oh, my poor dear, dear, good little Tulla. Oh, what shall I do—poor Tulla—"

Chapter Four

PAUL TELEGRAPHED TO HIS WIFE GIVING HER THE NEWS. "Come home as quick as you can." Björg replied by sending telegrams of condolence, to him, to her mother-in-law and to Pastor Garnaas.

The funeral was over, but Paul did not think he could leave just yet—on his mother's account; he was alarmed about her. She seemed completely crushed. Tua had now become little Tulla and nothing else to her mother—the little child she had loved, tenderly and rapturously—and forsaken and forgotten and neglected as the child grew up and did not turn out as she expected *her* child to be; though she had always had her daughter with her and looked after her well—in *a way*.—Never had Paul known that anyone could weep as his mother wept that morning at the clinic, when she threw herself upon the bed and took her dead daughter in her arms—and she sobbed and sobbed as though her whole being were wrung with sorrow; at last it was like the wild howling of an animal—

And yet it seemed to him that once before he had heard someone, a woman, howl in this wild and heart-rending way. Suddenly it came back to him—Lucy, the last night she was with him before he left her—

There was something in his mother's uncontrollable grief which struck him as strangely brutal—crudely indifferent to poor Halstein, who sat on the other side of the bed weeping quietly. So he got up and tried as gently as he could to loosen his mother's arms, which were clasped tightly about the body:

"Oh, mother dear, let her lie in peace now," he heard himself say. His mother shook him off with a gesture that looked like kicking him away.

LILLIAN came down from Syrstad to be with Garnaas and look after the children and the house for the time being. She was the one who had shared in Tua's life, ever since the girl began to grow up, and it was she who now revived memories of Tua's younger days—of how fond their father had been of her, and how active and kind Tua had been at home, and so sweet when they went about together to buy her trousseau. She had been such a charming bride, and so happy and solemn when she told her step-mother she was to have a baby—and Erik had been so moved at the thought that his little Sif was to become a mother—

Paul saw the desperate and furious agony in his mother's deep eyes. In her the death of her daughter had stirred anew the old, half-forgotten tiger-love of tender offspring—and behind the bars of ordinary human convention and regard for other people's sorrow, his mother sat staring like a tigress from whom they have taken her young, at those into whose care she had consigned her daughter.

AT the same time Björg's long absence began to cause him more uneasiness than he would admit to himself. To be sure, she was with her mother, and Fru Andora herself had no intention of returning to her husband just yet, from what he understood. But he did not at all like to think of what his mother had told him—that people were busying themselves with his domestic affairs, and that Fru Schjistad was dishing up a story of his and Björg's married life among her circle—which in a town so small as Christiania overlapped with all manner of other circles.

Nor did he receive any proper answer to his letters to Björg. And as yet he had not cared to go so far as asking her to return on account of gossip—

RUTH had four pictures in the autumn exhibition, and Paul thought he could do no less than look in for a moment on the opening day to see them with her. The portrait group of his children was the best—the two landscapes were quite sadly commonplace. Worse still was the big picture of the Hauga sæter with his father-in-law and himself in shooting get-up with dogs and guns as properties—jacket for cheap fiction.

From the exhibition they went into the Theatre Café. Upstairs on the first floor it was practically empty. Paul took pains to compose a really swell menu and find the best wine; meanwhile they talked of Tua's death and funeral, but Paul felt so depressed on his cousin's behalf that he really could not find anything else to talk about. He knew very well that she was not wanting in self-criticism.

Then she herself opened the subject:

"Of course I know I have my luck to thank that I've had so many commissions in the last few years. And you know that painting portraits to order couldn't have done any damage to my talent, if I'd had enough of it—one can see that from the work of older painters. It's simply due to my not having the strength to tackle that kind of problem that these pictures of mine look as if they'd been transferred to the canvas with a hot iron—as we did with embroidery patterns when I was young."

Paul turned red—she had put it so aptly that at the moment he could think of nothing to advance in protest.

Ruth leaned back in her chair and looked at him.

"Of course you'll never have time to sit to me—so I won't even ask you. But I believe I could paint a good portrait of *you*."

Paul thought in his heart that the figure she had made of him in plus-fours at the sæter was misery enough, but he answered:

"You know I'd be glad to sit, if it interests you. But it would have to be some time when I was up at Haugen—I always have more time there—"

"On the whole, you know," said Ruth, "I always do men's portraits better than women's."

Paul thought otherwise, but nodded agreement.

"That one of Jo—that's good, isn't it?"

"Yes, it's very good, I think." It was good, though it had rather the effect of a poster. But there was a diverting early nineteenth-century look about the long, raw-boned figure in a kind of plum-coloured suit, with red waistcoat and silver buttons, something at the same time countrified and dandified, and the face with its shock of black hair, its big, prominent nose and broad red mouth made one think of a masquerade.

At last he was able to get away to Copenhagen.

There was no one to meet him at the boat. And when he arrived at the hotel the hall porter handed him a letter from Björg, and was to tell him that Fru Jacobsen and Fru Selmer had moved out three days ago to some friends at Ordrup.

Paul felt his heart contract with a presentiment of evil. Something must be going on—

He tore open the letter as soon as he reached his room:

"Dear Paul,
    Unfortunately I could not get time to write to you before you left home, but mamma and I have got so sick of living in hotels that when we had a chance of taking a charming little flat which some friends of ours, Countess von Benningsen and her sister-in-law Fru Lehn, the Chamberlain's widow, who are spending the winter on the Riviera, were kind enough to offer us frightfully cheap, we moved into it at once. *I am sorry to have an unpleasant surprise in store for you,* but I shall explain all when we meet. Ring up when you are coming out so I can be sure of being at home.

                    Best wishes,
                    Yours affectionately,
                        Björg."

Paul turned the little note over and over. Then he rang down to the porter and asked to be put through to the telephone number that was stamped on the note-paper.

A Danish maid's voice replied from Ordrup that the ladies were out driving, but Fru Selmer had left word that she would be at home after four o'clock.

PAUL had always thought it detestable that women should submit to wear a kind of uniform at the orders of another person. So Björg's wish to see their maids go about in crimped caps and aprons had never been fulfilled. Now a smart little soubrette in black and white came and opened the door of the villa at Ordrup, took his hat and coat and showed him into a pearl-grey and lilac garden-room.

Björg rose from a little arm-chair in front of a little marble fireplace—she looked curiously changed, and had on a light brick-red dress. It gave him a shock—though of course no one could ask that Björg should wear mourning for a sister-in-law—

He gave her his hand, was going to kiss her—she made a little evasive gesture. Then he saw that she had had her hair bobbed and darkened her eyebrows—that was what made her look so changed.

"Well, of course you think it doesn't suit me?" was the first thing she said, on seeing his look of surprise.

"Yes, I think it really becomes you." It did suit her in a way; she had slimmed a good deal. She looked like the cover of one of her own ladies' papers—at a cursory glance.

Then she asked eagerly after the children, as she rang for the maid and ordered tea: "and will you tell my mother that Herr Selmer is here—"

"No, wait a moment, Björg—I'd like to have a little chat with you alone first, you know."

Björg looked up at him with a doubtful or guilty little air. Her hands flew up to the string of green beads she wore round her neck, fidgeting with it. Then she sat down on the edge of a chair and looked like a little girl whose conscience troubles her.

What the devil did it all mean—? Aloud he said:

"But look here, Björg—the idea was that you and your mother were coming home now— Could it be worth while to move out here?"

Björg looked towards the door, as if seeking help. Then she answered in a tone that was more offended than anything else:

"Well, I must say, Paul—*you've* been away from home a good deal the last few years. Our last year at Trondhjem, for instance—you let me sit there all alone with the children the whole winter. Have you forgotten that? So if mamma and I choose to stay here in Copenhagen this winter, where mamma can get such splendid treatment for her calcareous veins—do you think that's so unreasonable?"

"This winter, you say— Surely you don't mean that you'll be away from the children the whole winter—!"

"I was thinking that perhaps I could have them with me here," she said, losing heart. "Sunlife at any rate. There's such a splendid Catholic school here, run by some Catholic nuns," she added with tearing rapidity. "Fru von Benningsen's nieces go there and such a lot of nice children, so I thought perhaps you'd like to have Sunlife go there for a year."

"It's quite out of the question," said Paul shortly. "No, Björg, indeed I think you've been away long enough. You'll have to come home with me in a week's time. If your mother has to stay here on account of her health, it can't be difficult for her to find a companion or something of the sort—"

"Yes, but mamma's very far from well." Björg suddenly burst into tears. "I don't suppose you believe it—but she's had such *frightful* heart attacks."

"Well, I'm very sorry to hear it. But your children must come before your mother. How would you feel about it if anything serious happened to *them*, while you were here—?"

"Oh, you mustn't remind me of that!" She wept bitterly. Then she got up and ran to one of the doors: "Mamma! mamma, Paul's here—you must come in!"

Paul had a vague feeling that he was at the play—there

stood his mother-in-law, strangely rejuvenated and smartened up. She had grown a good deal thinner, but all the same she looked quite comic in a black velvet dress that only reached a little below her knees. He had never seen her legs before; they looked like pit-props in silk stockings and patent-leather shoes. Over her shoulders she wore a huge white fox—and then she too had altered the fashion of her hair. The pyramid on her crown was gone and the hair was twisted round her head like a scarf and stuck full of glittering ornaments.

She sailed towards him, as he stood looking blankly: "You're looking extremely well, Paul, how pleasant to see you! You had such a grand time together in the mountains, Jacobsen wrote. But how sad it was about your sister—poor Pastor Garnaas, I'm sure it *must* have been a blow to him!

"—But shan't we sit down? You'll give me a cup of tea, won't you, Björg dear?—Well, of course you're rather surprised to find us here, Paul!"

"Yes, you're right!—Father-in-law knows nothing about this either—he saw me off on the boat yesterday."

"No, we only made up our minds a couple of days ago, you understand. I've not been at all well of late years, as you know —but *how* poorly I was nobody really knows, for I'm not in the habit of complaining, so even Jacobsen doesn't know—and poor Björg, I had to spare her above *all*, when you think of the terrible trials she has had to go through lately—*first* her being put to that sort of trouble again, though she was not well enough at the time to be in that condition—and *then* her grief over the boy—! Poor thing, it's not to be wondered at if she's so pulled down, both physically and bodily—" Fru Jacobsen had talked herself into a flush of excitement.

Paul was not up to giving his mother-in-law an answer. And Björg sat on the edge of her chair and looked from her mother to her husband and back at her mother again with great round eyes.

"It's the real truth, Paul, what mamma says," she assented

188

in a frightened and woe-begone little voice.

"Well, but you've surely recovered by now—you look first-rate!"

Björg began to cry again, quietly and distressingly.

Fru Jacobsen said with emphasis:

"She is very far from it. The way you have neglected your wife of late years, in every sense—she absolutely needs the change! She must stay here with her invalid mother who needs her, so that I can take some care of her."

"It's quite out of the question, mother. She cannot stay away from her children any longer."

"No, but the children could come here—"

"Certainly not," interrupted Paul.

"You can see, can't you, that if for instance Björg should want a divorce, there's not the least doubt she would be given the children. After all, we have a State Church, I should think, so you can be sure you won't be allowed to keep the children and make them into Catholics, if Björg claims them—"

Paul turned to his wife:

"Will you be so kind as to tell me what all this means? What is this latest idea of yours—?"

Björg raised her head and looked desperately from one to the other:

"Oh, won't you tell him, mamma!"

Then she set up a loud scream and made a dash for the door.

Paul pushed Fru Jacobsen aside:

"No, no, mother-in-law—I don't accept any explanation from anyone but Björg!" He went after her.

It was a bedroom with two beds, the room next door, and it had a feminine smell; clothes and toilet things lay about everywhere and there was a glitter of glass and silver. Björg lay face down on one of the beds, howling. Paul sat down beside her on the edge of the bed and tried to turn her round:

"Can't you tell me what it's all about—dearest child—?"

"Oh, I'm in such despair—"

"Well but, good heavens, why not tell me what it is then? What in the world put this into your head—you can't be serious about wanting a *divorce*?" He couldn't help laughing—it sounded positively comic to speak of it now that they were alone. "What an idea—!"

At that moment his mother-in-law came in. She posted herself at the foot of the bed:

"Do you *really* think Björg's had such a grand time with you—planted there in the wilds of the country with a husband who's never at home and sees nothing in her but a breeding-machine whether she has the health for that sort of thing or not! I'd like to ask what kind of a husband you've been to her?"

"I? I've been an angel," said Paul, snubbing her. "Björg has testified that many a time. Haven't you, Puss?"

He lifted her up, holding her round the waist:

"Come along, put on your things and we'll go out somewhere. *No*, I say, mother-in-law. This is a thing Björg and I will talk over alone. She has been *my* wife for over ten years, so you must resign yourself to the limitation of your authority over her. She's not a child that you can do as you please with—

"—I say!" he had got her out into the hall, and she was weeping into her outdoor things, while he searched for his coat. "Is *that* your new fur coat—topping! And how sweet you look in it—and your hat? Have you got all your things?—Now we'll go—"

There was a little garden in front of the villa. A thin grey mist with a taste of frost hung over the road, but the ramblers on the walls of the house still bore a few roses. Above the half bare trees opposite there was a rust-red glow of sunset through the mist.

Paul stopped a taxi: "Where shall we go, Puss?"

"To Langelinje Pavilion," sobbed Björg.

"All right. I'm sure that's first-rate."

190

"UGH—what a sight I must be," she whispered, as the taxi pulled up.

Paul had found a table for them in a corner. "Shall we put off talking about the whole business till tomorrow, Björg?" he asked when the wine was brought. The next moment he regretted it—tomorrow, then she would have had a chance of talking to her mother, and then no doubt she'd be crazy again.

She looked so unhappy that it was pitiable to see her. Paul took her hand across the table:

"Let's see you smile now, Björg!"

"Oh, but Paul." She was on the point of tears again. "We *haven't* been at all happy together for many years. You *can't* say we have—!"

"Have you really been so unhappy, Björg?" he asked seriously.

"Yes—only think of last winter—when Erik died."

Paul nodded and stroked her hand.

"I couldn't face anything like that again!" The tears began to flow.

Phew. Were they going to talk about that again—?

"Listen to me, my dear," he pleaded in a low voice. "Don't you think, when you look at all the women who make a brave fight of it with a whole heap of youngsters—a fight which to many of them may look quite hopeless and meaningless, at any rate to those who have ceased to believe that every child born into the world is worth more in itself than the whole material world—since this is fated to pass away, but the child actually *cannot* die. You believe that too, Björg—you said so in any case, long before I could say that I believed it. And you believe too that Erik lives—he has already been given that to which we and the other children only hope to attain some day. But if you believe in an eternal life, you must also hold that you have been given your life in order that you may do something here on earth, since you were not taken away at once, like Erik—you are not simply to confine yourself to existing and trying to

191

while away the time till you have to die?"

"I swear I haven't done that either, Paul," she protested indignantly. "You can't say I haven't always been a good housekeeper—made a heap of things myself that Hjördis Schjistad or Evi or Ingse Meyer always get a dressmaker in for. And I'm sure I never thought of having nothing to do here either. Helping mamma and—learning fancy needlework I'd thought of—and clay modelling too—"

Paul had to laugh: "Yes, yes, that's all well and good. But it isn't what I meant. I meant something that Our Lord wishes *you* to do and that nobody else can do in your stead. You have sometimes complained that you had no talents like Ruth or Berit, or were not gifted and independent like my mother. But can't you understand that all such things must appear relatively trifling to those who believe in God and eternal life. The most they can be worth is of small account compared with a mother's work, if she can do it well. It is to our mother that we are confided in the first eight or ten years of our life—when we are really being formed. Unless we were taught to be receptive to it as children, we never learn a thing later, no matter how it is plugged into us.—So to apply such taunts as breeding-machine or the like to mothers is nothing but a blasphemy which is rather more idiotic than the rest—"

"Then you think mamma talks blasphemy, do you?"

"Oh, not at all. You know very well what I mean."

"Yes, everything that's *your* idea you call the will of God, and if I'm not enthusiastic about it, it's blasphemous—"

"They're not *my* ideas. And I dare say I've *not* shown enough consideration for you in the past, in many ways—though by the way you've said just the opposite, lots of times. But don't you think, to put it plainly, that it's rather cowardly of you, who have never known what it is to be ill or to have to go without anything, if you're so afraid of being burdened with a larger family—?"

Björg replied quietly:

"Well, but, Paul—people say you're so frightfully impru-
dent—as a business man, I mean. That you're getting out of
your depth in all directions, what with putting up new buildings
and trying new ways.—Yes, and it's true, I know it is, for you've
always got something on with contractors and people like that.
And then you've gone surety for a lot of your workpeople too—
Schjistad says you're a regular socialist that way—"

He laughed:

"That's exactly the opposite of socialism, Björg—it's dis-
tributionism."

"What may that be?" asked Björg suspiciously.

"Oh—it's a movement which aims at defending the individual's rights of property and private initiative—against capitalism and Americanism and standardizing tendencies—and State
interference and collectivism—you understand, defending every
single human being's right to have a place where he can be
master and slam the door in the face of any intruder—"

"Well, but surely everybody's agreed about that," she
said, almost offended.

"A great many are," Paul corrected. "And yet development
is taking another direction. Wherever people haven't a metaphysical foundation to build upon—if you know what that is—
so that they know they must guide development by their will,
instead of allowing themselves to be guided by what they believe to be the course of development—"

"Metaphysical foundation—is that Catholicism?" she
asked.

"Yes." Paul laughed. "Catholicism is a metaphysical
foundation, Puss."

"Then you must be what you said just now—?"

"Yes. I must. Though no doubt there are a lot of Catholics
who dare not believe it's any use. To stick up for the small
independent concerns and the freedom of the home and the
rights of parents against State encroachment and all that. And
there are many non-Catholics among the distributists. You see,

people have let themselves be scared into believing they must give up the hope of saving these good old things. Till somebody comes and explains to them that the good old things are built upon dogmas which at any rate have formed the foundation for the European conception of what each human being is."

"But," said Björg shyly, "suppose you should find it difficult to manage all that you've taken upon yourself—?"

"Well, then it'll have to be difficult." He shrugged his shoulders. "I shall have to get through it as best I can. But console yourself, Puss—it'll be a queer thing if I can't anyhow manage to provide for you and the youngsters."

Björg looked extremely preoccupied.

"There now, child! You're not drinking anything— There's no danger at present. Aren't you looking forward to coming home to Sunnie and Helge at any rate?"

Björg gave an infinitely long sigh. Then she looked up at him:

"Yes—" she said feebly.

"Now you're coming back to the hotel with me, aren't you?" Paul proposed, when they had got into the taxi. He put his head out and gave the driver the address.

"No, Paul, no—it won't do. Besides, you'll only have a single room—"

"We can get that changed in a jiffy. And they know you there, so there's no risk of being compromised," he laughed.

"No, I can't—think of mamma," she objected.

"We'll telephone to her—"

"And I haven't any night things."

"You can borrow pyjamas of me—then you'll look like Sunnie's big doll when she dressed it in real child's clothes. I'll run out the first thing in the morning and buy you a tooth-brush and comb—and this stuff too, if you want it"—he laughingly passed his finger over her painted eyebrows—"if you'll only tell me what you call it—"

194

"No." She suddenly lost her temper. "I won't. No, I won't, Paul. I'll go home to mamma. You *shan't* make me do anything of that sort," and then she began to cry again.

He told the driver to go to Ordrup. Björg wept miserably the whole way.

All the same he was in a good humour when he came back to his hotel. Heavens, yes—he was fond of her and she was fond of him; they were fond of each other, and it was both humiliating and shabby on his part to have had such bitter thoughts of her these last years, every time he found it a nuisance that Björg was not more intelligent.

For he had always known that there was no depth in her. But it must be his own fault that he had never succeeded in making their married life any better than it had been—like a series of little holiday love affairs, only with no variation of their object. And the kind of petting he had offered her was in reality a worse neglect of a wife than neglect naked and un-adorned.

He ought in any case to have managed his married life successfully enough to have made her his girl instead of her mamma's. But when they now came home again to the children, it might actually turn out that this little experiment in seeing the world for herself had taught her a lesson. Perhaps she would attach herself more closely to him now. And perhaps he need not have been so sure that it was waste of time to talk to her as to a grown-up person. That was the impression he had had this evening—she had taken in what he said, had asked questions, raised objections—

He *had* felt that he was fond of her, very fond, when she cried so bitterly this afternoon. For it was not just the same as when she had recourse to tears at home, in order to get her own way. She had wept like a real human being, who stands perplexed and distressed in a difficult and painful situation. My poor little Puss—

195

HE was in a far more peaceful and happy mood next morning in St. Ansgar's church than he had been lately at Mass. Perhaps too he had exaggerated his own irritability and impatience, reproached himself gratuitously with something which by no means denoted a fundamental defect in his soul. Perhaps his lack of humility consisted precisely in this: that he could not reconcile himself to the possession of faults which he found it difficult to master?

It was the first time he had been in church outside Norway, and it made him glad and thankful that here too he was able to go forward to the communion bench together with the others. The priest who said Mass pronounced his Latin with a strong Danish accent, and it was with a curious emotion that he heard the familiar words with this slight brogue.

It was the schoolchildren's Mass, the church was crammed with them. A big boy stood up and recited prayers in Danish, following the ceremony of the Mass. He liked this practice better than the one they used at home in St. Olav's church, where the schoolchildren prayed in chorus.

BUT when, later in the morning, he came out to the villa at Ordrup, it became clear to him that if he had gained some ground with Björg the day before, his mother-in-law had been pretty successful in winning it back from him.

Fru Jacobsen received him alone. Björg had had such a frightful headache this morning that her mother had sent her out for a walk. And then she began to lecture him.

—About how unhappy Björg had been with him of late years, and she should not submit to be ruined in body and soul for the sake of his principles, while he destroyed the welfare of his whole family with his wild ideas, which might do very well for Dagoes who got their living by going round with a barrel-organ or selling peanuts and vegetables in the street—and that was one way of being your own master—

Paul nodded gravely:

"You're right, mother-in-law. I'll make a note of that, if I should go bankrupt some day—"

The old woman was furious:

"Ah, but I'm serious, I'd have you to know. I'm not going to leave my child in the hands of a perfectly irresponsible person that nobody knows what he'll do next. And you'll find I shall take good care that there's enough settled on Björg and her children so that they shan't suffer any want if you choose to go and ruin yourself—"

"I think you've taken leave of your senses!" Paul gave an angry laugh. "Who on earth put it into your head that I'm in such a bad way? It's absolute nonsense—"

Fru Jacobsen's head rocked on her shoulders:

"Ha! I know more than you'd suspect! And Björg's still young and pretty, let me tell you, and can still make something of her life. It's not going to help you a bit if you try to seduce your own wife— I can't see why you're not ashamed of such a dirty trick!"

"Good-bye," said Paul, and went.

HE walked up and down a little way from the house. It was the same bitter, misty weather as the day before, with a faded glow of sunshine behind the fog. The trees along the avenue of villas were half stripped, with a few yellow leaves at the top, and a few frost-nipped flowers still bloomed in the gardens.

After a long wait he saw her coming round the corner. She gave a start on discovering him.

"Good morning, Puss. How's the headache?"

"Better, thanks," she said weakly.

He took her arm and drew her into a side road—exactly like the one they had left, with villas and villa gardens and naked trees and dusty withered leaves on the footpath.

"So you've told your mother *everything* we talked about yesterday?" he asked, as they walked.

She only looked at him, miserably unhappy.

197

"Well, after that you can well understand that I won't let you go back to her. Now you'll have to come back with me to Copenhagen and we'll leave by the night train. You're not to talk to your mother till we're in Christiania—that is, if it pleases her to come after us—"

Then she started her crying again.

"I can't do that, Paul. I can't leave mamma like that—it would be running away and nothing else—"

"Oh—you didn't mind running away from me."

She gave him a frightened look:

"At that time I had no idea I shouldn't be coming back quite soon—"

"Then is it entirely your mother's work, putting these fancies into your head?"

"Well—mamma has quite made up her mind that I ought to apply for a divorce," murmured Björg.

She stood holding on to a paling with both hands, and her tears dripped into the privet hedge of some total stranger's garden.

And it struck him as a terrible thing that all this to-do was about *her*. That little body in a brown fur coat, with the childish, tear-stained face—why were they fighting to get possession of her—? And could it be true that temporal and eternal values were at stake, according as she acted in this way or in that? Certainly she was to be pitied—but why couldn't he let her run, if she wanted to so badly—?

And as though she had read his thoughts, she said:

"Pooh, it's not that you care a bit about me, my boy! It's only because you're not allowed to have a divorce, I know that very well!"

"No, Björg, it's not only that. You know that I'm fond of you."

But he felt himself that it did not sound very convincing. Björg walked on, with bent head, and in a flood of tears. She did not answer a word more, and when they came to her garden gate he had to let her go.

IN the afternoon a telegram came for him: "Mamma had heart attack, can't leave her a moment, don't come out. Björg."

It was true—which he would never have believed. But when he came out to the villa he met a stout gentleman with ruddy cheeks and fair hair on the garden path—presumably the doctor. And the maid who opened the door looked at the same time frightened and deeply interested. Fru Jacobsen was very, very poorly, she informed him. *Probably she has brought it on by suggestion,* thought Paul.

The drawing-room smelt of cigar smoke and something medicinal—ether no doubt. Björg stole in; miserably tearful and shaken she looked. He did not get much talk with her— obviously it was of no use now.

So he sent out flowers and sweets to his mother-in-law and to Björg and telephoned and called and inquired how things were. But it was useless to think of getting Björg home with him now. And when a week had gone by he could not stay any longer in Cophenhagen.

At the last moment Björg turned up at the station. She brought a whole armful of parcels for him to take to her father and the children. She wished him a good journey. Her face was pale and harassed, and it was with an almost pitiable smile that she spoke of his coming again—

Only when he sat in the train going northward did the thought occur to him—surely there could never be a man in the case? But he dismissed it. There was at all events this good thing about conventional morality, that it kept the Fru Jacobsens and the Björgs from committing follies. And it was not very likely that any man would take it into his head to fall in love with Björg *now*—to the point of divorce and marriage. With himself it was a different matter: it was the habit of all these years, based on the memory of her early brier-rose charm. *He* could see traces of that in spite of all, where a stranger would see nothing but a fairly ordinary, doll-like little woman, who was no longer so young that her childishness became her. And she trailed round with that mother who was fit to scare anyone over the border—

Chapter Five

NEVERTHELESS IT ANNOYED HIM FEARFULLY TO COME HOME to Christiania without his wife. He told his mother about Fru Jacobsen's illness, and she replied "how tiresome" in her iciest tone.

Sunnie and Helge were pleased with their presents. They asked after their mother, but not very anxiously.

At last it came. His father-in-law rang him up one day: "There's something I must talk to you about. It isn't anything amusing exactly, but it can't be helped. I don't know whether you'll come out here, or shall I come up to you?"

"If you can come out here, you know the youngsters will be delighted. Take the 6.30, then you can get a lift with our trucks, and we'll meet at the office."

Of course it was about *that*. Until now it had never been mentioned between them, though Paul had been to see his father-in-law several times since he returned from Copenhagen.

Jacobsen looked miserably depressed when he appeared at Paul's office that evening. The back of his ulster was red with brick-dust, and as Paul was brushing him he hung his head with a strange air of embarrassment.

Paul had to find the night-watchman and speak to him before he left the works. The big lamps shone out into the raw November evening as they walked down between some long drying-sheds containing unbaked bricks that had been spoilt by the frost. The fog drifted and wreathed about the lamps. While Paul was talking to the watchman Jacobsen stooped down and patted his big Newfoundland. He looked as if he was seeking comfort from the shaggy black animal.

The children rushed to meet them the moment they stepped into the hall; they were wild with delight because their grand-father had come and they would be allowed to stay up a little longer than usual and had their best clothes on. Sunnie looked charming in her sea-blue knitted frock; every time she flung round, her light brown hair danced over her slight shoulders and thin arms.

Paul saw some little old man's tears, bead-like and hard, quivering on Jacobsen's prominent cheek-bones.

He was quiet and dejected at the supper-table. Now and again he looked from one child to the other, as they chattered delightedly about the things on the table, which were not the same as on ordinary days.

Afterwards, when they had all moved into the smoking-room, the children insisted on their grandfather showing them card tricks; Jacobsen knew four, and they were just as exciting every time he performed them.

"Grandpapa, aren't you well?" asked Sunnie presently, as she caught sight of his face.

"Grandpapa's tired," Paul hastened to say; "so now you'd better go up to bed."

"Oh, but you *said* we might stay up a long time—"

At long last he got them off upstairs.

"Ay, ay, ay," sighed Jacobsen. "She's so like Björg, when she was that age— Just like that Björg was, and oh, such a dear good child, and so pretty—"

"Yes, Sunnie's very like her mother."

"Ay, that time we were good chums, that we were. Then it was papa this and papa that, all the time. No fancies about her in those days—"

Gladys came in and interrupted—she was to say that the children were ready. Jacobsen went up with Paul to watch them at their prayers.

Sunnie's evening prayer had gradually developed into quite a protracted liturgy. Her grandfather sat on a little child's chair, with his clasped hands hanging down between his knees. He gazed with profound devotion at the little girl—she looked very angelic, kneeling in her white nightgown.

"First I read something out of the Bible to Helge," she informed her grandfather; "and now I'm reading about John the Baptist, because it's Advent, you see—"

"Read about where they chopped his head off!" crowed the bloodthirsty Helge.

"No, that's the twenty-ninth of August, you know," said Sunnie patronizingly.

"Beheading of John the Baptist!" Her grandfather's face lit up in a huge smile. "So you know that too, my lass!"

"Yes, I should think so—it's in the missal, that is—"

"But, father, what made Herod do it just because that girl said he was to—did he think she was so nice?"

"I expect he did. She had danced so nicely, you know," said his father.

"I think they look so idiotic when they're dancing," said Helge scornfully.

Jacobsen suddenly bent his head and covered his face with his hands. Sunnie waved her hand: "There, now you must be quiet, I'm going to read—"

"You'll stay the night of course?" asked Paul, when they were down in the smoking-room again. But Jacobsen said he must go home by the last train; there was the furnace to be seen to.

Paul waited while the old man explained at great length how unpractically the hot-water pipes were laid in his house.

"—Well, now mother's written," said Jacobsen at last. "I thought I ought to tell you about it. Maybe it was stupid of me, but it made me so mad, I tore up the letter and went straight down and pitched it into the furnace. Ay, this is—I'm so ashamed that my daughter's turned out like this!"

203

"I can guess what she's written—that she wants to get Björg divorced from me?" Paul asked.

Jacobsen bowed his head. A few small grunts came from him.

"Father-in-law! I don't think you need take it so much to heart. I don't at all think Björg herself is so set on it. When it's made clear to her that it's quite out of the question that she can claim the children—and it is so, I've consulted my lawyer about it—she'll come home again all right."

"You're sure of that—that they can't take the children from you?"

"Perfectly certain."

Jacobsen said quietly:

"You know how Andora is, when she's taken a thing into her head. And now she'd made up her mind that she's going in for all this gadding about and amusing themselves and driving round in motor-cars with swell people and dancing in cafés and all the rest of it. And if it's true what she writes, that Björg has gone so utterly crazy about this fellow—"

Paul answered after a little pause:

"That I haven't heard anything about—that there was a man in the case."

"Well now, it *was* stupid of me to burn her letter. Now I can't think what it was she called him, but I'm sure he's from Czechoslovakia or Greece or somewhere in those parts—some kind of diplomat—"

"Oh, bosh!" exclaimed Paul with a laugh of relief. "I don't believe a word of it."

It would have to be an odd kind of diplomat who would think of taking up with those two ladies. It must be all nonsense—

BUT he was both depressed and uneasy as he drove home after seeing his father-in-law into the train.

In a way it excused Björg and explained her recent manner,

if she had contracted a love affair down there. For the poor girl had really been both distressed and perplexed. At any rate it showed her in a more human light, than if her conduct had merely been dictated by subservience to her mother.

The motives of this conjectural new fancy of hers were not likely to differ essentially from those which had once impelled her to fall in love with him. At that time, in those calm and distant days before the war, he had appeared as the man who was able to secure for her the future of her dreams, a domestic idyll of easy circumstances. But she too had reacted to the war and post-war period—in her little way. She too had grown restless, but knew no other way than to try to climb upward in society— according to what she had been taught as a child to regard as ups and downs. And in her eyes all those were "on top" who were not obliged to do anything, who could throw money about and found amusement in anything which saved one from being alone with oneself for a while. So it was quite possible that this little person had allowed herself to fall into rosy dreams, if a fellow whom she took to belong to a set of this sort had shown her some trifling attention.

And if it was imaginable that a foreigner had allowed himself to be dazzled by her Scandinavian type or had been taken in by her and her mother's extravagance, Björg on the other hand was apt to see heroes of magazine fiction and detective novels in anything that had to do with diplomacy and titles.

He could not feel any real jealousy. His feeling was far more one of exasperation at her everlasting stupidity which had ended in placing them both in such an impossible situation. It was crude to reckon on such things, but he could not help taking this into account: that it was scarcely conceivable that Björg would be capable of going so far as to be unfaithful to him in a legal sense. She entertained an honest, upright and intolerant abhorrence for what she called "passion," since of course, in common with all Philistines, she guessed that passion has something to do with suffering.

Jacobsen had said he didn't think Andora had any intention of seeking a divorce for herself. But she was going to remain with her child and stand by her side as long as Björg needed her—whatever she may have meant by that. Perhaps in a way it was lucky that Björg had such a dragon to guard her.

Paul could only suppose that when these two foolish females had it in black and white from the lawyer that their claims were ridiculous, Björg would come back.

What their married life would be like after that it was useless to speculate.

FATHER TANGEN had been Paul's confessor ever since he was received into the Church. But while Paul was in Copenhagen this autumn it so happened that Father Tangen was transferred to a country parish, and Paul had chosen Father Kindrich in his place.

Of course he could not expect to have a confessor who "understood" him—he knew that very well and said to himself that the thing is to acknowledge one's sins, great and small, as honestly as one can and resist all conscious and unconscious temptations to excuse them.—Uncle Abraham had been right in thundering against obligatory confession on account of its being humiliating, and Halstein, who to a certain extent admired the institution as a kind of spiritual hygiene, knew a good deal less about it than old Dverberg had done. It was *not* any kind of bath or massage for the soul; it was put there to teach people what it means to humble oneself—learn to know yourself and keep apart from each other the facts and all the excuses and extenuating circumstances that one usually discovers when preparing for confession; confess your own faults and not anyone else's—then you may receive holy absolution with a contrite heart, as the formula has it. And if the priest could give him no other guidance than that which was purely general and dogmatic, approximately the same for all, he had no right to feel aggrieved on that account. A confessor who is at the same time a *"directeur spirituel"* is a supplementary gift which Our Lord sends if He thinks there is need of it.

It had been easy enough to say this, so long as he had Harald Tangen. His addresses in the confessional were always purely objective little statements of theology and psychology; to him all souls for which he had been made responsible were equally valuable, and he purposely laid all stress on what was common to them, without emphasizing individual distinctions. That was in any case Paul's impression, since the priest had always talked to him in a reserved and matter-of-fact way, without a shadow of unction. Paul had seen enough of Harald Tangen in these last years to perceive that his friend abhorred sentiment, because his own need was to prune rather than to foment his tendency thereto.

Outside the confessional he had never spoken to Father Tangen about himself; their talk was always of work and general topics, never about people.

With Father Kindrich it was quite another thing. He was a Rhinelander, and he belonged to a different time, and Paul thought him fairly unctuous and altogether too effusive. He had to curb himself from getting impatient, even in the confessional, but it seemed to him that the priest misunderstood every word he said. His impatience with people he didn't like, his hasty contempt of everything he considered stupid and vulgar, inflated sentiment and slovenly thinking—these were indeed sins of thought; but he had no idea that he gave himself away when such feelings came over him; he merely retired into himself. Father Kindrich admonished him exactly as if he were in the habit of behaving brusquely and disagreeably to every person he didn't like.—A long time afterwards it dawned on Paul that after all it was old Father Kindrich who had had the clearer view.

As he thought he must now speak to a priest to find out what attitude he ought to adopt towards his wife's vagaries, he went in the first place to visit Father Kindrich in his study one afternoon.

That he must refuse his consent to a divorce was clear; it was only what he himself had thought. Similarly, that if in spite of that Björg succeeded in obtaining the divorce, and even if she afterwards married another, he was nevertheless bound to her as long as she lived.

But it irritated Paul that Father Kindrich was so sympathetic. He overflowed with compassion for the young man who was put to such a trial for his faith's sake. Father Kindrich assumed as a matter of course that Paul's heart was deeply wounded by his wife's desertion—and that made Paul feel as if his whole soul bristled up.

He had never mentioned to the priest in so many words that it was particularly in his relations with his wife that he had discovered how small a store of Christian charity he possessed. He explained his omission to himself by the argument that it would have been equivalent to an attempt at self-vindication or to a denunciation of another person as an accomplice in his sins—in other words, to making a sacrilegious confession.

Now he felt additionally guilty, because Björg's faults and shortcomings were vividly present to him, while the excuses which might well be made for her, and the reasons he had for judging her leniently, appeared in a somewhat pale and abstract light. But that made it yet more intolerable to listen to the old priest. Since Paul was not one of the loose-living married men, examples of whom were not wanting among his congregation, Father Kindrich evidently took it for granted that the wayward little lady was his beloved spouse.

FATHER TANGEN had written to him more than once and mentioned each time that he would be heartily welcome if he cared to visit him one day. So Paul went out there one Saturday in Lent.

He was present at Mass in a queer little chapel—a wooden building something like an outhouse on a farm. Afterwards he had lunch with Father Tangen in his little presbytery, and then he explained his whole position to the priest.

Paul knew that Harald Tangen would have given his life at any time if he could profit Björg's soul thereby. But he also had some knowledge of the lady—he had visited them at Berven once or twice, though it was rarely that he had time to accept an invitation.

He could only repeat that Paul must refuse his consent to a divorce and continue to regard himself as bound, even if his wife obtained a divorce against his will. But Father Tangen advised him to take no further steps at present. He was inclined to think that Fru Selmer would come back of her own accord, if he refrained from asking her to do so. She would hardly cut herself off from her children. The mysterious diplomat seemed to be more or less a creature of the imagination.—Father Tangen too was evidently convinced that Fru Selmer would end by doing what was most advantageous to herself.

So Paul left off writing to her. Every time her monthly allowance was sent he enclosed a note saying how the children were.

Chapter Six

T**HAT SUMMER** R**UTH** W**ANGEN WENT TO THE** H**AUGA SÆTER**
with the children. Tua's youngest—two little boys—were
there too. Pastor Garnaas had been so unfortunate with
his housekeepers since he became a widower, said Lillian; the
first one had set her cap at him so deliberately and the second
was quite incapable. So she had set about helping him. She
asked Paul to take Kjetill and Tov into the mountains, if Ruth
was willing to have them as well as the others; then Guro and
Ambjör could go with her to Syrstad.

"You know how fond I am of those children!"—Lillian
looked up at him feelingly from the sweater she was knitting for
Ambjör. "For I *do* feel I have a sort of right to a *small* share in
all Erik's grandchildren, haven't I? But with Sif's children it's
peculiarly so; they're so *very* near my heart—"

"It seems to me you spoil them all pretty equally, Lillian,"
said Paul politely. "By the bye, has Sunnie written to thank you
for her peasant's dress—?"

"Yes—such a charming little letter! Oh, but you *must* see
it." She looked as if she would clasp her hands, and gave a deep
sigh: "Yes, Paul, they're two lovely children, yours! Thank
God you have *them*, at any rate!"

Paul tried to think of something else to talk about. But
then luckily the telephone rang, and Lillian was occupied for a
quarter of an hour.

This was one evening in May; she had asked him to come
and have supper with her. Afterwards, as they sat in her bou-

210

doir, Lillian unfolded her scheme to him. Alster was trying to get rid of Syrstad; it had not done well—a place like that had to be owned and run by a man who knew the business. How would it be if she bought instead a villa with an upper storey, in a good quarter, and let Halstein have the ground floor quite cheap and lived upstairs herself, then she could be some help to him and his children, and he could devote himself more to his work, without being worried by domestic cares—

"Hm. What does Halstein say to that?"

"Oh, you know what Halstein's like. So sensitive about such things. It's so exceedingly repugnant to his nature to accept help from anyone."

Paul nodded. It was his impression that his brother-in-law found the constant solicitude of his step-mother-in-law rather a nuisance.

"But when he *understands* that it is *I* who have to thank *him*—for you know it would give me an *object* in life, wouldn't it, if I could devote myself to Tua's children—"

His sister's little boys were well-behaved and easily managed— that is, they became so when they had spent a little time in the mountains. His previous impression of Kjetill, the twelve-year-old, had not been very favourable, but here he brightened up. The poor boy had evidently suffered from being transplanted to town. Now he ran about all over the place, fishing and gathering berries; he and Sunnie fetched home the goat and helped to put in the cattle at night—and Kjetill had done a man's work when the haymakers were here, said the dairy-woman. "I'm going to be a farmer, I am," said Kjetill. "Well, there are worse things than that," thought Paul.

Tov was a little younger than Sunnie. He was no doubt an uncommonly backward child, but very good. Helge was overjoyed at having this cousin who submitted entirely to being ordered about by the smaller boy. Helge was very fond of bossing. And he could do that to his heart's content this year, as Sunnie was occupied from morning till night in "nursing the baby"—the dairy-woman had a child of about a year old, and Sunnie had appropriated it entirely.

Paul had not been able to come up to the sæter so often, but Ruth told him about the children. She had such a charming way with them. What a waste of values it is, thought Paul, that it has only fallen to her lot to be a mediocre painter. How old could she be now?—five-and-thirty or so. She was pretty; it only improved her looks that life had left some traces on her dark and dark-eyed face.

PAUL was pretty late in getting away from the steatite works this Saturday evening; the electric circuit had been struck during the thunderstorm of the night before.

The days were already growing perceptibly shorter; it was gloomy under the trees the last part of the way through the forest.

The cattle-track swerved forward under Vassfjeld. Above the crest the evening sky was a pale gold, but under the steep side of the mountain with its grey screes the shadows lay above the bog. A few scattered old firs grew where there was a patch of drier ground; farther out white-bearded dead pines leaned above the yellowed sedges round the water-holes. So when he came up on to the neck of Vassfjeld and had the flat bare rock in front of him, the light of the whole wide vault almost dazzled him. A row of glistening little tarns trailed northward towards the Gröndal hill; here and there little red eyes of light gleamed in the distance—the Gröndal sæters. He felt a sudden desire to go in that direction, simply to experience once again how it feels to arrive at evening among a group of sæters, where one has never been before.

But his road lay to the westward—he had still three-quarters of an hour's walk before him.

THE sky was still bright, though it was fairly dark on the ground.

Big black bodies loomed up on the dusky slope, coming towards him—the Rust sæter cows. "They're still as bad as ever at coming home, aren't they?" he said to the woman who was with them.—In a different way it is good to come upon a place where everything is familiar.

Many stars were out already as he came up the Hauga sæter meadow. The brook murmured, with here and there a gleam, as the water caught the light of the sky. Oh, the good smell of a sæter—of wet pasture and goats and byre and wood-smoke. The houses lay hidden in the darkening slope, as long, low black shadows. The roof of the byre alone stood out clearly against the western sky which was still fringed with orange light. The cattle were all in, the byre door was shut. From within came a sound of dull thuds as the cows shifted and strained at their halters.

The separator was whirring in Magnhild's dairy; there was a light in the passage window there. Paul walked past the old hut, where his own quarters were, and up towards the new house. Through the window he saw the flickering light of a fire —Ruth was using the open hearth. The children were probably asleep—

Then the notes of a concertina fell on his ear. She must have visitors—? He hoped they were only folks from the other sæters.

His first sight on opening the door was the children sitting huddled together round the fire in their night clothes, the foot of a man and the concertina he had in his hands. The man cut short his playing and leaned forward to see who had come; it was somebody with a black forelock hanging over his eyes, big cheek-bones and a big, sharp nose—why, it was Jo Braastad-lykkjen!

"But—are *you* here!" said Paul in surprise; the other got up and gave him his hand.

"Yes, I came home to my brother's the other day. And then, you see, I thought I'd look up the sæter in the holidays—it's so

213

jolly here—"

"Well—glad to see you back. Did you come just lately—from France, I mean? I thought you were going to stay in Brittany the whole autumn—?"

Paul felt a little awkward the moment he had said it—afraid the other might interpret it as a reproach for not having called on him at the works. Braastadlykkjen had been abroad with a travelling scholarship since the new year, and Paul had helped him to bring it off. Now he had a vague impression that Jo was put out at seeing him.

Ruth came in from the kitchen:

"We didn't think you were coming this evening!" The lads from Kaldbakken had brought news of the accident to the power circuit when they passed that afternoon. "But sit down and I'll find you something to eat. Gladys has gone over to the Mo sæter. There *is* coffee here—" The coffee-pot was purring on the hearth. Ruth brought a cup, handed it to Braastadlykkjen· "Will you pour out, Jo?—Jo has a flask of home-made, so you can have a drop of medicine to pick you up, if you like," she laughed.

"Papa, *have* you remembered my blue wool?" came Sunnie's sing-song voice. "Ah, that *is* a good thing, now I can finish the guernsey for Little Ivar this week. Papa, you don't know how good I am at knitting, aren't I, Ruth?—it'll be fine!"

At last Paul and Ruth persuaded the children to vanish, and the grown-ups were able to settle down in front of the fire. Paul and Jo talked of the affairs of the steatite works and of Jo's travels and of the neighbours and of common friends in Christiania.

Ruth had pushed her chair back on account of the heat. She sat half in shadow and the light of the flames played over her shapely hands, which were clasped on her knee. She kept perfectly silent, only replying a few words when one of the others addressed a question to her.

It was long past midnight before they heard Gladys saying

214

good-bye to her escort at the gate. Jo Braastadlykkjen got up and stood looking rather doubtfully at Ruth Wangen:

"Well—I suppose I'll have to be going—"

"Aren't you going to stay here tonight?" asked Paul in surprise.

"Perhaps you'd better stay here now, as it's so late," said Ruth. "You can get a bed in Paul's hut, you know."

"Thanks, but—" No, he'd borrowed Vinsvold's hut, said Jo. And then Ruth had promised to see him home tonight, so as to row the boat back.—Vinsvold's boat was drawn up on the island, but he was to take Hans Kaldbakken's boat to get out there—only Hans had said he must send the boat back again at once, as Hans was to use it himself early tomorrow morning. So Ruth had offered to go with him and row—

Paul saw that Ruth turned red. That was an absurd idea anyhow—that she should come back alone from Djupsjöen in the middle of the night—!

"No, you'd much better turn in with me," suggested Paul.

Thanks— The only thing was, Jo mumbled, that Vinsvold had said something about coming up himself early tomorrow and he had no key to the hut; the one Jo had was the only one—

"But then he won't have a boat! And you'll never hear him, when once you've gone to sleep, however long he shouts to you from land."

"If you're not too tired—" said Ruth. She rose, went to the window and looked out. "We might both see Jo home. I should enjoy it. There's such wonderful moonlight tonight."

THEY had only a little way to go along the hill at the back of the Hauga sæter before they saw the lake lying before them on the lower ground, drenched in silvery moonlight.

The beauty of the night was positively unbelievable. The moon was almost full and stood high in the sky, filling space with a pale, as it were liquid light in which the stars were drowned. Long rounded summits, whitened with reindeer moss,

rose above the moor into the moonlight, and their immobility
and the colours of the night and the murmur of water through
the stillness seemed like another life beyond human life.

Paul kept wishing to himself, couldn't Jo hold his jaw now!
But he talked on and on—about the thunderstorm the night
before; the lightning had struck one of the big old firs on the
bog below Vassfjeld: "didn't you see it as you came up?"

Paul shook his head.

But Jo continued to hold forth: it always struck there. He
remembered in his childhood two dairy-women were killed
there by lightning; they had taken shelter under a tree. It was
the husband of one of them who found them, the other was his
sister—

Paul didn't care to say that he knew the story, but had been
told it happened sixty years ago.

On the stump of the tree under which the women had lain
there was said to be a cross carved: "Now I suppose that's a
custom that has come down from Catholic times, isn't it?"
asked Jo.

"I dare say."

"I'd like to know whether the Torsgar hill on the other
side of the bog wasn't called after Thor and his goats. You know,
they called it Bukkedal somewhere along there—"

It was said to be called after two reindeer hunters who
quarrelled over a buck one of them had shot, Paul knew, but
didn't take the trouble to answer.

For there was supposed to have been a group of farms in
old days, where the Torsgard sæters lay now. Before the Black
Death, no doubt. Jo had seen the site of the church—

Paul was reminded of the novel Jo had written. Many of
the descriptions were good in themselves and full of life, but
any other plot would have done just as well. He had written two
endings and read them both to Paul: in one of them Gjert rav-
ished Kari and then disappeared into the mountains. Many years
afterwards some reindeer hunters found a skeleton in a scree

with a gun lying under it. Kari lost her reason and wandered about among the mountains, crooning and singing. In the other ending Gjert and Kari came out on a brae where they had a view over the whole country-side: it was morning, just as the sun was rising; he walked erect like a young god, and she followed with bent head, tearful and smiling like a flower wet with dew. Where the paths divided they paused for a while—Kari took a few steps along the path that led to her father's farm—then she turned and ran back, weeping and laughing, till she rejoined Gjert.—Jo had had a sore struggle to decide which of these endings he ought to use. Well, well—his job was a sculptor's—

Paul sighed impatiently. On a night like this people had no business to be out on the mountains; if they chose to be out for all that, they might at least keep quiet.—There was a glint as of mica on some of the small stones in the path.

All at once a mighty long-drawn roar seemed to rise from the very earth—a bull bellowing long and loud, then another growling darkly. Straight in front of them they saw the beasts on a level stretch of grass by the path: two young bulls tilting at each other under the moon, grappling slowly with lowered horns and closing—one of them slipped aside, came again with a little crack, as their horns met. Elfishly superb they looked at their play, with the short black shadows under their feet. Four or five smaller bull calves lay or stood about on the outskirts of the patch of grass.

That would have been a nice thing for Ruth to meet as she came back alone, he thought. Though he knew that Ruth was not afraid of bulls, and the two which were butting at each other were the little bull from Haugen and another youngster that belonged to the Mo sæter.

They stood for a while watching the game. Then the two that had been at grips dashed off, and all the calves got up and shambled after.

They reached the lake. The path of moonlight lay broad upon it, and far out the island showed up in black shadow. It

217

was a longish row—out there and back again. A mad idea this of Jo and Ruth—

IT was half-past two before they had finished saying good-bye to Jo on the island and Paul and Ruth got into the boat again.

Paul rowed with long, slow strokes. The island grew less and less. The moon had sunk a good way—and Ruth sat in the stern of the boat, dark and slender; she said nothing, only now and then she bent her head back as though looking into the sky with her closed eyes. *Now* he thought there was no such hurry about getting home—

All the same, when they reached the shore and he had tied up the boat, they took the path home to the sæter. They walked quickly, side by side, and said not a word. The bulls were gone; they did not meet a living thing except a lemming that darted across the path.

It was good to be allowed to walk in silence, after all the chatter of that fellow Jo. Paul did not reflect that never before had he been silent like this, in Ruth's company. Cold it was now, so that they could see their own breath like a little light smoke in front of their faces, and the stillness all around was alive with a murmur of water on the moor.

As they stood in the shadow outside her door they instinctively spoke in low tones; they said good-night to each other and Paul took his rucksack. He had gone a few paces down the slope when she called softly: "Paul—"

"Yes—?" He turned round. "Was there anything—?"

"No.—Not really. Only, it's almost a sin to go to bed on a night like this—"

Paul stood waiting. He no longer felt tired, was quite ready to go and see the sunrise from one of the hills, if that was what she would propose. But she said:

"I don't know whether there's any water in your hut."

She went with him down the meadow, and when he unlocked the door of the old hut she went in first. The room seemed

218

pitch-dark to them coming from outside, and the air of it was warm and cosy within the timber walls. A streak of moonlight came in through the little window, lighting up a white square on the floor.

The carafe and the mug were empty: "oh, but it doesn't matter, Ruth." Paul picked up the pail from the passage and hurried out.

The spring was away behind the barn. Paul knelt on the flat stone and lowered the pail slowly into the clear, ice-cold water. The pool was a little world by itself in the moonlight, with colours unknown to the daytime—the water lay dark and deep under the light, smooth-worn slabs of shale; green weeds waved delicately where the spring bubbled up and glistened. The thick moss bordering the brook was a vivid light green by daylight, and the willow-herb which grew thickly round the pool was dark green with fine reddish stalks—now they were something different, for which no one could find a name.

Ruth had followed him out and stood facing him.

"It was a shame that you should have to fetch water yourself—"

"Oh, but that's nothing—

"—*Is* there something, Ruth?" He could not tell how he had come to ask such a question.

She shook her head slightly. They walked slowly over the grass.

Paul stood on the doorstep outside his hut, following her with his eyes till she had gone in and shut the door of the new house. She had been so odd—

He went on thinking about her as he undressed. She could never—? In the first place she was at least six years his senior, and besides, Braastan was good enough in his own way, but he and Ruth—no, that would hardly turn out well.—*Hadn't* they been just the least bit odd when he came in this evening? They had seen a good deal of each other in Christiania in the last few years. No indeed, he sincerely hoped Ruth wouldn't go in for any nonsense in that direction after all—

PAUL could not rid himself of a feeling of discomfort or uneasiness, as he was jolted along in Rasmus Nyplassen's cart on Monday morning. Jo had been to see them again on Sunday afternoon. One can't interfere in such things, but—

NEXT week-end he had to fetch the children; they were to go to school again. Ruth had offered to stay at the sæter and keep house for him during the shooting season—though Magnhild, the dairy-woman, could have done that perfectly; this year it looked as if he would be there alone. His father-in-law had refused, he was quite broken-down now, and nothing Paul could say had any effect. He had proposed to Hans to come up for a time, but Hans had ended by deciding in favour of an invitation from some friends who had a shooting in Valdres, and of course he would have better sport there than at the Hauga sæter. —But then there was that business of the portrait which he had promised Ruth to sit for—. He didn't feel a bit inclined— to give up some of the little leisure he could allow himself. But if she was so keen on it—

The children had a heap to say about Jo, when Paul came up. Braastadlykkjen must have spent the whole week at the Hauga sæter. And he came again on Sunday morning, lay smoking cigarettes on the grass, while Ruth was busy with the children's packing. And in the evening, when Paul drove away with children and nurse and baggage on two carts, Jo stood beside Ruth and waved to them from the front of the hut.

GURI and Ambjör were to join them at Haugen, so that Paul could take the whole flock with him, when he went into Christiania on Monday morning.

The first thing Paul saw as he turned in to Haugen was a strange pale-grey car which stood shining under the light of the big lamps of the stone-cutting yard. Then a door of the main building flew open, and Lillian came dashing out into the streak of light with a queer fluttering air:

"I *must* have a word with you at once," she whispered aloud to Paul, as she rushed past him, lifted Tov out of the cart and clasped him to her bosom with a ponderous, tragic gesture. Kjetill received a similar embrace, and Sunnie and Helge more ordinary ones.

"You've come too? That's delightful," he said to Lillian, and at that moment a young chauffeur turned up—it was Alster's —and helped him to unload the baggage, while Lillian and Gladys swarmed into the house with the whole crowd of youngsters.

Paul helped to take the horses out and put them into the stable, was just going across to make himself tidy, when Lillian came out again in the same wild state of excitement.

"Do you know!" She stood in the full light of the electric lamps, massive and solemn, dressed in a long riding-jacket and breeches: "Halstein is married! *Can* you imagine it—he was married last Tuesday! At Kongsvinger! To a nurse—a Fröken Nymoen! One of his old parishioners out there—!"

Paul could find nothing to answer.

"I *really* didn't think *that* of Halstein," groaned Lillian.

"He's been in a difficult position for many years," Paul hazarded. "Really had no one who could look after his home and the children."

"They say she has money. And that he saw a *great deal* of her while they were living there," said Lillian significantly. "She was constantly in the house—nursing Tua and so on."

"Ah, then he must have got to know her well—knows that she's a good sort who will do her duty by the children—"

"Aren't you the least bit scandalized? It's not much more than eight months since your sister died—"

"Scandalized, scandalized— But look here, I must go across and have a wash—"

Scandalized—that was as one chose to take it. Of course

he didn't like it, Paul thought, as he changed his clothes in his room.—But good heavens, something of the old tradition still survived that a clergyman always ought to have a wife and help-mate—parsons who were left widowers always *did* marry again, that was his impression. And if it was the case that for years Halstein had waited with his affection and his desire to be a good husband—on an invalid wife who had rebuffed him, in weariness and distaste, his action was not so very unnatural. He could assuredly justify it before God and his own conscience, as the saying is—maintaining that it was the best thing for all, in-cluding the children.

Loyalty—there is one kind of loyalty which is an affair of the will. And another loyalty which is beyond one's control— feelings and memories which no act of the will can root out en-tirely. But feelings and memories of this kind do not hinder a man from entering into relations with other women—on other premises. It need not imply any disloyalty to Tua's memory, even if Halstein had come to the conclusion that he would do best to marry again so soon as this.

Or else——. That a man really can feel he is done with a woman so completely, though he has lived with her for years and had children by her, is almost uncanny. He himself had been revolted by it at a time when he was young and had never before abandoned himself to anyone—when another's shame at being taken and forsaken and taken and forsaken again had felt like something in which he himself shared. That men had pos-sessed his beloved as he himself had possessed her—and then gone their ways, just as if it was nothing at all!

Now—well, now he acknowledged that he could not rid himself of his duties to Björg, even if his emotional nature did not acknowledge it. It was with a totally different part of his being that he admitted it. But otherwise Sunnie's and Helge's mother might have appeared to him as one with whom he had had a passing affair a long time ago and had almost forgotten.—

Supper was laid for them in his tenant's kitchen; Paul's

rooms were not large enough to house such an assemblage.

It pained him to see the two elder girls; their faces showed such a hopeless expression of defiant coldness under the curly pale yellow hair. Kjetill looked as if he had been given something altogether too difficult to think about, and Tov had been crying. But even Sunnie and Helge looked ill at ease. It was not a comfortable meal, though the children ate the waffles and cream with a good appetite.

It was really too bad if Lillian had been setting the children against their step-mother in advance. She ought to have the sense to stop it anyhow.

Sunnie gave him such a curious look, when she came to say good-night. And when he drew her to him and kissed her, she seemed to stiffen in his arm. Then she flung herself into his embrace with a sudden vehemence.

AFTERWARDS, when he and Lillian were sitting alone in his smoking-room, he told her so. She had been holding forth about Halstein, who couldn't even wait till Sif was cold in her grave.

"Anyhow don't say anything like that to the children, Lillian. You know it will be much better for them to be on good terms with their step-mother."

Lillian sniffed scornfully. Then she said, almost in tears: "And I love those children so! But now—you'll see, his new wife will take care to destroy the old intimate footing—of course they'll never be allowed to come to me any more. And Tov, poor little fellow, who has such need of someone who understands him, he has so little to say for himself. Do you suppose *she* will have patience with the poor little child—?"

"I don't see why not. If she's willing to take a widower with four children, it's only reasonable to suppose that she realizes the task before her. And I don't think you ought to make it more difficult for her. Let her have a fair chance, in God's name—

"Remember how abominably *I* behaved to you, Lillian," he pleaded. "You yourself have told me you felt it deeply. And

223

that father was terribly hurt by it. Are you going to help to
bring the same sort of thing on Halstein and his new wife?"

He saw that Lillian turned red under her paint:

"That was quite another matter. If Tua had left Halstein
in the same way as Julie left your father— But that he could
forget her as soon as she is dead—after all her years of suffering
and illness, *that's* what I think is so cruel! Dear me—if Julie
had decided to marry Doctor Wangen after Benedikte's death,
both Erik and I felt sure that you would all have come over to
our side, and you would have been the first!"

Paul had a sudden feeling of sinking into the floor—his
heart shrank and he felt a hot pressure over his eyebrows. His
mother and Uncle Halfdan—!

"And of course that was why she didn't do it after all," said
Lillian. "Not that I believe they would have suited each other
either, when it came to the point. Doctor Wangen was really
so insignificant—there I always agreed with Erik."

Paul wanted to get up and go, but dared not. He dared not
give himself away.

"But fortunately Ruth doesn't take after him in the *least*,"
Lillian went on with her chatter. "She's the very image of
Benedikte—well, she's very like your mother too, only less
robust, you might say, just as Fru Wangen was—more subdued
and fined down than Julie, I always thought. Your father thought
a *great* deal of that sister-in-law, he always said—"

Good Lord, how am I going to get away from this—

"No, I am sure," said Lillian with feeling, "your father too
would have thought it the best and—and—happiest ending of
all this, if you and Ruth came together at last!"

Paul felt as if he was in some kind of an earthquake.

"Because there isn't a living soul that can have anything
to say against it. After the scandalous way Björg has behaved
to you. And Ruth has quite won the children's hearts already—

"—No, when I *think* of Björg! How well I thought of her
to begin with! *Never* have I been so disappointed over *any*one!"

"You seem to be talking bosh!"

Lillian looked at Paul in dismay.

For a while neither said anything. Till Lillian began rather timidly:

"Yes, *that* you may be sure would meet with sympathy from everyone—if you and Ruth were to marry—"

"I believe you've gone off your head! I *am* married—Björg and I are not separated even—"

"No, but you *know*, you could get a separation without the *slightest* difficulty, after her running away from you and the children like that—"

"But I can't do anything of the sort," Paul shut her up. "As you know, I'm a Catholic—"

"But I'm sure Ruth would be glad to turn Catholic, if you wish it," said Lillian soothingly. "We have all seen how immensely fond of you she is—how splendid she has been with Sunnie and Helge—"

"No, stop it, Lillian. There is no such thing as divorce among us. Not that I miss it either."

"Well, but that can't be possible. There must be a way— the Catholic Church is supposed to be so brilliantly organized that it can find a means for everything! Look here, Paul— you're still a young man, in the prime of life. If Björg doesn't come back—what will you do then?"

"Oh, she'll come back all right. Besides, there's my work and the children that I'm answerable for. What else have *our* priests, but their work and their responsibility?"

"Oh yes." Lillian pursed up her lips. "We all know what *that* leads to."

"No, that's what you don't know," replied Paul hotly. "You only know of those who fail. You simply don't *want* to know of the work they do, the many more who are steadfast. And the others—*they* are not the ones I'm to imitate. Don't you remember what Jesus said to St. Peter on a certain occasion, when he was trying to poke his nose into John's affairs? 'It's no business

225

of yours,' he said—in plain language. 'Follow *thou* me!' "

Paul got up: "I won't hear any more of this. I'd better say good-night now—"

But at the door of his bedroom he stopped:

"You might tell me one thing though—*where* did you get hold of the idea that there was anything between Ruth and me? There isn't a shadow of truth in it. But is there any talk —have you heard anybody else hint at anything of the sort?"

"I don't quite know," said Lillian timidly. "You know what I am, Paul—I *never* gossip about other people's affairs. But I must say, I've had a sort of impression that all our friends are hoping it may come to something between you two—"

He stood in his bedroom, shaken and revolted.

And a positive shower of scales fell from his eyes.

The whole thing was so insane that he couldn't help laughing too. But it had simply never entered his head that anyone could imagine—

—That night when they rowed Jo over to the island and walked home together in the moonlight—no, hang it, it wasn't true; Ruth was his cousin, and it was utterly intolerable if he was to believe she wanted to give him an opportunity of making love. But now, when he recalled the whole of that moonlight night—their row home across the lake, their walk back to the sæter, the moment when they were alone together in his dark, cosy room, with the moon shining in at the window—he could not help seeing that everything seemed to have been staged for a declaration. Except that nothing of the kind had occurred to him— But what about her? As he thought of her silence it suddenly appeared fateful.

Nonsense. Ridiculous to let Lillian put such a thing into his head.

And then there was what she said about his mother. A crowd of little incidents cropped up in his memory and acquired a new significance. He had never been able to under-

stand his mother's admiration for that terrible booby, Uncle
Halfdan—that she could take him and his chatter seriously,
that she could stand him glaring into her eyes every time he
spoke to her—and he had that trick with all women. His father
had loathed him—

He suddenly had a vision of his mother, as he had seen
her one day when he was a boy—he had come home from school
—it must have been just after they had moved out to Linlökka,
as the house stood bare and yellow in the wind and the spring
sunshine; the trees of the garden were tiny, and the snow around
them was shrinking. His mother came out into the yard and
hung up some washing which flapped heavily in the blast. She
had kilted up her blue dress over the bright red petticoat and
rolled up her sleeves, so that the strong white arms were bare
far above the elbows—he remembered that once again it had
struck him as a revelation of beauty: his mother was so handsome! Round her head she had tied a red and yellow silk handkerchief, but the hair fell out from under it, and her great yellowish eyes shone out of the dark face. The expression in them
had been the same as he afterwards came across in a photograph
of her from the jersey period, full of expectation and challenge
and questioning of the future or of life or whatever one was to
call it—

She had had big gold rings in her ears too—he could not
remember ever having seen them except then.

In later years, when he came to think of her as she was
that day, he had had the idea that she was playing a game with
herself, she was something like a Drachmann gipsy wench—

Clever as she was, she was at the same time boundlessly
naïve, mother. But if she had contrived to see anything great in
Uncle Halfdan—!

He remembered her having said to him once that no woman
can tell the same story in exactly the same way to a man and to
a woman. And yet both ways may be equally true. Yes indeed—

Ruth had never been able to care very much for his mother,

he had seen that. No doubt it had been a dismal failure, that
time many years ago, when she was to try spending a winter
at Linlökka. If there was anything in Lillian's tattle, then Ruth
knew of it—

O Lillian, Lillian, you ought to get it hot for your tongue-
wagging!

Just now too—he simply hadn't time even to think of any
women's nonsense now. He felt personally ill-used and aggrieved by fate, or by Our Lord, just like a child, that this
should come now of all times, when he had more than enough
to do with his business. The threat of a strike at the brick-works
hanging over him—and he had made preparations for keeping
the second kiln going, at all events till into the new year, and
had made favourable contracts for chips and slabs with Nils-
moen sawmills. He had hoped that the place would run so
smoothly for a while that he could honourably retire from the
Berven affair. Then he could move up here entirely—for otherwise he would have to appoint an engineer to manage the works
at Haugen; it could not go on as at present, with himself
travelling backwards and forwards.

—For that matter he had had a distinct impression that
he arrived rather inopportunely for her and Jo that evening; of
course it was Jo that she was inclined to be taken up with—and
he discovered with a feeling of humiliation that *now* he wished
it might be so—and the next moment, that he was very far
from wishing it all the same. The lad was gifted and unreliable;
torn out of the surroundings in which he had grown up, he had
drifted about in another world in which he had no roots,
greedy of experience and sensation, lacking instinct for such
things as the unwritten laws which find sanction in each sepa-
rate stratum of society. God in Heaven, they didn't even speak
the same language, he and Ruth, even when they used the same
words—they had not the same meaning for them. And in reality
she was not an artist at all; what she had was just the capacity
for understanding art and becoming absorbed in it, but not

for understanding an artist or entering into his feelings. And
already she was too old for Jo—and in a few years, when she
was over forty and he was not much more than thirty—

Why was he so upset at the thought that Ruth might be in
love with Jo Braastadlykkjen—? It was quite natural after all.
She was his cousin, and with her in particular he had had a
strong feeling of relationship; he had seen a great deal of her
in the last few years, was very fond of her— There was no need
of Lillian's absurd ideas to explain it—

—Isn't it about time you said your evening prayer? asked
the Devil with a grin. All right, old 'un, don't worry about that—

O God, O God—*must* I discover once more what an ass I
have been!

PAUL went to bed, rolled himself up in his beloved skin rug and
discovered that he might as well give up all hope of sleep for the
present.

What an ass he had been—again!

But indeed he was not so sure what he was to make of Ruth
now—how much meaning was to be attached to her manner of
late, or how she had interpreted his. He had assumed as a matter
of course that she knew he was married and that there was no undoing it. But it did not look as if any others of his family had
taken that view—even his mother evidently believed in the rubbish that certain Protestant clergymen wrote in the papers, to
the effect that the Church refused to recognize any marriages
but those she had celebrated—

But, that being so, it could not be denied that his relations
with Ruth would bear more than one interpretation. They had
been a great deal together, ever since he had moved back to the
South—and during the last year they had been together constantly; they had motored together, dined out together, both
with the children and alone, Ruth had looked after the children's clothes, taken them to the dentist's and so on, and she
had spent the last two summers with them at his sæter—

And he disliked the idea intensely that all this must now come to an end.

He was fond of her and knew that she was fond of him—and please God she was not fonder of him than he had realized. Neither of them was now so young as to be liable to a great, flaming passion. They had both lived long enough to learn how seldom one meets another person of whom it is possible to be fond in a perfectly safe and trustful way, without fear of encountering in the other qualities of which one is oneself intolerant by nature. An alliance between Ruth and him would never admit of any violent excitement, nor on the other hand of any deadly disappointments or profound embitterment—if an alliance between them had been possible. They understood one another far too well for that. He understood her longing to strike roots in life; he was fond of her precisely because she was like that, made for building up and preserving. He appreciated her rebellion against the freedom in which she was imprisoned—her indignation with those who told her how she ought to use her freedom, she who was not allowed to become what she herself wished to be. And he felt humiliation on her behalf when he saw that she herself was aware of the false position she occupied with regard to her art; since she was not equipped by nature to practise it, but to love it and to be a mediator between it and other people.

But even if their friendship was not of a kind to take their breath away—a good, safe sympathy—he well knew that even this equable, warm feeling was capable of growing into something intense, shining and glowing. If they were not likely to provide each other with many surprises, they could no doubt have experienced many wonderful surprises in common. Now he was continually haunted by the thought of that night when he and she were out together, alone among the wild, moonlit mountains—

It was going to be quite impossible—he would never succeed in being his old self, when he met Ruth again. When he did not know for certain what she had put into his manner towards her. For *affectionate* was just what he had been towards her—though it had never entered his head to caress so much as her hand. But he was fond of her and had never dreamt of concealing it from her—it had seemed to him so much a matter of course that their friendship could never be anything but what it now was. He had not even reflected on it. But what if Ruth had not thought the same?

He could not continue to associate with her so closely as before, and if he now suddenly retired, he would offend her—

And then that arrangement that she should stay at the Hauga sæter over the shooting, and that silly portrait—. It had not occurred to him that there would be anything in it if he was there alone with his cousin for ten days or so, with the dairy-woman and the people in all the sæters round about. But now it was impossible, when he knew that charitable souls were already discussing their relations. For she and not he would be the one to suffer most.

This idea of the portrait had been distasteful to him all the time. For he hated to see her paint badly, and he winced on her account when she got bad notices, knowing how terribly she really took them to heart.

He was much fonder of her than he had known—. And his intimacy with her had been a playing with fire, he saw that now.

But how he was to put an end to it without wounding her, that he did not know—

LILLIAN was to drive back to Syrstad next day; she took all the four Garnaas children down to the station first. They had an oppressed air, as if they were ready to defend themselves against attacks from everybody, when Paul had them collected with the rest of his party in the train.

He did his best to show no sign and chatted with the children, but without much success; he was himself tired and depressed. The others' ill humour was infectious, so that even

Sunnie and Helge kept remarkably quiet the whole journey. Not a word did Paul say about their father's marriage to his nephews and nieces, though he felt himself that this was wrong. Keeping quiet about it like this was in a way equivalent to endorsing Lillian's opinion.

At last this journey came to an end; they had passed Bryn, the lights of the town gleamed through the carriage window along the Loelv valley, and Paul had lifted all the hand baggage out of the net; he stood helping Guro on with her coat—and then he found the opportunity to say to the two elder girls:

"Now you mustn't be so unhappy in anticipation. You may be sure, if your father has done this, it is because he thinks it will be best for you all. You know how fond he is of you. Now don't begin by thinking there is anyone who wishes you ill."

But he could hear how weak it sounded. For he remembered himself how it felt.

Ambjör answered scornfully:

"I'm not going to stay at home—I shall go to a boarding-school! She's done this because she wanted to help father to get us on, so they say!" The girl was puffing with rage.

"Well, but then you can see at any rate that she *means* well!"

But the discomfort of the situation weighed on his heart—all the pain that is brought on children without anyone being really able to help it! In the stuffy, over-heated carriage there was a smell of orange-peel and damp, dubbined boots, and a litter of waste paper and fruit-peel everywhere in the dim light that fell from the lamp in the roof. Paul felt all the most vexatious emotions of his childhood vividly stirring within him, as he directed the children to clear up the mess they had made.

Pastor Garnaas was at the station to meet his children. Guro gave him her hand and said: "Congratulations, father," in a chillingly hard, thin voice. Then the other three congratulated him, and Tov started to howl horribly.

Paul pressed his brother-in-law's hand:

"Good luck, Halstein."

They walked together up the platform, the whole caravan. Paul felt intensely relieved when he had seen all the Garnaases disappear into a taxi, the clergyman last, fairly down in the mouth. Poor fellow, he had only a new set of difficulties to look forward to.

Frans was waiting in front of the station with their own car. Paul made Gladys sit in front with him and sat behind himself between the two children.

They had come a good way beyond the town; trees and houses and fields appeared out of the darkness, came towards them in the light of the lamps and dashed past. Then Sunnie said all at once—she had been sitting as still as a mouse:

"Oh, father—I think it must be so *terrible* to have a new mother; don't you think they're frightfully sad now that they're at home with her?"

"You know it was sad that Aunt Sif was taken away from her children. But now God has taken her to himself. And it may well be that Uncle Halstein's new wife will be just the one to make them feel less sad."

"*You* must never do that, father!"

"But, darling, your mother's alive. You know that mother must stay in Denmark to nurse grandmother, so long as she's so ill."

"Fancy if God should think of taking grandmother next time," said Sunnie hopefully. "But Grandmamma Selmer says he's not likely to do that; she thinks he's only too glad, as long as he can get off having anything to do with her."

"Oh, you mustn't pay attention to what Grandmamma Selmer says in that way—she doesn't mean so very much by it." Paul hoped the child hadn't noticed that he smiled in spite of himself.

Sunnie flung herself into his arms so violently that Helge got a jolt and was shot into the other corner of the car, but he slept on just as soundly.

Chapter Seven

PAUL DECIDED TO GIVE UP THE SHOOTING THIS YEAR. THE
strike was still in the air, but he wrote to Alster hinting
that he would like to retire from his position at the Berven
brickworks. Just lately he had had a prospect of selling his
share in the works to a man at Fredrikstad who was in the business and would be glad to take over his position. It would not
be any very brilliant affair for him, but in spite of that he was
more than ready to close with it. This would then set free a
little of Paul's capital, which he could put into the steatite
works.

In these circumstances there was no temptation to exert
himself overmuch to get Björg home. This summer she had been
staying at a country house in Jutland where they received a few
elect as "paying guests." Goodness only knew how she and her
mother had worked it to get into that circle, but no doubt it was
through Fru von Benningsen and her sister: they were reported
to be a pair of extremely respectable old ladies, but they needed
all the income they could scrape together.—For the time being
Björg was at Skodsborg again with her mother, who continued
to take cures.

But now in any case he would do what he had long thought
of—see that Sunnie and Helge received proper religious instruction with a view to their first communion. Helge had to
start school anyhow; they could go to St. Joseph's Institute this
winter. Then he could shut up the big house at Berven, only
using a couple of rooms. He had to be glad enough to be able

234

to cut down any expenses.

It would also be cheaper to take a room in Christiania than staying at an hotel—he was at his town office every Thursday at least, and it was his habit to stay the night and go to Mass on Friday morning. Wilfrid Gotaas proposed half in jest that he could come to them—rent the same room that he had had in his student days. There was something in the idea which tempted him, and Paul accepted.

It was queer all the same, the first evening he went home with Wilfrid to Schwensens-gate; it was after a meeting at the St. Joseph's Society. Little Fru Clara had coffee for them, and Paul, who felt as if he had had more than enough coffee for one day, went politely into the parlour.

It was entirely changed. Gone were Fru Gotaas's plush furniture and carpets and palms and pedestals and little stands with plaster saints—all the things that had filled the air with dust, so that the sun always shone through a mist of little dancing, rainbow-coloured motes, when it was on this side of the house. Wilfrid had got himself new, shiny birchwood furniture and a tall standard lamp with a colossal orange-coloured silk shade. The old oleographs of the Heart of Jesus and the Holy Family had made way for photographs of van Eyck's Christ the King and Bellini's madonnas. On a kind of altar stood a big crucifix of light oak and imitation ivory between candlesticks and flowers.

Round about signed photographs of clerical persons stood or hung. Wilfrid produced an enlarged amateur portrait of a Carmelite nun with bare feet in sandals: "Monika, you remember her—here she is, Sister Joan of the Cross. If you ever require special intercession, you need only send her a few lines—" He said it as if it were a matter of ordering tea from England.

On the top of the book-case was a glaring white cast of the head of John from Trondhjem Cathedral. "We have lots of good books," Wilfrid showed him proudly—there were Belloc and Chesterton and Maurice de Wulff in English—many shelves full of the most recent foreign Catholic literature. In a corner by themselves stood some little worn covers with the leaves hanging out—his parents' library.

"No, we're obliged to be wide awake; our action is what the times call for," declared Wilfrid Gotaas. "For Europe has got to make up its mind either to take God seriously or to declare war against Him. Because, you see, it's unworthy both of God and men simply to believe He's out of date and takes care of all fools when they think it may be a good thing to call upon Him now and again. I say straight out, there can't be any other choice but between Catholicism and Communism for folks who use their brains at all. Either we must live solely for God or we must try how we can get on without Him. But as for an ordinary conventional life—just as if they think the world's a restaurant with a stand-up counter where you push in and help yourself, and heaven the private rooms upstairs where you're served with coffee and liqueurs afterwards—pish, is all I've got to say!"

Paul had no objection to offer. But he missed the old Gotaases. The very air of these rooms—a rather seedy smell of crowded life—had seemed so charged with charity and unaffected kindness.

At that moment young Fru Gotaas came in from the bedroom with their child, a little creature in a woollen combination. It was a pale, thin boy with fair curls who clung to his mother and whimpered, half asleep, when his father tried to make him take notice of the strange man.

"Yes, she had to have an operation afterwards," Wilfrid explained when the mother had taken the child back. "So we shall never have any more than him. Wouldn't one have thought that God might have let us have a houseful, us who would have been thankful for them? But His will be done. So that's why he's called Emanuel."

At last Paul was allowed to retire. Wilfrid Gotaas followed him into his room.

It was the same furniture. But all the little old devotional

236

pictures and images had disappeared. Above the bed hung a brand-new crucifix and on the chest of drawers stood two new saints, long and thin, in imitation of Gothic wood-carving. Wilfrid turned on the light and introduced them with a motion of the hand. They were Thomas More with his chancellor's chain, a red book and a green palm of victory in his hands, and Cardinal Fisher in a biretta, holding a palm.

"I bought them when I was in England—I have a special devotion to the English martyrs. Have you read Challoner's *Memoirs of Missionary Priests*? I can lend it you—it's one of the most magnificent books there is in the world, let me tell you—"

At last he dipped his finger in the holy water bowl and held out the drop to Paul by way of good-night.

Paul shrugged his shoulders—what business had he to criticize Wilfrid Gotaas, even if he thought the other's faith took a rather too self-sufficient form? In reality he too loved all this; he loved the Church down to the smallest things, symbols and signs, more and more as he got to know what they stood for —pivots for lines of thought which were all parts of a universal interpretation of life. He too loved all the consecrated trifles that the Church gives to her faithful, he loved the majestic liturgies of consecration which dare to command all created things to serve men when they serve the Creator. In reality it was only a love which is divine and a courage which has no bounds that could impel a church to venture this, after nearly two thousand years' experience of men's untrustworthiness and eternal craving for flattery, no matter whom or what they may have served.

But at the same time he could not help recalling how meaningless—or misleading—all these things look to those who have no knowledge of what they stand for. That is to say, to all his acquaintance of former days. He himself had smiled at them, when he stood outside and regarded holy water bowls and candles and rosaries and ugly little statuettes as a kind of hieroglyphics for the language of a dead past. Wilfrid had never seen these things without knowing what they meant; it was equally natural that he should treat them with blunt familiarity and that he should be inclined to brag of his store of them.

Thus when Wilfrid informed him in a rather offhand way that he had a special devotion to Thomas More, it was Wilfrid who in reality understood St. Thomas better than he himself did—he admired the chancellor from having read a great deal of his writings and of what had been written about him, and he had hanging at home a reproduction of Holbein's study of his splendid face. But the essential thing about Thomas More was that he had laid that head upon the block for his faith's sake; it was a secondary matter, not so unessential however, that it was one of the finest heads in the Europe of that day.

But he was entangled in a net of associated ideas. There were things that he had heard other people say, and although he had never believed in them, they had left an impression behind. Other people's notions, which he had never shared, had nevertheless left traces in his mind—in much the same way as he had got burrs sticking to his clothes in old days, when he went botanizing round those sinister ponds of his. When he thought he had picked himself clean, he always discovered that a lot were still left on him.

And it was due to the importunity of such associations that he sometimes felt shocked at the expressions of the prayer books. Words like faith and salvation, sin and grace, free will, even God's name, were to him so loaded with old idea-complexes that their meaning was distorted to one side or the other. He himself had never had use for them before; he had had no concepts to which he could attach them. But he had had some notions of what they might express in the language of various Christian and freethinking sects. There was hardly a word for religious concepts which does not express something different in the hierarchy of Catholic ideas from what the same word may mean in the dance of concepts of every other philosophy under the sun. But this made it impossible for him to converse with anyone he had known from his youth about his present thoughts and opinions. His faith in spite of all had penetrated his whole being and determined all that he thought and felt and did—not least when he was slack and lazy and lukewarm.

His mother had said to him one day not long ago—without the slightest connection with what they had been talking about previously:

"Tell me—what view do you Catholics take of spiritualism?"

"Spiritualism?" He had been taken aback, more at her tone than anything else. "Indeed I'm not very clear—I've never taken any interest in it. No doubt there's a lot of humbug and self-deception in it—but there are certainly supernatural powers behind the movement, encouraging it. Someone whose interest it is to send people searching after truth in a quarter where there is least danger of their finding it."

"Well, what makes you feel so sure about that?" his mother had asked, a little hurt.

Because the Church says so. But however anxious he might be to explain this to her, she would never understand that he could think this reason enough. That in the beginning it was pure commonsense conclusions that had impelled him to make inquiries of the Church—if there was any place on earth where he could hope to get sensible answers about anything on earth, it must be there. And that his experience had shown that it is of some use to ask: one receives answers. Therefore he was willing to accept the teaching of the Church about other matters concerning which it had not occurred to him to inquire.

Instead of this he said to his mother:

"After all we may put a little faith in the religious inklings of the whole of humanity too. Mankind has had a sort of awe of death, or has been indifferent to it. But to look hopefully on death because we believe that only then will life begin in earnest to be commonplace and standardized—that seems to me to smack too much of the taste now in fashion. It may be droll enough that folk have always had the belief that they were to go on living when once they were dead. But the news we get from the spiritualist heaven strikes me as a little too like the latest claptrap—about continuation schools and people who go cackling about one another and poking their noses into other people's affairs. I cannot believe that the God of the Philistines is the true God."

His mother said softly:

"But if one meets all one's dear ones again, as the spiritualists assert?"

"Then we shouldn't be able to stand them—not for a whole eternity. If we were condemned to be together always in a future life of that sort, without a hope of ever being able to bore each other really to death."

At that his mother had suddenly begun to cry:

"You mustn't talk like that! For I will tell you one thing, Paul—I myself am no longer so sure that there may not be something in all that I used to reject as mere figments of the brain—a life after death and God and so on—"

"But then can't you imagine," he had asked, "that there may exist something like an objective truth about God?"

"Oh really, Paul! How could we human beings acquire even an approximately objective knowledge of God?—With our tiny midge's brains!"

—And of course it may be right enough to talk of our tiny midge's brains, when once we believe in a personal God. And if one believes in revelation, then one may kneel down and confess that what we can grasp with our intelligence is so small that we may be tempted to call it nothing. When one has the dogmas expounded by St. Thomas Aquinas, one can *see*, as it were, what is meant by unfathomable mysteries—just as one thinks one can *see* the infinity of space when one looks upon the whole of Jotunheim standing sharp and clear and white with

fresh snow against the sky on a dazzlingly bright autumn day.
—But from his mother's standpoint it was misplaced modesty
to speak of men's tiny midge's brains—taking into consideration what she could have with which to compare human brains,
these are quite worthy of respect. It was only one of these
many figures of speech which have a meaning so long as people
cling to one Christian dogma or another; when these are thrown
over the meaning is gone. If men do but postulate a pantheon of
gods between themselves and the First Cause, they have always
been conscious of being sufficiently important to excite either
the envy or the love of their gods.

It was his mother too who had always maintained that the
belief in a life after death was merely dictated by the desire
for more life and more happiness. This is, to put it mildly, im-
probable—since most people have believed that life after death
was something they had to put up with, but certainly not a
thing to be looked forward to with joy. That idea as a rule
had first been imparted to them by Christian missionaries. Eternal life which is eternal bliss—that is a thing Christ promises
to *His* believers in *His* kingdom, where He rules absolutely.
And He disposes of it as an absolute monarch—to some He
promises it as a reward, if they will bear His cross and endure
with Him in all His afflictions; and to a robber He promises it,
because in dying he prays, forget me not—. It is only when people remember something of the hope of Christianity, but have
forgotten its fear, that anyone can believe heaven to be like
a suite of reception rooms upstairs, to which people are admitted
if they are dressed more or less according to the latest moral
fashion.

But now it appeared that his mother was trying to believe
what chimed in with her wishes. She wished she could find again
the child she had lost. It was obvious that she was at any rate
very much occupied with spiritualism for the time being.

And whether the feeling were sinful or not—he thought it
much better that his mother should remain what she was, a proud

241

old woman who proclaimed herself an arrant heathen. Disbelief
is always material sin, but formal sin it is not, if it is based on
venial ignorance. And his mother had always been in good
faith with her own ideas. He prayed for her every day, that
she might find the truth—but he confessed to himself that he
could not see how this was to come about—except by a miracle.
But can there be anything gained in a person coming to believe in a life after death—if it is only to be another edition of
this life on earth?

His poor mother was only thinking of seeing Tua again.
But mother and Tua together, let us say for twenty thousand
years—that was a hopeless thought. Unless they were both absorbed in one and the same blissful vision, God Himself who
alone can reconcile the irreconcilable, the inmost diversity of
human beings.

"United in Christ." He remembered his own ideas of former
days when he heard such expressions and to him they were only
the jargon of alien cliques. Probably he had been inclined to
think that when people said they were "united in Christ" they
meant that they were a set who had certain enormous advantages over other people now and would obtain even greater
advantages later on. And that they had a private yardstick with
which to measure all others—and doubtless also that they were
very willing to do good to the rest of mankind, provided the
others would leave it to them to decide what was good for
people.

United in Christ—by the memory of the water He turned
to wine in our cup, by the memory of the promises we made to
Him when drinking and kept so miserably, united in longing
for the day when He shall redeem His promise to drink the new
wine with us in His kingdom. United by the memory of all the
times He forgave us our sins and our cowardice and our un-
faithfulness—and we went away and were unfaithful again. By
the memory of all the times when our ears burned when the
talk was of His death and of the traitor who handed Him over

to the sinners: "Lord, it cannot be I—?"

Eternal life—he had certainly never entertained a desire to live eternally. Until it dawned on him what Christ meant when He called Himself the Life. An eternal life which is anything but uninterrupted insight into God—is hell, as one must discover sooner or later.—

His mother had been so healthy and engaging in her limitations—in her love of this life in good and evil, so far as her knowledge of it went. She had at any rate been consistent in rejecting all that was not of this world. Was she now—when she felt that even for her this was no longer enough—to stray into a world where shadows of the natural life posed as supernatural life? He could see nothing but sadness in it.

PAUL continued to lie awake. The light of the gas lamp at the street corner fell obliquely on the yellow wall behind the bed, and the shadow of the curtain stirred slightly. How well he remembered it.

And how far he had travelled from himself as he was in those days. In a way he had become a stranger to all the people who had been near to him at that time, and the new people who ought now to be his intimates, because they were fellow-believers, remained strangers to him in another way.

But only in a way. Twenty years ago the world had appeared to him as something solid, massive, impenetrable to his sight and senses. Firm and solid when he caressed it, firm and compact when he ran his head against it. Now it had gone with him as when one puts little bits of matter under a microscope, sees their complexity and knows how infinite it is, even if one pursues it into the interior of the atom. And by way of a supposition one may imagine: what if cohesion were done away with and everything dispersed—? In the same way he saw everything now—all of matter and all of spirit in its place in the procession of things out from the First Cause. But what he acknowledged regarding his own nothingness and his own value, since he too was a mote in this universe, had nevertheless given him another kind of love for men and another kind of love of life, a new way of being happy and unhappy. He could not feel this in the same way as he felt natural reactions—annoyances, as when he had to give up a plan he had made or when he was obliged to listen to people gossiping about other people or when he was concerned on his mother's account or depressed at the thought of Ruth or happy in his children when he looked at them. *That* was perhaps the nearest natural analogy to this feeling as it were of an upper and a lower stratum of the mind —for one is permanently fond of one's children in *one* way, but besides that one is fond of them in another way, when one looks at them and talks to them and touches them.

In the middle of September Henrik Alster came to Christiania. Paul met him at the station and was not a little surprised when Henrik helped a little lady on to the platform and introduced her: "Fröken Haakonsen, my private secretary." At the supper table in the hotel Henrik and the lady were on formal terms, till they had got through the soup and fish. Then they dropped all attempts at hiding their intimacy. Henrik was so much in love that it was embarrassing to make a third in their company —apart from how one regarded the moral side of the business. But he was far too fat, with humped shoulders, a red and fleshy neck, ruddy all over his little head, right up to the coarse scalp under his fair hair—he was ill suited for the part of this child's lover.

She called him "my Harry." She was pretty in the new standardized way, of middle height, slim, with charming legs. All the features of her little round face seemed copied from a design, and her short hair was combed forward into a little curl over each cheek—they made Paul think of shoehorns. She danced extremely well—it was really fun dancing with her. When talking to him she used her eyes in a way that gave the impression of having been learnt by heart. Paul caught him-

self in a very improper thought, but for Henrik's sake he really
hoped that at any rate when they were alone she might be able
to go a little beyond her lesson—

"Well, you understand," said Henrik, when Fröken Haakonsen had retired, "the idea is that we're to get married."

"I see."

"Yes, I don't suppose you approve. Though according to
your ideas it ought to be all right. According to them I was
never lawfully married to Berit. Nobody knows whether Hans
Herman is alive or not—"

"Does she know nothing about him?" He had to say something. "In old days he used to write now and again and ask after
Lillemor."

"It's now nine years since the last letter. Then he was in
Chicago."

They said nothing for a few moments.

"Well, unfortunately I'm committing no indiscretion when
I tell you, Berit's not behaved to me as she should. I agreed
to let bygones be bygones and to try and forget it—for the sake
of the children. I know that you're acquainted with the story.
But you see, the situation's not quite the same now. At that
time I had every reason to suppose that I'd finished with all
that kind of thing, and so we could just as well stay together
for the sake of the children. But now as a matter of fact I've
met a girl who's fond of me and I of her, and she's—er—well,
there's no past in her case, she's never been fond of anyone
before. And so I can't see that it can be my duty to sacrifice
Solveig's and my own happiness for Berit's sake—there's certainly no happiness to be ruined *there*, for either of us—"

Paul could not find anything to say.

"Solveig is a wonderful little person.—And strange as it
may seem in other people's eyes—she's really frightfully fond
of me. Just as I am, difference of age and all.—It may have
something to say to it that she's quite alone in the world; her
mother lives at Mosjöen. She lost her father when she was nine;

245

he was in the Post Office. So she has a great craving for affection,
has been longing for someone who would take care of her and
protect her—"

"Yes, that's very natural—"

"So when Lillemor's wedding is over—next month—I
shall no doubt leave home. Move to the Britannia for the time
being—"

Paul would have liked to know what Berit said. And then
there were Jacob and Elisabeth.

"Well, well," he said after all. "I can't help saying I think
it's sad. That you two—. When one's old friends break up their
home and leave each other like this. Berit and I were very good
friends once upon a time—"

"Yes, so she's told me. She's never been able to live without having admirers about her—I know that. And now of course
it's hard for her—she's forty-seven. But—every dog has his
day, and, my word, Berit's had hers, and a long one too. It
began as soon as she and I were married.—I can tell you, many
a time I thought you two carried your flirtation pretty far—"
he said bitterly.

Paul looked up:

"It never occurred to me—"

"No, I can guess that. Of course I know you didn't mean
anything dishonourable. And poor Berit was fond of me all the
same, at that time—very fond of me. We loved each other, yes,
we did. But to tell the truth, Paul—I did think at the time that
you showed damned little consideration for me. It's not my
way to make scenes—and it wasn't that I didn't trust you as
far as one can trust another man in such things, and Berit had
no secrets from me either at that time; she probably thought it
fun to have such a youthful and enthusiastic worshipper in all
innocence—but upon my soul you didn't consider me much
that time!"

All holy moral theologians, pray for me!

"I dare say I was inconsiderate. But, you know, I never

really meant to be. But I'm quite ready to admit that I was so—
from thoughtlessness, if you like. Of course I won't deny that I
was tremendously thrilled by her. I was pretty green then, and
she came to Trondhjem with a sort of halo of triumphs and
European fame and all that. So she made a fairly overwhelming impression on me."

"Yes, that was how I understood it too," replied Alster
in a conciliatory tone. "When all's said and done."

But Paul was in a singularly uncheerful mood when at last he
went home to his room in Schwensens-gate.

If Henrik had applied for a divorce as soon as he had discovered Berit's iniquitous conduct, he would have had nothing
to say. He would have done the same himself—if he had been
Henrik.

But that he had gone back on his word now, many years
after, because he had fallen in love with his stenographer—
that was really pretty bad. First he had swallowed the disgrace;
for the sake of the children he had agreed to go on living with
Berit after her exposure. And then, because he had got spoony
on this little darling, he had gone and dug up the old bones
and asserted against his wife all the charges that he had once
promised to forget and forgive.

What made it so sad was that Henrik was Henrik. So now
it appeared that he had been jealous and had felt hurt at the
time when Paul more or less voluntarily had been pushed into
the part of Berit's worshipper. But Henrik had never let him
see it, in either word or deed. And now he took up this too in
order to justify his rupture—on account of a new love affair.

As Henrik said, his relation to the divorced Fru Herman
was not what a Catholic understood by marriage. But that he
could think of alleging this in addition—after being married
to her for nearly eighteen years—

The chit, Solveig, was sweet in her way. But it must be
devilish easy for one of that type to confuse her own with

somebody else's sweetheart, if the truth were told. Björg with all her faults was still Björg—she had almost the air of a distinctive individuality compared with that type.

The wind stirred up eddies of dust and the gas lamps flickered in the deserted little streets round St. Hans' Hill. Paul let himself in at the dirty, draughty old front-door, and the wind shut it after him with a bang.

The idea that Henrik should stay with him at Berven at this time fell through as a matter of course. Paul motored Alster and his private secretary out in the mornings and back in the evenings, and then they went to the theatre and to revues and finished up at some place where there was dancing.

Fröken Haakonsen was a sensible little lady; she had a good head for business. That too must be tempting to Henrik —to get a wife who understood that side of life. Hitherto he had had a family who merely expected him to provide money for all they wanted.

Berit would probably move to Christiania when the separation was arranged, thought Henrik. She had been perfectly desperate to begin with, when she guessed that at last he had taken his revenge. She had come up to the office and made a scene there, and she had forced herself in upon Solveig at her lodgings and boxed her ears. For the present she would have to be allowed to keep the children, but when Jacob went to the College his father would no doubt get him back.

Henrik would not hear of Paul's giving up his position at the brickworks; that Fredrikstad fellow was a cantankerous brute who quarrelled with workmen, contractors and customers wherever he went. Paul was obliged to admit that he had heard something to the same effect.

It was pleasant enough to hear some appreciation of the work he had done here of late years. And Paul was himself aware that scarcely anyone could have done it better. In spite of that it had not been a very brilliant business—what with the

248

condition of the labour market and the taxes, and with the local clay which was to some extent pretty pebbly and required a good deal of preparation; on the average it was not particularly suitable for the production of pipes and roof-tiles; they could never expect to turn out large quantities of those articles.

Henrik asked him straight out why he refused to consider the proposal of the big stone industry trust to take over Haugen works. Of course he could continue his connection with the enterprise, if he made that a condition. He had done well up there in the good times, but as things looked at present he would find it more and more difficult to hold his own in competition. Paul had had too little capital to begin with; it had gone well enough so long as he had surplus profits to draw on for the necessary renovations, but it could not go on any longer in the old way. That side of the business which had always been Paul's chief interest—the manufacture of stoves and all kinds of articles of industrial art—had shrunk from year to year. Now he sold not much more than a third of the quarried stone as worked and raw steatite; the rest was ground up.

But then he must either appoint an expert manager or move up there and live there altogether. Vinsvold was capable and trustworthy and had acquired tremendous practical experience during these years, but this was no longer sufficient. The grinding plant was a regular factory, and the industries which were its customers—roofing paper factories, linoleum makers in England, and all the rest—constantly demanded new types of products, according as they themselves had to place new types of their goods on the market.

Paul was not in the mood to discuss with Henrik the profound reluctance he felt at the thought of possibly letting Haugen pass out of his hands. Henrik no doubt would regard it as a sort of sentimentality, if it meant all the world to him whether he was to own a small concern and manage it according to his own discretion, or allow it to be absorbed by a company in which he was himself interested. Companies were Henrik Alster's element, and he had always been glad enough of a chance to make a decent escape from an undertaking which was no longer profitable.

Perhaps it was a kind of sentimentality that he had felt himself defrauded, even when Haugen was doing well, because it did not follow the lines he had wished. The mill, where the men worked all day long in the noise of machinery and in a dust-laden atmosphere—it was really nothing of the kind that he had wished to start, though of course he too in a way loved having to do with machines—when the machines were his. He would not have been a man otherwise.

Out on the ground, where there were outcrops of steatite, one came upon sites of old workshops. The workmen had begun carving out a pot but had left it unfinished; it was still fast in the rock. He had found cups and bailers, loom-weights and spindles, or the men came and brought him these things. Many of them showed forms which might date from the Iron Age, but were just as likely to be only a hundred years old.

These were labour conditions which no one could bring back. He had helped to get up exhibitions of domestic industry and had offered prizes; he had taken part in judging cabinet work which mimicked the old styles or the models of furniture makers three or four fashions back; they were decorated with caricatures of flower-painting or carved in dragon style and baroque. The results had not been brilliant. Prospects looked poor for the old handicraft tradition.

He could not say he liked it, when the stone-crushing machine chewed up hundreds and hundreds of tons of the beautiful, sensitive soft stone, diversified and complicated and handsome as it was, though people who did not know it properly could only see that it was all alike and pale. There must be something madly wrong here—when raw materials all over the world are mashed and pounded up and used for mass production of goods that are both superfluous and hideous. There is no sense in the world being disforested because wood pulp is

250

needed for innumerable monster newspapers which consist mainly of advertisements.

There had been times when he thought he was no doubt ridiculous with these ideas of his, which he could not relinquish —that men if they chose must be able to be masters of the machines they themselves had invented. It must be possible to go back—not in order to halt at anything that was old, but in order to choose a point of departure in the past and proceed from that in a different direction. It was absurd that the same people who asserted the importance of the individual man's private initiative should blindly follow a development which makes private initiative a privilege of fewer and fewer. It was nonsensical to maintain that the family is the living cell of society and that intercourse between human beings is best learnt through intercourse between blood-relations, while at the same time agreeing to let the family be sacrificed every time a man is no longer willing to sacrifice himself for his family, and holding that the tie of blood is not to be binding if it galls.

But he had scarcely dared to put trust in his own opinions, because he had such a profound distrust of subjective opinions in others. And he had been afraid of sensitiveness in himself, because he loathed sentiment in others. Nor had he been able to imagine, any more than other people in this country, that there were more than two alternatives. Either one had to hold with the existing state of society, sickening as it was in many ways, full of injustice and at the mercy of a development which determined its own mysterious way—or one must take part in pulling it down and building a new one on entirely different principles. Only there was nothing in the new principles which made an offer to solve the fundamental difficulty, that human beings are human. If the masses in a society are allowed to share in governing and making decisions, the leaders must use all their cunning and blandishment to make the people think they are governing when they are really being led—and then there are no limits to the follies that are committed and the values that

251

are wasted. And if the little minority of talented men has its way, four out of five of them will sacrifice the masses to their own aims—whether these be materialistic or idealistic.

He had not known that there was a third alternative in the world and an army that would fight for it, a Church militant. It was a free corps which had chosen its point of departure nineteen hundred years ago and had never exchanged it for others. It was an organization which at the same time was an organism, a body, a person, and it said that society must build upon Christ and that it was going to be dear. But all attempts to build cheaply on that foundation had come to grief, because his life, as told in the gospels, is not a thing that is past, but a thing that is present: when the earthquake of Golgotha shakes the ground all that is jerry-built collapses; and while some work at the building, others must clear away the rubbish. But that which shall remain standing grows continually, for here is a means of making human beings more than human.

He flung himself into neo-Thomism and discovered that thoughts and feelings which he had suppressed in himself, since they seemed to lead nowhere, had already been thought out by others to their final consequences, and then it appeared that they had their place in a system which admitted even his inmost vital feeling. St. Thomas had a psychological explanation even for such a thing as his feeling about work—he defined art, *ars*, as an intellectual virtue, and virtue in his language means power. Art is the right understanding of the thing which is to be produced; every man is a worker, and as such has need of art, not in order to live well in a moral sense, but in order to do good work. Therefore art has always been something diffused and anonymous in every nation, except in the over-industrialized communities for which Puritanism is chiefly to blame. There the proletarianized masses have been prevented from exercising a power which is a normal part of a man's psyche, whether he be a bricklayer or a sculptor, a dyer or a composer.

Well, all he had got out of his own enterprise at Haugen

was that production increased at the expense of the work. He had helped a few men to have homes of their own and a few old people to stay on till they died in their own cottages and slam the door in the face of anyone they were not inclined to let in. They were people who would rather live unhealthily and alone than healthily with others in a home for the aged. But he too had been compelled to put up huts, and most of the people worked in the quarry or in the mill. Jo Braastadlykkjen was the only man to whom Haugen had been a stage on the road to freedom and the exercise of virtue.—Jo, by the way, was an excellent example of the difference between intellectual and moral virtue, as defined by the schoolmen, for all Jo's virtue was used in making his work better and better; the man himself never changed an atom.

But, as Henrik said, every dog has his day—he had had his day at Haugen. If he had to submit to seeing his independent concern swallowed up by a trust, he must bear that too. It would be a defeat. But he no longer believed that culture must succumb to mechanization; mechanization can be subjected to culture in proportion as men become aware of the real hierarchy of things. Whether men look for their salvation to something of their own invention or subject themselves to it, is all the same; it is fetichism.

However, he did not intend to give up Haugen just yet.

Chapter Eight

A T TIMES PAUL FURTIVELY REGRETTED THE IMPULSE THAT
had made him take his old room in Schwensens-gate as a
pied à terre. For one thing, he was now accustomed to
more comfortable and roomy surroundings, when for instance
he was going out in the evening and had to change his clothes.
And then it almost always happened that he had Wilfrid Gotaas's
company to church in the morning. He had not himself been
aware how utterly disinclined he was for conversation in the
morning. That Björg had never been in the habit of getting
up till after he had left home was a boon of which he had
never been sufficiently appreciative. Especially when he was
going to church he preferred to be left in perfect silence till
after Mass. He studied to bear it patiently when Wilfrid talked
incessantly the whole way from Schwensens-gate to St. Olav's
church.

Now he had both his youngsters there, on the schoolchildren's low benches in front. They waited for him when he came
out from Mass, flung themselves upon him and said good-
morning. No doubt they were a trifle homesick for Berven; they
had a rather Spartan life at the Institute; but they liked it. At
any rate they had a tremendous lot to tell their father every
time they saw him.

"Anyhow it's not so beastly going to school there," said
Sunnie, "as it was at Heimtun."

She had had lessons in a little private class out at Berven,
together with the children from the garage and the doctor's chil-

dren and a few more. And she had always declared that she "hated school."

"Oh, what nonsense! Fröken Holmsen was really sweet and kind, Sunnie!"

"Too sweet!" said the child cuttingly. "Ugh, when I think of how she patted our cheeks when we'd been good!"

Neither Sunnie nor Helge had ever tolerated any caresses from strangers. And he remembered he had been the same himself as a child. But he laughed at her:

"Well, was that such a crime? But it's a good thing if the Sisters never take such liberties."

"At any rate not in *that* way. Not so namby-pamby."

"Oh, you're a cheeky little thing!"

She was very keen on telling him all she had learnt in the course of the week in the classes on religion and pointed it out if the priest had explained anything differently from her father, when he used to teach her religion:

"But I dare say you've misunderstood some things because you were a heretic before," Sunnie consoled him. "Helge and I, you see, we're *not* converts."

"It's no shame to be a convert," said Helge. "Aloyisius, he's a Catholic *born* and he's a regular blackguard. And Sister Marie-Halvard's a convert, she told me so herself."

"Oh, you! Nobody's a Catholic *born*," Sunnie corrected her brother. "All people are heathens when they're born, until they're baptised."

"Father—it was Sister Marie-Halvard who cut my hair," said Helge eagerly. "Aren't I awful? She had never cut the boys before last Saturday, but it'll be better next time. I believe she used to cut the Sisters—but that doesn't matter so much, because they have their white caps and veils on all the time, day and night—"

"Oo, they don't have veils on at night, stupid!" scoffed Sunnie; "then they only wear the under hood—"

"Anyway I'm glad I'm at the Institute," remarked Helge;

255

"because there I don't have to listen to Sunnie all the time, for she says everything I say's wrong. Can't you let me say what I like, cheeky!"

They had suddenly started calling him father. Paul had never liked those sticky words, papa and mamma, but they used them in Björg's circle, and so it came about that his children said papa and mamma. Now it struck him—could it be Ruth who had told Sunnie and Helge they were too old now for that—?

It came upon him all at once that Sunday evening, as he was driving out to Berven, that this was unfair to Björg and unfair to the children. If she hadn't sense enough to see that she had duties to her children, the children had duties to her. She had not enough resources in herself to prevent life being painfully poor for her, if she was to go on drifting about in this way as long as her mother was alive and had her illness to keep her busy. And when once the old woman was gone, she would be left among strangers, a middle-aged, stunted child; and even if she came back to them, it would be too late. She had a right to what the children could give her; he hoped they would be such good Catholics that it would never occur to them to think otherwise; and it was his duty to do what he could to prevent their being robbed of their duty. However unlikely it might be that his home should ever again be happy in a tangible sort of way, there was something far more important at stake, as sure as they were once for all man and wife, parents and children, and there was no getting out of it by pretending it was not so.

He had liked it so much when the children began calling him father last summer. That the matter might have another side had not entered his mind.

As he turned into the yard at home he was struck for the first time by the look of the big uninhabited main building. There was a light in the kitchen window; but otherwise the house stood there with blind, dark panes which reflected a

256

little light from the lamp out in the yard, and the shadows of
some branches swayed on the long grey surface of the wall.

Going upstairs he opened the door of Björg's room. In
the light from outside he saw sheets lying and hanging everywhere; the atmosphere of the room was cold and clammy with
damp linen. The bare four-post bed was stacked with it. The
nursery alongside was ready—they came home now and then;
all the same, the whole place had the cold air of a spare room.

He saw himself how inconsistent it was: in theory he had
always acknowledged that if a man has once married and had
children, his first duty is to them; and if he knows that there
are other things in the world which are of greater importance
to him than being the father of a family, then he ought not to
marry. Perhaps, if he had been a Catholic from a child, he
would have discovered that the cloister was his calling. There
is a basic relation in life which a man must not violate, even if
he cannot fit himself into it; and if a person is not suited for
family life, he must find a way for himself without injuring
anyone's family.—During all these years of his married life
he had constantly escaped from his home in one way or another. He had stayed at Haugen, he had slept in town, he had
lived here by himself, he had sent his wife travelling or to some
sanatorium. In a way he had always had good reasons for it.
But at the same time he might have hit upon another arrangement, had it not been that he preferred it so.

That he had sent the children to the Institute was another
matter. If they were to grow up as Christians, they must at any
rate for a few years be at a school where religion was not one
subject among many, but the foundation both of daily life and
of the whole instruction. But it was not that he was glad to have
them off his hands; the children missed him sorely.

But Björg was right in saying that he had left her far too
much alone. He had neglected her always and tried to bribe her
and himself with his everlasting compliance.

That same evening he wrote her a long letter and asked her

to come home now, for the sake of the children and for all their sakes. He promised to mend his ways in everything, and to arrange in future so that he need not be so much away from home.

THE week after, Ruth came to town. She had stayed at the Hauga sæter as long as there were people up there with the cattle and after that she had visited some friends at Lillehammer. Paul had to go in and meet her at the station.

He took an afternoon train to town and went into St. Olav's church for a while. There was not a soul there when he came in.

It was childish, he knew very well, to feel he had been punished by God, every time the consequences of his own actions recoiled on him. The wrath of God is only one way of looking at God's being, when one strikes against it, coming from that side. God had thrown down the wall with which he had surrounded himself, given him light and air and stretched out a hand to him so that he might climb over the heap of rubbish. It is heresy to wish God to conjure away the ruins instead of letting a man clear them up for himself. It is heresy to confuse the forgiveness of sins with exemption from the consequences of one's own actions. He would pray for nothing but God Himself—more of God, more of love.

From the church he went over to the Institute, sat for an hour with both the children in the parlour. They chattered away without ceasing, interrupting each other all the time. Till all at once Sunnie whispered:

"Father—are you sorry about something—?"

"I? No, what makes you think that, Sunnie?"

"You don't say anything?"

"No, but how do you suppose I could get in a single word? You two never stop for a second—"

HE fetched Ruth from the station and they drove up to her studio with the baggage. Paul took the roll of her canvases to carry it up.

"It's heavy, this—you've done a lot of painting?"

"Yes," she said cheerfully. "I really believe I've worked well this last month. It was a pity you couldn't come up—I've rarely seen the mountains so fine as this autumn. But not many birds this year—"

"Yes, so Vinsvold wrote."

Ruth let herself in and switched on the light. She had put away the lamp-shades, so the light from the naked bulbs shone crudely over the big room, where everything that could be packed away was stripped from furniture and walls and dead flies crunched under their feet as they walked about.

In the middle of the floor stood a group of half-withered plants in pots; among them a tall oleander raised its spiky leaves and faded brown clusters of flowers. Ruth fetched a can and gave them water, explaining that Fröken Aaser, who had looked after them while she was away, had gone abroad a few days ago. She talked and talked about the people they both knew in the country. Paul noticed that she did not mention Jo. So he asked after him.

"Haven't you met him? It's a fortnight since he came to town." That she could turn so red for that.

"What's the matter?" She stopped and looked at him with the water-can in her hand. "You went so red?"

"Did I go red too?" Paul laughed.

She looked at him, smiled—but then she laughed too. And he realized with a consternation which was not altogether unpleasant that it did not take more than that to make them both feel they were on slippery ground.

"But look here—weren't you going to change? Aren't you hungry?—I am!" He remembered now that he had eaten nothing since the morning. "I came straight from the office and took the four-thirty train and so I forgot to dine." Perhaps he should not have said that, he guessed, on seeing the expression of her face.

259

"But poor you, are you as busy as that?" she said with an indulgent smile.

Paul sat on the canvas-covered divan under the naked electric light and heard Ruth humming to herself as she moved about the next room. It *could* not be true—they had not got into any mess. They were not in love with each other. All bosh, of course. What trick would his fancy play on him next? All the same he could not get rid of a sort of presentiment—

"Where shall we go for supper?" he asked, when she came back. She had on her fur coat, and he could just see something light underneath.

"Frogner sæter," she proposed. It was very late for that, but he said nothing.

"I wanted so much to show you my new pictures," she said, when they were in the taxi. "I believe they're good—some of them anyhow. Are you going back to Berven tonight?"

"No, I've let Frans have the loan of the car. He was to drive his sweetheart home to her parents' and pay them a visit. So I shall have to stay till tomorrow and take the train."

"If you feel inclined—and have the time—you might look in again tomorrow morning?"

It gave him a rather inconsistent feeling of reassurance to hear her thus take it for granted that they would be in a humour for looking at paintings together next morning.

IT reassured him again, as he helped her off with her coat, that she had not made herself so very smart either. At any rate she had long sleeves—her dress was of light, sandy yellow silk; it suited her very well, by the way.

There were not many people in the dining-room, the nearest tables were unoccupied. Ruth began talking about his children, the moment they had seated themselves.

"I think it's hard luck on them, Paul. And you know, you've said yourself you thought children had a better chance of developing even in an inharmonious home among their own people than in the most complete vitamin-free harmony among strangers."

"Did I say that—?"

"Yes, you did. One day when I was speaking bitterly of father.—By the bye, how's Aunt Julie?" she asked, as though it had occurred to her that moment. Again Paul felt himself blushing, and was angry with himself for it. But perhaps Ruth did not notice it; there was a red shade on the little table lamp.

"But I suppose they're not to stay there very long?"

"They must stay to the end of the school year anyhow. They're to be prepared for their first communion this year."

Ruth said quietly:

"I know that's the custom abroad. I always thought it a pity, when I saw the tiny communicants in their white frocks and veils. Really, you know—all that about religion is more like a kind of game to Helge and Sunnie—at least that's the impression I got last summer. Communion, for instance—they can't possibly understand what it is."

"None of us grown-ups can either," he said curtly. "Nevertheless we know by experience what we receive."

"Well, I won't say anything about that, because I know nothing about it.—But is it settled then that the children are to be—well, I suppose it means that they're to belong to the Catholic Church now?"

"Yes." Then he began to wonder whether she knew more of Björg's plans than he did. That might be the case with a lot of people. His mother-in-law had been home on a visit in the summer.

To change the subject he told her about Alster's visit. "So after all nothing will come of my moving up to Haugen."

"Well but, Paul, I don't understand that. That you can feel bound to stick to your post at Berven, when your own business is to suffer by it. I don't doubt your capability—but you can scarcely consider that you're indispensable at the brickworks. And Alster is interested in so many other concerns. If

261

you feel you're bound to stay on there because he wishes it—I think you're overdoing your loyalty to a friend of your youth enormously."

"You must remember that Henrik took me into his business when I hadn't much more commercial knowledge than a kitten."

"You had capital to put into it. Aunt Julie told me that—you remember I stayed with her that winter."

"It wasn't much."

"In the long run I'm certain that Alster has got more out of you than you out of him," said Ruth. "Yes, Paul. I've heard Trondhjem people say so too. They say that Alster is mixed up in so many affairs that there hasn't been any proper management of the builder's merchant's business, for instance. No partner who has had time to take a real interest in it since your time. It's doing badly."

"Yes, I know. But can't you understand that that's just why I can't come and say to Henrik that now I'm going to get out of this Berven business?"

"No, that's what I can't understand. Alster has turned into a speculator pure and simple—everyone says so who knows his affairs. There's no sense in your having either to neglect the business you yourself have built up or put in somebody else as manager, because you think you're under an obligation to try if you can save one of Henrik Alster's last assets. And anyway Berven Brickyard is not such a flourishing business, I'm told."

Paul laughed:

"Oh, as brickyards go.—I'd rather have the toothache than a brickyard nowadays, says our old builder, Rasmussen."

Ruth said seriously:

"Paul. I must tell you one thing. All your life you've had a disastrous tendency to quixotry. Yes, you *have*! Ever since you were quite a youngster and went about with clenched teeth as the champion of your ousted mother. As if any man in the world could have had the pluck to oust Aunt Julie—before she

had herself turned her back on him and given him to understand
that he was not the man she took him for. She has never in her
life been fond of anybody but you three boys, because of her
firm belief that you would turn out as she wanted you to—
there's actually a kind of artistry in my aunt; she tries to make
images of people out of her own head. And even now she doesn't
see how differently you have turned out—all of you! What she
specially has in mind is that your material—your flesh and
blood—is common to you and her, and therefore she still idol-
izes you. It means more to her than the form, which she had not
succeeded in determining."

"I know you and mother have never been able to agree."
Paul shrugged his shoulders in dissent. "But I don't see what
this has to do with what you were talking about just now."

"Oh, a great deal, Paul.—Then you were to be the champion of that little girl you got engaged to and broke off your
studies to build a castle in the air for her here on earth—at
Trondhjem. And when that came to nothing, it was business life
itself that was to be your adventure—"

"No, that won't do. As a business man I've certainly gone
in for fewer adventures than most people in these times."

"You mean you kept outside war-time speculation. Then
let us call it work. You're not a bit what one understands by a
born business man. The one thing for you has always been to
see if you could make a success of the career into which you
plunged out of quixotry. Am I not right?" she asked pressingly.

"I don't quite know what you understand by a born business man. For you can't be so naïve as to suppose that one who
is a born business man only thinks of doing business and not of
building up a business? Do you really think it's above all the
desire of gain that has brought about class-antagonism, for instance, in our day? No, it's the mania for records—and an age
which makes industry and big business the fields in which
would-be record-breakers find their best opportunity. Remember that industrialism and capitalism originated in a Calvinistic

milieu which at any rate in the beginning forbade rich men either to live—openly, at all events—or to let live."

Ruth smiled sceptically.

"Of course. Business life too has its romance and its romantics. Otherwise it would have been impossible for you to become even a moderately clever business man.

"But now you want to do with your children exactly what your mother tried to do with you. In spite of all you have not got the world to conform to your ideas, and so you have taken refuge in Catholicism; therefore the youngsters are also to be Catholics. Can't you see that to you the Church is what progress and evolution and the scientific outlook were to my aunt? Now, after the world war, people are getting afraid of progress and evolution and talk about the bankruptcy of science—"

"Yes, but we Catholics don't do that. We only want to get rid of a whole lot of superstition and determine for ourselves what is to be developed and what ought to be allowed to progress—disafforestation here in Norway, for instance, or agriculture. And science is no more bankrupt because people have had to learn at last that it cannot hand them out a view of life, than it was when it had to give up casting people's horoscopes. A certain section of the public ceased to take an interest in astronomy when they found that the astronomers could not undertake to read their past and future in the stars, and they will cease to be interested in geology and biology when they see that scientific men can never spoil the trade of clairvoyants and fortune-tellers—"

"Yes, yes, Paul—you can reconcile that with *your* Catholicism. But don't imagine it's the same in the countries where it's the religion of the people. Honestly I don't believe that all the women and girls and workpeople that I've seen running in and out of the churches in France and praying to the Madonna take such a tolerant view as you do of the scientific outlook and suchlike heresies. Nor their priests either."

"My dear Ruth, you can hardly have such accurate knowl-

edge of what they believe—or what I believe, which is precisely
the same—about the Madonna, as you call it. On the other hand
there may be widely different questions about which they and I
don't know what the Church has said, or whether it has found
itself competent to say anything at all. A woman who knows it's
a misfortune when a cancerous tumour develops, and a piece of
good fortune when a child develops, has perhaps never heard
of what is called the doctrine of development in the popular
language of this country. And even if she has heard of it, she
may never have been sufficiently interested to inquire what the
Church says about it. And many priests are perhaps not so
frightfully interested in scientific and popular-scientific explanations of the world, because they have an explanation of
the world which really explains it.

"You can surely see, *I* merely think it's only reasonable
that mother has sought an explanation of all she has seen and
felt and experienced and wondered about—her defeats included.
I think she has rested satisfied with an explanation which is not
reasonable. I myself never heard any explanation of anything
which I thought sounded credible, until I began to listen to the
Catholic Church. I am quite simply a Catholic because I believe
that the Church—besides all it gives one later—begins by giving sober information about absolute truths. Even if the truths
in themselves are not sober, but fairly wild, and the absolute is
infinite and inexhaustible."

Ruth shook her head:

"You simply have no idea how unlike you are to these
southern Catholics whom you imagine to be your co-religionists.
You can be sure they're not all of them so scrupulously careful
about their personal morality. And in reality you're as far as
you can be from fulfilling that ideal of modesty and humility
which your priests set up."

"No, I know very well I'm not an ideal Catholic. And perhaps I'm subject to scruples—in the same way as a convalescent
is timid at first, when he's learning to walk again. Also because

I have no turn for modesty. I can't stand anyone, even God, seeing how badly I walk.—Humility, that's something quite different, Ruth! Humility has nothing to do with consciousness of
sin really. One may learn a little about humility by discovering
what it means that one is a sinful man. But one may just as easily
be made arrogant by it. Our sins are our own—and indeed a
man would have to be queerly constituted not to find some pet
sin or other among his sins, and to think it after all quite a gal-
lant or becoming pet sin—at all events greatly to be preferred to
other people's pet sins—

"She whom you call the Madonna—you know we believe
she was born undefiled by sin and lived and died sinless. And
that nevertheless she is the only created human being who has
been perfectly humble. So humility in itself does not consist in
acknowledging one's sinfulness, but in acknowledging the relation between oneself as creature and the Creator. 'Be it done
to me according to Thy word.' Therefore her Creator was able
to make the Virgin Mary His collaborator, when He became
incarnate in the human race. And since He is the same yesterday and today and for ever, she has been that always in His
thought and is so always—"

Ruth looked at him with a curious smile—at the same
time bright and melancholy:

"So then—I have to fight for you with the Madonna herself, have I, Paul?"

He dared not answer, for he was not sure what she meant
by it.

"Paul!" She took the stem of her wine-glass between finger and thumb and twirled it round. "Will you answer me
quite honestly and sincerely? Have you never a feeling that it
is *you* who have established yourself in a world of unreality?
Dare you actually believe every moment of your life that what
you see is reality, and that all the rest of us are so shortsighted
that we see no more than a few inches of reality above and below
us? Think of that time we were at Hans's and Evi's last spring on

his birthday. There was your mother and there was Herr Hansen and there were a lot of Hans's and your and my acquaintances of our young days, and a great many more. Doesn't it sometimes seem to you unthinkable that you should be the only one among such a collection who knows all about it? Your contemporaries, Paul—with red necks and big stomachs already, many of them —Haagen Nicolaysen as bald as a billiard-ball. You've worn quite well—it suits you to be a little grey at the temples. Don't you ever feel that it may be you who have not been able to give up certain youthful notions that the world has got to disclose itself to us—while all the rest of us have learnt our lesson and resigned ourselves to the fact that we are to find out very little in this world and must make the best of it—?"

Paul made no answer, but his thoughts went to his mother and her experiments in spirit-raising.

"Some kind of religion many of them have, no doubt. I suppose most of us have a feeling of awe for something unknown. I have for one. And that cousin of yours, Evald Dverberg, he's mixed up in all manner of Christian work and vigilance societies and so on. But don't you think it would seem too fantastic even to *him*, if you told him you believe all that about a little Jewish working man's wife who lived in the days of the Emperor Augustus and must have slaved hard, carrying in wood and water and crushing corn in a hand-mill and baking cakes of meal and oil which you wouldn't manage to swallow a morsel of, if the Virgin Mary sent down an angel with a tin of them for you? Can you associate the thought of such things with a being who alone of all humanity is supposed to have realized the relation between Creator and created?"

"Evald is at all events an orthodox Lutheran, so he must believe in any case that Mary stands in a unique relationship to her Creator, since she became His mother."

"And for all that you are on no closer terms with Evald Dverberg than you are with me or Nikko or Wirstad. Don't you think that's strange?"

267

"Yes. But that's owing to purely human prejudices and sympathies. Evald and I could never bear one another. But as a matter of fact we have of course something absolutely crucial in common—"

"No, Paul"—Ruth laughed aloud. "You have nothing on earth in common with that awful jellyfish! But you think you're bound to sit there looking resigned and talking such terrible drivel. That's exactly what I want to make you think about— are you going to live your whole life in such an anæmic and abstract and colourless belief that you can persuade yourself that you have the least atom in common with Evald Dverberg? While isolating yourself from all of us with whom you share sympathies and habits and tastes and prejudices and weaknesses and tacit affections and loyalties—our whole way of thinking, however we may differ in opinions? Paul—will you go on get- ting farther and farther away from us all—never turn back and settle down where you really belong?"

He felt himself blushing again:

"If you mean, do I think I can ever be anything but a Cath- olic—no, I cannot."

"Do you never have any feeling that you have landed there because like your mother you won't acknowledge your defeats? You got engaged to that strange girl—and when she vanished you got engaged to one who was even more of a stranger to you and all that was yours. And now that she too has run away from you—that sort of worldly and voracious little creature soon gets tired of you and disappointed with you, because you simply can't shed what you've inherited from cultivated parents—you choose the Virgin Mary!"

"Yes—for His sake whose mother she is."

"And what about the two children whose father you are?"

"We shall share what you call isolation."

"And you dare condemn them to that—? If you think it may compensate you for the emptiness and loneliness after you've thrown away the greater part of your best years on a doll

—dare you consign your children to the same fate while they are young? The boy too—dare you bind Helge's youth, when he grows up, to an old faith? Dare you, Paul?"

"Yes, I dare. I didn't choose my faith in order to fill up any emptiness but that which results from not finding any truth in the world. If I didn't know that what I believe in is the truth, there would be no need for me to condemn myself to any isolation—" As he said it he was terrified at his own words.

"What would you have done then?"

She sat straight upright, and Paul thought there was something marvellously fine in the challenging look she sent him. Her hand which lay on the cloth was trembling. He had an overpowering feeling that it no longer rested with him to determine what he should say or leave unsaid:

"What would you have done, if you hadn't been a Catholic?" Her voice seemed to come from far away, with an insistent summons. "Paul—don't you understand that I would rather you told me *that*, than that you said *nothing* to me!"

He looked down at the fruit-knife which he was fingering.

"Then it would have been only too easy for me to forget that I'm married to her whom you call a doll. But now I know that nothing can be undone simply by forgetting one has done it. And that a person whom God has created is something more than a doll, whether we can see it or not."

"And therefore you daren't drop the doll and take a person instead whom you know to be a person? And who thinks of herself, in all modesty, that she too is created—and created to be something more than a man's doll—"

"That's the whole point of the story, Ruth. That no one is created merely to be another person's doll. Everyone is created for something else—and ultimately for the same thing."

"Oh!" She shook her head violently. Then she whispered:

"Do you think I'm bold? Do you think that, Paul?"

"No," he said in the same low tone. "I think you're—. You know I'm awfully fond of you, Ruth."

She made a little gesture of helplessness:

"You say that! And I know it's true.—Do you think I'd have bullied you into saying it, if I hadn't known I should be able to force those words out of you?—And so you daren't say any more?"

"No. I ought not to have said that either. But I knew you knew it. But, you see, I *cannot* do away with the fact that I have bound myself."

"Oh—" She looked at him for a moment in silence. "It's not only for my own sake that I'm sorry, Paul. I'm almost more sorry for your sake. How can you believe in the truth of what you've just said? That you *cannot* undo what you have done. Nobody else believes such a thing, Paul. If you had even said you *would* not get a divorce and marry again—for the sake of the children or some such reason. But because it's part of a religious system which you have taken over cut and dried—

"—You're smiling?" she whispered, hurt.

"Something Sunnie once said came into my mind. She was in a temper and called down to me from a window: 'I can spit down on you, but you can't spit up at me.'"

"WILL you please telephone for a taxi," Paul asked the waiter.

"We can always pick one up as we go along," said Ruth. "I'd rather walk a little."

He would rather not, but he couldn't say so.

There was a fog outside. As soon as they had gone a little way from the restaurant its lights became a feeble glimmer high up in the white mist, and the forest was all they were aware of. Withered birches stood out a little from the dark wall of firs. The stillness in which they walked was as it were a stillness of tiny sounds—the trickling of moisture all through the forest.

Neither of them said anything and they made for another brightening of the fog—a lamp which lighted up a patch of the trees by the roadside and puddles and yellow birch-leaves in the gravel, and so they went on from that lamp to the next, a long way in front. There was hardly anyone about.

Presently she said:

"Now you must never take it into your head, Paul, that you've driven me to do anything silly, if you should hear for instance that I've changed my plans. It may be I shall go abroad at once and let my exhibition wait till the spring. I shan't do anything stupid, I'm too old for that. I'm not in despair or anything like that—I went through too much of that in my young days.—I'm sorry for your sake and for my own, because I believe you're rejecting your real life which *might* have become something rich and good and fine, in order to follow a will-o'-the-wisp.

"Of course it's never amusing to be turned down by a man. But I may tell you that I'm fond enough of you to bear it without regretting that at any rate I made an attempt to bring you home from what you've strayed into. If I *hadn't* done it, I should have regretted it always."

Paul said quietly:

"I can understand that, Ruth, for I would have done the same in your place—at least, I hope I would have done so. And I know that you and all the others must look on me as a sort of suicide. We are accustomed to pray: 'that thou wilt send out thy Spirit and renew the face of the earth.' And undeniably everything puts on a different face for us. I cannot even tell what I may see in it at last."

Then he saw that she had tears in her eyes, and he knew of nothing that he dared say to her. The worst of it was that he felt *he* was not unhappy for not having dared to accept what she offered him. It was no temptation that he had put behind him. His longing was towards the new face he had seen, and he would not have gone back to what he came from, even to save his life.

Though it was terrible to have caused her pain. And shameful to have done a thing that looked like putting a woman to shame. It always makes one feel mean to play the part of Joseph.

The shriek of an up-going train approached through the

fog—the cars rattled past—a shower of long sparks dripped from the trolley-wire in the raw atmosphere. Paul began to shiver. And when a taxi came along the road behind them he stopped:

"Shall we take this if it's empty? It's muddier than I thought—"

She consented with a sort of resigned movement of her whole body. The taxi was free, and glad of it he was.

As they drove down he wondered what he was to do about those pictures of hers. He thought he could hardly ask whether he should come in tomorrow or not, and to stay away without saying anything wouldn't do either.

So he asked her after all, as they stood outside her door:

"Those new pictures of yours—I wanted to see them, you know—"

"Oh no—let that wait till another time."

Paul walked on alone up Drammens-vei. At the first cab-stand he came to he took a taxi—he had a sudden idea that he would go straight home to Berven and avoid meeting anyone.

Chapter Nine

About three weeks before Christmas his father-in-law died quite suddenly. He was on his way up to the little hut he had on Harestu lake; in the waiting room at the station he collapsed while talking to a man from one of the other huts, and it was all over directly.

Björg telegraphed that her mother had received such a shock that she was dangerously ill, Björg could not leave her. So Paul had to make the funeral arrangements alone; he and Sunnie and Helge were the chief mourners, and the rest was made up of Jacobsen's old friends and Selmer's family and friends.

Though he had been fond of his father-in-law as of few others he had known, he was somehow not so very distressed at Ole Jacobsen's death. He had had a bad time these last years, and not too good a one before, in all likelihood. And if any man had lived honestly and uprightly according to such lights as he had here on earth, it was his father-in-law—in him there was no guile.

"It may well be that grandfather *is* with God already," said Sunnie, the morning they had been to the requiem for him.

"That may well be." Paul hoped so. Jacobsen had had his purgatory already in this life.

His death led to a good deal of correspondence with Björg. So Paul was not greatly surprised when she sent him a long screed some days after her father's funeral, informing him that now she intended to have a divorce, with or without his consent.

273

Then came something new: "You may just as well know that
there's another that I've got fond of. He's an out and out gentleman, but not like you, who never appreciated me at all. He's a
director and we're to live here in Copenhagen, thank God, for it
doesn't suit me to live in the country, you must have seen that
long ago."

She wrote of the children: "You've taken them away from
me already when you put them into a Catholic school so that
they were bound to become strangers to me." But she would
claim to have them with her in the summer holidays: "Valdemar
(my future husband's name is Valdemar Christensen, I may tell
you) is so fond of children, he has two children of his own
which are with their mother, but he has promised me to do all he
can to give Sunnie and Helge a good time when they come here
in the summer." Then she made some bitter little reflections to
the effect that it must be to his advantage too that in a year's time
he would be let off having to keep her any more, since he was
always in financial difficulties.

—No doubt it was his fault that it had turned out like
this. But still he could not quite see how he could have acted
otherwise.

He knew in a bitter and desolate way that he had always
wished Björg to feel happy and contented; it had always made
him glad if he could do anything to please her. But he had never
been able to coerce his nature into desiring anything of her.
Even during his periodical little fits of ardour he had always
known that he would have been quite unable to work up any
longing for her, if he had not had her close beside him.—If at
any time he had seen her sorrowing like a real grown-up person
—but he had not. Even when they lost Erik he had not been able
to come in contact with anything serious in her, although he
knew that she did suffer in her own way.

And now his feeling for her was the same. Even if he had
not believed that this affair with a director in Copenhagen meant
a fresh calamity for her poor ill-used soul, he would neverthe-

less have been saddened on her account; it was hard to believe
that any good could come of it for Björg even from a purely
worldly point of view. But he *could* not think of her without a
sense of boredom falling upon him like an oppression. If it had
only been a question of his own feeling of happiness or misfortune, his indifference to this Herr Valdemar would have been
cruelly complete—

In the following spring Julie Selmer went to Paris at Easter;
she wished to visit her youngest son. Paul saw at once, when he
met his mother at the boat, that it had been no pleasure trip for
her.

He had fetched her with her own little two-seater, and as
soon as she had taken her place beside him she said:

"Ugh. The first thing is—I wouldn't write it to you, preferred to tell you. The first thing is that Sigmund's got married.
Three weeks ago. And not to that Mrs. Errold, but somebody
quite different. Danish. Lykke Lönstrup was her name."

"It seems to me I've heard that name some time—"

"Yes, she appeared here too. In revue, I believe."

That was it! At the Dovrehall—in his student days. Even
then she wasn't altogether young—

"For that matter she gives me the impression of being a
woman of spirit. She's determined to get Sigmund away from
Paris. Home to Norway for choice. She's not afraid of hard
work. She's tried her hand at all sorts of things, since she had
to give up the stage. Given singing and dancing lessons. Now she
makes dolls, you know, the kind they have lying about in
drawing-rooms. But her idea was, if they could find some place
not far from town. Then she'd start a kennel. She has gone in
for that too before now—"

Paul drove out past the old villa quarter which lay scattered among forest lots. Lean spruces straggled among the
houses, whose paint looked faded under the strong spring sun.
Down below the fiord shone with a white glitter that blurred

the outlines of the islands. Then the road ran among fields where patches of snow were still thawing on the withered pasture and the plough furrows were full of water which reflected the blue of the sky. The light and colours of early spring—yes, he knew this road well on such a day. Aspens and osiers reared their heads to the fresh blue sky and were filled with flickering light among the silver clusters of catkins. Red cottages among the fields, farm roads and paths which vanished mockingly behind a copse. He knew every tree and every mossgrown rock.—Of Sigmund his mother had not yet said a word.

He himself had Hans's affairs in hand. He had tried to hide from his mother as much as could be hid. But he did not know how far he had succeeded.

They lunched together in the little pale-blue, white-panelled dining-room at Linlökka. Heavens, how charming and innocent it looked, the old yellow coffee service with little white reliefs that stood on the shelf of the wainscoting. The fragile crockery had lasted on while five generations of them had lived and died.

"How long can it be since you last saw Sigmund?"

"Let me see—wasn't it the autumn of 'sixteen that he came home and gave concerts? I haven't seen him since he was at Trondhjem on that tour."

"I don't believe you'd recognize him now, if you met him unexpectedly." Julie was gazing vacantly before her. "He's grown so terribly fat. Bloated. And his hair's quite thin." She gave a little shudder.

"He has a good many pupils, hasn't he?"

"Yes, but—. I'm afraid he won't get very much to do here. He's got so—erratic."

She knew of course that Sigmund had been ill, Paul was sure of that. Hans, who had been in Paris fairly often of late years, said it had been a pretty bad case and not properly treated in the beginning. He was well now in a way, but it had left him a wreck. It had shattered him psychically even more than physi-

cally. This was natural enough, for a son of hers. They had all
learnt that health was power and honour, salubrity was purity,
and bodily defects were sin and defeat, without even being
aware that their mother taught it them. And he himself still
clung, in a part of his feelings, to this pagan morality of his
mother's. Something still whispered within him that it was in
any case a hale morality. But he had been spared the experience
of how it must feel to be one of those it condemned.

Poor mother—she kept her head up. Sorrow and disappointment and bitterness had wasted her, but she shut them up
within herself and never let a sound escape her. Her hair looked
even whiter, now that her face had grown browner and more
wrinkled, quite a purple brown under the deep-set eyes. And he
felt a lacerating tenderness for her, precisely because it was her
present self that he loved. It was not her fault that she did not
know the only One before whom it is no shame to bend. And so
long as that was so it was a good thing that she remained unbent.

But against death this paganism is helpless. There is no
longer an abode of the dead which is worthy of Death—no
realm of shades with sorrows worthy of the human soul, no
Hades or Hel which it becomes us to remember with offerings
to the dead and songs of lamentation. It is true that Christ has
harrowed Hel.

His mother's plans were quite simply—and she put them
before him without any beating about the bush—that they
would have to buy a property somewhere outside the town for
the superannuated Danish variety star who had been willing to
take Sigmund as he was and look after him. "Oh, she's a capital
person in her own way," said Julie.

"By the bye, I have messages for you from the Braastadlykkjens," said his mother, just as he was going. She walked
with him down through the garden. "He would really have preferred to come back to Norway with her, because Ruth's going
to have a baby, and he says he hasn't much faith in French
doctors for that business. But of course, as Ruth says, other

277

people have babies in France. Well, it won't be before September, so they can change their minds several times before that."

"Are they all right otherwise?"

"Yes, I think so. We spent an evening with them—it was very pleasant. Thank God Ruth got married at last—she was getting to be quite an old maid—"

Well, but it wasn't his mother who had ever seen very much of Ruth.

HANS SELMER's affairs looked more and more hopeless the deeper he went into them. Evening after evening he sat up till late at night working on them with Hauan and Nikko. He was now sincerely thankful that Arnt Hauan had settled in Christiania some years before—well, he had been that all the time for that matter. Nikko had been Hans's lawyer for several years, but Paul could not discover that he had done very much to prevent his brother going so completely to smash.

The worst of it was that Hans had taken to some kind of beastliness. Curiously enough, and thank God for it, their mother didn't seem to have any suspicion of it yet. She had seen so little of Hans lately. He himself had been afraid of it for a good while. Evi had noticed it: "Fancy, I believe Hans is never quite sober now," she had chirruped, looking at him with her most unfathomable expression. "He scarcely touches alcohol, but he has something which he *takes*. That's so easy for a doctor, you know."

He had met her outside the church one morning in March —he could scarcely believe his eyes when he came out and caught sight of Evi standing there, handsome and elegant and altogether lost at that hour of the grey and frosty morning. "It was a good thing I met you. I don't know what I'm to do, Paul.— Fancy, Hans hasn't been home for three days and nights and nobody knows where he is. Isn't it terrible?"

He went home with her and at any rate got it clear that Hans three days ago had telephoned to the clinic and said he

had to go away for a few days, but didn't say where. He had
given the same message to his consulting room. He had made no
arrangement for a locum tenens—Doctor Lande, who usually
took his practice, had not heard from him. He must have rung
up from a kiosk or something of the sort.

Paul feared the worst, but apparently that had not yet occurred to Evi. She sat erect and charming as a statuette, wondering what had happened:

"Do you think he can have been overstrained—so that he
had a nervous breakdown and lost his memory? One reads of
that so often in the papers nowadays. I've seen so little *of* Hans
in the last few years—he's always been so busy that he hardly
ever had time to talk to me—

"Besides, you know, I'm so slow at taking things in. Oh
fancy, Paul, it makes me so sorry at times that I can't be more
clever! I do *hope* Little Erik won't take after me in that way—

"For you understand—since my health has been so poor
after I had Little Erik, I've never been able to be anything much
to Hans. Before that he used always to say to me, 'look here,'
he said, 'you've not got to worry about anything, all you've got
to do is to be lovely.' " She blushed violently. "I really do wish
so much, Paul—that I could be more for Hans. But that's what
he *said*, 'you have nothing to do but to be lovely.' But don't you
think too, Paul, that it's terribly sad for me that I'm such an
invalid—for I really *am* so fond of Hans, and I do want so much
to *be* something for him." Her beautiful face was like that of a
mourner on a tombstone relief.

Merely with the idea of leaving no stone unturned Paul had
rung up the stations along Hallingdal, where he was sure they
knew Doctor Selmer. And so he actually found out that Hans
had gone up to the hut he shared with a couple of friends in the
mountains near Gol.

He prayed that it might not be too late, as he made his way
there on skis with the guide, but he had no great hope of finding
his brother alive. And if he had not made away with himself,

Paul could not imagine what kind of reception his brother would give him, bursting in on him headlong and uninvited in this way.

What he was least of all prepared for was that Hans should receive him without a trace of emotion—utterly slack.

In the course of the day he showed a little more life. His coming up here was a kind of impulse that had come over him, in his overworked and depressed state. Yes, he was overworked; yes, he had used stimulants for the last year or two; no, it wasn't cocaine, but something else, a new preparation. Yes, he'd been losing and losing. He had no doubt he'd be able to live on his practice—but there was his position with regard to Evi; he'd gone through all her money, and he had debts to any extent, and it doesn't do for a doctor to go bankrupt, and Evi would think it such a disgrace; well, so would his father-in-law. He had lost the last of his capital when the bank there went broke; he had just enough to live on. But Hans believed that after all Evi would be quite happy if she could go back to her father and the little town and the kind of life she had been accustomed to before. And she had the boy.

Probably it had been his intention to take his life here in the hut, but he hadn't had the energy to do it. And now that his brother came and offered to put things straight—

At the end of the evening it came out that there was a woman in it too—the wife of one of his friends. And he was afraid Evi might hear of it.

Paul knew there had been a good many similar affairs in his brother's life.

It began no doubt with that unfortunate childish engagement to Molla Nicolaysen. She was charming and witty, a good sort, level-headed, a flirt and fairly cold by nature. They discovered independently that they didn't suit each other, but each thought the other had been kept waiting so long that it wouldn't be honourable to break it off. At this point Hans plunged into an affair with a much older married lady, who took care that

Molla came to hear of it, and she put an end to the engagement, in violent indignation. Hans broke with his mistress, but immediately took a fresh one, a sort of demi-monde lady. And then he was appointed assistant physician at the hospital at Veiholmen and met Evi Hansen.

What shocked Paul was that Hans made light of Evi in a way, because she had never possessed any other means of expression than her body. Whether this was a notion he had acquired through being so long engaged to the virtuous but cold Molla, while at the same time cultivating a different kind of erotics—or was it purely and simply the damned Norwegian puritanism which distrusted all pleasure and delights of love? First it was held to be sin and shame in itself that two people could be downright scorchingly fond of each other. Later on eroticism was extolled, but only as a symptom of rebelliousness and egotism. Nobody ever seemed to reflect that it might also be a gentle, faithful and inarticulate young woman's only language.

Paul was reminded that once through an accident he had come upon Evi as she let Hans embrace her. She had looked radiantly lovely—her elastic figure and every line of her beautiful face triumphant in a happy transport. It was true he had wondered at the time what kind of a mysterious and accomplished young lady it could be that Hans knew so well. Nor had he found out till afterwards, when he got to know his brother's wife, that she was the sweetest little person and so simple that she reminded one of the innocence of trustful little animals—

At that time she could never have had to struggle with words and sentences to let Hans know how fond she was of him. And now Hans dismissed her like this, because illness had deprived her beautiful, expressive body of speech and she had no means of making him see how unchanging was her love for him.

HANS himself fully realized that the best thing he could do was to enter a home for treatment; otherwise it would be difficult to cure himself of this drugging habit. They could say he had gone abroad for professional studies. He knew of a place in Germany which was excellent.

The clinic would have to go, but there is always somebody willing to take over a clinic. The same with the villa on the Holm; he would have to get rid of that, however big the loss might be. This would do something towards cleaning up his affairs, but there was still a long way to go. And a lot of gossip there would be, even if they managed to arrange everything privately. It might be difficult enough for Hans when he had to work up his position again. But it was no use worrying about that now.

They sat opposite each other in the railway-carriage on the way to Oslo. Hans Selmer slept, leaning back in his corner. He's a very good-looking fellow, thought his brother, with a strange coolness. Quite different from the rest of us, really. He was tall too, but slightly built, narrow-shouldered actually, but he did not give that impression because his whole figure was elegant. His face was oval and pale and his complexion no longer that of a young man, the cheeks had fallen in, the mouth was handsome but weak. He had almost black hair and it was smooth. He wore it brushed straight back off the forehead and rather long, in the new fashion which Paul thought distinctly untidy.

Skirt-hunter, he had mentally called his brother, at the time they were schoolboys and Hans was always running after little girls. In that department there was no doubt Hans had always acted exactly as he felt inclined at the moment. And Paul had acted according to his ideas of self-discipline and cleanliness, not taking up with women whom one really cared nothing about. It was impossible to say that Hans had fared worse by following his impulses than he himself by living according to his principles. Being the lover of his friend's wife would have been too much for him—but Hans had managed it well enough. It is a fairly irresponsible thing to try to bluff boys into morality on the pretext that certain virtues will profit them in everyday life.

Whether they bring one success or failure in this world is purely accidental. Or rather, it is not that—they bring one the good things of which Our Lord knows a man to be in need, but these need not be the same as what people call success.

Once when Hans was awake he said:

"You know, I'm pretty sure Lillian has decided that Erik's to get something extra in her will, because he's named after father."

"It's a question whether Lillian has very much left," said Paul curtly. "She burnt her fingers fearfully over that Syrstad venture."

"By the way," asked Hans again; "supposing Evi doesn't care to go home to her father's while I'm away—do you think she could stay with you, she and the boy? It's no use suggesting mother; Evi simply feels so unnerved when she has to meet mother that she's like a mouse in a hole. But I think she feels pretty confident with you."

"Yes, with pleasure." Though in truth he didn't know what he was going to do with the helpless little creature out in the country. He would have to get Sunnie home from the Institute, he thought with a smile, so as at least to have one moderately capable female in the house.

THERE was nothing for it but to give up Haugen. The family would have to see about consolidating its diversified affairs on a narrower front. It was no worse for him than for many another man in these times.

He must try to get out as much as possible in cash. When his works had been taken over by the big company he did not want to have more to do with them than was necessary. He had no desire to show himself there constantly, meeting people with whom he had made friends. On the whole he had got on well with his staff, but that was because he had been his own master. Unless he had the final word, co-operation was not in his line—he knew that.

Nor would he keep the sæter, if there was any chance of getting rid of it. When better times came, he would always be able to find some place in another part.

The children were to be confirmed this spring. They had been instructed as to the sacrament they were to receive, but they were rather more excited about having to choose for themselves a name and a tutelary saint.

Helge had chosen his without hesitation: "Christopher— because he's the patron of motor-cars."

Paul had in fact put a little plaque of St. Christopher and the Child Jesus on his car, but he regarded it more or less as a joke, even if seriously intended, that the old soldier from Asia Minor had been appointed patron saint of motor vehicles.

"Let's hope he'll make it a little safer for pedestrians to move about among you," said Sister Marie-Halvard. "And that you won't smash yourselves up unless you're in a state of grace." She had come into the parlour to talk to Paul about Helge's report; every day there was something against him.

"Then is he quite impossible, sister? That's bad, isn't it?"

"Oh, it's not so bad either," said Sister Marie-Halvard. "He's a nice boy. But restless and given to fighting. So it may be bad for the one who has to have him in her class," she laughed.

Sunnie raved about so many different saints that she found it hard to decide which to take—the little Theresa or Agnes, Cecilia, Margrethe Marie Alacoque, Birgitta, Sunniva—they all had qualities that it would be fine to imitate.

"Blandina," suggested her father, and told her about the martyrs of Lyons and Vienne.

But one day Sunnie came and announced that now she had chosen a name, and her father was not to know what it was till he heard it in church.

"Lisa Eberhard has chosen St. Hildegard of Bingen. Doesn't that fit her splendidly? For she was so frightfully learned, and I believe Lisa will be the same, she's so clever. Mine was learned too—but she had a lot under her who weren't a bit clever when she lived on earth. No, it's *not* St. Theresa. Nor Birgitta either." Sunnie was dancing with joy. "You'll never guess, father!"

It was impossible to hear at the back of the church what the bishop said to each one of the confirmees. But when he came out with the children afterwards and had wished them joy, Sunnie clung to his arm:

"But I say, couldn't you hear it—Paula! Aren't you frightfully glad? And oh, I want you to *call* me that. Sunlife, that isn't a name really—ish!"

There were no pictures of St. Paula to be had in the shops, Sunnie explained; she was not much known nowadays. But Sister Marie-Halvard had painted a card for her of St. Paula. "Only think, father, when St. Jerome was translating the Bible into the Vulgate, he read aloud to her every evening what he'd translated in the day, and then she corrected it, if there were any mistakes."

Randi had been very clever at drawing caricatures in old days; her attempts at drawing devotional images were not always equally successful. The high-born abbess from the Aventine and Bethlehem looked in any case as if she was not to be trifled with.

THAT summer Paul took long motor drives with the children every Sunday after church. Generally they took with them some schoolfellows from the Institute or some of the Eberhards. Hadeland, Hurdal, the districts about Öieren, both sides of the Christiania fiord—it was amusing to renew acquaintance with places he had walked through in his student days and had not seen since. He guessed it was a terrible disappointment for the children when they were told they would never go to the Hauga sæter any more. So his idea was, in the summer holidays, that they should start on Saturday and drive to the different small towns where there is a Catholic church and go to Mass there; that might interest them.

They took food with them and ate somewhere by the road-side, or stopped at some of the little rustic hotels that reminded Paul of walking-tours in his young days. At that time it had been fun to put up at one of these places—always. He had never been able to stand the big tourist hotels that he had known later. Now once more he arrived on Saturday evening at a little ramshackle wooden hotel with verandas front and back where nobody could sit for the draught or the broiling sun, and he and the children had supper in a bare little dining-room. They got weak tea served in a dull plated tea-pot and regaled themselves on scraps of cold meat that tasted of nothing on earth and sweating cheeses. Afterwards they strolled along a road white with dust, while the rosy blush of the evening sky faded behind distant wooded ridges and its reflection in a little lake paled and grew dark.

Then they climbed up a hen-roost ladder and were shown into narrow little rooms which smelt of sun-baked timber and paint or sometimes had a vaguely unpleasant odour. In some places there were hard iron beds which clanked in a dislocated way when one turned over, and in others there were narrow old-fashioned wooden beds with bulging down coverlets and coarse sheets with crochet-worked borders, and the bed was intolerably hot as soon as one got into it. There were plain wooden chairs and wash-stands which rocked as you used them, and on the walls were portraits of the King and Queen and Crown Prince Olav in a sailor hat and white blouse, and theatrical and senti-mental pictures of soldiers in khaki and misses and lovely young girls—from the first years of the war, while it was still regarded with official enthusiasm in all the belligerent countries.

From the next room he heard the children splashing and brushing their teeth, and Sunnie lecturing Helge and Helge re-senting it. Then they said their evening prayers, and then there was a creaking of the beds and they knocked on the wall to him and cried good-night for the last time.

There were filling-stations everywhere now, and electric

286

light in the rooms, and cars dashed past on the road outside.

Early next morning they drove into the nearest bright little town and went to Mass in a tiny chapel, where the little congregation showed a happy and inquisitive interest in three Catholic strangers. Sometimes they were invited to break their fast afterwards with the Sisters of an Order in a tiny little parlour, and after High Mass they went and called on the parish priest.

But that his daughter was now to be called Paula was more than Paul could learn, and Helge protested: "Pooh, it's only because you think such a lot of yourself. You'll have to see about being a saint first—do you think I'm going to call you Paula when you sit there scratching your midge bites in church—do you think the holy Paula did a thing like that?"

ONE day he took the children out to Bærum to see Sigmund Selmer and his wife.

He was not a cheerful sight, the youngest brother. He and Paul had been very like each other—tall and broad-shouldered and well built, with the same type of face: their mother's broad, low forehead, straight eyebrows which turned sharply down at the temples, grey eyes with a splash of yellow, a big mouth with narrow, finely outlined lips. Sigmund too had had that dry, shiny, nut-brown hair with rebellious curls which had to be kept closely cut if he was not to look like a lady-killer.

Now it was thin, and the little he had was left so long that it looked tousled. There was not much left of the eyebrows either, and his eyes were sunk in pouches. His face was puffy and blotched, and his hands were swollen. His clothes hung on him anyhow.

His wife was small and thin and round in the back, with a short neck and a curious old-fashioned projecting coil of reddish fair hair which lay so low on her neck that it gave her an odd humpbacked appearance, though she had no hump. Her head was large and perfectly flat on the crown, and her face was like wash-leather, loose and mobile all over; her eyes had the colour of milk and water. But she was pleasant to talk to and cooked admirably, and they were both very kind to the children; Sigmund played to them after dinner, and as they were going Aunt Lykke came and presented Sunnie with a big doll. It was an atrociously perverse-looking object with a little cheeky, squinting face that looked almost uncannily alive, and arms and legs outrageously long and loose. But Sunnie was delighted with it. And then Aunt Lykke promised her a pekinese puppy next winter.

"If father gives me permission to have it," said Sunnie a little anxiously. "For I can't have it with me at the Institute, you understand." No doubt she had heard her father express his dislike of lapdogs.

THE last half of the summer holidays it rained almost without ceasing. Paul guessed that the days must be pretty long for the children out at Berven; he was only home for a little while at dinner-time and often came back fairly late from the works in the evening. And it was not like the mountains, where they could be out of doors whatever the weather; it was wet in a different way down here by the river with big trees round the house on every side and tall grass and a clay soil, so that the roads were a sea of mud in rainy weather. The children kept getting colds and seemed to be pretty cross and troublesome, from what the maids said.

They talked all the time about Haugen—what fun it had been when they could go into the quarry and the mill, how slippery their shoes got from talc dust, and now Helge would never get any more rides in the skip on the cableway. Vinsvold and Ivar Rud and Old Anders and the men from Mo, the people at the works and those they knew at the sæter, the names of cows and farms and peaks and lakes—they uttered every word as though with a caress.

They had letters and cards from their mother and wrote to her now and again, but they avoided speaking of her, at least in their father's hearing. They often talked of their grandfather, but Paul doubted whether it had made any particular impression on them when they were told about a month later that their grandmother Jacobsen was also dead. They pronounced both names before praying "Rest eternal grant them and may perpetual light shine upon them" in saying their evening prayers, and Paul himself, as in duty bound, mentioned his mother-in-law in the prayer for the dead. He had caused some masses to be said for her soul—and he assumed they were needed.

ON one of the last days before the children were to return to the Institute the whole family came to visit Paul at Berven. It was a farewell dinner for Hans and Evi—he was to accompany her and the boy to Veiholmen in the following week and then go on to Germany.

His mother, Hans and Evi with Little Erik, Sigmund and his wife—Paul had not been able to bring himself to invite Lillian as well. As it was, it might be quite enough for his mother, without her having Lillian looking on. But he knew that Lillian would be deeply hurt if she came to hear of this family dinner-party, and he was sorry for his step-mother now; she felt lonely and rather bitter since she no longer had Garnaas and his family to look after.

But they all put a cheerful face on things, and Fru Lykke was really an acquisition on an occasion like this, splendid at keeping conversation going. At dessert Sunnie was taken ill and had to leave the table. "I'll come up and look at you when you've gone to bed," said Hans.

He went upstairs when the others moved into the drawing-room for coffee. But not long after Hans came to the door and called Paul.

They went into the dining-room, where the maid and Frans's wife, who had come in to help, were clearing the table.

"This is rather bad," said Hans Selmer. "It's inflammation of the lungs that's developing, there can't be any doubt of that."

Frans's wife put in:

"She was shivering so that her teeth chattered when they got out of the car—" Sunnie had gone with Frans when he drove to the station to fetch Sigmund and his wife.

Paul went up to the night nursery. Sunnie had fever and a high temperature, and it hurt so when she coughed, she complained.—Yes, she had been so frightfully cold this afternoon, and then she had been so sick, and now she had a headache and felt sort of horrid all over.

Hans said:

"I can take Evi and Erik away at once. Then I'll drive into town and get what's necessary and come out again. Unless you'd rather have another doctor?"

"No, thanks, if you can manage to come back—"

"She's so strong and healthy, there's no cause for anxiety at present anyhow," said Hans. "But of course inflammation of the lungs is always a serious business."

Julie said she would stay the night. The rest of the party broke up. When Hans Selmer came back at half-past nine Sunnie was very ill; she was delirious and had severe pains, and in the morning her expectorations began to be tinged with brown.

THE illness ran its course, and it was a fairly serious attack.

On the night of the fifth day Sunnie's temperature dropped suddenly from over 104; in the morning it was down to 97.5. In the course of the day it rose again, rapidly as night came on.

Both lungs were now attacked; Hans was not at all pleased, Paul could see, and the nurse said so too.

As he was starting for the works that morning he asked his brother: "Well, it looks so serious now—I think I'll have to telegraph to her mother."

"If you think she ought to know," said Hans curtly.

"All right. If there's any change, send the car for me instantly."

No message came for him. No change, was the answer every time he rang home. Two o'clock came; staff went to dinner. Paul stayed in the office. He would wait till the others came back and finish what he had to do for today. So long as he was here, so long as he was at work, it seemed unreal. But when once he came home he could not bear having to leave her again. He had done it every day—for an endlessly long time, it seemed to him —but each time he had thought, this must be the last time, I shall not be equal to it any more.

This anxiety which neither increased nor decreased was almost paralysing in its effect. Literally so. He could do nothing but such things as were pure routine. When he prayed it was as though he were alone in the world, and the prayers which took shape within him were blown away into the empty air, and those he had learnt and used every day, fell withered to the ground. "Sacred heart of Jesus, who Thyself hast tasted the bitterness of death, have mercy on all who are to die tonight." Actually he was far from believing that Sunnie was among them. But it was inconceivable that the tension could last on and on in this way.

Helge was walking by the row of currant-bushes when Paul came home about six. There was such a warm radiance of golden sunshine over the thick, dark foliage down here by the river, and the boy stood there so peacefully eating currants—it was like two worlds, one within himself and one outside, and they were equally unreal. The feeling of emptiness and clarity in his head and his whole body no doubt resulted partly from want of sleep —only he did not notice it so much when he was at work.

Helge had joined him, and now they walked hand in hand up through the garden. Paul heard the boy say:

"Can't I go back to the Institute just the same, father?— it's so slow here when Sunnie's ill—"

Paul looked at the boy. It was as though he had not been aware of him till now.

"We'll have to see, Helge."

291

If she died, he would not send Helge away from him.

If she did not die, he would not send the children away from him again.

HE had been sitting with Sunnie for many hours, had dozed a little at times, and started up every time she coughed. It was very dark in the room; someone had hung a red and yellow silk handkerchief over the lamp, so that the light seemed to be only smouldering behind it. But some flies were buzzing round the electric bulb and hitting against the glass with a little ringing sound, and Sunnie's breathing wheezed and wheezed in her chest.

The nurse had gone downstairs to have something to eat, but when the child had another fearful fit of coughing, Hans came in from Paul's bedroom. He took her in his arms, gently pushing Paul aside; he could hold her better than her father. She moaned faintly in a heart-rending way.

Hans laid Sunnie back on the pillows. Her face looked dark red in the subdued red light, swollen and distressed; her eyes were blood-shot and tired out with coughing.

"Uncle Hans," she whispered in her worn, sick voice; "do you think I am going to die?"

"Not a bit. You're not so bad as you feel, Sunnie. You mustn't go thinking of such things," said the doctor sternly.

"Oh, but—now I've made up my mind that I'll offer myself to Jesus, to be His sacrifice. I should like to die—for His sake. As a sacrifice."

"You mustn't talk like that. Sacrifice—can you imagine that God wants anything of that sort? God would much rather you got well again, you may be sure."

"Then He wouldn't let so many little children die. If He hadn't some use for them besides letting them grow up. But He's glad when we come and offer ourselves of our own accord."

"Hush, be quiet now—you mustn't talk so much.—Can't you get her to stop, Paul?"

292

"Isn't it true, father?" She slipped her hot hand into his. It was soft and clammy with illness—and this change from her firm and scrubby childish hand gave him a sudden shock as though it were the beginning of incomprehensible things.

She had a fresh fit of coughing which cut off what she was trying to say. When she was a little quieter, Paul bent over her:

"What would father do without you, Sunnie?"

She raised her arm, put it round his neck and drew him down to her. A damp and acrid heat rose from the little body among the bedclothes, and her breath smelt in a way that suddenly brought him face to face with the horror of death.

"I can't tell you what it's for," she whispered close to him. "But you'll be able to see that when I'm dead. It's something I want to gain, you understand—for a soul—"

Paul felt as though something opened within him—a gulf, and his own self tried to find foothold, but he sank powerless— the child drew him with her into something unknown, entirely supernatural. A mystery which until now he had only seen from the outside opened and swallowed him up. He was convulsed with horror—but felt he was entirely in the power of the other world—

"You must do it too, father—offer me up—"

He knelt with his face buried against her side, heard how her chest was being racked.

"I cannot, Sunnie," he said in a rapid whisper, and held his breath with pain.

"Yes, yes, yes!" Her voice became flurried and impetuous. "You *must* do it. I've done it already, you understand—I began many days ago. You must help me. Say: My God, I offer her up to Thee—"

"Stop it, man!" His brother seized him by the shoulder. "I believe you've gone perfectly crazy!" Hans was trembling with indignation.

The cough came back. "Do it, father," shrieked Sunnie in the middle of the fit. Hans held her up; pushed Paul aside.

"Say—" she waved her hand, trying to reach her father.

"Yes, yes, yes, Sunnie, I'll say it." He sobbed once aloud, buried his face in the blanket at the foot of the bed. "My God, I offer her up to Thee"—the sweat broke out all over him, and for a moment he seemed to be whirled through darkness by a great wind of flaming light, so that he lost consciousness—

Hans had grasped him by the arm and now he was standing at the foot of her bed; then his brother drew him away to the table in the window.

"You—you—" Hans was whispering, but his voice shook with excitement. "You mustn't go clean out of your senses. Surely you can control yourself, man—not take the life of your child with such—disgusting hysteria."

Paul gave a little shake of the head. He saw perfectly clearly that Hans must look at it in that light. *He* could see his brother's point of view—that other state, the inner reality through which he had been whirled for a few dizzy and stifling seconds—that was a thing of which he could say nothing, no one could, there were no words for it. But his natural vision was as it were a painting on the outside of life's reality, and it had flaked off. What had happened to him he did not understand—for an instant both he and the child had been close to God, himself in a way that was terrible, the child calmly and without fear. And now she was dying—. At the same time he knew exactly how it must look in his brother's eyes. Disgusting hysteria, that was clear.

"I have not the right to be arbiter of my child's soul," he heard himself say. "In the presence of God one human being cannot command another."

"Offer herself as a sacrifice!" Hans made a grimace of abhorrence.

The disproportion was in fact so great between the stiffness of words and the cosmic things they stood for, that Paul himself had a taste in his mouth as if he had been sucking a rusty copper coin. But nevertheless there was no word which could express anything of this—

It was true, though even now he could scarcely understand it himself. He had not dared to restrain his child, when she insisted on disposing of her own soul—

There was a gulf which no words and no explanations could bridge over between him and his brother here. And he himself could only glimpse in a half dazed way what it meant that one human being could offer to die for another—though for Sunnie there was nothing strange in it, he understood. And how Hans looked at it he also understood—as he himself would have looked at it once.—

I can spit down on you, but you can't spit up at me—

But the moment he thought of that, it was as though he saw all the days of Sunnie's little life before him in a flash, and he thought, no, God help me, I cannot lose her—

Just then she called to him from the bed:

"Father—can't you ring up the church—so that I can have extreme unction?"

"Yes, I'll do that, Sunnie. I'll go down and ring up the presbytery."

Hans followed him out to the landing:

"You don't mean to tell me you're in earnest—with a sick child—that you're going to fetch a priest and set about preparing her for death etcetera?"

"Wouldn't you say that she's in danger?"

"The inflammation is far advanced and her heart is now affected. And of course you won't make things better by encouraging her to a continual series of these extravagant scenes."

"If her life is in danger—I cannot refuse my help in seeing that she has the last sacraments."

"I never heard anything like it! If it had been a grown-up person I'd have said nothing but everyone to his taste. But a child—. I call it downright sadism, Paul."

Paul nodded.

"Yes, I understand that you can't think otherwise."

While Paul was telephoning to the presytery his brother stood on the opposite side of the writing-table and watched him with an expression of gloomy and brooding antipathy.

"Yes, she's coughing a great deal.—Well, if she may take a little water to swallow the Host with, she can certainly communicate.—Yes, I can send in the car at once, then you can be out here by twelve o'clock or soon after.—Yes, thanks—yes, thanks. Thank you."

Hans Selmer shook his head resignedly.

Then they went upstairs again to Sunnie.

"—now and at the hour of our death, amen—now and at the hour of our death—" It cannot be true.—Now and again she seemed to doze a little between the fits of coughing. Then she lay awake for a while, but said not a word. Paul was not quite sure whether she was clear or not; in any case the fever was very high, and she groaned constantly.

Hans came in to look at her at intervals. Once when he wanted to give her some medicine she pressed the crucifix which she held in her hand closer to her breast: "Not yet, uncle—" The doctor stood still for a moment—then he turned and went away without a word.

Her father sat looking at her, trying to understand it: She is waiting to die. She is not afraid. Underneath the wanderings of the fever her soul is at work making ready to depart. When she has received the sacraments, she will go—

It was nearly eleven o'clock. Paul asked the nurse to tidy the room a little and wash Sunnie. He himself moved a small table to the foot of the bed, laid a cloth on it and fetched the crucifix —it was Fru Gotaas's—the candlesticks and bowls of water and holy water, cotton-wool and breadcrumbs. The nurse stole inquisitive glances at his preparations.

It was horrible in a way, he thought. The connection between these prescribed forms and the incomprehensible reality, between the absolute sovereignty over her soul possessed even

296

by so young a child and the firmly defined path leading to this freedom, was beyond understanding. He himself moved as it were on a borderline where he did not feel his own feelings—

Then he heard the car hooting at the bend.

HALF an hour later it was all done. Sunnie had sunk into a sleep even before her father had finished clearing the communion-table.

Paul was to drive the priest back to town himself. *If only I don't fall asleep at the steering-wheel—.* It was the new Norwegian priest, Father Falk. Paul had seen him in church, but never met him before. A little, slight, dark-haired man with sharp features and blue eyes. He made a sympathetic impression, spoke so softly.

"Thank you, I won't take anything," he said to Susanna when she came into the hall and whispered that there was coffee in the dining-room. "But you drink some coffee, as you're going to drive. I would rather sit at the back of the car, then I can sleep on the way. You see, I have a Mass at the hospital at six o'clock. I shall make a memento for your little girl tomorrow—"

WHEN Paul reached Berven again in the grey dawn, Hans opened the front-door to him:

"She has slept the whole time. Just at the moment it doesn't look so bad."

Paul went upstairs and lay down half undressed outside his bed. He fell asleep at once, and when he woke it was late in the forenoon. From the nursery he heard his mother's voice; she was talking to Sunnie.

"She's much brighter now," said Julie. "Thank God." She was arranging some grapes she had brought, and placed the bowl on the table with the crucifix and candlesticks which were left there from the night before. "Those are handsome candle-sticks, let me tell you, Paul!"

The change was unmistakable, he saw as soon as he went

up to the bed. There was quite another look in her eyes, and her face was different too.

"How do you feel now, Sunnie?"

She looked up at her father with an expression as though there were something she could not understand:

"Oh—I haven't any more pain to speak of—"

When he went into the dining-room there was a note for him: a telegram that had been telephoned on from the office: "Arrive Sunday morning boat Björg."

He sat fingering this slip of paper when Julie came in. She took the cosy off the coffee-pot and poured out for him. "You'll get fried mushrooms in a moment; I brought some out.—You got some rest then?"

Paul handed her the telegram.

"Did you send for her?" asked Julie with a frown.

"Yes, when it looked as if it might just as easily have taken a bad turn, I did so."

Julie was silent for a moment:

"I think it would have been better—since *she* could forget her own children—if the children had been allowed to forget her in peace and quietness."

Paul made no reply. The events of the night already appeared to him in a strangely unreal light. Besides, he was by no means certain what Sunnie's intention had been that time. It might be simply that she had heard of voluntary self-devotion— and so she had seized upon it and done it to please God.

That they never talked of their mother did not necessarily mean that they did not think of her a good deal. He himself would never have mentioned his father if the grown-ups had left him alone.

But he would not say anything to Sunnie yet. Wait and see first if she really came. It would be like her not to—

"I suppose you think there's been a miracle, don't you?" Hans chaffed him, when Paul came back in the evening after taking

298

his mother to the station.

"No, I don't know about that——. I have heard that the illness often takes a turn for the better when the sick person has received extreme unction. But of course I have no personal experience of these things."

"With pneumonia patients one often meets with surprises. It may follow so many different courses. But it really does look as if that entertainment last night has had a favourable influence on Sunnie. Let's hope there won't be any further complication. But I say—don't stage any more of your holy shows for the child! Hang me if that wasn't about the worst thing I've come across."

Paul couldn't help laughing—he was so nervous too:

"Yes, you may well say that—"

ON Sunday morning he was walking up and down the quay among the others who were waiting for the Danish boat.

"Yes, I've come in to meet my wife," he answered the stout fair man who had come up and said good-morning.

The weather was perfectly wonderful. The white sunshine floated idly on the oily water of the harbour. The town in its sabbath-day hush lay beneath a thin blue haze, but above it the hills were clearly outlined and the woods showed autumnal yellow patches against the blue sky.

"Fine morning," said the stout gentleman. "Nice calm trip they've had. Not that my daughter's ever sea-sick—" and then he went off into the story of a voyage from Antwerp in a devil of a storm. Who the deuce is he? Paul wondered absently.

The boat came slowly in to the quay—there came the swish of the hawser—and there he caught sight of her by the rail. She had on a black fur coat and a black veil like a widow's on her hat—oh yes, for her mother, of course. She was greatly changed, that was his impression—

He took his place in line with the others and waved up to her, as the boat made fast.

"How is she?" Björg called.

"Oh, she's much better now. Hans is very pleased with her, considering all things. And you—you've had a fine passage?"

Then there was the Customs and passports and all the rest. But at last he was actually walking behind a porter with her baggage, side by side with Björg along the dusty pavement of the quay, among dusty grey goods sheds on which the morning sun was shining. He thought she was smaller than he remembered; that was probably the effect of the short skirt and the tiny hat. She looked downhearted or frightened, walked with bent head.

The stout fellow in grey stopped them, bowing to her.

"Who was it—do you know?"

"My dear—why, that was Lieutenant-colonel Dahldorff. Don't you remember, they were staying at Korstad in 1917 the whole time we were there? His daughter was on the boat—"

"Have you got a new car?" she asked; he had had the baggage put in.

"Well, it's the second year I've had it. Chevrolets are handy, you know, if they're not exactly Rolls-Royce—"

They drove out through the east end of the town. Her big veil fluttered all over the place. On reaching the country he stopped:

"Shall I help you? Tuck it into your coat, so—" She dabbed her eyes with a handkerchief; her complexion was pale and rather grey, and her features had sagged—her cheeks, her mouth. The eyes were no longer clear—grey and opaque like pebbles. Poor thing, you must be fatigued by the voyage.

"Poor Björg, you must have been fearfully alarmed about her?" he said as he helped her with her coat. The fur was rubbed off in many places, the buttons worn bare—it was surely the old one he had given her many years ago.

She took her seat again, as though cowering, and he drove on. She was sniffling and drying her eyes all the time beside him.

"I say, Björg," he begged her; "do try not to take it too

tragically—"

Then they arrived at Berven.

Paul took her outdoor things and hung them in the hall.
She sank down on the little settee, a melancholy figure in black,
stooping so that her fair hair fell forward in a bunch, shading
her face. Her neck was shaved and she had started a side parting
and stopped curling her hair; its colour had faded. For the first
time a suspicion crossed Paul's mind that perhaps she had not
even had a good time, according to what she understood by
good.

Susanna opened the dining-room door: "Breakfast's ready.
—Welcome home, ma'am—"

"Dear me—are you still here, Susanna?" She looked up
shyly at the maid.

"Oh yes, I've been here all the time—but now you must
come in and have some coffee, ma'am—"

"I'll go up meanwhile and see if Sunnie's awake," said Paul
reassuringly; "and tell her. You must try to eat something
first—"

At that moment Helge came downstairs from the first floor.
He hesitated on seeing a lady sitting in the hall—then he came
on slowly and stopped at the foot of the stairs.

"Yes, Helge, mother's come home," said Paul.

"But bless my heart—is that Helge—?" Björg straightened
herself, flung the wisp of hair off her face with a toss of the
head. Helge came forward slowly, took his hands out of his
pockets and held out one of them:

"Good-morning, mamma!" He made his nicest bow.

Björg held out her arms—then drew the boy to her with a
loud, sobbing cry:

"Oh, but how big my little boy's grown—why, I hardly
know you again—"

Helge stood bolt upright in his mother's embrace, glancing over her shoulder at his father as though seeking help there.

"Don't cry so, mamma," he begged her, bashfully.

"Now you must go in and see that she has some coffee," said his father, and then he went upstairs to Sunnie.

The nurse was busy washing the floor.

Sunnie had been lying with her face to the window; now she turned her head. Her face was now pale and transparent; she was free from fever, her father could see; her eyes were dark and preoccupied.

"Are you feeling better—?" The phlegm in her chest sounded different, looser. "Do you know who's here, Sunnie—?"

"Is it mamma?" she asked calmly.

"Yes. Has anyone told you?"

"No."

The expression of her eyes was so curiously distant and calm that he dared not say anything to her. He bent down and kissed her hair:

"Now if Sister Haldis will just tidy things up a little, mamma will come up to you—"

"Yes."

Paul went down and put on his coat: "I've got to go to the office," he said to Björg at the door of the dining-room. "I'm badly in arrears with the work, you understand, these last few days."

He had to get away to some place where he could be alone.

Björg went about the house as though she were shy of them all. She avoided Paul, she was bashful with Susanna, who had been in the house ever since her time, and bashful with the new maid, bashful with Hans when he came out. And when she was upstairs with Sunnie all she seemed to do was to sit on a chair by the bed and say nothing—after a while she stole out again and sat in a room by herself. Perhaps that straight-combed lock of hair which kept falling sideways over her face had something to do with her dollish look, and the short-skirted black dress made her small. She reminded Paul of a cat that has run into a strange place; it may keep to the house, but is always on the watch,

distrustful of everybody and everything, ready to bolt if anyone approaches it.

Paul saw that she took long strolls in the garden with
Helge. The fine autumn weather held day after day. The river
gleamed at the foot of the garden where the gnarled old apple-
trees were full of red and yellow fruit. Helge picked up wind-
falls in the grass and carried them into the kitchen; it kept him
busy all day long.

He ought to have been at school long ago—he was to be
moved up into the second class. He was a big boy now with
close-cropped brown hair which curled rebelliously, freckles
across his nose, gaps in his teeth. He would have to keep Helge
at home this winter, send him to the local school—it was a three-
days-a-week school, which was one thing in its favour.

Sunnie was making good progress, but Hans urged caution.
She received many letters with little devotional pictures from
the prioress and sisters at the Institute, and she had had a book
about St. Elisabeth of Thuringia from Father Falk and cards
from Father Kindrich, and from Father Tangen a tiny little rosary which went into a walnut-shell. Grandmother had sent her
the Inger Johanne books, and Aunt Evi and Uncle Arnt Hauan
sent sweets and Aunt Lykke an extraordinary kimono. Fröken
Alsaker, who was in father's office in town, had given her a
crucifix made of olive-wood from Jerusalem, and Lisa Eberhard
wrote long letters and sent her a pair of pink slippers of her
own work and an English book. From Uncle Henrik she had had
a wristlet watch and from Uncle Sigmund a powder-box.

Björg came and looked at all her daughter's presents:
"What a lot of people are kind to you, Sunnie—?" then she
sighed and looked away with sad, strained eyes.

She was to be pitied; she must feel like an outsider, and
she no longer had anyone to assert her right to a share in the
child.

She had now been here a fortnight and Paul had not seen
any letter come for her, except one or two which looked like

303

bills. She was not well—there was something weighing on her besides the fact that she was like a stranger in this house which had been her home.

One afternoon, as Paul was on the point of going back to the brick-works, Susanna came up; there was a man here who asked if they would buy a whole sheep's carcass—?

"You'd better ask the mistress about that, Susanna," said Paul, and went off.

AT supper that evening he noticed that she looked at him surreptitiously, but dropped her eyes whenever he looked at her. She was so nervous that her hand shook.

"Paul," she whispered at last, staring stiffly at her plate. "Do I understand that you wish me to look after the house the time I'm here?"

"Not unless you want to, of course. For the present, perhaps, it won't be for very long, as I thought of proposing that you should take Sunnie with you to a sanatorium when she's well enough to go out. You know it's very raw here by the river in autumn, so I think she ought to be away for a time."

"Yes," said Björg faintly. "You know I should like that very much.—The only thing is," she mumbled still fainter, "I haven't any clothes for that—"

"No, but it wouldn't take so long to get them?"

"But afterwards," she asked in a trembling voice; "what am I to do then, Paul—when I've been at the sanatorium?"

"You know very well what I think you should do. But I can't force you."

She collapsed altogether. Paul got up and pressed the bell.

"Come, we'll go into my room. Then they can clear away."

She went before him through the big dark drawing-room. He had a glimpse of her rounded back and shoulders. She looked so miserably afraid that he was quite in despair himself. Well, well, what kind of a scene was she going to make now—?

"Sit down," he said; "then we'll try to talk this over calmly and sensibly; will you do that, Björg?"

She obeyed and sank into the chair he pushed forward, trembling with apprehension. Then she flung her hands to her face and shrieked aloud:

"Oh! Oh, why, why, why didn't I go home with you, when you came to Copenhagen to fetch me!"

"Yes, it can't be denied that would have simplified matters considerably. But it's too late to cry over that now, Björg. Can't you try to calm yourself—"

"Oh—oh. But it was mamma"—she was weeping—"poor mamma was always so confiding.—Poor thing, she couldn't see that they only thought of getting money out of us—and they didn't mean anything by it when they pretended to admire her and made so much of me, and the ones we used to go about with, she thought they wanted our company because they liked us. She couldn't see that they didn't mean anything when they said they thought so highly of her and found me so charming and attractive and such a real Norwegian type—

"I *wanted* to go home with you, Paul, I can assure you, I said to mamma that it was you I was fond of after all and I longed to see the children. But mamma said it was perfectly certain that if you were a Catholic and I belonged to the State Church I could claim to have them with me. And then, you see, there was one who made love to me so desperately, he was a commercial attaché—no, there *wasn't* anything wrong between us, Paul, I can take my oath of that, he didn't even propose to me —I dare say it was only his foreign manners that made him flirt so much with me. But you know what mamma was like, she thought the best of everybody, especially when they were sort of high up and so fine and gentlemanly. She said you were not a bit fine really, you only thought you were, and you were so rough—and then all that kneeling and praying and making the sign of the cross when there were other people there, that was vulgar and immodest, she said; if you'd been a really fine gentleman you wouldn't have thought of behaving in that Dago

305

fashion. And I must say I thought it looked funny too, Paul, I felt quite ashamed lots of times—

"And then she said I was being ruined by living with you, because, you see, we weren't a bit suited to each other in that way, and you hadn't any consideration in that sort of thing. So it would be much better for me to get a divorce while I was still young and fresh and could start life again and get married to someone who was suited to me so that my nervous system could recover—"

That was it, by all the devils in hell! How could he have forgotten that?—it's just the kind that won't hear of it when it's called passion, who are ready to accept anything if it's supposed to be good for the health. They're just the ones to advise a child to change her husband as one changes one's medicine—

"But I *would* rather have gone back with you. I know I was angry with you when I went away. But when I saw you again I felt that after all you were the one I was fond of—I thought you were so nice, and you'd really been so kind to me before—. But then, you see, mamma got so ill and I couldn't leave her—

"But I can tell you, I've learnt now what people are like! There aren't many after all who are so unselfish and dependable as you. Oh, if only I hadn't stayed in Copenhagen and let everybody make a fool of me—. But I must tell you, Paul"—she had another fit of weeping—"I've had such a hard time, you've no idea what a cruel hard time I've had! So I must have been punished already for the wrong I've done—"

Paul racked his brains for something to say to her, but for his life he couldn't find anything. It was almost idiotic—and it was terrible. And what of himself—who had set his mind at rest with the thought that Björg would always manage so that nothing should disturb her comfort and self-sufficiency. That he could have *believed* she would pull through, when she had no one to make things easy for her—!

"Well, well, Björg," he said softly. "It's partly my fault. I ought not to have given up so soon, when I knew how little

306

experience of the world you had—"

"No—" she was weeping more quietly; "of course you knew what the world and people are like, much better than I. So it wasn't right of you either—you *ought* not to have given up—"

But will some devil be kind enough to tell me how I should have set about getting you to understand it at that time?—whispered the devil who provides sinners with excuses.

"There, now you must calm yourself, Björg—not cry so terribly. Anyhow you can't think of leaving your children again, now that you've come back to them—"

"No, if I may stay—" she whispered.

"May? They're your children. They have a right to you."

She sat still for a moment, catching her breath.

"What I wrote you about"—her voice was quite husky with crying. "That's all over, you understand. A good while ago. For it wasn't true that he was divorced. And he said just the same as you—that the children had a right to him. And so he went off to Aarhus. That's where his wife lives. He said exactly the same as you."

Paul did his best to swallow his rage.

She was so stupid as to be scarcely rational. And at the same time he felt dismayed, now that he guessed how she had suffered—perhaps much more than he would ever come to know, and certainly without understanding it, like a child that is exposed to misfortune—alone and without resources among strangers. When he thought of this, he had a dim sense that she was his after all; it was not merely compassion that he felt for a fellow-creature, but he was bound to her. As he had felt every day since she came home, when he saw that she was afraid of them all and stole about as if she were always ashamed of herself—he had felt a kind of solidarity with her—

"Come now, Björg." He stroked her hair, went on stroking it. "Try and be a little calmer."

"You can't possibly be the least bit fond of me any more?"

307

she whispered, glancing up.

"Yes, Björg, I am." It was true—though to be sure it was in a different way. He bent down and, because her whole face begged for it, gave her a light little kiss.

"Take a cigarette, it'll calm you. You shall have a whisky and soda, that will help you to sleep, when you go up—"

"O God, how I've cried and cried these nights," she said, gazing before her with wide hopeless eyes. "Lying in my own lovely room again and thinking that the children were asleep close by and you in the next room, and then I thought of how happy I might have been—"

PAUL stayed downstairs till he imagined she must certainly be asleep.

He looked in at Sunnie first. A little lamp was burning on her bedside table among books and images and rosaries. The child was asleep with her face turned to the light; she held a little red book between her fingers. Of course she ought not to be reading at night—but the nurse's breathing came deep and regular from the sofa bed in the corner. Paul took up the book. *My Changeless Friend*—ah, it was the one Lisa had given her.

It was heart-rending to see how like her mother she was, as her mother had once been. Sunnie was now very pale of course, but her face was the same soft, full oval, and she had the long eyelashes which lay so placidly against her cheek. Her hair had the golden sheen of youth; the thick plait lay upon the child's delicate shoulder and low breast as though it must weigh them down.—That Björg's hair looked literally withered—it was lustreless like winter grass—did more than anything else to make her appear so broken-down.

In the early days of their marriage he had sometimes felt a wondering tenderness for her, as he looked at her asleep. As though he divined—against his better judgment as he thought at that time—that something mysterious lay concealed in every

308

human being, if only one could see it.

Sunnie. He recalled her the other night, as she sat up in bed, flushed with fever, with the reflection of the candles on the communion-table in her dark eyes, her expression as she closed them and opened her mouth, while the host in the hand of the priest made the sign of the cross over her face: "*Accipe, soror, Viaticum Corporis Domini nostri Jesu Christi, qui te custodiat ab hoste maligno et perducat in vitam æternam—*" His only thought had been that this would happen—God swept aside all evil in the world as with an almighty gesture and led His little sister in to Himself. He had not even had a feeling of sorrow at the time—God's will and the child's will flowed freely past him, without his daring to wish it otherwise.

"My Changeless Friend"—he laid the book among all the other things on the bedside table—recalled Julian of Norwich's words that the love of God is like a mother's love. These little blessed and consecrated objects—the little porcelain figure of Mary with the Child, the bronze relief of the Heart of Jesus on a slab of onyx, the framed post-card of Christ from Limpias, the rosaries for every day and for holy days—he still saw how ugly they were as things, though he knew their value as pledges of a spiritual connection. To the child they were the dear and precious objects of the home, hallowed by a mother's hands. —The knick-knacks of her home in Storgate had been hallowed to mean something peculiarly fine and precious to Björg, because her mother had handled them.

HE was in his own room beginning to undress, when Björg opened the door between their rooms:

"Paul—I can't get to sleep—"

He turned round, unpleasantly surprised. And a wave of cold disapproval came over him—Lord save us, what a sight she is: in a kind of pyjamas of yellow silk embroidered with black dragons! All at once it appeared perfectly absurd that he could really have anything to do with the dressed-up, tear-

309

stained object that stood there—

"I believe there are some of the powders left that Hans prescribed for Sunnie. Go back to bed, I'll come in and give you one."

It was with a sense of absolute repugnance that he opened the door of her big, shadowy room. The pink gleam of the bedside lamp on the crumpled pillows of the bed, the stuffy atmosphere heavy with perfume—the whole room sickened him with its thick carpet and crowded Louis-seize furniture and the abominably wide bed with its hangings and gewgaws.

"Here you are—dormiol—I don't know how much you ought to take—have you any idea yourself?" He handed her the little box and put a glass of water by her.

"Can't you stay here a moment?" she begged in desperation. "It's so horrid to lie here alone and do nothing but think and feel miserable—"

"Take your powder, then you'll be able to sleep."

"Yes, but do sit here a moment—" she pulled him by the sleeve, and Paul resignedly sat down on the edge of her bed and let her take his hand. She gave a plunge so that she lay flat on her back looking up at him:

"I know I've behaved like a wicked woman, you understand that—but it wasn't *all* my fault, Paul—

"It wasn't always so easy for me to be married to you, let me tell you. You were always teasing me and making fun of me—just as if you never took me quite seriously. You thought I was stupid, I saw that all right—and I was really rather clever, looked after my house properly—nobody ever thought I was so stupid till I was married to you, I was always one of the smartest in the class when I was at school—"

He gave a little laugh and said deprecatingly: "Oh but, Björg! It was only meant as—" It wouldn't do to say truthfully what it was meant as; so he said: "You were so like a little girl in your ways.—I don't believe I ever meant any harm by it. I thought you always understood that I wanted you to be

310

happy and comfortable and in a good humour—"

"At any rate you didn't think I was anything to show off. When your business friends came to town you hardly ever invited them home. Henrik gave parties for them, he did, but you asked them to lunch at the Britannia or motored them about —even at that I wasn't always allowed to join you. With the solitary exception of the Grossmanns, it was just as if our home wasn't good enough to be seen by your gentleman-friends—"

"I chiefly thought of saving you trouble," he murmured. That was not absolutely true. But he had regarded it as a trifle. To her, then, it had been a slight.

"Oh no, no," she was in tears. "I could see well enough you didn't think we were quite the right thing. You and your people were so much better and more refined.—*Can't* you understand how it was—when we mixed with folks over in Copenhagen and they were nice to us and made a fuss about us, and if we were different they thought it was only because we were Norwegians—there was nobody who looked down on us. And how could I *help* thinking a man was properly fond of me, when he was just as polite and attentive as you, and just as generous with presents and thinking of ways to entertain me—but not the least bit superior, none of that treating me like a child, but absolutely as if he *looked up* to me—. He *was* really a gentleman in his manners, and never let mamma and me feel the least bit awkward. Yes, Paul, you can't deny it, you are a little snobbish in that way, you thought my mother was common, and you *did* look down on me and my family—"

"Have you ever noticed that I looked down on your father?" he asked seriously.

"No, papa and you, that was something different. But then you were men. And besides, papa thought in his heart it was all nonsense, mamma wanting us to assert ourselves as people of good position."

"You see, Björg—" he patted her hand; "your father was fond of us all. He was fond of those he liked and fond of real

311

things. Perhaps he and I thought that much of what you and
your mother attached so much importance to was—well, trifles
and make-believe. So I came to treat you as a child, more than
I should have done."

"That's not true!" She flung herself round again, buried
her face in the pillows and sobbed. "Mamma was fond of me,
she was—properly fond! She worshipped me, mamma did. Nobody else has ever been so fond of me as she was. And now I've
got nobody—

"Oh, can't you be a little bit fond of me again, Paul, you
don't know how unhappy I am—oh, if you won't be fond of
me I don't know what I shall do—"

"I am fond of you." He stroked the stubble on her neck.
"I am fond of you. And the children, you know—"

She threw her arms round his neck, drew his head down
close against her breast, groaning out his name. Paul let her
go on for a moment—then he gently freed himself.

"There, Björg. Take your powder now—you must try to
be calm."

From the depths of the pillows she murmured:

"Can't you come in and stay with me—I'm so afraid—"

"No." A spasm shot through her whole body. "You're agitated and—and—. You must see about getting to sleep now—
or you'll make yourself ill. Here—be sensible now." He felt his
face go white and cold.

She raised herself on her elbow—looked at him in mortal
agony with a face that was flushed and wet and swollen. She
looked awful with her bristly shock of hair plastered down
over her tear-stained eyes. Then she yawned and let him shoot
in the powder, took a drink of water and sank back into the
pillows with a groan.

"I shall stay up for a while," he said softly from the
door. "I shan't go to bed until I'm sure you're asleep."

He was trembling all over, as he stood by the open window
in his own room. God in heaven, this is going to be a worse busi-

ness than I imagined. She was so—so absolutely revolting he thought her, as she clung to him—and at the same time he had never before felt so completely that they were both human be-ings and that the bond between them was unbreakable—it was an actual fact.

It had always given him an intuitive loathing to read of saints who drank the water in which they had washed lepers and things of that sort. Paul shuddered violently: now he could see the point of it.

It was an unspeakable relief, the day he could take Björg and Sunnie up to the sanatorium.

Björg had gone about like a picture of misery these last weeks. He could not really blame the poor creature for having assailed him with demands for affection—she was so pro-foundly and obviously unhappy. She had come into his room too, late one night; but as Helge slept there she had been obliged to keep comparatively quiet. He had got her to go back to her own room, and then he had talked to her: it was not his inten-tion to start any brother-and-sister relations; he had no great belief in the durability of such a state of things. But he was not going to take part in any hysterical scenes of reconciliation. They would have to accustom themselves to living together again and doing their share for the home, seeing that the chil-dren's life was brought back to its normal groove, then every-thing would shape itself in time.—She had listened to him in absolute silence.

He sent her in to Oslo to arrange about clothes for the chil-dren and get what she and Sunnie wanted for their stay at the sanatorium.

That she had a heap of debts in Copenhagen he found out by degrees. She and her mother had evidently lost their heads altogether down there. When Jacobsen's estate was more or less wound up it appeared that there was not very much left. They had not yet been able to sell the villa at Ullevaal. So what Björg inherited from her parents went in paying debts—and then she had started making fresh ones. She could have lived on the sums he remitted to her every month during her absence—but she and her mother had acted as though they were on a permanent pleasure trip. And the company she had frequented had grown worse and worse—swindlers of both sexes in the end; she was utterly uncritical.

Of course the responsibility was his. He ought to have seen that as soon as those two women weighed anchor and put to sea they were bound to run on the rocks.

HANS and Evi got away at last. Hans after having impressed on him caution, caution and again caution with Sunnie: "I take it for granted that after all you would rather keep the youngster yourself than see her go to heaven, when you've thought it over. Thank God it turned out as it did, say I.—You see now that God isn't quite so crazy as you people try to make him out."

These days had brought Hans and himself nearer again, Paul felt; he noticed an unaccustomed warmth in the other's manner. Hans was of course delighted that Sunnie had got over her illness. And Paul wondered whether Hans did not feel a kind of secret bond between them—his view of it would probably be that Paul's religion and his own dependence on that stuff he took, whatever it was, were two different forms of the same thing.

Evi had been out to see Sunnie and had called on Björg. They sat making spasmodic attempts to find something to talk about and both looked equally forlorn. This was one of the moments when Paul thought it might not be so insuperable to patch up his married life after all, enough to make it work. Her incapacity disarmed him; it seemed to him, even if he had not been a Catholic, he must have discovered sooner or later that he had no right to allow one like her to go her own way.

His mother said one day—it was at his office in town:

"I wanted to come out one day to see Sunnie. But now I prefer to wait till Björg's gone away again."

"Björg is not going away," said Paul shortly. "It's decided that she's to stay."

His mother looked at him, and he looked at his mother. The sort of glances that cross like rapiers, in the language of the novelette.

Then Julie said slowly:

"Do you know, Paul, I've often wished that you had married Lucy. Of my prospective daughters-in-law she was after all the one I really liked. In many ways she was impossible. But all the same I was fond of her. She was *human*.

"Of those that my sons have really married I must say I prefer Sigmund's wife—"

No, of course: the proposition that all people are human beings is in reality mystical theology. In any case one must have a living faith and good training in living according to one's faith, before one gets out of the habit of making exceptions in practice. His mother at any rate confessed frankly and honestly, that human beings are all those with whom I can discover that I have something in common; but there is a limit—

In her own way she might have been just as much of an ass to have for a mother-in-law as the one he had had.

Björg had been at the sanatorium with Sunnie about three weeks when she rang him up one morning. She seemed quite desperate over something or other, crying into the telephone and begging him to come up as soon as he could. Oh no, there was nothing the matter with Sunnie.

Well, well, what could have gone wrong now—! Some of the visitors up there might know something of her doings, perhaps she imagined they looked askance at her, perhaps they really did so. In any case it could do no harm if he motored up there one day and showed himself on the scene. Then he would see Sunnie too. She obstinately signed herself Paula when she wrote to him.

He drove up a couple of days later. It was glorious weather, the whole world bright with rime when he left home, and the morning sun was veiled in a light frost-fog through which the blue sky showed palely.

Sunnie came walking towards him on the road a mile or more below the sanatorium. Her cheeks were red from the fresh air; she looked so sweet in her blue and white knitted guernsey and cap, with her long plaits hanging down in front.

"Have you come to meet me? Hop in then—"

"And what about mother, is she quite well?" he asked as they drove on.

"No, poor mother is not at all well. I don't know what's the matter with her. She went to Oslo on Thursday and was away till Saturday. And do you know what I did, father?—I went by motor-coach to Hamar and slept with the Sisters; oh, I can tell you, they are dears, and such a darling little chapel; and then, you see, I could go to Mass and holy communion again the first Friday in the month—wasn't I lucky?"

Björg looked so wretched, as she crept into the hall to meet him, that he was quite alarmed. But why it was absolutely necessary for him to come here in hot haste did not appear: "It's so horrid being alone here, I've had such sleepless nights—"

Nor could he quite gather what she had been doing in town. First she said she had not been to a doctor; but then she said yes, she had been to a doctor, and "then I went up to papa's grave." It was not very like her to go to town simply to visit her father's grave. But perhaps her conscience smote her on his account.

She ate nothing at lunch, and not a sound was to be got out of her while they were in the dining-room.

They sat upstairs in her and Sunnie's room until dusk. Paul spoke of leaving, he could not stay to dinner.

"Father, when are we coming home again? Ugh, it isn't any fun here, there's nobody I can make friends with. That Milli Wilhelmsen is such a bore—"

"Hm—I don't know what your mother says—"

"I say, you might put on your things"—Paul noticed that Björg was trembling in a way that was quite shocking. "Go out and slide for a bit, before it gets too dark."

"Well, Björg, what is it?" he asked when they were alone. He could not hear that she made any answer.

"What is the matter with you? Aren't you well?"

"No—" Her teeth were chattering with fear.

"Well—is there anything seriously wrong?"

It was a moment or two before she replied:

"I—I—I didn't believe it when I came home—I hoped so much I was mistaken. Otherwise I wouldn't have dared to come. And I wanted so much to see Sunnie again.—And now it's too late to get anything done, they told me in town—"

"Are you mad—?"

"—and now I don't know what in the world to do—" she collapsed altogether and sat doubled up.

Paul stood still for a moment. It gave him a fright when he touched her with his hand—she trembled so, it was as if she were no longer human. She drooped still lower when he put both hands on her shoulders.

"There, there, Björg. Don't be like that.—It makes no difference, you know that."

The next instant he could have bitten off his tongue for saying it. There is surely a limit to the insults one can put on a woman. Even her here.

Björg breathed a faint whisper:

"Do you mean—may I stay at home all the same?"

"Well, yes—you needn't ask—"

She began to cry, quietly and painfully, and Paul stood waiting. Then Björg said, between sobs:

"At any rate I can promise you this—I'll never again set myself against your making the children Catholics. Or say anything about your being one. For now I can see that you're a true, living Christian."

Oh, God!

317

BOOK THREE

Chapter One

THE DRAWING-ROOM AT BERVEN LOOKED VERY DARK BY artificial light; in the ordinary way they only used the lamp on the table in front of the sofa, and the big, heavy furniture in the Gothic of the 'seventies was upholstered in dark green rep which absorbed a great deal of light.

Paul sat down at the piano and lighted the lamp on it:

"If you want me to accompany you, you'll have to come now!"

Through the open door to the dining-room he saw part of the table, which was littered with satin and tulle in glaring colours, and the sewing-machine directly under the lamp.

"One moment, father," said Sunnie's voice.

"We're just trying on our costumes," cried Lisa Eberhard. "We're coming now!"

"Yes, but I've got to catch the half-past nine and I must go up and dress first." He began playing through the accompaniment to the hymn to Venus. It was every bit as tame and innocent as Cecilia's song about Christ.

The wicked Manilia appeared at the dining-room door, in a sky-blue tunic with a gold border and a tiara of imitation pearls on her black bobbed hair. Neck and bosom were hung with ropes of beads of every possible colour and length. She advanced with her stomach thrust out, holding her thin, bare, childish arms close to her sides and clenching her fists. The dark little face with its upturned nose wore an expression of cruelty and freezing scorn.

321

After her came the holy Cecilia in a white, long-sleeved garment that reached to her feet. She had wound a towel turban-fashion about her fair head, and she walked with her hands gracefully crossed over her bosom and her eyes turned to heaven.

"You mustn't keep your hands like that the whole time," criticized the saint's father.

"No, only when I'm taken into the bathroom to be strangled," Saint Cecilia explained; "and then look here, this is how I lie when I'm dying"—she let herself slide down on the dark green carpet and lay on her side, her body slightly bent and her hands extended, one of them with three and the other with one finger pointing.

The wicked Manilia brought a little plaster figure of Maderno's St. Cecilia for comparison: "You must keep your legs close together all the way and the right foot only a little bit behind the left. Can't you screw your head a little more under you? We have to see something of your cheek when we look at you from the back—"

"I don't do that till I die. When I say the long speeches to Aurelia and the handmaidens and Marcella I must look at them, mustn't I?"

"And then we strew some towels with cranberry juice on them over the floor," explained Manilia; "and then she has her neck painted to look as if she'd been beheaded three times."

"Yes, but come along and sing, if you want me to play for you," said Paul. "Come on, Lisa, we'll take the hymn to Venus first."

Sunnie sat on the floor, leaning against the sofa, and listened with admiration while her friend sang of Cyprian groves and the delights of love—

For months the girls had been full of this piece in which they were to play the leading parts—for the benefit of something or other in St. Halvard's congregation. Paul knew by heart this version of St. Cecilia's life and death, adapted for convent schools. All the beheading was done in the entr'actes.

Up in the nursery sat Helge with all his school-books spread around him, bronzing the axes for the lictors.

The baby was asleep in his cot. His little face was perfectly white again.

"Has Bubbe been quiet all the time?"

"Oh yes," said Helge, wiping the bronze off his fingers on the seat of his trousers.

When Paul came downstairs again, Sunnie and Lisa were jazzing round the drawing-room—their little faces as solemn as the grave. One had fair shingled hair, the other's black mane was bobbed and curly—two lanky, long-legged youngsters in short school frocks. Their costumes were thrown across chairs.

"Now don't stay up too long—and tidy up after you before you go to bed." It was the proper thing to say, though Paul knew he might have spared himself the trouble. It was exactly the same, Fru Eberhard said, when Sunnie was given leave to spend the night with Lisa in town.

He was to meet the others at the Bristol after the theatre; Herr Hansen and Evi were in Oslo for a few days and had invited Björg, but luckily Paul had had a business excuse. Six hours of their company would have been rather much.

Dancing was in full swing in the lounge. The waiter showed him to the table reserved for Herr Hansen. He had just time for a whisky and soda.

Nobody he knew here this evening, as far as he could see. Mostly young people—as became these new dances. Paul sat following one couple after another with his eyes and listening to the music without taking it in. Many charming young girls among them—there was especially a little slightly-built one with auburn shingle, in a figured, blue-grey frock. How delightful she was. He knew the face of her partner with the long hair brushed straight back—or perhaps it was only a resemblance, they were so much alike, the young men nowadays. But surely it was that friend of Anton Todderud's. Funny to think of it—Brother Fidelis O.F.M. in frock and sandals and this fellow here, and neither wanting to change places with the other. Brother Fidelis was now gardener of his monastery and wrote enthusiastic letters about the life he was leading; there one saw what prayers and work could accomplish in this world. But his friend too looked quite pleased—the girl was entrancing.

When the others arrived he supposed he would have to do his duty and dance. Not that it wasn't always amusing to dance with Evi. But he couldn't get rid of the idea that the modern dances were not suited to people of his generation. Of course, in a way he was always glad when Björg got some amusement. But—

No, it certainly didn't suit that fat fellow there, for instance, jazzing with the tall blonde lady in yellow—a head taller than the man almost—

But bless my soul—can it be she? He wasn't sure, but she really reminded him of Lucy—very much. No, it couldn't be, all the same—. She would be six or seven and forty now; if it was she, he could not be expected to recognize her after so many years. Was that her husband perhaps, either of the two fat creatures, both pretty awful, who made up her party—?

Nobody could say that couple cut much of a figure among all the slim and well-trained young people who glided round and round to the blatant music—

Though the lady was handsome in a way, but somehow too big and heavy for this setting—not stout, but thin rather than slim, with superbly modelled shoulders. Her lemon-yellow dress came high up over the bosom, but was cut low in the back, almost to the waist—the colour was not a happy choice to go with the rather faded face and the unnaturally golden hair. So as far as that went the lady might very well be Lucy —he smiled at the memory; she had never known how to dress.

But the short hair became her—she wore it waved and brushed off the face without a parting, and in that way it set

324

her off well. The fashion is by no means ugly if they only cut the hair short enough; it's the hair that is neither one thing nor the other and straggles down from a parting that looks so unattractive in most women, or the sort of curls that are plastered over the cheeks. But as that lady in yellow wore it—it was pretty—

Lucy had had such a finely shaped head, he remembered. When she took out the pad, combed out her splendid cinder-blond hair and plaited it for the night, she became another being, something far finer—a woman, instead of a girl who made desperate efforts to be a lady.

Yes, it must be she. Those were her feet too—classically formed, but on far too big a scale to look well in any kind of modern foot-gear. She had on yellow silk stockings and gilt shoes—in some colossal size—

Yes, it was Lucy sure enough. So that was how she looked now—

They had stopped dancing, she and the fat man, and were coming this way. Too late Paul took his eyes off her—Lucy checked herself for an instant, and he had half risen and bowed before he knew what he was doing, and Lucy bent her head. Then she went on to her table, where the other red-faced lout sat waiting.—Lövstö, that was the name of her husband—.

Paul finished his drink, looked at his watch—the show ought to be over now. Time after time he caught himself looking that way, though it was no business of his—and all at once Lucy said something to her companions, got up and came across to his table—

Paul had got on to his feet, and she gave him her hand:

"I felt I must come and speak to you, when I saw you knew me again—"

"That was really nice of you.—So you're in this part of the world—?"

"Well, yes, I've been in Oslo five years now.—Do you mind if I sit here a moment—?"

325

"Please do—"

"You see, I have a little business here. I'm separated from my husband and so I have to provide for my children.—I've seen you in the street a few times these last years, you were walking with a biggish girl with long fair plaits—is that your only one?"

"No, I have a boy of ten and another little one of two."

"She's charming, your daughter. You so seldom see little girls with such long hair nowadays that you can't help noticing them."

"Well, I'm sorry to say she no longer wears her plaits either. Of course she had to be shingled like the rest—"

"Oh, I think that was a shame almost—she looked so pretty with them."

There was a pause.

"And you," asked Paul; "are you getting on all right—?"

"Oh, you know, it isn't so easy when one's all by oneself with two little children and hasn't any connections, either family or anything else. But I get along.—I've started a little shop in Övre Slotsgate, 'La Sultana,' I don't know if you've ever noticed it. Times are so awful, that's about the only thing one can be at all sure of doing any good at, but there's such a heap of sweet-shops now—

"But perhaps you're waiting for someone—?"

"I was to meet my sister-in-law here—Hans's wife—and her father and my wife, they're coming from the theatre." Paul began to wish she would go back to her own party.

"Hans isn't in Oslo, is he? I wanted to take Roy, my boy, to him—he's had so much illness, it's his stomach—but then I was told Hans wasn't in town any more."

"No, Hans has become a wanderer in his old age. He went to Germany for some research work some years ago. And from there he joined a scientific expedition. To Brazil—far up in the interior—they're to be away three years according to the scheme."

326

A youth came and announced that Herr Selmer was wanted on the telephone. "You'll excuse me a moment—" He dashed out.

It was Herr Hansen, who said they had met some friends of his at the theatre—the Taraldsets—and had gone home with them: no closing-time there, he-he. Would Paul take a taxi and come along. The address was some unearthly place a long way beyond Holmenkollen.

When he came back to the lounge, he saw that Lucy was still sitting at his table, and the one she came from was empty.

"Changed their plans, of course. But I say, you mustn't let me detain you."

"Oh, those two—they've gone. They were going on somewhere else, and I didn't care to stick to them any longer. They were only some old friends of ours from Bergen—they'd asked me to sup with them here. But then I said I had to get home to my children and that you'd find me a taxi—"

Very well. It was none of his business how they did things in those circles.

"But don't let me keep you, if you're going anywhere—"

"Oh, there's no such hurry. But look here, won't you have anything—?"

"Well, thanks, I don't know—a glass of sherry perhaps—. Tell me, Paul"—it was the first time she had spoken his name—"are you just as fond of dancing as you were when you were young?"

"Oh yes, I like to have a dance now and again. And you dance?" He was simply forced to suggest it: "Do you feel inclined—shall we try—?"

She got up at once, took his arm and they made their way among the tables.

It was a tango. They glided out over the floor. Her dancing was not so frightfully brilliant, but she had had lessons, he could tell that. Her dress was cut so low at the back that it was impossible to hold her without coming in contact

327

with her bare skin. It was rather droll all the same to know that it was she, this lady he was dancing with. She had shaved herself under the arms. And her hand—why yes, it was queer. Ah well—nothing lasts—

The music stopped, and he led her back to their place. Without a trace of emotion he recognized a little star of converging veins that she had on her back just below the right shoulder-blade.

The wine had come; he poured out:

"Well—your health, Lucy."

"Anyhow I've made up my mind about one thing," she said; "Eva Marie, that's my little girl, shall learn to dance, I'll manage that somehow. Maybe lots of things would have been different, if I'd been able to dance and do all the things other people can do, when I was young."

"They must be getting big now, your children?" asked Paul.

"Roy's ten, and Eva five—"

"But I thought you had—. I had a glimpse of you in the street at Bergen in 1911, you were pushing a pram—"

"Gunnar, yes, the eldest." She was silent a moment. "We lost him. You see, we were frightfully well off for a bit during the war, Herman made such stacks of money, and he worshipped Gunnar, the boy was to have everything he could ask for. I was afraid of his having a bicycle, only seven years old, you can imagine, and there was an ugly corner where the road to our house joined the main road. But it was no use talking, he *was* to have his bicycle. And then there was an accident, you understand, he ran straight into a motor-car. He was terribly mangled—he died that night. I thought I should have gone out of my mind altogether. It's not to be wondered at that Roy's turned out queer, poor boy, and not strong; I was expecting him when it happened with Gunnar—"

"Poor Lucy—that was terrible for you—"

"Yes, I daren't think of it. Gunnar was such a handsome,

plucky boy too—I was so fond of him, more than I can tell you. You remember I always used to say I didn't care a bit about having children. But one doesn't know what it is till one gets them. I can't make out to this day why I didn't die. I got quite queer—was like that for a long time after.—But, I say, what's the time? I've got to catch the twelve-fifteen. Yes, it's no fun having to be away from the children all day long, sometimes I can't keep myself from picturing all the things that may have happened while I've been away from them. Why, do you know, Paul, I'm living quite near your people—the upper part of the Aamots' house in Smaalens-vei. I've often wondered if I should see any of you in the train. I've seen your mother now and then, but never any of you—oh yes, Sigmund I've seen twice, but he didn't know me, and then he was with a lady, who must have been his wife—"

"I've really been far too seldom to see my mother of late years."

"And of course you've got your own car?"

"Not now. No, we have the railway, and now there's a garage by the station, so we have only to telephone when we want to hire—"

"Your mother has a car, I've seen her driving it. Oh well, you know—Fru Aamot sees to Eva a bit, while Roy's at school, but after that he's at home, and Roy's so sensible. But all the same I'm anxious, you can understand.

"But perhaps you've got to go now? Indeed, I'll have to go too if I'm to catch my train."

Paul waited outside in the entrance, and she appeared, in a Burberry and snow-socks.

"Now I can drive you round by the station before I go up to Holmenkollen."

They exchanged a few commonplace words while they sat in the taxi.

"It was pleasant to meet you again," she said, as he helped her out at the station. "Good-bye and thanks."

329

"Good-bye."

WELL, well, he thought as he drove back again. So that was Lucy. It's quite possible that our memories undergo some transformation as time goes on, but that is nothing to the changes that time works in ourselves. Confrontations of this sort can never be very pleasant. Poor creature.

His image of her had been so absolutely dated—to the pre-war period with its narrow horizon and its optimism and the homely idyllic atmosphere within which even the most primitive and human feelings had to confine themselves. He himself had had no optimism which the war could take from him. But what a difference it had made all the same to live among people who believed in the perfectibility of mankind—

His thoughts went to the little girls—the wicked Manilia strutting about among grandmother Selmer's Gothic arm-chairs, with a demoniacal smile, as she described her daily amusements: they consisted solely of feeding her eels with slaves and watching gladiatorial combats and arranging persecutions of Christians.

The saintly Cecilia crossed her hands more charmingly than ever on her bosom and looked up at the ceiling:

"O my noble Manilia! Could I but convince you that each one of these poor creatures whom you in your ignorance so cruelly illtreat possesses a sublime, dearly-bought and immortal soul! Ah, my Manilia, not only my pure bridegroom Valerianus, my dear brother Tiburtius and our beloved father Urbanus, but I too and these my sisters in Christ who by the conventions of this world have been given to me as slaves—we would all joyfully offer up our lives, if thereby we could save a single soul. And not merely that of the meanest of your slaves, but even your proud, deluded soul, Manilia!"

Hm. Like to know how a literary prioress will tackle it when she has to choose a subject from our time and concoct a piece suitable for performance by the girls of a convent school.

Father Falk maintained that the historians of the future would lump together the first three millenniums after Christ as one period—the assaults of the heathens against Christianity and the rise of heresies within the Church. The earliest heresies make their appearance in the Mediterranean countries. Small type: something about Gnosticism, Nestor, Arius. The first tidal wave of heathens comes from the northern outskirts of Europe—small type: the Migrations. The next and far more important heresy is Islam, which at the same time lets loose the next assault on the Church by the peoples of south-west Asia. From the middle of the first till towards the end of the second millennium. Within the Church there arises at first a series of speculative, pre-eminently intellectual and mystical heresies: Cathars, Albigenses. After that, in Central Europe, whose Christianity was comparatively recent, various attempts to amalgamate its doctrines with the primitive heathen ideas of these countries—so-called reform or protestant Christianity. Small type: Calvin, Luther; their connection with the heresies named after them is however historically uncertain. Meanwhile, towards the close of the second millennium, the last and most powerful assault on Christianity takes place. Small type: in its early stages the movement is sometimes given the name of Bolshevism. Of this however practically nothing is known beyond the fact that it was the prelude to the advance of the Asiatic peoples and their conquest of what is now Western Eurasia. In the course of the twenty-third century the destruction of what had been Europe was completed. The last pope of European descent, St. Pius XX, suffered martyrdom A.D. 2237, and the American and Chinese cardinals assembled in Nova Roma, Alaska, chose the Benedictine abbot, Petrus Yang-tse-kiang, as pope. Dying Europe was incapable of producing further heresies—the growing intellectual paralysis showed itself in a return to ancient and primitive religious conceptions: animism, the interpretation of dreams, fetishism, the worship of the spirits of ancestors and of eponymous heroes who were erected into local divinities

331

of fertility.

Father Falk did not usually continue his history of the world beyond the year 3000, when the Dominicans of Samarkand began in earnest their missionary work among the Ostyak-Samoyeds inhabiting what had once been Norway. These naturally claimed to be descended from the ancient European Norsemen, and the new cathedral on Spitsbergen was adorned with a huge mosaic of Saint Olav at the field-telephone in his headquarters at Stiklestad. And it was only a sour and learned old Benedictine or two who objected that at that time they still had nothing but the wireless telephone.

A WEEK or so later, when Paul was in his town office, Fröken Alsaker came and said there was a lady outside who asked if she could speak to him. She had been before and had been told that as a rule he was there on Thursday afternoon and Friday morning.

Paul felt he had known it was she, when Lucy came in.

"Well, you must really excuse my coming and bothering you like this, but it's a thing I thought I'd better try and see you about. I ought to have begun by thanking you for the other evening, by the way—"

"Don't mention it. You got home all right?"

She sat opposite him in the old leather chair. She wore a little black cloche hat and a black coat with fur trimming— it looked well on her, though the black emphasized the fact that her looks had gone off and she was no longer young. She sat with her hands clasped about her hand-bag, looking down—he knew that attitude of hers so well—

At that moment the telephone rang and Paul picked it up: "Yes. Oh yes. No—but we've already agreed about that with the builder. Oh yes, he accepted that. No, Friday—no, that can't be managed. Well, then I'll look into it again—I'll ring you up from the works tomorrow. Yes, of course. No, we don't know anything about that. Very well, I'll telephone to Larsen at once.

Just so—just so." He put down the receiver. "Well now, Lucy—"

She said, in a low voice:

"Well, I'm so desperately sorry, Paul, at having to come here and worry you, but it seemed such a stroke of luck that I should meet you just as I didn't know which way to turn. You see, I know absolutely nobody that I can ask for anything, they're all broke, those I knew who had something, and I haven't had a farthing from Herman since before Eva was born—"

He felt he had known this too. He was so used to these people who called at offices and asked for help. And he had no business to feel—as he felt—because it was Lucy who asked it.

"You know that if there's anything I can help you with," he said in an even tone, "I shall be glad to do so.—You may be sure," he added, as she was still fumbling with her handbag.

"Can you lend me six hundred crowns?" she whispered without looking up. "It's a paper I have that's fallen due.—If it isn't too inconvenient for you—?" she added below her breath.

It was inconvenient right enough. But he said: "Oh yes, I can do that"—and was on the point of ringing for Fröken Alsaker.

Then it struck him that he would rather not take this money out of the cash: "You'd just as soon have a cheque for it, wouldn't you?" He wrote the cheque, and when she had put it away in her bag, she whispered: "You'd like a receipt, wouldn't you?"—he shook his head: "No, no, Lucy, that's not necessary."

"But I would rather pay you back," she said softly, "if I ever have a chance to do it.—Well, now I suppose you think I'm a regular—" she looked him straight in the face for the first time, and her expression affected him to such a degree that the feeling of painfulness and humiliation vanished. This was earnestness and this was sorrow. Ah yes, she must be one who was fighting with her back to the wall.

"Don't think of such things, Lucy—don't be sorry about it. Do you think I don't know how difficult it is for many people nowadays—?"

"Perhaps it isn't easy for you either?" she asked seriously.

"Do you know anybody for whom it is easy just at the moment?" He laughed. "But we jog along somehow. And things must get better some day."

She sat looking at him with her clear eyes, inured to sorrow:

"Well, you know, I try to think so too. I say to myself that it's difficult for everybody. When Herman went to smash I thought, well, it's no worse for us than for all the rest. But then he went off, you see; he'd got me to come after him to Oslo when we had to leave Berkeley Hill, he wrote that he'd got some agencies, but when I came here with the boy, and it was just before I was going to have Eva—I found Herman gone, and I had exactly sixty-one crowns and thirty öre besides my trunk. But at that time Jonsa was still alive, and so we could stay there till I went to the maternity hospital. And from there I went to a lady who took children at nurse, I didn't get any wages and it was hard work being there with all the washing, but it was because I could have Eva with me, you understand, and Roy was at Jonsa's. But then she died, and this lady wouldn't keep me with two children, when she could get another with only one baby. A friend of Herman's got me a place as waitress at a hotel on the Bergen railway, two summers running, and there I didn't do badly, but I had to pay for the children where they were, and in winter-time it was hard to get a job. I don't know how I'd have managed if I hadn't had a few things left that I could sell, furs and jewellery. But then I got word that my father was dead; I hadn't heard anything from home for ever so long, but then I came into nearly three thousand crowns, and then it was I made up my mind to start the sweet-shop. And it's getting on pretty well too, if only I could have got some place to live in town that wasn't too dear, because the ticket runs away with a lot of money, but there's scarcely any place where they'll have you if you've got children.

"So if you should hear of anything—you're sure to know a lot of people who have to do with houses and that—two rooms and kitchen that might do for us, I'll ask you to be so kind as to think of me—"

"Yes, I'll do that, Lucy. It's not impossible—"

He showed her out by the door leading directly from his private office into the corridor. He stood at the window and watched her as she crossed the street and disappeared round the corner.

It was sad—but it was no use meditating whether things might have turned out differently. And he ought to be thankful he had been able to help her out of a tight place.

That one helps another person if one can—that had always seemed to him a mere matter of course. And it was only because he knew in himself that he could scarcely have brought himself to ask anyone for help, that he felt this humiliation or sensitiveness about *her* having come to him on such an errand. He could not help wishing that they might both have been spared it. But that was nonsense. He might indeed wish that she hadn't required it; the really painful thing was that she was so hard up. But he had no right to think disparagingly of her; it might well fall upon him to help her, if she had no one else.

Chapter Two

WHEN SUNNIE CALLED IN ON HER WAY FROM SCHOOL TO walk home to dinner with her father, he knew there was likely to be some reason for it.

The office was a long, low timber building with a steep, weathered roof of tiles—a hundred years old; it had stood here while the other buildings were altered and repaired and modernized, and the works were extended and closed down and started again, and the neighbouring works at Aasland had been part of the same concern, had been sold and bought back again. Paul had a sneaking fondness for the old house: it belonged to the time when men could cut three windows and a door in a wall in such a way as to make a handsome building of quite an ordinary little cottage.

His own office was a low-ceilinged little room with two small-paned windows; he felt at home there, but then he was at home in any room that was his own and devoted to work. Perhaps this dated from the time he came to Trondhjem as a beginner and was rather proud of having an office and was ambitious to show the world, but above all himself, that he was very capable of giving a good account of himself in what was funnily enough described as the practical life par excellence. Later it had come to this, that any place where he could get away from his home was to him a sort of sanctuary.

The June day was broiling hot and the room was in a golden mist of dust and sunshine. Sunnie had such an air of summer health as she came strolling in to her father: her apple-

green linen frock did not reach to the knees and her bare arms
were burnt brown. The child was sunburnt all over and it made
the red colour of her cheeks so pretty; her hair, which was now
neither short nor long, varied from an almost silvery fairness
on the outside to golden and nut-brown under the thick folds—
can it really be a good thing, thought her father, that little
girls never wear shady hats nowadays? And she's too big to
go about with so few clothes on—her light-brown stockings and
shoes were exactly the same colour as her skin.

She dropped into a wooden chair right in the sunshine
and began to rummage in her school satchel—an old portfolio
of his that she had annexed; none of the children used anything
else now, she asserted.

She held out her report book with her cheekiest smile:

"Do please look through it at once, then it'll be done!"

Paul cast his eyes over the document. He had never been
really sure of what all these abbreviations stood for, but he
could scarcely believe that the reports were as brilliant as the
children wanted to make out: "Mdl., Sunnie, that can't be anything very grand, can it? And seven bad marks in one month,
my girl! Two for impertinence, Sunnie!"

"Ugh but, father, what am I to do—?" He could see she
was just bursting to tell him of her exploits. "One of them I
got when Fröken Holmsen was away ill and then we had that
brother-in-law of hers, Herr Sæther, to take her place, and just
imagine, he made us write an exercise in *landsmaal*,* though
that's never been a subject in our class, but then he's a language
fan, you understand. And so when I had to write about a visit to
a sæter, I naturally spelt it *sæther*, because I thought, if he
spells it that way, it *must* be right, and I said so. And then the
others laughed and that made him so wild—"

* "Country language," based on the country dialects, as opposed to
the *riksmaal*, which is the more usual literary language of Norway. Both
forms of Norwegian are taught in the State schools. For more than two
generations a fierce controversy has raged around this language question.—Tr.

Paul shook his head and tried to look serious.

"And then the other time we had the Crowbar. Oh but really, father, she *is* exactly like a crowbar! Dry and cold and stiff as a bar of iron. Well then, Fröken Rud if you like; just imagine, she brought in Catholicism, do you see, and then she asks me, 'Now isn't it true, Sunlife, that when Protestants have been into one of your churches they come with a broom afterwards and sweep it out?'—and so of course I answered, but I really said it quite nicely and modestly. 'No, they generally use a vacuum cleaner now; you know, modernism has made such great strides in the Catholic Church,' and at first she took it quite seriously, but then Knut Pedersen began to snigger— and then I can tell you the Crowbar got waxy—"

"Well, but seriously, Sunnie—yes, I'm quite serious," he laughed. "Don't you remember what it says in the catechism about our duties in our state of life? Now your state of life is a schoolgirl—"

"Oh but, father! It's so beastly going to that school—I know everything already—yes, I *do*! That's why I get such bad reports, there's no other reason, only when I have to learn the lessons I think I know them already, and so I don't worry to learn them properly—. Ugh, it's so hopeless, and when you have to think that you've got to keep on at school so *long*! Why, just imagine, if I'm to take my matric I shall be nineteen before I'm done—how old were you when you went to the university, father?"

"Seventeen. And your Aunt Tua was a little over sixteen. Yes, I can't deny that I thank Our Lord I got away from school in decent time."

"And the most bare-faced thing about it is," said Sunnie with emphasis, "that these kind of school people think they're at liberty to force their society on us year in and year out. They *must* be totally wanting in self-criticism!"

"Agreed, Sunnie, but as it is so, you must accept it as a mortification and be good and stick to your work all the same."

338

Sunnie was hunting busily in her satchel:

"Just imagine, father, Lisa's to go to England in the autumn, to a convent school kept by the Dominican nuns of the Third Order"—she had found the prospectus and handed it to him: "Albertus Magnus College—"

"That's a hell of a name for a girls' school!" Paul exclaimed in astonishment.

Sunnie looked at him reproachfully.

"Yes, I know, it slipped out. Then is she going in for philosophy now, the talented Lisa?"

"I expect *that's* only for the big girls who are going up to the university. All the Sisters who are teachers have been at universities. But there's a school for children too and—and a golf course and tennis courts, and they have a chaplain who says Mass every morning, and the Sisters say the office in the chapel, and any of the pupils that like can come too—"

"In other words, you would like very much to go to Albertus Magnus College with her?"

Sunnie nodded.

"And leave us all?"

"Not for more than a year, father—at present, I mean."

She looked at him—then she smiled, a gentle, radiant little smile.

"Shall I tell you something?—Wouldn't it make you frightfully happy if I became a nun?"

"No, God knows it wouldn't."

Sunnie looked at her father in surprise—her lips opened slightly:

"*Wouldn't* that make you happy!"

"No, Sunnie.—In general, you see, I don't believe a convent life is much in our line as Norwegians—at any rate as we are now. I've certainly tried to bring you up as good Catholics, as far as I was able—but it hasn't been easy, there are so many things that counteract it in this country—besides, I'm not a very good Catholic myself. We are so accustomed to think of what God is to give us—instead of asking what we can give God; it seems to be assumed that if we give ourselves to God in a general way, all the rest is too trifling to worry about. And you know, my dear, there's nothing wrong in it either, so long as we don't do anything that is sin—we are allowed to keep for ourselves some of our time to spend as we please and money that's our own, and we may decide what we will work at and how we will dress and so on. Think of that, my child—do you think you'll be able to face it: all your life long, having to get up always at a fixed time, always having your work arranged for you—never being allowed to have your own way, which you're so fond of, my Sunnie—"

Sunnie said quietly:

"But whatever work I was put to, it would be for God. And as I don't know of anything, father, that I'd want to do more than anything else? If there was anything that I felt I could do for God out in the world—. But if I went into a convent, I'm certain I should be just as happy doing whatever they put me to—whether they took me for the school or for nursing the sick or in the kitchen or to be porteress and attend to the telephone. If only I were allowed to choose God, so that He must give me everything directly with nothing between us—and people, so that I could never think any of them were more my own than God's own. Not you and not mother either." She turned crimson. "So you see, if I went into a convent I should have the *right* to a time when I could pray, without anyone taking it from me."

Her father made no answer.

"Tell me, father. Do you remember when I had pneumonia? Do you remember that you agreed to it then? That I should offer up my life to God?"

"I remember that very well, Sunnie.—But to tell the truth, I was not sure whether you still thought about that."

"Yes, I think of it always." She rummaged in her satchel again, found a shabby little book and took out a book-mark

340

which she handed to her father.

It was a dirty old card with a communion picture on it: a thin and mawkish figure of Christ giving the sacrament to some thin and mawkish children, supported by weedy, anæmic angels. Underneath was printed: "Jesu, our only joy be Thou. As Thou our prize wilt be."

"I can't remember where I got it from—from Aunt Selma, I expect? But it seems to me I've had it always. At any rate I remember I had it in a drawer when we were living in the Holms' flat at Trondhjem." She gave a little laugh. "Well, of course it's only something I've dreamt, I know that—but when I was little I believed I'd been given it by Jesus Himself, and He really looked just like that. I thought we'd been in a church, and as we were going He came and gave me His photograph."

Paul shook his head:

"I took you with me once to St. Olav's church at Trondhjem, when we were living there.—And now you say that, I remember something about your being given a picture by another little girl who was in church."

Sunnie put away her card:

"Of course you can guess," she said quietly, "I'm not thinking either that it can be now. As long as mother wants me to look after little Bubbe. And really what I should like most of all would be if we could have some place here in Norway where they took children like him, and I could be one of the sisters there.—I didn't really mean to ask you if I could go to college either. But I thought, when I told you about it, you would anyhow help me by wishing it—you would pray too that I might be received in a convent at last—"

"I pray that your lot may fall as is best for you." Paul had changed his office coat and taken his hat. "Come along, Sunnie.—At any rate you're too young to think of the cloister for many years yet."

"I thought you'd have been so glad about it," the child sighed.

THE blue sky was scored high up with light, feathery clouds and all around the air was a-tingle with the song of larks. They took the path that led along the edge of the banks above the river. The meadow stood high already, full of wild flowers among the grass and bordered with a pale green foam of wild chervil where they walked. The cornfield showed a dense green of long blades, with great patches of yellow charlock among them. Houses and clumps of trees on the level ground already had their summer look of being submerged in the growing fields, and only here and there a cloud of dust far away reminded one that roads ran through all this flowery verdure.

Paul could not have said what he wished for his daughter. That she might continue as she was, young and charming and good, *"halb Kinderspiele, halb Gott im Herzen."* The awkward position at home did not impair the children's innermost joy in life. They made no secret of being often bewildered and saddened, but in their inmost hearts they were happy, healthy and full of confidence in life through good and evil.—This was exactly the opposite of his own childish experience: at that time his life had been full of delights and festivities, amusement and excitement, but deep within him there was as it were an empty patch of unrest and doubt, not that people for the most part meant well, but that they had any clear idea of what they were doing or saying.

Helge he had thought of sending to the Benedictines or the Jesuits for a few years, perhaps in England; a Norwegian boy would have the best chance of feeling at home there. The boy was a smart little fellow, he had a turn for languages and was interested in history. He was getting pugnacious, sceptical and stuck-up through going to a school the whole spirit and tone of which was muddled and neutral, characterized by the old middle-class optimism which was beginning to be harassed by doubts of its own illusory individualism, but in fact could see no alternative to this but collectivism and self-surrender. When Helge had matriculated he would let him go to the Catholic universities abroad; that is, if he could afford it when the time came. While he was young the boy should have a chance of getting to know Catholic Germany, Catholic England, Catholic France—the whole Catholic action for the return to the faith which was Europe's life, while the nations held fast to it, and Europe's malady, when they were false to it. The boy should be given every opportunity of finding his place in the movement, whether as layman or priest.

But of Sunnie's future he had never thought very much— he had merely hoped in a general way that she might always be able to live in a place where she got all the sunshine there was and where the air she breathed had not been used by other lungs—and there must be beasts and trees and plants by which she could tell the passage of the hours and seasons.

One day she had discovered in a drawer of his bureau the garnet rosary which Randi Alme had given him in Paris many years ago. He himself had never used it—it was so heavy. Sunnie had pestered him for it, but he would not give it her: pure superstition of course, because many who had owned it had ended in a cloister. Such a life might be excellent for one like Anton Todderud; behind his *gamin* exterior the lad had had a fund of spiritual energy and venturesomeness; or for an intelligent and a capable lady like Randi; everyone said she was a splendid nun, her work would certainly leave its mark in the congregation. But little Sunnie was only her mother over again, so far as that was possible for a little creature who was God's child instead of Fru Jacobsen's. All the same he could never believe it would suit her to bind herself to follow the rule of an Order; she should not have to renounce all the little acts of charity towards herself which in themselves were innocent.

Two men were lying underneath some bushes, where a little path led down to the river through the alder thicket. The elder man touched his cap. Paul knew him well; it was a tramp who passed this way regularly four times a year. Quite a sympathetic fellow as far as that went, but he was simply no use for anything but tramping. Paul exchanged a few words with him: "All right, by six o'clock I shall be back at the office—"

His companion had a little restless, ape-like face—with a rather imbecile look of the Mongoloid type. He stared at Sunnie. Paul flushed with anger when he saw the expression of the fellow's face.

The poor brute couldn't help it.—As a rule most of the men who passed here on the road were decent enough, and in the course of time he had got to know many of them pretty well. The more dangerous class of those who through lack of something or other fail to find a place among the workers prefer the towns. Or perhaps it is the towns which are more dangerous for the abnormal. Still, he was always anxious about Sunnie out here; he didn't like her to go anywhere unless Buste, their deerhound, was with her.—It was absurd letting little girls run about half-naked like this. Every conventional fat-head jabbered about its being a sign of a more wholesome and innocent and less stuffy outlook. Just as if everybody didn't know that most little girls get their knowledge of sex from exhibitionists and from the sort that edge up to them and say nasty things when they stop to look into a shop window, and scare them in doorways and staircases. Stories of assaults had been current already in his and Tua's childhood—in school yards and playgrounds; and things had certainly not improved since that time, from what he heard in Oslo—east or west, there was nothing to choose. It was not hypocrisy, it was sheer stupidity and nothing else that caused the old-maidish souls to cackle about long skirts and modesty and short skirts and innocence and no skirts and again innocence—without knowing what they must have known all the time, as well as anyone else. In all ages there are men who look at young girls with eyes that tempt a father to trample them down like so much filth.

At any rate one can see to it that one's daughters do not run about half-naked. But it was impossible to talk to Björg

344

about anything of this kind. So Sunnie had to be dressed like all the others.

It wasn't always so easy with Björg and the children.

She had been away from them for years; that was a thing which could not be undone.

And religion was a tie which bound him and the children even closer than the tie of blood; that feeling of isolation which is never entirely absent from Catholics in absolutely non-Catholic surroundings, caused him and the children to feel as though they lived together in a house defended by invisible moats; even their nearest relations and best friends were on the other side. It is incredible what a difference it makes to one's views and judgments whether one believes in an objective or a subjective truth, whether by "future" one understands time in the ordinary sense or something infinite and timeless. It is a difference which determines one's view even of the smallest trifles—only that the others very often are unaware of it. To him it was a discovery to which he was not yet fully accustomed; to the children it was a matter of course—but in the face of all others it was a fellowship without flaw.

The gulf divided the children even from their mother, but no one could alter that. And their mother she was.

Björg undoubtedly had had her own religion too, in the sense of a conception of the world-order, and probably it had been the most decisive factor in her mind, though consciously she might not have been greatly occupied with it, and it had not been a religion which made any great demands on its adherents in the way of cult. But she had always assumed that there was a God in heaven and that he was good and just: if people behaved decently, did nothing that was forbidden by law and the opinion of other decent people, then God took care that things went well with them; that they had a positive right to expect.

Now she saw the chastising hand of her God in all the evil that had befallen her; now her God was like a strict and extremely unamiable criminal judge who dealt her tit for tat; for each particular misdemeanour she had been guilty of, God condemned her to a misfortune.

He had taken Little Erik, because she was so angry when she found he was coming. He had taken her father and mother, because she had deserted her children. She had been frivolous and dissipated while she was in Copenhagen, therefore it had come about that everyone knew her to be a contemptible person. And as a punishment for being unfaithful to her husband she had had a child that was deformed and feeble-minded.

Poor Bubbe—she was doubtless fond of the boy in a way, but she was ashamed of being his mother and frightened of him when occasionally she was obliged to attend to him. For he was constantly ill, and each time Björg was beside herself with despair—Paul did not know how much of it was due to her being fond of her child in spite of all, and how much to her fear that God might be after her again with his punishments.

Poor Björg, her misfortunes had affected her as measles and chicken-pox affect savages who have acquired no immunity from such ailments.

Almost the saddest thing about it was that now he knew he had always cared for Björg in the way he now cared for her— a creature of whom he had once for all undertaken the charge. But this feeling, which at bottom was an affectionate feeling, had been overlaid by various little amatory episodes which always ended by disclosing how little they understood one another, and by the irritation he felt when at times she bored him so immoderately.

If he had even been able to help her to rid herself of the terrible notion of that angry and cruel God of hers. Guilt and punishment and atonement are not to be explained on so simple a system of book-keeping. True, each for himself must say "mea culpa," through my own fault I have deserved it. But sorrow and pain are at the same time something different, since God chose them for His own lot when He would save the world, nor did He spare His mother's heart the seven swords, nor exempt from martyrdom those friends in whom He trusted most. Anton Todderud had said once—it was when Paul tried to persuade him to think it over a little longer before entering on his noviciate—that the miracles of the saints were above all a sort of system of signalling: here is a safe path, they said as it were with signal flags, to those who were doubtful how they could cross the morass.

When first it became clear to her that her boy was not normal, Björg had declared in her despair that now she too would become a Catholic. She began to take instruction with Father Falk. But she gave it up when neither the priest nor her husband could promise her that then "all would be well again"—as she meant by well. Her mind still retained the stories she had heard as a child about drunkards who were converted and whose homes became idyllic, and repentant Magdalens who made good marriages. That it might turn out that the reformed drunkard lost' his employment through other people's fault, and that the Magdalen was perhaps looked at askance to the day of her death by the other wives in her circle—these were things Björg did not understand God permitting, if he was really good. She continued to believe in each one for himself.

She and Helge got on quite well. There was something touching about her pride in this big, brave boy of hers. He had been a chubby, fair-haired youngster when she left him; it had seemed like a pathetic pleasantry that the little object she decked out in nursery suits of pink or pale blue embroidered with cats and dogs was to grow into a man; "little daddy" her women friends called him when they petted and made a fuss of him. When she came back Helge had definitely grown into a boy, an enterprising little fellow who was quite able to talk about the things that interested him—books he was reading, carpentry and carving that he worked at, and motor-cars and aeroplanes and ski-running and jumping. But about himself he was very silent and reserved—perhaps his mother did not realize how reserved

Helge was, and his father was glad the boy was so.

On his own initiative he was always very regular in going to confession and communion, and Paul had seen that the boy spent much time over his prayers morning and evening. He was extremely careful to behave correctly in church, and he had learnt to be apt in ministration. But he was not given to talking about anything which concerned religion. This made his mother feel safer with Helge than with Sunnie, who found it hard to leave off talking about God for long at a time.

Another thing which made Björg shy with her daughter was that Sunnie gave so much attention to her sick little brother; Sunnie loved him and thought him sweet, just as he was.

Paul himself was surprised at it, but he too was really fond of the poor little fellow—Johannes was his name. It would have been far more difficult to put up with the presence of this child in his home if it had been a normal boy who perhaps one fine day would have given evidence of an alien nature. In that case no doubt he would have had to try to bear it with patience and kindness, but it would certainly not have been easy. As it was, little Johannes was not merely a stranger to him, but a stranger in the world, and Paul was fond of him with a feeling that did not resemble what he felt for his own children—more like the best feelings he had been able to entertain for Björg, but stronger and less turbid; the child was absolutely innocent.

He had had an odious scene with his mother on the boy's account. He himself had had a suspicion from the very beginning that the child was not normal—it had such a disproportionately big head with a tiny face, the feet too were misshapen—bear's feet the nurse had called them.

Gradually it became unmistakable that Johannes was indeed an idiot, and then his mother had proposed that he should have him sent to a home "for the sake of the other children."

"Sunnie will get more highly strung than she is already. I don't know how you can stand seeing her hanging round that horrible changeling—fondling it."

"Sunnie's not too highly strung. And if it's agreed nowadays, for one reason or another, that we can't go back to the ancient practice of killing off such children as Bubbe, why then someone has got to hang round them, as you put it. And it's surely more reasonable that a sister should do it, who is fond of the poor creature, rather than a stranger. Nobody has the right to turn his difficulties over to others, unless he is absolutely forced to."

"He's not your difficulty," said Julie roughly. "And his mother will be only too glad to be rid of him."

"I'm not so sure of that. Björg is certainly fond of the boy."

"She! Who could run away and leave two little children. She has never been fond of any living creature but herself."

"I don't suppose she intended to run away from her children," said Paul wearily. "But she easily forgets what isn't constantly before her eyes."

"Then she'd forget Bubbe pretty quickly, when once he was in a home."

Paul shrugged his shoulders.

"Maybe. But that's only one more reason for not putting the child out."

"Is this sadism, or what is it?"

"I can see that it may appear so to you. But the thing is, I believe nothing that is done can be undone. It would only be putting off the evil day, both for her and for me, if we tried to get rid of the child in that way."

Julie set her teeth with a click:

"It isn't that I don't see through Björg pretty well!" She looked him in the face with eyes full of hatred. "If you had been man enough to treat her with honest brutality and played the tyrant with her, she might perhaps have turned out fairly decent. And I'm not going to say much about your scaring away what little wits she had, when you turned round and began to carry

349

on so that one would think you imagined yourself at least a sort of St. Paul Number Two!" He could not help smiling; and then his mother flung out her hands, trembling with indignation or despair: "But to think that you can't give it up and become a sensible man again! Throw her overboard. She'll go to the bottom one way or the other—it won't make her any happier if you're willing to wear yourself to death dragging along this wreck of a woman and a child that you don't know who's father to. *You* can't tell how many times she's made a cuckold of you—"

At that she herself set up a loud, terrified shriek, flung her hands before her face and fell to sobbing violently. She looked up once into her son's hard, white face: "Well, now I've said something you'll never forgive me—"

"Oh yes, mother, I do that."

"Yes, I know, like a Christian." She sank back in the old arm-chair, in an agony of weeping. "But let me tell you, you can spare yourself the trouble. I'm not going to be content to be nothing to my own son but just a neighbour whom you forgive because it's Christian to do so! Then I'd much rather you never forgave me and never wanted to have any more to do with me—"

"Good heavens, mother." He took her hands away from her face and forced her to look up. "That would be too much for either you or me. Neither of us could manage that, mother."

She kept hold of his hands, as he stood before her; little by little her weeping grew quieter.

"It's only because I'm so fond of you, Paul. I can't bear the way things have gone wrong with you all. And I hate everything and everybody that does harm to any of mine. I *am* like that. And I don't care to be any different."

"No." He stroked her tear-stained face once—the wrinkled cheeks were so soft and old-womanish, but the eyes were blazing with life and passion deep down in their wide sockets. "But probably most of us are the same by nature." So it's not to be

350

wondered at if the world is so damned like hell.

But when she had left him he locked both doors. He remained seated at his writing-table. Of course it was only because he was so fearfully tired and worn out that he trembled like this—it would soon pass off.—But at times it was as though he could not rightly recall what were his wishes and intentions in all this. It looked so utterly useless.

How much Sunnie and Helge had understood he did not know. But that they had had their own thoughts about their mother's absence and return and the birth of their little brother, was sure enough. They never said anything, and he certainly would do nothing to entice them out of the silence which was their best defence.

But a day or two before their summer holidays the children came home from school, Helge with a swollen protuberance instead of a mouth and nose, and a blouse all covered with blood. Paul was in the hall when they arrived.

"What a sight you are, boy! Have you been fighting?"

"Yes," said Helge. Sunnie slipped past them and upstairs.

"At the school?"

"Yes." Helge followed his sister, and Paul heard him go into the bathroom. After a while he went up to see how the boy was. He stood with his face in the washing-basin, puffing and gurgling, and the water was red with blood.

"You've had an ugly mauling," remarked his father.

Helge looked up from his towel:

"The fellow I fought with doesn't look very pretty either," he answered reassuringly. "He bled just as much."

Paul asked no more. But when the children came in to dinner Björg uttered a shriek of consternation:

"But Helge, what a sight you are! Have you been fighting?"

"I tumbled down the steps over at Heimtun. And then my nose started bleeding."

"But gee, how terribly you've hurt yourself, my poor boy—"

Sunnie was looking down at her plate, red as fire.

At that moment the telephone rang. It was the dentist's wife asking for Fru Selmer.—Björg came back to the table in a great state of excitement. Everybody said it was so marvellous, the film they were giving at the picture-house that afternoon; she and Inga had agreed to go together to the six o'clock show, "and you can both come with me—"

"I can't go to the pictures with a mug like this," said Helge.

"I've got to do my mathematics," said Sunnie.

"But you'll have the whole of tomorrow to do them, Baby—"

"Yes; but I must go through the whole term's work, you see; I've forgotten such a fearful lot."

So Björg went by herself. Paul sat in the veranda reading, when Helge came strutting awkwardly towards him. The boy plunged his hands into his trouser pockets, took up a position facing his father and regarded him seriously, with a slight curl of his swollen lips.

"I say—father!"

"Well. What is it, Helge?"

Helge came a little nearer the table, drew his hands from his pockets and began to finger the papers that lay there, then the coffee-pot—pinched a lump of sugar. At last he said:

"I say, father—can't we be let off going to that Heimtun school any more?"

Paul put down his book. He looked attentively at his son:

"Is it anything *special*, Helge? Anything more than the usual?"

The boy nodded.

"I had a row with Audulf, you see. You know, the son of the garage people. Well, we went for each other *properly*, you understand—the end of it was we fell down the steps, both of us. Then we had Fröken Holmsen for the next lesson, and she

352

tried to pump us and wanted to know what we'd been up to. Fell down the steps, we said. But of course the idiot couldn't let it go at that, she kept on asking if we'd been fighting. Well, and then some of the others said we had. But then she insisted on knowing who'd started it. And then she wanted to know *why* I'd gone for Audulf. Then Missi Imerslund told her; she'd been by and heard."

Helge stopped, and his eyes filled with tears. He swallowed a few times, but his voice was trembling with rage when he began again:

"Then she comes up to me and *pats me on the head!*" He jerked his head as though to shake her hand off. "Then she said Audulf was to leave the room and I"—Helge made a face—"I was a brave, *chivalrous* little boy.—And then she wanted to grab hold of me again, but I gave her a whack across the hand—"

Paul put down his pipe and sat looking at the boy.

"Well, of course I know it's sin," said Helge defiantly. "But it's true, father, I could have *throttled* her! I did make her ashamed of herself though, the beast!"

He helped himself to another lump of sugar and stood as though waiting.

"No," said his father thoughtfully; "it's quite clear that you can't stay on there.—You'll have to keep cool, Helge—behave as if nothing was the matter till the exams are over. Then I'll find another school for you and Sunnie to go to in the autumn."

"Thanks," said Helge.

He was standing so close to his father that Paul was able to stroke his hard, round boyish head once. His hair was reddish brown, bristly with curls like the forelock of a young bull-calf. Paul felt a strong inclination to take the boy in his arms and kiss him, but dared not; he never kissed Helge except on coming out of church when they had both been to communion.

HE went up to Sunnie a little later; he had promised to help her with her mathematics. A feeble little whimper answered his knock; when he opened the door he could not at first discover her anywhere in her little room.

Then he saw her lying over in the corner by the little sofa with her head buried in the cushions. By the side of her fair shingled head sat that horrid perverse doll with the long, dangling arms and the squinting smile.

She got up when her father came in, went up to him and allowed him to embrace her. Paul drew her over to the sofa and sat down, and his daughter snuggled closer to him and laid her head on his shoulder.

"I can't do anything for it, Sunnie," he said painfully. "I don't know what I'm to do to make things easier for you."

Sunnie dabbed her face again and again with a wet handkerchief.

"If only mamma doesn't get to hear of it. That Helge's been fighting. Ugh, that doctor's wife is such a chatterbox. It's so sad that mamma's always so low and depressed about everything—

"Father, do you think mother will never be a Catholic?"

"No one on earth can tell that, Sunnie."

"I've tried to explain it to her so often too. And about Bubbe. That he is innocent. 'Enfant de Dieu' they call such children in France, Father Auberive says. But mother doesn't like my talking about anything of that sort."

"No, but then you mustn't do it, Sunnie. You're a big girl now, you must have sense enough to understand that you're not to worry her—"

Sunnie sighed:

"It's just as if I worry her *whatever* I say."

Paul stroked her hair again and again.

"Sunnie?" he asked softly. "Would you think it very awful if I were to sell Berven?"

Sunnie straightened herself, gave a little sigh:

"*Rather* awful I should think it, if we were not to live here any more. *Must* you, father?"

"Oh, must—. I *can* presumably get rid of it now. The commune have their eye on it for a home for old people, you see."

"Then are we going to live down by the station?" she asked anxiously.

"I must tell you, Sunnie—your grandmother wants me to take over her business entirely in time. And you know that the works here have not shown any profit the last few years. And my position here has not been altogether pleasant since Uncle Henrik went broke. I can't hold on to Berven, it's more than I can afford. And the brickworks here, you see—with only one kiln working, and that not all the year round, and Aasland, where it's questionable whether it would pay to bring the works up to date—it will be more rational to let the whole concern come under the same management as Jensmo. Do you understand?—I would rather propose it myself, before anyone else suggests it."

Sunnie looked at him seriously. After a moment she said:
"Then shall we be moving to Oslo?"

"Or just outside town."

"That'll be livelier for mother." She gave a little sigh. "And easier for us to go to church."

Paul pressed her lightly to him. He had dreaded speaking to the children about this. He dreaded leaving here himself. He had left Trondhjem with a light heart—and there his life had been relatively happy and carefree. But he loved this home at Berven, and he knew that the children loved this old house and the garden and the river and the roads across the plain. Thank God then that Sunnie took it as calmly as she did. He never had any anxiety about Helge—the boy's character had already hardened so that no outside influence was likely to do it much harm.

"Shall we take a look at your mathematics now?" he asked presently.

"Yes, please, if you have time."

IN the following week when Paul was in Oslo he went out to see the Eberhards in the evening. He wanted to find out a little more about that college with the imposing name.

Karl Eberhard laughed. There was really no question of Elisabeth going to England. His sister the Carmelite nun had sent them a lot of prospectuses, in case they might hear of any girls who were thinking of going to a convent school over there. Lisa would have liked it well enough. "If I had been able to afford it, you know." But the boys' education must come first.

Their home looked the worse for wear, and Fru Margrete-Marie apologized for their dinner-service—it was cracked and chipped. Eberhard laughed at this:

"That comes of keeping a glass and china shop. You know the saying, Selmer—the shoemaker's wife never has a sound pair of shoes."

But it was always cosy and pleasant with them. All the eight children were brisk and healthy. In point of fact Paul thought Lisa the least attractive of the crowd; she was a pretty girl, obliging and very useful in the home, but a great deal too forward. Margrete-Marie brought in her youngest, whom Paul had not yet seen. The whole family were in raptures over this little Magnus, who had made such a dilatory appearance.

Sunnie was always delighted when she was allowed to stay at the Eberhards' and sleep on the sofa in the little parlour, where Lisa and Gertrud and Birgitta slept on the floor or on camp-beds. And they were all fond of her here, her father could see that. Here she had a place of refuge such as he with all his affection could not give her. And that was a bitter thought.

Eberhard walked with him along Storgate, and then Paul asked if he would accept the offer—if he decided to send Sunnie to the college in the autumn, he would invite Lisa to accompany her. If, that is. It wasn't worth while saying anything to the girls in the meantime.

So it turned out. At the end of August Paul crossed the North Sea with Sunnie and Lisa. It was the first holiday he had had

for a very long time, and he had not been abroad since before
the war—except of course to Denmark and Sweden. And the two
pretty and charming girls were the most entertaining company.

They were so delightfully interested and overwhelmed by
everything they saw—from the moment they landed in Newcastle and drove straight to the Catholic cathedral for Mass; the
children had never dreamt of so splendid a church! "Pugin, isn't
it?" asked the learned Lisa as soon as they came out. Paul had
to confess that he didn't know. And in the hotel where they
lunched afterwards the dining-room was decorated with the
most incredible pillars of green majolica. And the streets of this
foreign town, and the shops, and tiny little children who called
out to each other in English. It was amazingly good for one to
have the company from morning to night of two young human
creatures who were happy all the time—and one of them was
Sunnie, Sunnie beaming and keen and overwhelmed afresh each
day by all these new sights. At each meal it was as amusing as
ever to sit and watch them as they studied maps and guide-books
and discussed where they should go next—to the Roman Wall of
which they had read in Kipling, and cathedrals and castles and
old villages and ruined abbeys.

Bless my soul, how sweet they are, he thought evening after
evening when he had said good-night to them—after they had
roamed about for a whole day in the green Northumbrian country. They had passed from one village to another, with its old
church and old grey stone houses which were marvellously
beautiful and new little houses of red brick which were marvellously ugly, by the banks of shallow little rivers and over
green slopes with great clumps of trees and quick-set hedges.
They had had tea in little tea-gardens and in cosy roadside inns
and in comfortless tea-rooms, always the same excellent tea
and the same terrible cakes and white bread that tasted of nothing at all, accompanied by cold ham and Cheddar cheese. And
Sunnie radiant as ever, as she poured out the tea: "Oh, father,
isn't this enchanting? Don't you think we're having a grand

357

time?"

Every single morning, when he had been to Mass with the two girls in a strange church, where they were not strangers, he prayed as he thought he had never been able to pray before. Once away from his daily worries, he felt in the depths of his soul how in these last years every day had brought him things which he himself had scarcely remarked or understood fully: every day had had its worry which he had felt, but below the surface his life had been renewed, so that he did not realize that his gratitude was only a childish stammering about things the value of which he had hardly begun to appreciate.

But for his daughter he prayed that it might always be granted her, not only to be happy, but to feel that she was happy.

SECRETLY he had rather dreaded the visit to the Carmelite convent, but it was obvious that Lisa must go and see her aunt, now that she was in England.

And one fine day he actually found himself with both the girls in a bare room with yellow walls. At one end of the room, instead of a wall, there was a grille of thick iron bars with long spikes, and behind it was a thick curtain. The furniture of the room consisted of a table and a few stools which reminded one of the waiting-room at a little out-of-the-way station. Above the door hung a crucifix and on the wall were oleographs of St. Theresa of Lisieux and St. John of the Cross.

Sunnie and Lisa looked about them with eyes gleaming with expectation. Paul stood at the solitary little window of the parlour. Outside there was a strip of black, sooty ground in which a few evergreen bushes were planted, and beyond this melancholy patch of garden rose a blind, soot-flaked wall.

Sunnie came up and put her arm through his. Her travelling dress was so neat and suited her so well—in a dark grey tweed with a light fleck in it; she had unbuttoned her jacket, showing a white silk blouse and a long chain of dark, faceted coral which he had come across in an old curiosity shop and given her the Christmas before. She had been delighted with it and wore it always. That her happiness should reside in a place where there were neither pretty clothes nor coral chains nor friends of both sexes and dancing and flirtation, perhaps leading to love—he could not bring himself to wish. But he knew enough to realize that it was not impossible. It might mean happiness to Sunnie, and in that case all the glories of this world would only be a kind of make-shift which could never give her satisfaction. He pressed her arm lightly to him: "Well, little one?"

The curtain was drawn aside and there stood two figures in coarse brown dresses with broad scapulars and black veils hiding their faces.

"Oh, Mr. Selmer," said one of them, in English; "how very kind of you to come and see us and bring the young girls!"

The two masked nuns whispered together, and then threw back their veils. Paul was utterly unable to tell which of them had once been Monika Gotaas of Christiania. Both had the same clear, pale complexion with a faint tinge of red in the cheeks, the same expression in their limpid eyes—they looked young, but it was a kind of youth which had nothing to do with time or years.

"And so this is Elisabeth," said one of them, but they smiled in unison. "Oh, I haven't talked Norwegian so long, I hardly don't think I can any more—and you've come to see your aunt in Carmel—and this is your daughter, Mr. Selmer—"

The girls pulled up their stools close to the grille; their glances ranged inquisitively over the two nuns and the little room behind. Paul had taken a seat a little farther back; at present he could excuse himself from taking much part in the conversation. The girls and the Sisters got on without him. Lisa had a great deal to say about her family and about Catholicism in Norway, and she produced snap-shots, of which her hand-bag was chock-full. There was a kind of turn-table at one end of the grille, and by this Lisa passed the photographs in to the nuns, and the nuns passed out their breviaries and some coarse earthenware mugs and bowls, which they used for meals, for the children to look at. They laughed at Sister Joan's Norwegian and Lisa's and Sunnie's English and at everything the Carmelites told them about life in the convent:

"Oh, it was so cold last winter!" Sister Joan laughed. "Tek, tek, tek, we heard from all the cells in the morning; the water in our washing-basins was frozen, you see, and we had to break it up and try if we could wash ourselves with bits of ice. Oh, how we laughed!"

They sat there an hour or so, but then they had to leave; there was to be sacramental benediction in the convent church at five o'clock.

"I have often thought of writing to you, Sister Joan," said Paul. "Wilfrid said once that I had only to write to you and ask for your and the Sisters' intercession, if I was in any special difficulty."

"Oh, but we pray for you and all yours every day." The Carmelites looked at him with their clear, distant eyes. "I constantly hear from home, so we can follow everything that's happening in our prayers. We have Norway days and Norway week and a heap of acquaintances whom we shall never see till we meet them in heaven, we hope—"

"Well, but say a special prayer for me now and again besides that, Sister Joan. One finds it difficult at times, when one has actually lived half one's life without believing in *anything* —only in oneself, with all possible reservations—to take things as a good Catholic ought."

Sister Joan nodded.

"Of course. I have always thought that when Our Lord converted Nicodemus, that was the most remarkable of His miracles. Of life and death and health and disease and angels and devils He was master. But to men He had given freedom of choice, whether they would have Him for their master or be

360

their own masters."

Then the three visitors went over to the church. It was brand-new and shone with stucco and gilding and light stained oak. Sunnie and Lisa were allowed to peep into the nuns' choir, which was divided from the choir of the church by a grille.

Paul waited kneeling in one of the front benches while the children were at the grille. He had a glimpse of the Carmelites within; now they had put on their long white surplices. The children spent a long time whispering with them.

People were beginning to come into the body of the church, many children, a few working men—there were coal mines outside the town. A half-grown boy in a brown livery with gilt buttons—a hotel page-boy, probably—knelt down by Paul's side, hid his face in his hands for a while, then took out his rosary and let the beads slip through his fingers, while keeping his eyes fixed on the tabernacle with an expression of perfect peace and concentration.

Then Sunnie and Lisa came back, with flushed and radiant faces, and bobbed down on the bench by him. Suddenly Sunnie raised her forefinger to her lips and blew a little stolen kiss up towards the altar—then hid her red cheeks in her hands with a little titter of delight.

FOR ten days he had been running about with his young companions; then he delivered them at Albertus Magnus College. It was at all events a fine place—a block of old red-brick buildings with a forest of chimney-pots on the roof. It stood in a park with green lawns which sloped down to a little brook, where willows overhung the shallow, glistening water.

In the dormitories there were white curtains round all the beds, Sunnie told him eagerly, and she would have to get one of those enamelled buttons with the school crest, the Dominicans' badge in black and white. The Prioress, a tall thin lady with big front teeth, in the dazzling white habit of the Order with black veil, looked strict, but Sunnie said that Mildred said that she was so easy to get on with. Mildred, why, that was the fat girl with bobbed red hair and tortoise-shell spectacles—they'd already talked to her quite a lot, she was such good fun—

His last morning, when Paul was to take the motor coach which left for York at half-past seven, Sunnie had got leave to meet him in the little Catholic chapel up in the town, a quarter of an hour's walk from the school. She went on to the hotel with him and they breakfasted there alone.

"You mustn't be sorry, father—I shall be coming home again in a year, you know. And I'm much too young to come to any decision yet—our reverend mother says the same."

"All right, my dear. As long as you feel happy here, everything will be well."

Outside the shallow valley was filled with a light, thin mist. The big trees along the river were blurred and dark, and the slopes were beginning to show green through the fog, behind which the sun shone, white as a moon. It was going to be a glorious day. Paul walked back with Sunnie past old houses and gardens and garden-walls over which hung huge dark elms, to the gate-lodge of the school.

"No, my child, I won't have you crying." He kissed her on the mouth and eyes. "You're just to have as lovely a time as you can, this one year anyhow. Hush now, little silly—oh yes, I shall miss you all I have time for, and then we shall think of each other morning and evening, and you'll remember us in chapel—and now do stop crying, Sunnie."

"And then you must all remember to put Miss Paula Selmer on your letters. They'd laugh themselves sore, everybody here, if they found out my name was Sunlife!"

Paul stood watching his daughter as she ran along the avenue, her dark school frock swinging about her slender legs. Oh yes—he was glad he had sent her here—.

Then he heard the roar of the motor coach at the bend of the road—he had arranged for it to stop here and pick him up.

Paul had planned a couple of days in London. One morn-

ing on coming back from church he found among his mail a letter which had been sent after him from place to place down
through England.

It was a lady's hand which he thought he ought to know,
but he couldn't remember where he had seen it before—only
that he associated it with some unpleasant memory or other, so
he left the letter to the last.

It was from Lucy—of course. She wrote that she was sorry
to have to trouble him again, but she had no one to give her
any advice, and she was in such a desperate situation—could
she come up to his office and talk to him anyhow?

The letter was thirteen days old. And it would be regretta-
ble if she should think he had not answered because he didn't
want to have any more to do with her. There was no address on
it, and for the life of him he couldn't remember what that shop
of hers was called. So he sent a picture post-card and addressed
it to the station at home. Not till he had sent it did it occur to
him that Upper or Lower Slotsgate would have found her just
as well.

Chapter Three

PAUL STILL HAD LUCY'S LETTER ON HIS MIND. HE WOULD hate her to think he had purposely left it unanswered.

A day or two after his return from England, when he was at his town office, he looked up the telephone book. "La—" something or other. But he couldn't find anything that would suit. Perhaps she hadn't a telephone.

He had a kind of idea that there must be a little sweet-shop at the house in Slotsgate where Hauan had his office. In the afternoon, on his way to the station, he looked in—at any rate he could buy some candy for Björg.

It was quite a little, narrow shop—no more than the width of the door and the shop-window. Both the side walls were filled with shelves on which stood gaudy cardboard boxes and beribboned baskets, and there was a glass counter with jars of sweetstuff running the length of the shop. It had not struck him before what a dull life it must be to stand all day in a shop like this weighing out candy and caramels and being obliging to customers.

He was served by a young girl with a waved shingle. She was alone in the shop. The door of a back room stood ajar, but there seemed to be no one in it.

Just as he had paid and was going Lucy came in from the street. She stopped abruptly on seeing him—and Paul felt with vexation that the little shop-girl must guess there was something behind it.

"Gracious—are you here?" she asked in a surprised whisper.

"Yes—I just wanted to hear if you received a card I sent you from London about a week ago—"

"Yes, thanks. It was kind of you to let me know you had been away," she said in the same low tone.

"I thought, you see—you might have had something particular to say to me."

She stood looking at him. She was dressed all in black; it suited her well, but she was fearfully powdered, with reddened lips and black round the eyes. The hair under her little hat was crimped in waves and had an artificially golden sheen. But so many wore it like that nowadays. And her eyes had the same heavy look that he knew so well. He suddenly felt quite unreasonably annoyed over a row of round yellow boxes with idiotically grinning moon-faces on them which were ranged on the shelf behind her.

"If you can spare a moment?" she asked with hesitation. "Could I have a word with you?"

She brushed past him in the narrow passage between the counter and the shelf—she was unpleasantly scented—and led the way into the little back room. It contained the scantiest of office furniture and looked out upon a narrow yard with goods-hoists.

"No, you see, Paul," she said, when she had closed the door behind her; "I regretted it as soon as I had sent that letter. You must excuse my writing it. But it was one evening when I was simply out of my wits—. But you know, when I didn't hear from you, I regretted it still more, for then I thought you must be angry with me and—and despised me too.—So I must thank you for sending me that card."

"But that you wrote about?" he asked presently. "That you were in a difficult situation. Are you still, Lucy?"

She looked at him with a mortally sad expression in her great grey-blue eyes. Then she shook her head:

365

"I managed that time.—Herman's in town now, I must tell you—my husband, you know. And now he's worrying to get me to go and live with him again. But I told him I found it hard enough to keep myself—the expenses are so big in this business that I don't know if I can manage to keep it going much longer. So he needn't imagine *this* is anything to count on. *He* hasn't any regular job and not much chance of getting one either.

"But then he had just had a job, and so I forced myself to get a hundred and fifty crowns out of him for the children. But for that I had to let him have them with him a whole Sunday— he has a friend who's got a motor-boat. But my God, I was frightened till I'd got them safe home again. Not but what Herman's fond of the children, so I knew he'd look after them, but he drinks, you see, when he can get hold of anything.

"But then I pulled through, with a little extension."

Paul said quietly:

"It so happens that I could give you a little assistance just now, Lucy. You see, I'm thinking of selling that place I have in the country. We're going to move into Oslo in about six months. My mother wants me to take over her business—she's getting old now, you know."

Lucy nodded. She was looking down in her lap.

"I've met your mother. Roy was so frightfully ill again this summer; the doctor had to come to him several times a week for four weeks. And he must have told your mother about it. So she came up to me one day in the train and sat down beside me. She was so nice to me. And then another time she said, if there was anything she could help me with, I was only to tell her—

"And so, as I didn't get any answer from you, I thought one day—well, I went up to Linlökka in the evening. I borrowed two hundred crowns of your mother; it was just enough to see me through it with what I'd got from Herman.—Your mother said she thought Eva was such a good child. I'd taken Eva with me."

After a pause Paul asked without looking at her:

"Did you say anything to mother about our having met?"

She too looked another way:

"No, I didn't happen to mention it."

"Is that Roy?" asked Paul, for the sake of saying something—he nodded in the direction of a framed photograph on her desk.

She handed it to him:

"No, that's the one we lost—Gunnar." He ought to have guessed that, by the way; the photograph was pale with age, it showed a little boy in an old-fashioned sailor's blouse.

He had been looking, without knowing it, at some account books that lay open on the desk. But all at once he became attentive:

"Look here, Lucy—have you any objection to telling me who keeps your books for you? Do you do it yourself?"

"Yes, I'm obliged to. I can't afford any help except my little errand-girl—she serves in the shop when I'm obliged to go out—"

"Then do you *know* book-keeping?"

"I helped Herman a little—the last part of the time before we went quite to smash. So I learnt something then. And Jonsa taught me a little. But I'm not very good at it." She turned red.

"Well but, Lucy, let me tell you—in case of accidents— you'd better get your books in order. You know there's a law about that sort of thing. Shall I suggest something?—I could let my girl clerk come here a few evenings to help you. Fröken Alsaker—you must have seen her that day you called last winter. She'll get your accounts in proper order and show you how to keep them. And then we shall get a general idea and see if there's anything I can do to put you a bit straighter."

Lucy dried her eyes once:

"I'm not sure that it's any use, Paul. But at any rate it's frightfully kind of you. Oh well, many a time in old days when I was living here in Oslo I used to think it was awful that I

hadn't anybody to hold on to. But then I had only myself to look
after. Now I've got the two children's future to think of. That's
almost worse. Though I don't believe I'd be able to live now if I
hadn't them."

"You'll see, Lucy, something'll turn up." It was fairly
hackneyed as a consolation, but what was he to say—?

"Well, you know, Paul—if you *could*—help me a little so
I could get along, myself and the children—then perhaps I
should think it wasn't true after all what I've thought sometimes,
that I was *bound* to come to grief. Every time I've been on top
and getting on well for a bit—it was only to make me feel it all
the more when I had to go under again."

"You mustn't think like that, Lucy."

"I say, that lady clerk of yours you were talking about,"
asked Lucy suspiciously; "is she that sort too—Catholic? I noticed she had on one of those brooches with the Virgin Mary—"

"Yes, Fröken Alsaker is a Catholic and a wonderfully good
woman—a real saint. So you can quite safely depend on her,
Lucy."

"She won't go talking about you and me, will she?"

"Never in this world."

As he was going Lucy said:

"I say. I suppose I'd better not come and see you at the
office any more? I mean, in case I might meet your mother, for
instance?"

"You may just as well ring me up on the telephone if there
should be anything," he said shortly.

The girl was gone and the shop shut. Lucy let him out and
they walked together a little way down the street. "But look
here, Lucy, I'll have to take that car if I'm not to miss another
train—"

BJÖRG sat in the veranda reading when he came home. Paul
gave her his usual fleeting kiss on the cheek: "Have you waited
tea for me?—but, my dear, you shouldn't have done that—" He

368

could not get rid of a feeling that there was something improper
about it, as he gave her the bag of sweets he had bought in
Lucy's shop.

Later in the evening, when he went upstairs for something,
he looked into the nursery where Bubbe was. The boy had been
given chocolate, he saw—he had dribbled it over him. So Björg
had been up and put a bit in his mouth.—Poor thing, she was
fond of him after all.

"Ugh, where did you buy that candy?" she asked later,
when they were walking in the garden. "It was absolutely stale!"

"I'm sorry. I popped into a little shop and bought it on my
way to the station."

Björg regarded the prospect of moving to Oslo with unmixed
delight. She evidently hoped too that her husband's income
would grow again, when he took over his mother's business.

Paul himself had no illusions on that point. At his mother's
death there would be four to share her property. With his
brothers he could certainly arrange matters. Hauan advised him
to claim repayment of the help he had given them some years
back. But Paul had little desire to remind them of it so long
after—he had made no conditions at the time. And Sigmund
needed all he had got; he had a few pupils, but what he earned
could scarcely pay for his clothes, and he had to go to a
watering-place every summer for his rheumatism. Lykke slaved
hard with her pekinese and Alsatians and chickens and ducks
and what not. Now she talked of starting a fox farm.

Hans would be able to manage, when he came back, but
neither he nor Evi had any turn for economy. And then there
were Tua's children who were under age.

It was going to be something of a job to get it straight. But
he must congratulate himself that it was a job he could undertake.

He had not got back all he had invested in the Haugen
works by a long way, and what he had put into the Berven brick-

works was practically lost. But this experience was no different
from that of many other men in these times. What he got for
the villa at Berven would mostly be swallowed up in providing
another house.

His mother had talked of letting him take over Linlökka.
But that did not appeal to him. It meant being dependent on
trains again. Though no doubt he could afford to get another
little car. But he didn't care to live at Linlökka—not with Björg.
When his mother was no more he would prefer to remember the
place as it had been. Besides, a regular little town had grown
up round it now; it was not as it was in old days.

Björg was in favour of investing in a flat in town. But he
had not lived in the same house with other people since he was
twelve years old.

However, he humoured his wife; they might at least look
at Pastor Garnaas's flat and talk it over with him. Halstein
would be glad to have it off his hands and go to live among his
congregation; this new wife of his was so active in parish work.
She and her step-sons got on well together, Halstein said, one
day when Paul met him in the street. Ambjör and Guro were at
a boarding-school.

So Paul and Björg were invited to supper at Pastor Garnaas's one evening at the beginning of winter.

It was pleasant enough—that is, he bore it with politeness
and good humour, but Björg seemed quite to enjoy herself; it
always made her happy to spend an evening out.

The new Fru Garnaas was sympathetic. Halstein he had
never cared for particularly, though the man had a heap of excellent qualities, as he had always been ready to admit. But what
one of them had viewed with faith and confidence had always
been regarded by the other with the deepest aversion and dread,
and it could scarcely be otherwise now, though Paul had long
ago lost his taste for entering into discussions with a man whom
he could not meet on a scrap of common ground.

"After all we worship the same Jesus as our Lord and Master," Halstein had said to him once, shortly after Tua's death.

But that was exactly what they did not do, thought Paul. Since one of the few things we can be sure of, if we reject the authority of the Church, is that Jesus for the most part was speaking of Himself, whatever may have been the subject of His discourse. And that being so, it makes all the difference imaginable whether He is creator or created.

This evening the two ladies were discussing a play; Fru Garnaas had been to see it with her husband. A number of the clergy had been invited to the theatre in order that they might pronounce on it from a religious point of view—presumably because the action of the piece was supposed to take place in a future state. The characters were all dead and were travelling by steamship to another world, where they were received on arrival by an exceptionally consequential and self-satisfied official who was given the title of censor; he rehearsed for the benefit of the poor souls a lot of gossip about their earthly life, after which the immigrants had their passports endorsed by him.

"Well, I really do think it was awfully solemn and impressive," said Björg. "And I can't see how Paul could say it was simply ridiculous."

"Ridiculous? Indeed, that's the last thing I should call it." Garnaas was rather hurt. "That with your religious views you can't sympathize with an attempt to present the idea of immortality in a way that accords with modern conceptions—that I can quite well understand. But ridiculous—I must say, I could never think that of a work of art which preaches belief in a life after this."

"But that's precisely what seems to me ridiculous," said Paul; "preaching as a solemn belief that after this life we enter on a new one which is just as stupid and full of futilities. And I can't understand why none of you parsons protested—you're not so peaceably minded in the ordinary way. For it's the most arrant blasphemy of both God and man to suppose that in eternity men will continue to judge men."

Halstein looked annoyed:

"Naturally it's not the most exalted idea of eternity. But don't you think it's in any case an advance, a sign that materialism is losing its influence—when people begin once more to be interested in the problem of a life after death?"

"There is much good to be said of materialism. If only it had not been an untenable standpoint which may easily become a station on the road to Satanism."

"Then you did not regard it as an advance when after Tua's death your mother raised her eyes towards the unknown, trying to get in touch with the spiritual world?"

"No, and I'm glad she's given that up. Since there are such things as unclean spirits. The material world is at any rate something which God has created, even if it was never intended to suffice us. I believe too that it is better in the sight of God to delight in it, while knowing that more than one lifetime of it would be too much for us—than that one should cling to it so closely as to seek for a shadow of it even beyond the grave. I believe that so long as a man has felt no impatient desire to see God as He is in Himself, it is healthier for his soul if he thinks one human lifetime is enough for a man."

The baby made himself heard from the bedroom, and Björg went in there with Fru Garnaas.

Pastor Garnaas looked at the other:

"That sounds very fine indeed, Paul." He smiled rather sarcastically. "But I wonder whether you mean it, when it comes to the point.—If you had lost your little girl a few years ago when she was so ill—would you have rejected so scornfully any idea of meeting your child again, even if it were not to be in a heaven where you would both be brought immediately before the very face of God?"

"I hope so in any case. If she was only to awake to a life which resembled this life, I hope I love my children well enough to wish they might never awake again."

Once more Halstein Garnaas looked at him, and Paul had a

strange feeling that never before could they have come so near
to one another.

"But what if you had lost—a wife whom you had loved
with all the strength of your being, with all the idealism and
warmth of your youth?—Well, it's not that I would say anything disparaging of my present wife; Bergljot is an excellent
person. But it's not the same as the bride of one's youth. If it
had been your lot to win in marriage the great love of your life
and then to lay her in the grave—I wonder whether you would
have said the same as you said just now?"

Paul looked down:

"Perhaps not," he said softly.

JUST at the moment, however, he was not in the mood to see anything overwhelmingly desirable in these old loves that rose up
out of their graves. He had a suspicion that Lucy's concerns
were going to bring him many grey hairs.

Fröken Alsaker and he had arrived at the conclusion that
this business of hers ought certainly to pay its way, if only she
were clear of debt. The turn-over was not so bad. And by degrees Paul had got rid of the most pressing items.

He had seen a good deal of Lucy in the course of the
autumn and winter; it had been unavoidable, though God knew
how little he liked it. It wouldn't be the least amusing if they
were to be talked about, among folks who knew they had once
been engaged, for instance. If Björg came to hear of it she
would be jealous, and in present circumstances he didn't really
know if he could meet jealousy on Björg's part with Christian
forbearance.

But it was his actual intercourse with Lucy that depressed
him most.

At times he thought that only now was he beginning to understand her. She had allowed all her experiences in life to wash
over her, while she stood immovable, a rock of pessimism. And
it was like a kind of perverse spirit of pride in her—never had

a misfortune been able to take her unawares. That too must be reckoned a form of strength—her perplexing and passive attitude in the face of all the evils in life.

But in that case he could only have tormented her in their young days with his opiniated talk of being man enough to make the happiness of both secure? She had wept so pitiably when he was about to leave her in order to work for their common future. Had she thought him naïve and inexperienced beyond all bounds, and been incapable of finding words to warn him?

So it was not in *him* that she lacked confidence. He had had no more sense than to be offended—amongst other things—believing that she judged him from her experience with her other men. But it was life she was judging, according to her experience of it.

She was devoid of hatred too. Many a time she must have been irritated with him and with his relations—with their activity and their belief that anything could be any use in the long run. Suspicious and afraid—with all the heathen's fear of anyone who conducts himself in such a way as to draw the attention of the gods. But she did not hate. He remembered that she had spoken of her two earlier lovers with a curious objectivity: they had deserted her, because it suited them best to be rid of her, and every man for himself.

And this husband of hers, who had vanished, leaving her friendless and without a penny, with one child on her hands and another coming—and who now wanted to join her again because he imagined she could keep him—of him she talked calmly and without bitterness, ready to be just even to him. Herman was really kind by nature, but he was brutal to her when in a temper. He had often treated her badly in the first years of their married life, because he was jealous of her past. But when he got so frightfully rich during the war, he had been wonderfully generous to her, said Lucy—she was to have everything she could think of, in fact he had worried her to go on spending all the

time. He was fond of the children, had loaded them with presents as long as he had anything to give. When he had no more,
he cleared out. He was really an easy man to live with, except
just when he was thinking of her past or had been drinking—
but he was rather given to that. And so on.

Only for Paul himself had she possibly felt at times something resembling hatred—after the event. Because he had tried
to teach her to hope.

At other times Paul would think—bosh, it's only that I
haven't learnt any more wisdom than to try if I can trick her out
as something extraordinary, a kind of nature spirit almost. Because she was once my mistress, and because I insist on making
out that story to be something altogether exceptional. She is
quite ordinary, a poor weak woman, not specially endowed with
the means of defending herself, but tough, in a way, in spite of
that.

SHE would talk, by the way, of those years of profiteering as
though she really thought she had had a splendid time. She
wanted no encouragement to describe all the glories of Berkeley Hill: there had been a little cottage called Birkely on the
site they built upon, and so Lövstö renamed it, to sound
grander. She had had two parlour-maids and a nurse for Gunnar, "So then I had plenty of time to myself. I read a lot, I can
tell you—we had such a nice library and over a thousand books
in it, I'm sure," and she had bought pictures by the dozen and
had gone to all the concerts. "I went and heard Sigmund too,
when he played at Bergen, and I sent him a huge bouquet of
forty roses. Didn't he ever tell you? Herman was awfully proud
of me, because everybody thought I had such a swell and stylish
manner, I was much more ladylike than lots of the other men's
wives. For you see, I copied your mother, I always tried to be
like what I'd seen her, as you can imagine." Paul could not quite
imagine it.

He had met some of the profiteering fraternity at the time

and had heard plenty of stories about them. But Lucy in her placid, indolent way gave him details of the inner life of that circle which fairly took his breath away.

"Cocaine cocktail—what do you say to that?"

"Oh, Satan in hell!"

"I thought you weren't allowed to swear if you were a Catholic," said Lucy reproachfully.

"No, but it's not swearing to give the name and address of a well-known personage when one hears him mentioned."

"Do you think it was so *wicked?*" asked Lucy, rather frightened. "Oh well, I dare say there was a good deal that was pretty sickening really."

Some kind of responsibility for her he must have, after the relations which had existed between them. As far as he knew, the Church recognized the clandestine marriages of non-Catholics, if they were contracted on the assumption that they were to last for life. And it was not his fault that Lucy had not assumed the same as himself. In any case, he was the only one she had who could help her at all.

JULIE SELMER was laid up with influenza at the end of February, and Paul went out a couple of times to confer with her about various business matters.

She was up again, but Hans Selmer would not allow her to go back to the office for another week. He had returned from Brazil at the new year and was staying with his mother for the present. Paul went out to Linlökka one evening, with the intention of staying the night. At the station he had caught a glimpse of Lucy; she was evidently going out by the same train. He took care not to get into the same carriage.

It was snowing—the flakes floated down, fine and thick and dry, around the big lamps as he got out on to the platform at home. Paul stayed for a few moments chatting with old Fru Kastrud, so all the other passengers had left the station when at last he got away from her.

376

The birches were domed in airy whiteness under the fresh snow as he walked through the little street of the village, and the snow was still falling. Their short cut to Linlökka was snowed up, so he had to go part of the way down Smaalens-vei, where the sound of Kastrud's sleigh-bells lost itself far ahead. Stupid of him not to have asked for a lift—

Paul had left behind the last of the street-lamps and came all at once into the country. On the higher side of the road a good deal of building had taken place of late, little wooden houses of a story and a half with little gardens in front, but to the west of the road the great fields still stretched, white and intact, and far away under the edge of the woods on the other side the lights of Linlökka twinkled through the driving snow.

He made out two dark figures ahead of him on the road—it looked as if they were fighting. A husky male voice roared angrily, and a female voice gave one feeble scream. Paul shouted hallo and walked faster.

He was still a little way off when he recognized one of the voices as Lucy's.

"Hallo, Fru Lövstö—is anything the matter—?"

The man was a tall, big fellow in a fur coat and fur cap; his breath smelt of liquor as he answered Paul's greeting:

"No business of yours! What the devil do you mean by speaking to my wife when she's walking with her husband?—get out of here, quick!"

"Certainly, if your wife wishes it."

"Oh, do go away, Herman," Lucy pleaded querulously; "I've told you I don't want to talk to you—can't you go now!"

The man swore and blustered and tried to close in on Lucy.

"No, let the lady alone now," said Paul. "You hear she doesn't want to talk to you—"

"What the hell are you butting into our affairs for, eh?" He swayed in Paul's direction as though he was going to fly at him, but suddenly bumped into Lucy, making her stagger and nearly fall—there was ice on the road under the fresh snow.

She screamed, and the fellow lurched against her and caught her in both arms.

Paul flung down his suit-case, laid hold of the man and hung on to him while Lucy freed herself. She was still whimpering: "Oh, do go, do go, Herman—you shall come another evening and see the children—"

"Leave off annoying the lady, man. Let her alone, I say—"

The other yelled and damned and called Lucy foul names, as he struggled in Paul's grasp and tried to kick. A big, ugly fellow he was, and seemed pretty drunk. So Paul heaved him into the ditch, and there he lay floundering in the snow, howling and scrambling to get out.

Paul picked up his suit-case:

"Come along, Lucy, I'll see you home."

They walked on. Lövstö's roaring grew feebler in their rear. Paul noticed that Lucy was very much upset, she seemed to be trembling. She walked with her head bent against the snow, which was driving fast; they had it right in their faces.

"He won't lie there and get snowed under tonight?" she asked with some concern.

"Oh no—it's early in the evening and there's a lot of traffic along this road.—I can't say he made a sympathetic impression, on a casual acquaintance," he could not resist saying.

"No, poor fellow, he had a good deal on board tonight.—Ooh, he's worried me so cruel lately," she sighed.

"This is where I live," she said, stopping outside a little garden gate. A few paces off, within the little, newly planted garden, stood a wooden cottage. The only light came from the balcony room in the attic.

"The Aamots were going to the theatre tonight," she said as she opened the door. "They won't be home till the last train. Ooh, I hope Herman's not going to come along and make a row outside here. I'm always so afraid of what he may be up to, when he's like this. A fortnight ago he was here one evening and Aamot had to threaten to 'phone for the police—

378

"You couldn't come in for a minute, could you?" she begged miserably.

"Yes, of course I can."

"Then you'll be able to see the children," she said in a more cheerful voice, as she led the way up the narrow stairs. "I'd like you to so much."

They entered a tiny hall, and Lucy opened the door of a moderate-sized room. It was warm and dark in the corners under the sloping roof; Paul had an impression of cosiness. In the middle of the room under a hanging light with a pink silk shade stood a table laid for three. And on the other side of the table stood the two children looking at him.

"You must come round and say how-do-you-do nicely—"

The little girl was quite sweet, chubby, rosy-cheeked and fair-haired. She gave him her hand with a curtsy and said "good-day" nicely in a thin, clear little childish voice.

The boy was slight and rather small for his age. Anything but handsome—with a big, rugged head on a skinny neck. His close-cropped hair was almost white, his face with its big, knobby forehead and hollow, blue-veined temples had a yellow cast. He had short, compressed features, a strong mouth with narrow red lips, and dark eyes with a kind of dull metallic glint and deep blue shadows under them. He looked as if he might be fairly wide awake—and destined for one thing or another.

He greeted the visitor reservedly, went off at once and took his place by the side of his mother.

"Roy always has the table laid by the time I come home." Three yellow tulips stood in a glass in the middle of the table; they gave a curiously grateful effect. "Well, you see what I have to offer—can't you sit down and have a cup of tea with us—?

"I'm a bit afraid of being alone in the house with the children," she went on, under her breath, when she saw that he hesitated. "You can just put your things on the sofa there—"

"Thanks, but they're so wet.—Anyhow I must 'phone to mother and let her know I'm not coming till later—she's expecting me."

Lucy showed him the way to the telephone through the dark
rooms downstairs. "No, thanks, Lucy, you needn't switch on
the light—"

It was his mother herself who answered from Linlökka.
Paul explained the situation to her—with a queer, uneasy feeling at his heart, as he stood there in the dark at the little un-
familiar writing-table.

There was a pause before Julie Selmer replied. Then her
voice came, easy and straight to the point:

"But look here, Paul, don't you think it would be better
if you all came over here? Ask her if she will bring the children,
then you can come here all together."

Obviously that would be better. And Lucy agreed, with
some reluctance.

She stood at the glass door to the balcony when he came
back: "Look there—"

Outside in the falling snow stood a big dark figure on the
other side of the road—he was looking across at the house.

They stood there in the dark looking out through the glass
door. Between them was a pedestal with a fan-leafed palm on it
—when Paul moved his head it pricked him on the ear and
rustled very faintly.

"He's found out, you see," said Lucy in a whisper, "that
I've begun to keep company with you again, and that's what
makes me so afraid of what he may be up to. Because it's you
he was most jealous of. That was always what he went on about
when he got wild and let fly at me—"

"I see. Well, that was what one might expect."

"Yes, for you see, he knew all about Carling, for they
were pals, and so he knew besides that there'd been somebody
before Carling. But about you I'd always said that you never
had anything to do with me in *that* way, I took my oath to that,
for I didn't want him to think you were like the others. So I
said you'd never so much as tried to get me to do anything like

380

that, all the time I'd been engaged to you—you'd never been anything but gentlemanly and considerate."

He moved rather hastily, making the leaves of the palm rustle. Lucy went on quickly:

"Because that's how you *were,* you know, and then I couldn't stand—" her voice failed for an instant. "Herman would never have understood that there could be anything but beastliness in that there—"

"Lucy, don't you think I'd better 'phone for a sledge for you?" he interrupted her sharply.

"Now I believe he's going." The figure in the snow turned and began to slouch along the road in the direction of the station.

"But then he found some old letters of yours, you see. I don't know if you noticed there were some missing when I sent you back your letters?"

Paul shook his head. "I burnt the whole bundle and didn't look at any of them."

"There were two letters you wrote me that were not like the others. The others anybody might have read and it wouldn't have mattered." Her voice was thick with sorrow and scorn. "But there was one that you wrote from a place where you'd gone for the shooting—Ronglan it was called, I believe—about a tarn with some water-lilies. And then there was one about that house you wanted so much to buy—and you wrote about how it would be when we lived there. And I hadn't the heart to send those two back. I hid them under the padding at the bottom of my work-basket—"

He vaguely remembered.—One night when his longing for her had come upon him with the force of a tempest, and he had got up at last and written to her—something about the lonely house under the Lade crag where he had dreams of their living. If her husband had got hold of that, it wouldn't be much use her pretending any longer that their engagement had been altogether platonic.

381

But in general he had taken pains to write so modestly and reasonably that complete indifference could hardly have expressed itself more chastely.—Had that been her interpretation of it—?

"But look here, let me see about a sledge. Eva Marie can't go tramping through all this loose snow."

He couldn't stand any more of this just now. Talk about old loves and spook séances—he was perfectly sick with disgust and sorrow. But in any case he admitted that he might well congratulate himself on his mother's declaring herself willing to act as a kind of chaperon, so to speak, for this galvanized friendship of his with Lucy.

He rang up the posting station, but there was not a sledge to be had.

He went upstairs again to Lucy. She was on her knees putting on the little girl's socks and snow-boots, when Paul chanced to hear Roy whispering to his mother: "Did you see father— he was outside here just now—"

THEY went southward and took a cross-road which led through the fields to the meeting house at the edge of the woods. The snow had formed great drifts, so that Paul had to carry Eva most of the way. Lucy and the boy trudged behind, hand in hand. The situation was as preposterous as it could be.

Julie met them at the front door, when at last they reached Linlökka. She shouted a welcome, and the maid came with a broom and helped to beat the snow off them, while Julie took off Eva Marie's outdoor things. Everything was now as natural as possible.

It was warm and bright and cosy to come indoors; the little girl soon made herself at home, when once she had discovered that Josua, Julie's big St. Bernard, was not dangerous. She could pat it without being afraid. Next moment she was on the floor beside the dog, hugging him.

At supper she chattered in quite a lively way and made a

mess of herself with jam, and Lucy admonished her in a half-whisper to keep still and not be such a pig. Otherwise she said little and looked serious. The boy looked about him now and again with rapid, prying glances—they were strange, those dark, metallic eyes of his. Paul could not remember afterwards what he had said to Roy—but the boy smiled suddenly, and that smile pleased Paul quite inordinately. And the child's mouth with its thin red lips was really finely outlined—the only handsome point about the boy.

Afterwards, when they had moved into the drawing-room, Julie installed Lucy in a comfortable chair in front of the fire—it was one of Paul's steatite fireplaces dating from the palmy days of Haugen. On the mantelpiece stood a photograph of his children, taken as a souvenir of their first communion, Sunnie all in white with wreath and veil, and Helge in his starchiest clothes with a ribbon tied in a bow on his left arm. Their grandmother had asked for it herself—to Paul's great surprise. But the children looked very nice in it. Lucy took it up, looked at it a moment, but said nothing.

Presently Eva Marie came and wanted to sit on her mother's lap—she was getting sleepy. Roy had found some picture books to look at. And Julie had settled herself in front of the fire and kept up a quiet conversation with Lucy.

Paul sat down on the sofa over in the corner and took up a book which lay there. It was *Spanisches für die gebildete Welt*. He had brought his mother several of Alban Stolz's books, thinking that in any case she must be able to understand the marvellous wealth of temperament in them, the multiformity of the man's mind with all his affections and prejudices and shrewdness and asperity and charm and aspiration and impetuosity. But his mother had fixed her attention almost exclusively on that side of the old priest's writings which bore the stamp of his age—she was not very keenly alive to the timelessness of his soul.

There were one or two passages that recurred to Paul, and

he tried to find them. One about a boy's voice that Stolz had heard singing in a Spanish cathedral, and he compares this child's voice to a dewdrop: no sooner is it fully formed than it is doomed to perish. And another place, something about the transitoriness of beauty—youthful beauty, and the loftiest human beauty, that which may glorify a corpse in the brief respite between the hour of death and corruption.

Roy came over to him with the big book he had been turning over: "Where's this, I say?"

It was a big German work with reproductions of photographic views. The picture Roy pointed to was of a road running through a desolate plain. A gigantic crucifix reared itself in solitude against the sky, which was full of bright clouds. It was a splendid photograph.

"Wegkreuz bei Dachau in Oberbayern," Paul found in the index. "That's in South Germany."

"I thought it was in Judæa, I did," said Roy in a hushed voice. "Have you been there?"

"No, I'm sorry to say; I've never been in South Germany."

"When I'm grown up I mean to go everywhere."

"Well, it wouldn't be bad, if one could do that," said Paul.

"And then I shall learn to play," said Roy. "Can you play?" he nodded in the direction of the piano.

"A little. Nothing to boast of, but—"

"Do play, won't you?"

Paul laughed.—How is it one is always so flattered when a child asks one to do anything? He went over to the piano, rummaged in the music-stand and came across some sheets of manuscript. It was something of Sigmund's—an Elegy.

His interest grew as he got into the piece—there was a section which was very fine—some beautiful modulations—

"I say, mother, do you know when he did this? I've never seen it before that I remember."

"No, it's a thing he composed last autumn."

Roy had stood by staring intently at Paul's hands:

"It looks pretty difficult. But I'm sure I could learn."

Hans Selmer came in; he had taken the last train. He greeted Lucy and Roy without a sign of surprise. But soon after Lucy began to talk about getting home. Hans telephoned for a sledge for her, and Lucy woke Eva Marie, who was lying asleep on the sofa, and put on her things.

They had seen her safely off, and Julie proposed a whisky and soda before her sons went to bed.

Paul looked at his watch: "Thanks, not for me, mother."

"You don't mean to say you're going up by the six o'clock tomorrow? After such a late night—"

"Yes, but you need only let me have the alarm clock in my room. I can come out again in the middle of the day and talk over what we didn't have a chance of discussing this evening."

On Ash Wednesday he had always been to church, every year since he was received. He would not miss this solemn opening of the fast; together with both his children he had gone up and received the sign of the cross in ashes on his forehead: *Memento, homo, quia pulvis es, et in pulverem reverteris.* Helge would be waiting for him in church tomorrow, and Sunnie would be sure they were there, when she went up to the altar-rails in the chapel where she was.

"That boy of hers," said Hans Selmer, as he mixed himself a drink, "he'll grow into a fine Bolshevik!"

"Yes—he's pretty well bound to," said Paul. "Unless they've got control here by that time. Then he's bound to be something else."

Chapter Four

I T SO HAPPENED THAT PAUL DID NOT GO OUT TO LINLÖKKA
again till Thursday. Hans had persuaded their mother to
take a couple of weeks at Holmenkollen; she left for town
just after midday, and the sons went back to the house; Paul
had promised to see to one or two little things that had gone
wrong with the bath.

Fröken Alsaker was to have been with Lucy that evening,
but had had a telephone message: Fru Lövstö could not come to
the shop today, her boy was ill. When Paul had finished his
plumber's job he rang up the Aamots to hear how Roy was.

He had been so poorly on Tuesday night, after they came
home from Linlökka, said Lucy; and when she returned from
town on Wednesday evening he was so exhausted with sickness
and fever that today she felt she couldn't leave him. "Fru Aamot
would be sure to give him a look now and again, but still it's
so slow for him. But I say"—she hesitated—"I suppose you
haven't time to look in for a bit?—It's so depressing," she
added, as he did not answer at once, "I'm so frightened about
Roy and have to sit here all alone with nothing else to think
about—"

When too late Paul regretted having said yes. After all he
had never meant that they should meet like this every day almost. It wasn't even fair to Björg, who sat at home at Berven
without so much as a suspicion that his first love had cropped up
again in his life in this way. And he had always been annoyed
with Lucy for trying to force candy and chocolate on him to

386

take to Helge at the Institute—

Her little sitting-room turned out quite comfortable by daylight—with a sloping ceiling and a door to a little balcony. The flat was a sort of half-story forming the upper part of one of these new little villas. Presumably there was a bedroom at one end and a kitchen with an electric cooker at the other.

She had served coffee on a little table in front of the sofa in the corner:

"It was so nice of you to come! I've wished so much all the time that you could have been here just once—so that you could see what my home was like. I'm glad you've seen my children—

"But perhaps it was wrong of me to ask you?" she asked timidly. "You look as if you were annoyed—?"

"I? No, far from it."

Roy was asleep, and Eva was out on her skis. Eva, she had so many little friends out here—

Outside the sky was a pale blue with mother-of-pearl clouds edged with gold from the setting sun. In the big field over towards the forest and Linlökka a faint greyish pink light fell on the snow, which was now giving way—there had been a slight thaw during the day and outside on the balcony a few drops fell at long intervals.

When there was no more to be said about Roy's illness he found it difficult to hit upon anything they could talk about. It struck him that any topic might lead round to things which were best left undisturbed.

His eye fell on a little painting that hung on the wall opposite and he went up to look at it:

"But, Lucy, this is a perfectly charming picture you have here—" It was a study by Jörgen Sörensen, a view of Vestre Aker in spring.

"Yes, isn't it pretty?" She was pleased. "I bought it one time when I was in Oslo, and I was so fond of it that I took it away in the bottom of my trunk when we had to leave Bergen. I thought sometimes whether I should sell it, but I didn't know if it was worth anything—Jörgen Sörensen, is that a well-known artist? But I thought it was so pretty—and then it shows Sogns-vei, you know, and I remembered those old oak-trees so well. It was you who told me they were oak-trees."

Paul was annoyed to find himself turning red and put his face close against the picture.

"Paul—will you have it?" she asked suddenly. "I should so awfully like to give it you. Now that you've done so much for me—"

"No, Lucy, you mustn't do that. You can guess I don't want you to part with anything you have left." What the devil was happening to him today?—but the whole situation here was so topsy-turvy.

Lucy said in a low voice:

"It's so awkward for me, don't you see—I do nothing but take and take from you Paul, and I know very well I'll never be able to give you anything in return—"

She turned crimson under her powder, and then he blushed too, and was furious with himself and with her for it.

"I read a book while we were living at Berkeley Hill," she said, lowering her voice again. "It was about a lady—well, she wasn't altogether straight, you understand—but she'd been forced to accept help from a friend of hers, and then she thought it was mean to accept anything from a man and not give him something in return."

Yes, you'd like me to believe that, he thought angrily. I dare say I read that kind of nonsense too, in days when I was green enough to think it rather fine in its way. He'd have to see about getting out of this, before things got utterly idiotic—

Lucy said, in a trembling voice:

"When I read that I thought to myself that I had really thought the same, only I've never been able to express myself so well."

Paul waited a moment:

"Do you mind if I smoke?" He lit a cigarette and extin-

388

guished the match in his coffee-cup before replying:

"You mustn't think like that, Lucy. Good heavens, what would the world be like if one person couldn't help another without demanding a return? Or if there should be nothing in the world which could not be used in payment."

She bowed her head, her hands lay loose in her lap. The smooth light collar that was turned over her black dress made her look younger. The light was fading outside and great clouds had gathered and blotted out the last of the sunset. Against the darkening square of the window he saw the fine shape of her lowered head and the line of the neck passing into that of the back.

"No—I'll have to go soon—"

"You won't have any more coffee?" She got up and lit the lamp over the round table in the middle of the room. "I shall have to see about doing some work—you'll excuse me—"

She took a big basket of linen and put it on the table before her, sat down and fumbled for something. It was a huge pair of tortoise-shell spectacles—

"Why but, Lucy!" he exclaimed involuntarily, between laughter and dismay.

"Do you think they're so ugly on me?" she asked apprehensively. "I can't see to sew very well by candlelight now," she murmured, taking off her glasses. Then she threaded a needle, took up a white garment, a boy's shirt, and began to sew.

Paul sat still; he could not take his eyes off her. It went to his heart, like a little twinge at every breath he drew—how terribly well he knew every single one of those movements of hers. The way she held her work, and the way she plied her hand with the needle, and a little, constantly recurring movement of the lips, and every line of her body as she sat thus—

It was as though all the intervening time vanished like smoke in some perfectly insane way, leaving as the only reality himself sitting here once more with her in this cosy little room, she with her work under the lamp, he in the shadow looking at her—

He had never watched any other woman sewing. He had a kind of vague impression of his mother thus engaged. If his life were at stake he couldn't say how Björg looked when she was sewing.

But Lucy—it was as though he had never done anything else when he was with her but take her and make her his own. From their blindest, most ardent moments to the most peaceful and empty hours when he followed all her movements almost unconsciously, as she walked and stood and sat and busied herself with little everyday things—it had always been the same, his passion which held her, receded a little and came again like the beat of waves on a beach.

The fine rounding of her head and the lovely arch of the neck. The weak, undecided profile; the mouth with lips tightly closed, moving very slightly without a sound. The forward drop of the shoulders was so supple, and the upper arms pressed the bosom slightly so that it became a nest. Her whole body was held in a stooping position, as though sheltering her lap. The whole woman was silently eloquent of the knowledge that was hers—

—It's no use. It's no use trying to fight against it—there is no escaping what is to come upon us. Misfortune, degradation, all evil lies in wait for us, and it's no use trying to resist life. You wouldn't listen to me when I said so—well, have you come to feel it now? The only sure thing is the happiness that you find close beside me. Wasn't it good when I held you in my embrace? Then we cheated misfortune so long as we hid from the giant with no heart in his body. Do you believe me now—have you learnt that I was right?—

But this is sheer madness—. Here I sit, and the old feeling wakens in my blood and in my body—and I'm getting mad for her. And I fancy I love her again—that I love her still—

"I really must be going." He looked at his watch. "I have to catch the half-past seven train to town."

390

But the blood throbbed in his ears, and when he got up he thought with a sweet sense of powerlessness that Lucy must surely guess how it was with him.

"Well, thanks for coming." Lucy gave him her hand—he let go of it quickly. God in heaven—he felt quite giddy, it was all he could do not to take her in his arms and kiss her.

Going out of the flat she took a shawl and wrapped it about her:

"I'll go down with you. I must call in Eva Marie at once—it'll soon be dark."

She switched on the staircase lamp, which gave enough light in the little hall below to turn the glass panels of the front door a deep, pure violet.

"Fancy, I believe it's beginning to snow again," said Lucy.

"Lucy." His heart was hammering terrifically. He knew he ought not to ask it; he flung all his resolutions to the winds. "*Why* did you do it? Why did you break off—disappear—?"

"Don't you know—?"

She stood a few steps from him on the little dimly lighted staircase—to his agitated senses she was like a pillar, her pale face a mask of unfathomable, mysterious sorrow.

"I know nothing at all." He shook his head.

"Has Hans never told you anything?"

"Hans?" Instantly he remembered his brother's face that day at the station, the blush that passed over it, the look of embarrassment—and a thought which had then tried to work its way to the surface of his mind, but had been forced back again—. And he felt he was suffocating—

"No. Did *he* know anything?"

"Yes, I should think he did. For he came to see me one day, and then he discovered it—that I was ill. I don't know if you remember, I had such frightful bronchitis the last autumn before you went to Trondhjem. It got a little better in the summer. But then next winter, just after new year, I began to spit blood, but I'd been coughing a long time. I got pretty frightened, you can guess, and I made up my mind to go to a doctor—"

Paul stared at her. A slight spasm passed over Lucy's face:

"Well, then there was a Saturday, you see, Hans was to call for me at Fru Skaaning's and we were to go out together to Linlökka. But in the morning I was so bad I couldn't get up and go to the shop. And when Hans came at midday I must have dozed off for a bit, because I hadn't time to say 'come in' before he opened the door, and so he caught sight of my handkerchief before I could put it away, and there was blood on my pillow too—it was the first time it had come up all blood—"

"Jesus—" he whispered.

"Well, then Hans got frightened, and he said I must go to a doctor straight away. I asked if he couldn't examine me, but he said no, I must certainly go to a qualified doctor, and I'd have to go to a sanatorium, he said, and I must write and tell you about it. Then I asked him if there could be any danger in it for you, and he said yes, it wouldn't do for us to be married until I got well again, I might infect you, and if I got in the family way it would be frightfully dangerous for me afterwards, and the child might get tuberculosis too.

"And then it didn't seem as if it was any use to go on thinking about anything. I thought maybe you weren't so fond of me any more either—your letters didn't seem so loving somehow, and you'd made so many friends up there that I didn't know. And I knew you wanted us to live together properly when we were married, and have children. And instead of that I should be obliged to tell you that I had to go to a sanatorium, and you'd have to stand the expense of that and be obliged to go on waiting several years more maybe.—And when you'd thrown away all your youth for my sake, and all you'd get for it would be illness and misery and poor miserable children.—No, then I thought it would be better if I made an end of it—"

"O God! Oh, why didn't you tell me!"

"No—I knew you'd only have said we should wait, and I
392

must go to a sanatorium, and we should get married all the same in the end. I knew what you were like—

"All the same though—sometimes I would get thinking that maybe you'd end by getting tired, if you had to wait so long. You were only human after all. But then I thought that—. Then I'd rather do it myself—"

Outside the snow was now falling fast—great wet flakes dashed against the glass of the door. Paul had turned away and stood looking out—he rested his forehead against the glass a moment:

"What you must have gone through! And I knew nothing, nothing!"

"I did think maybe I'd be able to tell you—when you were in town for Sif's wedding. But then, you know, we went home to my place—and so I didn't manage to tell you you mustn't touch me. And afterwards I was so terribly afraid that now you might get consumption too—. And I thought then I'd never get myself to tell you—"

"Was that why you took—him, the other one?"

Lucy did not answer.

"But that was just the same, Lucy? You might have infected him. And you had a child by him pretty soon after—"

"No, but I wasn't fond of him, you see. And when he'd been running after me for half a year, though he knew very well I was engaged to someone else. So I thought he didn't deserve anything better. And when I was going to have Gunnar I thought I shouldn't come to care much for a child I had by Herman. But when I'd got him, you know, then it was different. I did go to the sanatorium after that though, and then I was in the country for some time with a cousin of Herman's. They were really awfully kind—I got pretty fond of Herman too that time.

"But you know, what first made me take him was that I thought I couldn't be going about Oslo and keep on at the shop and risk meeting your step-mother and your father and all of you in the street or anywhere, when it was all over between you and me. I didn't feel equal to that. And so when Herman absolutely would have me at any price—"

Paul stood still and looked at her, and with the corner of his eye he saw the whirling snow outside and had a feeling that it was drifting upwards.

"But that Hans never said anything," said Lucy. "I do think he might have done that. I really thought he had.

"Because then I don't know what you can have thought about me." She bit her under-lip, her face quivered on the verge of tears. "You must have thought I was a regular good-for-nothing girl."

He threw his arms round her, pressed her to him and kissed the trembling mouth which opened as she wept. Oh—this was Lucy—at last, at last he had her in his arms again, he was kissing Lucy. He hid her head against his breast and bent it back again and kissed her on the mouth and on the eyes and the cold cheeks. They were so strangely sleek and woolly from the powder she had had on them—

"O Lucy, Lucy—oh, if only you had told me—"

"Ah, if I'd only known I was going to get well again," she whispered. "But anyhow I'm glad you know now. That it wasn't because I'd left off being fond of you—

"So you don't despise me any longer, Paul? Because you did, didn't you?"

"No, Lucy, I love you."

He took both her hands—they were cold as ice; she was standing here in the passage with only that little shawl over her. Then he kissed her hands and held them to his face a moment. "I'm glad you told me at last. Oh, but if I'd *known*—"

He drew her to him again.

"Must you go?" she whispered when her lips were free.

"Yes.—O Lucy—" then he released her and went.

He hurried along the road, and when he had gone a little way he heard her voice calling through the driving snow: "Eva—you're to come in now, Eva Marie—"

THE snowstorm stopped almost as suddenly as it had begun; it had left off snowing altogether as he came into the yard at Linlökka. The lamps were alight both over the front door and on the wall of the shed, and Hans Selmer was engaged in clearing a pathway between them. It affected Paul in a curious way—just as if he had surprised his brother performing some penitential exercise: it had always been left to himself or Sigmund to do jobs of this kind; Hans had always skunked out of lending a hand at any practical work. And here he was doing it, in his town clothes.

"Well, now it's all we shall do to catch the train," said the doctor. He threw the broom and snow shovel inside the door of the shed. "Bring down my case, will you—I believe I left it on the table in the boys' room—"

They had to run most of the way to the station.

"We shouldn't have caught it after all, if it hadn't been late," said Hans contentedly, as the brothers got into an empty second-class carriage just as the train started with a jerk.

"You won't come out to the Evalds' then?—I'm sure they'd be pleased if you would."

"No, I can't. I don't want to miss the St. Joseph's Society—it's the first meeting in Lent."

"No, no," said Hans, opening a review he had taken out of his case.

Paul sat with the last number of *Credo* before him, trying to take in what he read. Then he put down the magazine:

"I say. I went to see Lucy this afternoon."

"I'm sure you did. Well, you know best what you're doing. Otherwise I should have said—don't you think that kind of thing may land you in a lot of unpleasantness?"

"She told me something I'd never had a suspicion of before. That when she broke off with me her lungs were attacked. And that you knew it. You went up to see her, she said, one day when she was in bed and had had a hæmorrhage—"

"Yes, that's quite correct. I had the devil's own job with

395

her—I tried to make her go to a doctor straight away."

"I really think I ought to have been informed," said Paul.

Hans Selmer made a gesture of impatience—flung his review into the corner of the seat.

"She kicked up such a row that the end of it was she got me to promise I wouldn't say a word to anyone—for the time being anyway. I was awfully cut up about it, as you can guess— for your sake and for hers. It seemed such a pity—I was very fond of Lucy—we all were. While all the time we were furiously annoyed with her. She was enough to provoke a saint.

"At first she couldn't understand why I wouldn't examine her. You know, she was just the kind that thinks any medical student's as good as a qualified doctor, and when it comes to a point they'll trust a quack as likely as not. I have a strong suspicion too that she'd been to some of these natural healers and wise women, but she cried and took her oath she hadn't. But I offered to take her to Professor Hvasser, and I'd got permission to bring her after his consulting hours. We were to meet there the first time, and I sat and waited for her for two hours; the one who didn't come was Lucy. The second time she was out when I called to fetch her—she'd wandered about the streets and sat and howled up at Vestre Akers cemetery and didn't come home to her room before twelve o'clock at night. Yes, I was sitting there, so I know. Then she declared she was better, said she hadn't had any more hæmorrhages—and when I talked about getting her examined she shrank up—just like some cold, tough, naked snail when you touch it.—Yes, that was a business! And I was young and foolish and in a fearful stew on both your account and hers."

"But how was it you said nothing that day I met you outside the station?"

"Tut!—There was a minute or two before your train went and dogs making a shindy and people we knew hailing us every moment. No, but I did begin a letter to you. But as you know, I've never been much of a hand at writing. So before I'd finished

composing that epistle to you I got an absolutely deranged letter from her in which she told me she had married this Lövstö
fellow. And then I didn't see what use it would serve if I wrote
and told you all this after the event."

I should never have married Björg. But he couldn't say
that.

"Nor did I know whether it was this that made her break
it off. It was a good while after. The end of February or beginning of March it was when I went to see her, the day before the
school ski-ing match on Kastrud's hill; that was why I had to
go home, I'd promised to be umpire. As I told you, she declared
she hadn't spat blood since that time.

"And that business with Lövstö had been going on a good
while. Though to begin with she wouldn't have anything to do
with him—she rang me up several times, and I had to see her
home from the shop, because this fellow was in the offing and
she was afraid of him. My word yes, what a hell of a time I
had!"

"Some of you ought to have let me know about it," said
Paul.

"Yes, that would have been the only right thing to do, of
course. But I suppose I thought, afterwards at any rate, that
perhaps it was just as well it turned out as it did. I knew of
course that you were awfully fond of her. There was something
about her that made one that. But Lord save us, what an impossible creature she was all the time, you couldn't talk sense to
her."

"But didn't mother know anything about it?"

"Does any of us ever know what mother knows? But of
course it's unthinkable that she shouldn't have guessed something. But presumably what was most in her mind was that you
might be infected with tuberculosis."

"You want to go to Akers-vei, don't you?" asked Hans, as
they got into the taxi.

397

"No, thanks; will you tell him to put me down at the printing works. I want to look in at the office."

BUT when he had let himself into the office he stood still inside the door without turning on the light. He stood listening to the stillness all over the big building; in the daytime the whole place resounded with the droning from the machine rooms—a steady rhythmical hum as an undertone to the rattling of hoists and lorries in the yard and the noise of the street and the shrieking of the packing-case factory opposite.

Through some association of ideas he came to think of a film Björg and he had seen the other day. Grey and spectral pictures of a man with madness and terror in his eyes; he had hidden himself in an elevator shaft, stood flat against the wall, while the men who were after him tore along the corridor of a big office building. Then the counterbalance behind him began to move up—the elevator was coming down.—Disgusting, he had thought it.

Paul went over to the window to pull down the blind. Lights were still burning in one or two windows of the packing case factory. It was quiet in the street too, but round the corner the traffic still rumbled with a noise that rose and fell rhythmically as the street-cars clanked past, ringing their gongs at the crossing.

It was late to go to the St. Joseph's Society now. But he knew all the time that he didn't mean to go. He simply could not face sitting there among a lot of perfect strangers who were in a good humour, chatting and laughing at Father Auberive every time he said something funny intentionally or unintentionally. They were strangers—or rather, it was he who suddenly felt that this evening he would be a stranger among them. There were men he liked and men he didn't like, there were Norwegians and foreigners and half-foreigners, men from widely different classes and surroundings, good and moderate and not particularly good Catholics—so far as such things are within human knowledge. Now he saw, as though an uncannily bright light were thrown upon it, how unessential all these differences had been compared with what brought them together: the faith, the Church, Christ. In any case they all *submitted* to be in the hands of God, they accepted His bread, they prayed for His spirit. It was really true that the faith made them all something else, besides what each of them was in himself, a man with his own defects and limitations and good qualities and absurdities—and this something else was what was essential in all of them. It was so real that he shuddered at seeing it now, that they actually were parts of a unity, cells in a mystic body— how mystic he had never come near guessing till now, when he felt as though half-buried strata of his mind had been suddenly exposed by a convulsion, instincts and feelings belonging to a half-forgotten past rose up and protested—he would not be such a part, he would claim to be sufficient to himself and sufficient to another human being.

Compared with this it was a small matter that they reacted differently to that Will—grace—which flowed towards them from the primeval depths of existence. That one man accepted it, feelingly, intently, full of longing and affection, while others let themselves be carried along, resisting, yielding light-heartedly to every temptation, but still hanging on. He recognized, with a clearness that was almost intolerable, what the Church was—an organism with morbid and healthy cells animated by the same mysterious common life, either powerful or weak; but it made all the difference between life and death whether one took one's part or dropped out. It was the same difference as it makes in an army—of good soldiers and splendid soldiers and grousers and skulkers—whether one does one's duty or is already a deserter in one's inmost secret intention. It is the same as feeling solidarity with one's nation—the leaders, the common people, those who work and those who shirk—or planning one's flight to a foreign country, under an assumed name.

Rubbish, I haven't done that at all. I don't intend anything of the sort. Only I can't help what I *feel*—a homesickness for a time when I believed the world to be merely what I could perceive with my senses. And my own mind, which saw what I saw with my eyes and felt what I felt with my senses, was the only mind of which I could know anything. I believed that every man was the centre of the world for himself—even when he devoted himself with all his being and all his power to a cause, to another person, to all men, the only thing that every one of us could be certain of was that I am I. And that two of these I's could meet, as a fusion of two cells, become a union of two within the same many-coloured world-integument, that was the marvel. But I did not believe in any mind which encompassed everything and watched over what we do and how we are drift-ing, towards or away from a place which is appointed for us. I believed every human being was a world to himself. I did not know there was a God.

But, my God, this is only a *feeling*. I know it is *not* so. Faith, in the sense in which faith is certainty, had never been so strong with him as now, when he wished he could fly back to the ignorance of his youth and take Lucy with him and live with her in his old world of fiction and illusion within the many-coloured shell of the whole beautiful world of the senses.

He flung his cap and gloves on to the window-ledge, pulled down the blind and switched on the lamp on his desk. He took out of his case the papers which his mother had signed; some were to be posted and some put away in the safe. But after that he sat still with his overcoat on, without the energy to go and fetch envelopes.

All at once the faint odour of perfume penetrated to his consciousness—it hung about his coat and his hands. He had grown so accustomed to her using this scent that he no longer found it unpleasant—he really liked it, in fact.

It was utterly incomprehensible—already as unreal as something he had dreamt. That he had been sitting with Lucy in

400

her little room—he recalled her face in the lamp-light as she took off her spectacles with a rapid, submissive gesture, because he did not like them. It seemed to say that she was so entirely his—and the old love, the old, eager, exuberant love welled up from the depths of his being and drowned all thoughts and all consciousness but this, that there sat Lucy and that she was *his*, and why should he do anything but take her.—And when he thought back on it now, the old eager desire rose up in mind and senses and filled him once more.

—It must, it *must* not be true that they had misunderstood one another so terribly, and had so little confidence in one another that she dared not tell him what was wrong with her, and he had believed her to be one of those who could not remember a man when she no longer saw him and felt his arms around her. It must not be true that she had suffered so miserably and he had had not the slightest inkling of it—and they had gone their different ways and acted foolishly and tried to carry it off as though it were nothing to worry about that they had lost each other. O beloved! how you must have suffered—but you ought to know how it was with me.—I dared not confess it even to myself, I was fool enough to imagine I should be no real man if I allowed myself to grieve for a thing like that. It was just as though all colours were a little faded and life itself had lost its savour, when you were gone. Oh, if you had only known how fond I was of you. Then you would not have done it.

But ptt! twenty years, what's that, when it wasn't true after all that we didn't care for each other? We have been so wickedly stupid, but now I have held you in my arms again and felt once more your dear face against my cheeks and your strange, delicious kisses—

Paul hid his face in his hands. But this was sheer, downright, unadulterated madness. But it was more than he could bear, when he thought of what she must have gone through that time. And he had known nothing. And the others, who told him nothing! Her ineptitude, oh, it had brought him to the point of

401

fury many a time. And her love had been so inconceivable—
her generous abandonment like an ocean into which he sank. It
had been strong enough to brace her to do what she did for his
sake—and she had been stupid enough to think it was best for
him that she did it!

It was fearfully hot in here, Paul felt, and discovered that
he was still sitting with his overcoat on. He got up and took it
off, unlocked the safe and put away the papers that were to
go there, set to work putting the rest into envelopes. Then he
carried them out and laid them in the basket on Fröken Alsaker's desk.

—But there was nothing new in it—there was no sense in
his carrying on as if he had discovered for the first time that
people can ruin their whole lives like this, simply because they
haven't more sense. Simply because they are no better—the one
dare not think well enough of the other, dare not expect too
much of a fellow-creature. Love, love to the utmost of one's
power, that one can do, or cannot help doing; but whether one
can depend upon the loved one is a thing one never knows. Now
he was wild because Lucy had not ventured to trust in him more
implicitly—but God! what had he not thought of her when she
disappeared like that. No, not that either, for God knew, somewhere in his soul a kind of belief had always lain concealed—
that perhaps he did Lucy wrong, if he had known all. But all
the same, he had harboured the other thoughts too—and what
had he not believed, no, not believed either, but thought, the
moment she named Hans—

It was precisely that which was so terrible—that we never
know: we choose to believe in another person, but we *know* all
the time that it is hazardous to do so. Or we choose not to believe;
but then we know that perhaps we are wronging a fellow-
creature. Greater certainty than this can never be ours.

But he had known that, at least since he began to grow up.
And it had come like a deliverance to accept the explanation
which the faith gives of human nature: it is something marvel-

lous which has been broken by a fall, a growth with irrepress-
ible upward tendency; its nature is to expand and blossom like
a plant, but the seed itself is infected with mildew. It is true
that men are equal and men are brothers—we are all the exiled
children of Eve and are all born with the taint of her womb.
Like the plants in a garden which has once been invaded by
blight: it does not prevent them all springing up from the soil
as luxuriantly and beautifully as ever year by year; the first
little white specks on the leaves have no very dangerous look,
the first roses burst out apparently perfect and healthy, but the
blight spreads, thrives as the plants thrive, till everything is
mouldy and mildewed; at last the buds themselves are rusted
and drop off dead.

But it was nevertheless an explanation which restored
man's honour—he can no more refrain from striving to grow
than he can free himself from the taint which clings to all that
is human and grows with all human growth. All good will falls
short of its aim, but it renews itself. Every human enterprise
ends worse than it began, but the world is always full of good
beginnings. But it is not the earth that is an odious trap from
which no one can escape with his life—the dogma of the Fall
restores its honour to the earth, and it is not unworthy to receive again the King of honour. The first of our race crept away
and hid themselves from Him under the bushes, when He walked
in the garden one evening in the beginning of time. But He has
returned to the garden, and the children of men, who meet Him
there in the dawning, take Him to be the gardener, as Magdalen
did.

Paul hid his face in his hands again.

Lord Jesus—I believe this. Thou knowest that I believe it
and Thou seest that I wish I did not believe it. It is Thy truth
that I rebel against—and it is my own untruths that I wish I could
return to. I have known Thee for all these years, I have believed in Thee and prayed to Thee and accepted Thy gifts. I
imagined that at last I had acquired a *little* love for Thee, a

little joy when I was able to overcome a difficulty for Thy sake. I believed that I had really come to hate and fear evil, not because I know that I myself must expiate my sins in this life and after death, but because evil mars that which Thou hast created, and because sin is sin against Thee and crucifies Thee and thrusts the sword into the heart of Mary, who does not share our guilt.

O Mary, conceived without sin—thou knowest that my desire is to be able to persuade myself that we are all immaculately conceived. So that every man answers for himself and the Devil can take the hindmost—and I have the right to hate and despise all who do what I think is despicable, and the right to be sufficient to myself and sufficient to the one I love. Holy Mary, Mother of God—thou couldst have parted company with all the rest of us, if thou hadst wished, but hast not done so—pray for us!

There is nothing left of my faith but a refractory conviction that it is true, and I would wish it were not so. The Devil does as much as this—believing without love, without joy. As I believe now, so shall all Thine enemies believe one day—

Jesus, Jesus—I believe that Thine is all power in heaven and on earth. I know that we are all in Thy hands. Have mercy upon me, that I may be able to love Thy hands—not because they are almighty, but for the marks of the wounds in them.

Paul got up, looked at his watch. If he went home to Schwensens-gate now, they would still be up, and he could not avoid going in and taking coffee with them. Wilfrid would give him an account of the meeting—and then it would end in his talking about Emanuel.

It had given him a shock to see how Wilfrid and Clara had taken the boy's death. Not a complaint had passed their lips, when once it was all over. But Fru Clara's eyes filled every moment, and Wilfrid's face grew greyer and sharper every hour, while the body was lying at home—dressed as for a children's party in a suit of white silk with new white shoes on the feet;

they had given him a big wreath of snowdrops on his head. The candles round the coffin flickered and flickered with the continual opening of the doors—there was a succession of grown-up people and children who came to kneel for a while at the priedieu by the feet of the innocent child.

It had seemed to him that the liturgy for the death of young children makes hard demands of the parents. Nothing but candles, flowers, songs of praise. It is a hard thing to ask of a couple who have lost their only child, to take part in a song of thanksgiving to God, for raising up the poor man out of the mire and setting him among the princes of His people, for making the childless woman to dwell in His house as a happy mother of sons.—Now, when he thought of Lucy's two children, he understood it better.

When they said the three Paternosters at the grave—one for the dead child's relatives, one for the souls of all those buried in this churchyard, and one for that person among those present who was next to die—he had thought that perhaps the last prayer was for Clara Gotaas. She looked as if she could not bear much more.

But now she nodded agreement when Wilfrid talked of their adopting one or two children.

Roy, that would have been the worst that could happen.

For of course, those moments of aberration this afternoon —they were only a mirage which could not last. Even if he had not perceived subconsciously that it was so, they would none the less have fallen under the law.

Nothing of what had happened to them in twenty years could be undone. He could not jump back through time and place himself at her side in that unlucky spring. He could never relieve her of the burdens under which she had then struggled: the terror of death, the hope that she might escape for his sake, the convulsions of disgust and horror that she *must* have gone through before she prevailed on herself to go with that man— of whom, by the way, she had made use with a cynicism so grim that he was forced to admit he did not understand it.

"Irritating," Hans had called her. Well, no doubt the others had felt it vaguely as something irritating. The brutality, the suspiciousness, that had lain like streaks of rock in the soft mould of her patient spirit. Now he remembered a kind of vision which had come over him at times, when he was about to fall asleep and she slept already in his arm. He thought they were in a little open valley flanked by long slopes which ended in a low wooded crest; there was a little lake which mirrored the sky, and a silent, placid stream made its way through the valley. Sleep came upon him like a twilight which turned the green meadows grey and changed the reflection in the water from day to night, and her breathing against his shoulder was the faint sound in the rushes, and the last gleam of consciousness in him was as it were the starlight in the depths of the lake. He and Lucy were in this valley, but at the same time they were in some way the landscape itself.

But just as he felt the wonderful peace that there was in her—a peace which scarcely had anything human in it, but was more like the power that forests and plains and the twilight have over one's mind—he ran up against her little furtive distrust of people, her patience with the rascally side of life, her crude indifference to all that was strange to her. His youth tore itself raw on this, well cared for as his spiritual skin had become under his mother's health and cleanliness morality. But if he pleaded with her, trying to get her away from all this, Lucy looked at him with a trace of contempt in her compassionate smile. It was she who knew how the earth was accursed for men's sake, and he was an inexperienced boy who said Paradise be hanged! I've only got to give it a good pull and I'll open that gate right enough.

But that was twenty years ago. And even if he had not arrived at the faith which he now held, he could never have preserved the simple-mindedness of his youth all this time.

Even if he had not been a Catholic, he would surely have

come to the conclusion, when he had got over the first shock of seeing this resurrection of a dead and buried love—that after all he could not very well get a divorce and marry Fru Lövstö.

He would no doubt have thought of it—of doing what he had considered discreditable and lamentable when Henrik did it. He too would have made the excuse that Björg had first been unfaithful to him. Years after he had said that they must keep together in spite of it.

But he had Sunnie and Helge. And she had had her Lövstö; it was no very attractive thought to take a wife after Herr Lövstö. But there is a nasty word, "protector"—a disgusting position, that of the self-supporting divorced wife who has a "friend." God help him, in future he would be able to understand that even for this state of things a human explanation can be found, an excuse.

What cannot be excused—! No doubt he too could have got his conscience to listen to excuses. In his and her case the circumstances were so extraordinary. Probably all circumstances are extraordinary to those who are involved in them.

Only with regard to Roy he would never have been able to silence his conscience. To disgrace his mother in the eyes of a boy—for that there could be no forgiveness. Though he had known men who seemed to think it might be excused. But if they said that in good faith, he at any rate did not understand them.

He noticed he was hungry and remembered he had had no supper. It was too late now to go out and get anything. Besides, he could not have faced it anyhow—he had a queerly definite feeling that this night he was to be alone and was to go through something. But he had to go and get a drink of water.

The tap was out in the corridor. A light was burning over the sink. As he stood there he caught a glimpse of something moving on the floor at the far end of the passage. Ass! he had given a start, and it was only a cat. It came leaping towards him with the faintest sound of its little paws; curled round and round his legs and rubbed its head against his boots, with

arched back and tail straight in the air. "Hullo, puss—where
do you come from?—poor puss!"

The cat slipped into the office with him. And when he
knelt again before the old sofa, the cat jumped up, scratching
the leather with its claws; it stole in between his arms, rubbed
its head against his collar and his face, purring loudly.

It was a little tabby with a dirty white chest and white
paws. Its ears were full of white hairs inside. The little animal's
ear was so marvellously beautiful, it was alive.

In this whole building, where he was the only human being
tonight, there was nothing that was not lifeless; machinery
everywhere, heating apparatus, the staring, motionless electric
light, the mountains and bales of ice-cold paper in the ware-
house, everything was removed by process after process from all
life and all organic beginnings. Only this dirty little cat lay
here, moving its tail in little jerks and tingling with life in every
hair.

And in some way or other the contact with this living
creature awoke all the feeling of rebellion and longing within
him again. It *should* be as he had once believed, that men were
own brothers to the animals, could divest themselves of all
that distinguished them as of a garment and take up their abode,
naked, carefree and sinless, in forest and lake, as happy, innocent animals. Live, only so long as the blood-stream pulses
through the body, be happy when one is in sound health and all
one's senses are awake and keen and respond to the light and
the smell of the earth and the woods and the good scent of
lichen on sun-baked rock and the caress of wind and water on
the naked skin—knowing nothing better than the earth and
knowing no evil of it—and believing that one can possess and
embrace all this in another human being.

The earth and a life which is all our own as long as it lasts,
and is over when one dies, going out like a candle.

He thought he could never have seen till now what was im-
plied in the eternal rebellion against God. It was not men's ever-

lasting protest, renewed a thousand times daily, against man proposing and God disposing. He now looked down into the very foundation which lay below this—we wish to be rid of God, we refuse to hear anything of one who has created us. We claim to know nothing and to be able to exercise our imagination freely concerning the unknown island in space on which we are stranded; we have come to a no man's land from no one knows where, and no one knows that we are here. We wish to ask, but not to receive an answer, to invent and to believe that as we invent, so shall it be. It will be hell; hell is where God is not. So hell must exist, God's mercy must acquiesce in the provision of an asylum for such as desire to remain for all eternity outside all order and without God above them, sufficient to themselves for ever and ever.

It would certainly be a place that would beat all the hellfire preachers could picture—a place where every man will become what he must become when he is allowed to follow his own line to the very end. And certainly he did not wish that. But here he knelt, praying God to help him, merely because he was afraid—afraid of being abandoned to himself, afraid because he was a man and no one knows what that is, if he is no longer so simple as to dare to judge other men.

But this must be to have reached bottom? Now I can understand for the first time what it means to be a sinner—!

The rest had only been child's play.

Not that one or two things hadn't seemed hard, in these last years. Teaching himself to live with Björg and never forget that she too was a human being. All the same, it had not been so insurmountably difficult to look on Björg as a Christian man should do. What paganism there was in him had never been aware of her existence.

To be sure, he had been convulsed with secret revolt at his humiliation. That word his mother had used one day—certainly it had struck home; it had struck home in such a way that nobody should ever know how he felt it. His mother should never find out that he could not forget that. Forgive her—that was not so difficult. It was always easiest to forgive his mother when she went too far. Then he seemed to feel more than ever how fond he was of her, for then he felt that her power over him extended no farther than he himself would let it.

Other people he could appear to disregard, for he had always done so. He could not become entirely insensible to gossip about himself, but he could pretend not to mind it. This was nothing new that he had been forced to learn, but an old thing that he had learnt to understand better. Nobody has such knowledge of another that it is worth worrying oneself how people judge one another. In the last instance everything is a matter between a man by himself and God.

But what that meant he saw now, and that he would not endure.

Why, good heavens, that he had kissed Lucy and told her—as was the truth—that he loved her, that was wrong naturally, but it was only like the little stone that loosens and rolls down, bringing a whole rock-slide with it—till the naked soil is exposed, that one has never seen before. The very foundation of sin: I will be my own master. I will not hear of any indebtedness. After that every man does as he pleases according to the nature he has been given. There are as many as seven deadly sins sitting in a row and waiting for a partner—

Seven ladies who may all be attractive in certain lights, but just at the moment he did not find any of them particularly tempting.

In his present overtired state his thoughts took the form of images, as when one is on the borderline between sleep and waking. He saw a stretch of muddy road with wheel-ruts and footprints, and half-trodden into the mud lay a little mirror with a celluloid frame such as is sometimes given away in a shop as an advertisement. It was shattered as though something had passed over it, and it was bloody and soiled, but the fragments reflected a glimpse of the sky. And his soul was like a child that

stood there screaming and making a fuss: it was mine, it was
mine, and it would not see the sky above it; it was merely angry
and inconsolable over the little mirror that had been broken to
pieces.

HE had fallen asleep several times as he knelt there by the sofa,
with his arms and face resting on the seat. And he had woke
again with the cold and the stiffness of his uncomfortable position, and each time he tried again to pray. But all his praying
was only like throwing sand up into the air, it fell back and
scattered over himself.

God, Thou hast really been all to me. I have believed Thee
to be my saviour and the saviour of the whole world. There was
a remedy for all the world's misery, because all was in Thy
hand. I believed in Thee in Thy church; it was the ark in which
there was a place for all that would live. When the priest raised
the bread and wine, our gifts which Thou wert to change into
Thy gift, I prayed, change me also into something which is of
Thee. When I bowed before Thyself in the Host, I thought the
whole world must end by bowing before Thee, when it learns
to know Thee. When I received Thee in the holy communion, I
prayed, remain in me and let me remain in Thee. I thought,
Thou canst not reject any man in the end, for I did not believe
that anyone who rejected Thee knew what he was doing. I
thought, there are no limits to what God can do with the world—
make it new, make it good—I believed it to be true of all who
are against Thee, that they have never known Who it is they are
against. It is true that we who call ourselves Thine have little
faith, have little love, we are not good—. We are not good, we
are sullen and slow and ungrateful and petty. We shirk our
duty, presuming that those who are filled with passion for Thee,
the saints now living and those who are dead, are the salt of the
earth and the light of the world, no man knows how much they
can do—the rest of us can surely take things a little more easily.

But that anyone could know Thee and yet be against Thee,

that I have never really believed till now.

And now everything in me is against Thee, because Thou art the truth. And a dream that I myself scarcely believed to be more than a dream, is not true; and what I myself knew to be unreal is not real; and she and I and all men are as Thou hast created us and as sin has marred us; the images we ourselves form of men who do not exist, have no existence.

Thou dost command that we deny ourselves, because we are unreal; and now I would deny Thee because Thou art real, if I could do it.

I will not submit to Thy will, because it is the only one which is a creative will. Is it *so* hard to have to submit oneself and see that we can only live and act in that which *is*—we cannot create anything which is not?

O God, O God, give me back a little love for Thee, for I cannot bear to believe in Thee, if I do not love Thee—

God knows how it is with *her*, he thought at one moment—is she awake too tonight? But if she is, she is certainly happier now than she was before she had a chance of telling the truth about *her* love.

So no doubt she wished—oh yes, he knew very well what she wished: for he had said that he loved her. So no doubt she expected him to return to her. There was nothing to be said to that; being as she was, she could hardly help thinking, why shouldn't they?

That he could not—that did not concern his quarrel with God. He had lost Lucy—there was no undoing that. There were Sunnie and Helge, there were Roy and Eva Marie—there was Björg too for that matter and the other man, Lövstö, though just at the moment he could not feel that they were very real.

It was on account of all that might have been, if only it had not been impossible, that he now felt himself ill-treated by both God and the world.

Lucy—. It seemed that the more he found out about her,

412

the more there was he did not know. She too was a mysterious thing that he must leave to God. Well, God knows how all this is going to end.

HE lay down on the sofa and spread his coat over him. It was damp and his boots were wet, so he was chilled through when the cat woke him a few hours later by jumping up on him again.

He tidied himself a little, as well as he could, brushed some cat's hairs off his clothes and let himself out.

It was still dark, there were a few stars in the little strip of sky above the street. It had snowed again during the night; here in the side street the thin covering of fresh snow lay untouched, only showing the tiny footprints of a rat under the gas-lamp. The tall, dark house-fronts were whitened with snow around the black, flush windows. And from the next street came the sounds of men at work clearing away the snow.

Paul went by the back streets. Here and there a man was about already; at long intervals one heard a solitary taxi and the rumble of a street-car. And now and again a light leapt out behind drawn blinds, where people were getting up.

In Akers-gate a few more people were on the move—they looked small and black in the broad desolation of the street. The church was not yet open. He believed there were some seats in the little summer-house behind the sacristy, but if he sat there to wait he would certainly fall asleep, and that might lead to a choice piece of scandal—pleasant for Helge, if it came to the boy's ears.

There were lights in the presbytery—they got up there at five, he knew—and lights in some of the windows of the hospital and the Institute. No doubt this was the time there was Mass for the Sisters. For a moment he had thoughts of trying to get in. But then he gave it up. Probably it was quite unusual for strangers to be present at their Mass.

He walked on up Akers-vei. The sky was turning blue be-hind the snow-decked trees of the graveyard when he reached the

413

bare stretch between the cemetery and the fields that slope down to the Akers river. The whole valley lay glittering with the thousand lights of the town; in rows and in clusters the lights spread up over the white slopes of the east side. The air was still blue with night over the city, but along the horizon the sky brightened to green while he stood and watched, and behind the dark mass of Gamle Akers church the stars were swallowed up one by one by the growing light, and the building stood out in the daylight with its brown walls and its roofs white with snow.

Again the despairing weariness came over him. If it makes not the slightest difference, whatever men may do—whether they come together or shun each other, they always carry with them the same boundless capacity for doing things, the same incapacity for attaining their desires, unless they are inhumanly easy to satisfy. The same confidence in being able to control each other, and they cannot control themselves. Never to be able to escape from God without sealing oneself up in one's own hell. Always in revolt at there being no third way—

How in the world can it have arisen, that talk about God being men's ideal? Certainly nothing of what one sees in reality points to that. A creditor rather, whom we try to forget as well as we can, and when that doesn't work any longer we try if we can cheat him or come to an arrangement—

WHEN he came down to the church again the little door in the tower was open. It looked as if there was not a soul there when he entered the nave. It was quite dark, all but the little speck of red light high up in the choir.

Paul went right up to the steps before the communion rail and knelt there.

Suddenly he became aware of the singularity of his position—all through this night he had assumed in spite of everything that he should go to communion in the morning as usual. Bitter and rebellious had been his thoughts; he had seen his own obstinacy as fragments of a broken mirror, and he himself had

not cared to pick them up. He had counted on God coming to
him after all—God might as well walk on the broken glass, God
could stoop down and pick them up for him—

It can't be pleasant to be Saviour of the world, when one
single human being raises such troublesome hindrances and still
expects to be given another trial. My God, when everything is
in Thy hands, why hast Thou voluntarily placed Thyself in
the hands of men—?

God could have forced men to walk in His ways as obediently
as the stars. But He enters the world of men, clad in the old
habiliments of Adam, and lays aside His omnipotence at the
door. The thought took his breath away. It was as though he
could *see* it: the contrast between a universe moving in constant rhythms according to eternal laws and the everlasting
lawless tumult of human wills; it was a kind of vision—a
glimpse of omnipotence ruling the cosmos and going about
begging in the throng of human souls, a beggar who asked to
be allowed to give and to deal out some of the mysterious wealth
of his own being. As when rays of sunlight suddenly break out
from under a thick bank of cloud, lighting up a whole band
of glittering points on the surface of the sea, so he saw God's
incarnation—with a world of inexhaustible mysteries in each
shining spot: the Child stood in the mother's lap and was reflected in her eyes; it was infinity sinking into humanity, but a
humanity so clear and pure that it offered no resistance to light.
But round about the two rose a crowd of faces with eyes, eyes
that were half obscure like glass paste, and eyes that were hard
and opaque like pebbles, and flint-like eyes that threw back the
light in angry glances. The Child grew to man's stature, but the
wall of faces with eyes in them grew around him. The Man lay
with his forehead on the ground in a darkening land, the rocky
walls of the grotto and the clouds above him were all faces with
eyes; the Man rose, knelt upright a moment and took the
measure of all his enemies throughout all ages. Then total darkness fell around the dark cross, and the darkness grew yet

deeper, and in an inconceivable darkness God was hidden from God—

There was a darkness in which God had forsaken God. But men He has not forsaken—

Paul lay prostrate before the communion rail. From the realm of unfathomable mysteries and from the real presence a few steps away he felt the will which closed around his will. It swept over him like a flood and he felt himself swallowed up—by that of which fire is a symbol in this world; his soul was blinded by something of which light serves as a token here on earth. It was as though a burning bush drew him into itself, closed around him, consumed him, and yet he continued to exist—then it released him again, then it was no more, but it left behind a paralysing sense of happiness.

He remained lying motionless, felt that he had grown still to the very foundation of his being. Something had collapsed within him and depths had formed in the inmost parts of his being, and there this stillness would always reign, even when mental tumult was all his consciousness could feel—

SUDDENLY the electric light leapt out all over the church and he became aware that people had come in. So he would have to go back to his usual place. But somehow it seemed beyond his power. And now he found he had been weeping, but he did not know when.

A choir-boy in a red cassock and a short white surplice came in, carrying the long pole with a coil of taper at the end which the boys called the rat's tail. With profound gravity he struggled to get the altar candles to light, and Paul followed his efforts with a kind of tension—there was one candle which simply would not burn.

Then more choir-boys came, followed by the priest, and Paul had to go back. Helge was already kneeling in their place on the bench. He glanced up at his father an instant, seemed rather surprised, but then turned his face to the altar again.

Presently, seeing that his father had no missal with him, he pushed his own worn and dirty prayer book over to Paul:

"You can borrow mine," he whispered, "if you've forgotten yours. I know it all by heart."

The book was open at the Norwegian hymns before Mass, and the organ began. Ah yes, it was the first Friday in the month, Paul remembered; that was why six candles were lighted on the altar and there was a whole flock of choristers—Mass would be sung—

He was too much agitated by what he had gone through— could not follow the Mass properly; God, I don't even know how I am to set about giving thanks for this. It was something he had neither hoped nor desired nor prayed to be given. Now that it was over he felt shy at the thought of giving thanks for it.—

My Jesus—I was willing to betray Thee. But forgive me, crush me, break me to pieces and remake me so that I may really be as Thou wilt and can really desire Thee above all else. It was the very temptation of temptations, the temptation of unreality which is far more alluring than anything else in the world—and Thou hast given me an answer to it such that I scarcely dare look up to Thee, for I know not how I am to thank Thee—

He stayed in his place when Helge went up to receive the communion. There were a great many people—three rows full —as always on the first Friday.

When they stood up for the reading of the last gospel, Paul saw that Helge had been crying.

"What is it, Helge?" he asked anxiously, as they sat down again. He had never seen the boy cry in church before, and it gave him a shock.

"I'd looked forward to going to communion with you. But you didn't go—"

"I must confess first. But surely you know, you mustn't cry for a thing like that. It means little, you know, compared

417

with what you yourself have received—"

"No, but I always look forward to it still more the days when you go up too."

People were beginning to leave the church. Sister Marie-Halvard came up and touched Paul's arm: "The prioress told me to ask you if you would come across to the Institute and have breakfast with Helge?"

"Thanks, Sister, I have to confess now. But perhaps Helge may have leave to stay here meanwhile? Will you do that, Helge, stay here and pray for me while I'm at confession?"

Helge nodded.

There were a good many waiting by the confessionals. Paul decided to enter the first that was available when his turn came and make his confession to the priest who happened to be there. What exactly he was going to say or how he was to explain what had happened, he hardly knew.

The last thing he saw, as he entered the confessional, was that Sister Marie-Halvard was kneeling by the side of Helge.

Instinctively he held back the heavy curtain far enough to be able to see the ever-burning lamp up in the choir and the golden door of the tabernacle. He kept his eyes fixed upon it and did not know who was sitting behind the grating to answer on God's behalf, when he had finished speaking.

The voice behind the grating said:

"My son, you know that Our Lord has said we must work out our salvation with fear and trembling. Those are His words to us through St. Paul. He who would save his soul must be prepared to fulfil the conditions that apply. We cannot so much as pretend to be working so long as we are not familiar with fear or will not submit to feel fear effectually. Here on earth we can possess no other knowledge of our relation to God but that which is based upon fear. Now you know, dear son, that God's will to save us is changeless, adamant." It was Father Falk, Paul realized; the other priests were not in the habit of saying "my son," but Father Falk had been at an English semi-

418

nary for a time. "What we need to learn until our dying day, so that we never forget it, is that we can never be entirely sure of ourselves. And it is my positive opinion that, as surely as you have reason to be unspeakably grateful to God for having permitted you to learn something of Himself through an experience which lies outside our daily spiritual life—so surely have you reason to thank Him for giving you an opportunity of finding out how unreliable you are yourself—as are we all. I know that you have been faithful to Our Lord in your acts; perhaps when it came to the point you would scarcely let yourself be tempted to forsake God in deed. Therefore it is certainly good for you to have been shown where the danger lies—in your capriciousness, in the waywardness which leads to intellectual sins.—As a penance therefor you shall say a Magnificat.—You need not say it till afterwards, when presently I have given you the holy communion. And then receive your Saviour in the sacrament of the altar with joy at having been permitted to learn a little more of the nature both of fear and of hope. Remember that the Church here on earth is a Church militant. A grown man of normal faculties must know that where there is war, there must be danger, and fear is not to be avoided—and it is not the same as either cowardice or despondency, and it is no excuse for an attempted flight.

"—Ah, by the way, that lady you spoke of. You must of course avoid meeting her again, if that is possible."

"It is not. I have promised her my help in a purely business way; she has nobody else here in town who can help her."

"I see. Well, then you must bear in mind that you know what you may do and may not do, presumably better than she does. So you know that the whole responsibility in this affair rests upon you. And then you know—watch and pray.

"Now I will give you holy absolution—"

Paul bowed his head and the shrill, boyish young voice began: *"Misereatur—"*

419

HELGE looked rather down-hearted when at last the three went across to the Institute together, and Sister Marie-Halvard gave a little laugh:

"Won't you breakfast with us all the same? Because, you see, otherwise poor Helge won't get an egg for breakfast—we can't provide them all round—"

"Thanks, Sister, but I can't."

Before anything else he must go and get shaved and make himself fit to be seen—and then he must get a cup of coffee before going back to the office.

They separated at the school gate, and Helge called out from the steps: *"Laudetur Jesus Christus!"*

"In æternum." Paul smiled faintly. The poor boy vexed his grandmother so terribly with his Latin tags—on this point she was exactly like that nurse of Holberg's, in *Barselstuen.* For that matter he vexed his grandmother simply by being what he was —by having a standpoint on which he stood with both feet, small as he was, regarding her with respectful contempt—there was no other word for it.

Chapter Five

IT WOULD CERTAINLY BE DIFFICULT ENOUGH TO MEET LUCY again, Paul knew that. But just at present a fortnight went by without his seeing her; he was too busy. No doubt he had become more or less acquainted with his mother's business of late years, but this was not the same thing as having it at his fingers' ends so that he could take it over. And whenever he had a moment's leisure he was on the go with Björg looking at houses.

He had had a fairly long talk with Fröken Alsaker about Lucy's business. Another thousand crowns had to be found, but then all the old debts would be got rid of and in Fröken Alsaker's opinion it ought to pay. That is, if only Fru Lövstö would take care not to get swamped by debts again.—That was just it. Lucy hadn't much idea of carrying on a business. She could not see that what she had bought on credit must be paid for out of the money she took. She could have got on better with payment in kind.—But time enough for that.

Paul could not provide this sum without selling some pieces of the Herrebö china that he had collected in the course of years. He had begun to buy before it became the craze that everybody who had made money out of the war must collect antiques. Amongst other things he had got from a dealer who used to call on him at the office in Trondhjem was a big dish, decorated with a harbour view in blue—an experiment which was rather foreign to the usual style of the factory. It had been illustrated several times in publications, and Skaare the dealer

421

had offered to take it in exchange when Paul had called recently to look at things which he could not afford to buy.

He took that and two plates with manganese brown decoration into town. And in case Björg might miss these Herrebö pieces, he bought two big bowls from Kellinghusen—he had long fancied them, and Skaare had brought down the price again and again; but Paul had made up his mind once for all to limit his collection to older Norwegian handicraft and industry. In their days of prosperity Björg too had developed a certain interest in old things and had herself ransacked the old curiosity shops. True, she was only a very superficial judge of them. And it was to be hoped she knew nothing of the difference in the prices paid for Herrebö and Kellinghusen.

From Skaare's he had to take a taxi direct to the station—he had a meeting at the brickworks at one o'clock. So he sent the money to Lucy by registered post from Berven. After that rather more than a week passed without his being able to go into Oslo, and he heard nothing from Lucy; but Fröken Alsaker let him know by telephone that it had been settled as arranged.

The first day he was back at his office in town, Lucy rang up, just as Björg was sitting there; they were to go and look at a house at Vindern. Lucy began by making excuses for not having written: "I was thinking perhaps I'd see you again soon, you see."

"I've been so busy lately—"

"You're not going out to Linlökka one of these days?"

"No, I shan't have time for that."

"Roy has been so poorly—at last I got Hans to come and look at him. Hans wants to take him in and have him X-ray'd —that's what I wanted to ask you about, do you think I ought to do it? It seems so awkward because of Doctor Lund, but I don't think the diet and medicines he's given have done much good. Do tell me what you think I ought to do."

"Well, it's not so easy for me to say. But if you've called in Hans, I suppose you'd better do what he says. But look here,

I'm engaged now, there's someone here.—Oh, not at all. I hope you'll excuse me. Then I'll hear more when we meet. I hope the boy will be better."

"Who was that?" asked Björg when he had rung off. "It sounded as if it was a lady?"

"Yes—it was somebody you don't know."

"One of Hansie's lady friends?"

"Yes, that is—we all of us knew her, in the old days when we were living at home with mother."

He went to the Central Theatre with Björg that evening; there was a detective piece which she was keen on seeing. Lucy was there—with her husband. Next day she rang him up at his office at Berven. She had never done that before.

"But dear me—you don't owe me any explanation of that. Of being with your husband."

But she insisted that she must and would explain to him how it came about that she had gone to the theatre with Lövstö, so Paul had to promise that they should meet next time he was in Oslo.

It was with no little dread that he set out two or three evenings later—Lucy had got him to promise that he would call on her in Övre Slotsgate. He did not quite know on what sort of footing she expected their next meeting to take place. Now indeed he could see how unfortunate had been his behaviour that evening—he was afraid he had made matters still more complicated for Lucy.

She had shut up the shop when he came, and she led the way in the dark into the little back room.

"Won't you hang up your things? For you're not going again at once, are you?" Her voice was—oh, how well he knew that hushed, expectant tone.

While he was hanging up his hat and coat Lucy stood in the middle of the room under the crude, unblinking light— never had Paul seen a hanging light with a white glass shade look more detestable. She was wearing the same dress as he had last seen her in—a smooth dark frock with a light collar turned over it. He was reminded of the time when she was really young; then she had dressed in a much more old-fashioned style, with hair puffed up and a high neck and long skirts as they were worn in those days. Her youth was stuck into these trappings as a flower is stuck in moss. There was something spurious about this youthful get-up now that she was so faded and experienced. But at the same time there was something charming about it, and terribly sad.

The room had been put in order, so that its tidiness positively screamed at him, and on the desk by the window stood a vase with some sprigs of mimosa. That brought back another memory—she had sometimes brought him mimosa at the time he was living in Munkedams-vei; he had never cared to tell her he didn't like the scent of it.

She raised her bent head as he came up to her, and Paul guessed, with a stab at his heart, that she thought he was going to kiss her. So he took her hand and kissed that.

She looked at him:

"You're angry with me, aren't you?" she said in a low voice.

"No, why should I be angry with you?"

"Oh. There might be so many reasons. You've often been angry with me when I didn't really know what I'd done that you didn't like." Heavens—she talks as if she'd already wiped out all the time between, he thought in consternation. "I thought maybe you were annoyed with me for going about with Lövstö. But that's what I want to explain to you."

She fetched an uncorked bottle of wine—it had been standing on the floor in a corner—and took two glasses out of a cupboard.

"Will you have a glass of wine? It's sherry—I remembered you don't like port."

Involuntarily Paul glanced at the window to the yard.

The curtains were drawn—and those bright yellow curtains were evidently brand-new. He felt inclined to laugh and cry too—

"No, you see, I can't stand this business with Herman any longer. I mean to be properly divorced from him now, so that I shan't have him coming and making a row outside where I live and all that. Then there's this, that he's got a cousin in Buenos Aires who's written that he can find him something to do in his business, but he can't send him the money for his journey. And so I was thinking, if *I* could offer to pay his ticket for him. I asked Hans how things were in South America, as he's been there.—Well, that's how I came to be with Herman again, you see—to talk about this."

Paul said nothing.

"What do you think about it?"

"You know, Lucy," he said quietly, "that I don't believe in divorce. If your husband is such that it's impossible for you to live with him, out of consideration for the children and yourself, then that's another matter. But it doesn't mean freedom—"

"You can guess," she said in the same low tone, "I don't mean that *you* should make any change in *your* arrangements on my account. But it would be better to get Herman out of the way, I think. I'm afraid he might take into his head to do something to you too—"

Paul shrugged his shoulders.

"What else did Hans have to say?" he asked. "I told him what you had told me.—Did he say anything about that?"

"Well, I believe he thought I oughtn't to have told you. But when I'd talked to him for a bit he admitted that it was quite natural. And he's very good about Roy.—Roy likes him. He likes you too for that matter—"

"That's very—nice of him."

"I say," she whispered. "When you come out to Linlökka next time—won't you come and see us again?"

"I think I'd better not." They looked at each other for

425

an instant. "That would be playing with fire, Lucy." He gave a wry little smile.

"Well but, Paul." He saw that she was trembling slightly. "What do you *want?* Do you think," she whispered, when he did not answer, "that it could be so—awful? For I know your wife has not acted so very well to you—"

He made a rapid deprecating gesture with his hand. Lucy went on:

"You've only got to confess, haven't you?" she whispered, turning red as fire. "If anything more had happened the other day, for instance—you could easily have got an indulgence for it?"

Paul laughed nervously:

"No doubt I could. Since it would have been a—surprise. It's another matter, now *that's* over—"

"Over? Do you mean your love for me?" she whispered.

"No, that's never likely to be over," he replied, almost indifferently.

On seeing the pained, perplexed look in her face, he said seriously: "That's never likely to be over. And that makes all the difference in the world, Lucy. Now I should know every single time I went to see you—I *cannot* be with you without wishing that everything had been different. There could no longer be any question of a surprise."

She sat perfectly still, but her expression and her eyes—

"Oh, for God's sake don't cry," he begged her softly, turning away his face.

"Well but, Paul!" The timid surprise in her voice cut him to the soul. "What good does it do if you're so fond of me as you say?"

"I don't know, Lucy. None, perhaps. If it ever does no good for people to be fond of each other. Perhaps all the same it may one day mean something to you—to know that I have never loved anyone else as I loved you and as I shall love you always."

426

Lucy got up. She took a step or two—over to the window, stood there a moment. It looked as if she did not quite know what to do with herself. Then she came back and stood before him, tugging with one hand at the fingers of the other.

"No, no. If you think like that, you know I can see there's nothing to be done. But I must say I think it's sad. For you know, Paul, I've been through a good lot. I haven't always been as good as I ought to have been, I'm sorry to say. But I would rather have kept straight. I thought myself it was all pretty dreary and beastly—with all the others. It was only you that it was—different with. And now it's got to be all over for good?"

Paul nodded. Then he could not help looking at her, and he felt his face stiffen with pain. Good God, she was lovely—there was a kind of innocence in this—as it were a gleam of that animal innocence he had yearned for. But at that moment he remembered dimly that day on the Hurdal lake, when she had hidden herself from the innocence of his ignorance. Alas, it was so infinitely sad—

"O Lucy—" But he could not bring himself to say it would have been better if they had not met again.

His uttering her name seemed to put more heart into her. She stretched out her hands and cautiously touched his shoulders with the tips of her fingers.

He caught them, laid them together and held them in both his hands—kissed all her finger-tips which were visible. Then he let go, crossed the room and put on his coat. Lucy followed and stood looking at him with her expression of quiet perplexity.

"No, no," she said again; "if you think that, then I suppose that's how it is."

"Besides, you must remember, Lucy," he tried to laugh, "I shall soon be an old gentleman, with a daughter almost grown up."

"Yes, but she's going to be a nun, I've heard, so she need never have known anything about us—?"

427

Paul burst out laughing—bit his lip sharply to stop it. He was within a hair's breadth of bursting into tears. That would be the finishing stroke, if he was to turn hysterical.

Lucy let him out by a little door which led directly from her back room into the gateway. At that moment a man stepped out of the elevator just opposite. It was Arnt Hauan. He bowed, rather stiffly, to the couple standing there.

"I say," said Lucy. "Does Herr Hauan know that you and I have been engaged?"

"Yes, of course he knows. He and I were good friends long before that was over.—Why do you ask?"

"Well, you see, I pay my rent at his office. And that was the first thing I did when I got the money from you the other day. I had it in the registered envelope, and you know the notes were enclosed in a sheet of your business letter-paper. And as I was standing there at the cashier's desk, Herr Hauan himself came up, and he must have seen it, for I thought he gave me such an odd look—"

Well, never mind that, thought Paul as he went out into the street. Though on second thoughts he did mind a great deal what Arnt Hauan might think or not think—

PAUL was glad of it when it turned out that he might just as well buy a house as take over a flat with shares in the building. They had found a little villa in the neighbourhood of Vindern; the house was built in the early 'nineties, in the dragon style then fashionable, solid but ugly, with a minimum of modern conveniences and in rather bad repair. When Sunnie came home from England he and Helge would have to be content with two alcoves to sleep in, but for the present they could have one of the three rooms upstairs. Paul looked forward to having the boy at home again. So did Björg, probably; at all events she looked forward to living practically in Oslo.

The house was only separated from its neighbours by a fence. Perhaps this would be rather a drawback with Bubbe—

he had been somewhat restless of late. He would try to walk, but this seemed to set up pain in his deformed feet; they swelled up. So he crawled on all fours instead. He could not talk intelligibly, but he was much given to babbling and uttering strange discordant noises, and now and again he had those uncanny fits of screaming, when he seemed to be in pain. On his account it was going to be rather tiresome to have one's neighbours on top of one like this.

The garden was overgrown; there were several big old fruit-trees. Otherwise it was laid out in that fashion of the 'nineties which with such incomprehensible efficiency excludes comfort and beauty. The paths curved in just such a way that it would never occur to anyone to walk on them, and there were groups of ornamental bushes which were planted so as to be no ornament. So at any rate he would have that to fill up his time in the long evenings—putting the garden into shape. The paths he would do away with and let grass grow everywhere. Paul saw himself going to work in shirt-sleeves and overalls—standing at the fence and chatting with men who were doing the same in the gardens alongside. Well, well, you have not progressed so far that this may not be a good exercise for you. Learn to look with sympathy on villa gardens and friendliness among neighbours—these things make for happiness with many, so you can't be allowed to shrug your shoulders at them.

Björg was not well enough to undertake much of the packing up and moving; in the end Paul sent her to a sanatorium and put the whole move in the hands of an agency. He promised to bring Helge up to see her at Easter; it was comparatively easy to reach the church at Hamar from the sanatorium.

Julie Selmer had invited Sigmund and Lykke to make a trip with her to Copenhagen, and proposed that Paul should stay at Linlökka meanwhile, until the house at Vindern was more or less in order. This would be pleasant for Hans too. Paul had to take Bubbe with him. Alvilde, his mother's old maid, was very kind to the sick child, and Hans wanted to have him under observation for a time—to see if there was a possibility of doing anything which might at any rate bring about some improvement.

On Palm Sunday Paul took Helge with him to High Mass in the Dominicans' church. As they were going out after the service a tall, slim, red-haired lad with handsome, clear-cut features came running after them and clapped him on the shoulder:

"How are you, godfather! It was a good thing I met you, I was just going to write to you!"

"What—are you in Oslo, Jack?" To his shame he had not kept up correspondence with his godson Jacob Mosling Alster since Henrik and Berit were divorced. The last news he had had of the boy was that he was to go to the College at Trondhjem and to live with his father.

"But what are you doing here—in church? I thought you were a communist?"

"Well, so I am, godfather. And if it is God's will it won't be so many years before I join the communistic students' society that St. Dominic founded seven hundred years ago. I was received into the Church a week ago, and I'm so happy I simply can't believe it's true. *Ah, comme le bon Dieu est bon!* Isn't that so?"

That was a saying of Father Auberive's. He had been through the war and the prisoners of war camp, like many another priest, so he at any rate knew what he was talking about. For that matter Jacob too might have had sufficient experience, young as he was, to realize what he meant in saying God was good.

Father Auberive in his white frock came and joined them on the pavement. It was he who had celebrated Mass, so he was still fasting and pale with tiredness, as full of laughter and chaff as usual. He invited them to come into the convent and have coffee with him.

Jacob Alster's tongue was never quiet while they sat at the

little cloth-covered table in the library, which was the only
room the monks had to meet in. It was all about communism,
which represented the white blood-corpuscles in the social
body; the Renaissance and the Reformation, in opposing the
system of religious orders, had brought blood-poisoning upon
Europe; where the phagocytes are destroyed, it is obvious that
no wound can heal. It is the Devil's cleverest trick to have produced a culture of anti-Christian communism, so that Christianity may perish of pernicious anæmia—the white corpuscles eating up the red ones, the natural family cells.—It was Karl Adam
and Hilaire Belloc and Nicolai Berdiaeff and Franz Zach and
Maritain and Christopher Hollis and Henri Massis in one continuous stream.—

To begin with, his mother had objected very strongly when
he wished to turn Catholic, but his father had been very sympathetic. All he asked was that Jacob should wait two years
before entering on his noviciate. "It's a long time to wait, of
course, but with God's help even that time will pass. Godfather, how can it be that you, who have been a Catholic so
long, haven't yet entered any Order as a tertiary? Wouldn't
you like to have some books anyhow, so that you can see what
is required and what one gets by being a tertiary? I'm sure
you would discover that it's just what you need to enable you to
work still more energetically for your sanctification—

"—And you, Helge, you'll be a monk too, won't you, when
you grow up?"

Helge shook his head solemnly:

"I don't yet know what I shall be. I shall find that out when
God thinks it suits Him to let me know."

"Yes, but you must pray for light; don't you know that,
boy!"

"Don't tell me, sonny," replied Helge, without moving a
muscle.

Paul had been given the little *officium* and a whole pile of
other little books, when at last he and Helge got away. It was

431

arranged that Father Auberive and Jacob Alster should come out and spend the evening with him at Linlökka next day. So Paul rang up Father Falk and invited him too.

It was a very cheery evening. Jacob was fairly boisterous, of course; he would have been the same, thought Paul, at Jacob's age, when the faith was penetrating into the inmost empty and tender places of the soul—the boy's whole mind was foaming and splashing over. "I just wish I could make a fool of myself for Christ's sake! When I think how *He* was made a fool of for our sakes!"

"You will certainly have your wish fulfilled," said Father Falk. "But let Our Lord Himself arrange for your appearance in the part of fool—don't start on your own account. We all have our chance of that, if only we are good and obedient children of God."

It appeared that Jacob asked his father confessor about everything, even what kind of tie he should wear. "Can't I be let off taking whisky in my soda, *mon Père?* I hate whisky, but of course I take a little when I'm in company with non-Catholics." Paul couldn't make out when Jacob had had time to associate with non-Catholics in the last six months. "Non-Catholics misunderstand everything of that sort—they've been saddled with the curse of puritanism. If God lets them feel that they've got to practise asceticism, they jump to the conclusion that if a thing isn't good for me, it can't possibly be good for them. And then they do their level best to see that nobody else shall get anything out of it either. They're so dead set on looking after other people's asceticism besides their own."

They were going back to town by the night train from the south—the train by which Paul was expecting Hans and Evi. But he could not see his guests to the station, as he had let Alvilde go to bed and Bubbe was restless. So he only went with them through the garden—stood for a moment at the gate watching the three as they took the short cut across the fields.

It was dark outside; the snow was almost gone, but the ground was grey with rime. The sky was black and studded with restlessly twinkling stars. Along the road a few little fixed points of yellow light shone from the houses.—He had seen nothing of Lucy since he came out here.—The three were down on the pond now, he could hear them laughing and shouting on the long slide.

Bubbe was screaming when he came back to the drawing-room. Beds had been made up for him and the child in the little room leading out of it, as his usual upstairs room had been got ready for Evi. It was a matter of course that no one else ever used his mother's bedroom.

Paul went in to the child and helped him to sit up, supported by pillows. This always seemed to relieve the mysterious pains—nervous pains, Hans said they were. Hans suggested that perhaps an operation might do some good.

Paul wiped the perspiring, yellow little face. A soul that had been sent out lacking any serviceable equipment for accomplishing anything in this life. So in any case he was excused from doing any wrong. Paul lit a candle and placed it on the table at some distance from the bed—he had discovered that this was one of the few things the poor little fellow enjoyed, sitting and looking at a living light. He nodded at it with his big, heavy head and blinked his eyes to get the full benefit of the rays and gurgled with pleasure.

Paul returned to his seat in the drawing-room and began to dip into the two little books that Sunnie had sent him: "Our reverend Mother says they are so splendid, especially as you think so much of Mother Julian and the other English mystics."

They were Walter Hilton's *Scale of Perfection* and the anonymous *Cloud of Unknowing*—two second-hand copies full of underlinings. Paul read at random: "And therefore lean meekly to this blind stirring of love in thine heart. I mean not in thy bodily heart, but in thy ghostly heart, the which is the will."
—"All manner of bodily thing is without thy soul and beneath

it in nature. Yea! the sun and moon and all the stars, although they be above thy body, nevertheless they be beneath thy soul."
—"What is heaven to a reasonable soul? Soothly naught else but Jesus God.—For He only is above the kind of a soul."

—The clock in the dining-room struck half-past twelve. So evidently Hans and Evi had not come by that train after all. To make sure he ought perhaps to sit up another quarter of an hour. He took up Hilton again, turned over the pages—

Suddenly the telephone rang on his mother's desk. Paul put down his book and went across to take the message—with instinctive reluctance; the sound of the bell tore so brutally through the midnight stillness and the subdued light. It must be Hans.—"Hallo!"

"Is that you yourself, Paul?" It was Lucy's voice, strangely stifled. "Paul—Herman's outside and I'm quite alone in the house with the children. I'm so afraid he's going to break in. I've rung up the sheriff but can't get an answer. Can't you come over—?"

"All right. I'll come at once."

As he came back from the hall his eye happened to fall on Hans's revolver, lying on the table. Jacob had been looking at it—had emptied the magazine and reloaded it. Paul slipped it into his pocket, without any clear intention—. Then he went out by the veranda and ran across the fields.

An intensely homelike feeling closed in on him as he slid across the pond. The blazing stars over his head were faintly mirrored in the ice, he knew rather than saw how the rime-covered rushes by the bank were frozen in—and beyond the dark slope of the fields lay the row of little fixed lights, the houses by the station, low down with a border of deep shadow, the forest which one could not see, between him and the starry sky. He had walked and run along this path a thousand times, the planks under his feet gave a familiar sound as he dashed over the level crossing in the hollow. And it was with the vaguest emotion of excitement or uncertainty that he turned off from his usual path to the station and ran by the side of a wire fence through frosted grass that gave a faint hiss, across the lumpy, uneven field to the main road.

Aamot's house showed a light from a gabled window under the roof, and as he approached the garden gate he heard some dull, muffled sounds coming from within, together with the shrill screams of a child. It made him wild—

A pane of glass in the front door had been smashed in, and the door was unfastened. Broken glass jingled under his feet in the dark hall—and he took the stairs in a few bounds. A light showed through the chinks of a narrow door over in the corner—beyond the hall-door with the pink-shaded light—the screams were close at hand and he flung open the little door—

He looked into a room which was like a dream of horror and frenzy. It was a long, narrow room with a sloping roof on one side, and under this slope stood Eva Marie in her little bed, screaming. Right under the window some big dark shape loomed against a lamp—the back of a man who was kneeling on top of a low couch; he looked like a bear crouching above something it has brought down, and the victim still stirred and gurgled—

"I'll kill you, I'll kill you," a boy's voice shrieked, and it racked him in every nerve, he felt he was losing the last scrap of consciousness, but he *saw* that it was Roy who was jumping there in his bare shirt, and it was he who was shrieking and hammering at the monster with his fists—

Then he didn't really know what happened, until he was reeling this way and that in the narrow room, grappling with a big fellow whom it was impossible to get a proper hold of, as his coat was lined with fur and he was fat and his breath stank so horribly.—He had seen her face, dark red and bloody, with a look of horror in the eyes, the head hung over backwards when he got those loathsome paws away from her throat—he dared not take a proper look.—Then he had been flung against a sharp edge and had got a blow on the jaw, and then they had closed— the fellow was strong as the devil to wrestle with, but he

435

managed to force him towards the door—

"Open the door—" he called to Roy, in a shriek of fury, for the other was resisting so violently, trampling on his feet and trying to kick. Roy flung the door open, they fell over the threshold—and Paul tore himself out of the other's grip, gave him a shove, and the man in the dark fur coat disappeared down the stairs with a thundering crash. Paul locked the door behind him and stood for a moment leaning against it, groaning and trembling.

He tore off his overcoat and threw it on to the child's bed close by, picked up his hat which had been trampled to a shapeless mass and flung it the same way: "Hush, Eva Marie, don't scream like that, there's nothing to be afraid of now—"

Right under the window stood a low couch; the bedclothes and Lucy's head and shoulders had been pulled down on to the floor—her arm lay outstretched, white and long. The dark, blood-stained head gave out unearthly sounds which froze him with terror—then he went forward quickly, raised her head and stood with her whole body in his arms, the ghastly head against his chest:

"Can you come here, Roy—put the bed straight, so that I can lay your mother in it—"

The boy laid the bedclothes on the box-ottoman, smoothed out the sheets—there was blood on them—and put the pillow in its place. For an instant Paul pressed his face against the bared yellow breast from which the nightdress had slipped—then he covered her shoulder and laid her down. Roy spread the blanket over his mother, smoothed the top sheet—ugh, what a lot of blood there was on it—.

Paul stood for a moment not knowing what he ought to do —try artificial breathing or let her lie with her head on the pillow, then perhaps the blood would leave her head.—Her breathing rattled and came with sharp little bursts—she wheezed faintly.

"Bring a basin of water—and some towels—"

436

He began to wash the blood off her, cautiously—there were great red marks on her throat, and scratches—her face too was scratched.

"It's *him* all that blood's come from," Roy remarked calmly. "I expect he cut himself when he smashed the glass. And then when mother tried to open the window and shout for somebody, he pulled her down and got her by the throat. If you hadn't come I almost think he'd have made an end of the whole lot of us—"

"Hush now!" Paul was trying to wash the inside of her mouth. He took away the pillow, laid her flat and applied a wet folded towel loosely to her damaged throat.

"I'll have to go down and ring up the doctor—hush, Roy, there's nothing more to be said now. Yes, yes, yes, be quiet, boy —I did come in time, yes.—Go to bed, Eva Marie"—he lifted up the little girl, who had climbed down on to the floor, and kissed her warmly as he put her back in bed.

The moment he switched on the light at the top of the stairs and saw the dark thing lying huddled together at their foot, the cold certainty sank through him, that the man was dead. He went down, strangely stiff all over—took hold of the heavy body and straightened it out a little, but the touch of it seemed to take the power from his arms. Its face he could not distinguish properly, it was in the shadow. But he thrust a hand inside the coat and jacket, felt outside the waistcoat—oh, he knew it all the time, it was all over. And this was his doing—

"Is he a goner?" Roy, still in his shirt, was standing on the stairs above.

Paul gave a start, and shouted, beside himself with horror:

"Go in, will you! Go up, do you hear—go up to your mother and Eva—"

Is he a goner—the hard, uncaring boy's voice stuck in him like a knife, as he switched on the light in front of him and went through the neat little rooms with their plush furniture and palms which met him with a cold stare.

437

Then he stood at a little oak-stained desk with a big tear-off calendar facing him and spoke down into the telephone to young Lund, the doctor's son:

"—but straight away. There's one dead. And I don't know how it is with Fru Lövstö. It's an attempted strangling. Herr Aamot's house—the last house along Smaalens-vei—the doctor's been there before. At once, please—"

Then there was the sheriff. Just as he was going to ring up he remembered what Lucy had said—she couldn't get an answer from there. No, of course, he was at Fosser at his parents'-in-law—it was today, the golden wedding—

From far away he heard dance music and the buzz of voices, as he waited with the receiver to his ear—someone had gone to find the sheriff.

"—you, sheriff? This is Paul Selmer. I'm speaking from Aamot's house. I find I've killed a man."

"What's that you say!" He heard Kastrud's horrified voice. They were old fellow-students, Svend Kastrud and he. "But good Lord, man, how did you come to do that—?"

"You'd better hear the whole story when you come. But hurry up, do, so that I don't have to wait too long—"

He must go up to Lucy again, see how she was. He would have to pass *that*. He stayed where he was, by the desk.—God, he thought in despair—there's a dead man lying outside in the passage, it's true, I've done it—he seemed to come tumbling out of a fog of drifting devilry—how can all this have happened—?

A motor-cycle stopped outside. Paul went out into the passage. Only when he saw that the little figure was a woman, in spite of breeches and gaiters and leather jacket, with little fair curls on the cheeks under the hat and goggles, did he feel how he had hoped for the presence of another man—Doctor Lund's broad person and warm voice. This young lady's voice, saying "It's the doctor," gave him a quite disproportionate feeling of being abandoned by God and man.

"Well, there's nothing to be done here." She got up from examining the dead man. "And the other case—is she upstairs?" The doctor disappeared up the staircase. Paul stole into the Aamots' drawing-room, and there he collapsed over a table, lying with his face against a plush table-cloth. "I *must* go up and hear how it is with Lucy"—but he could not.

NOT till he was sitting in the car by the side of the sheriff did he come to his senses. The night air roused him.

"We must call in at Linlökka, so that you can take what you want with you," said Sheriff Kastrud as he started the car.

And Bubbe and the candle, Paul remembered.

"It might have been just as well if you'd left that revolver of yours at home," said the sheriff as they drove. "Even if you didn't happen to use it—"

No, what did I want with it after all, he thought. Frighten him—? But I never imagined it would turn out like this? If I'd remembered I had it on me, I expect I'd have used it—

The sheriff went in with him through the veranda. The room stood as he had left it, an age ago. Cosy, in a subdued light from two lamps, a faint smell of tobacco and hyacinths. On the table by the corner sofa lay the two little green books from Sunnie.—Seek God, not with thy bodily heart, but with thy ghostly heart, the which is the will. It felt like a bitter mockery to recall that now. Nothing in the world is above man's soul, except God.—Lucy, Roy, the dead man, himself—he saw them all as naked souls, thin, ghostly grey wisps drifting against a background of coal black, and the blackness was God; it looked like black to him, because he was blinded, could only see the ghostly dance; but he had thrust them out into this darkness—

Bubbe was asleep, fallen forward in his cot, and the candle stood on the little table, burnt down almost to the socket. Paul set about packing his toilet things in a suitcase.

"You've had visitors, I see?" said the sheriff from the other room. "It's a great bore she should have rung up *after* they'd

439

gone—otherwise it would have been clear that there was no previous arrangement about your going to see her. Because, you know, people have been busy about you two—"

"I suppose they have."

Alvilde came in, dressed, and took Bubbe:

"This is a very bad business." She was perfectly calm—it was reassuring simply to see her standing there with the boy on her arm. "Such a shock for the mistress too, when she hears of it. But perhaps you'll be home again by that time. It'll only be for a day or two, won't it, sheriff?"

"Take another drink, won't you, Selmer, before we go," proposed Kastrud. "It'll do you good to have a stiffener. Which is your glass?"

"WELL, you can guess, it may take some time," said the sheriff, as they drove off again. "It may be a matter of bodily harm resulting in death. But of course auntie Audhild can repeat everything you two said on the telephone. You know, when Fru Lövstö rang you up at such and such a time, she was listening in, sure. Oh, those exchange people are wicked at listening in, you know. So everything considered, I don't think you need be so very anxious."

Paul did not answer. He was not in a state to feel any interest in that side of the matter—that would come, he knew, and so would the thought of how they would take it at home. The newspapers too, it dawned on him. But that was too complicated to think about yet.

"I say, Kastrud, if it's allowable to ring me up there, let me know tomorrow, as early as you can, how Fru Lövstö is. Whether her injuries are very serious—"

"Well, you know, you can't use the telephone when you're detained in custody. But I can give the jailer a message.—Smart woman, that Doctor Heier—good-looking too. Clever, I should think—"

"Yes, I'm sure she is. Another thing—would you ring up

Veiholmen as soon as you get home? In case Hans is still there.
Tell him about it and ask him to go and see my wife."

The sky was growing light as they drove into the street of
a little town with low, light-coloured wooden houses and big
trees standing in old gardens. The breeze had a grateful tang of
the sea in it—between the houses there was a glimpse of the
fiord outside, it seemed to be rolling in towards the morning
light.

"Here we are," said Kastrud, and stopped the car. Paul
stepped out. On the other side of the street stood a big yellow
building with verandas, the hotel; it was many years since he
had been there. And immediately opposite was a trim white
wooden house on a high stone foundation, by the side of which
a wide gate in a high plank fence was unlocked.

"And here we have jailer Olsen. Good-morning, Olsen;
well, this is him I rang you up about. Custody, yes—Selmer.
Yes, it's a tiresome business—"

The jailer was small and inclined to stoutness—Paul
thought there was something comforting about him; yes, he reminded him of his father-in-law. He felt at once how physically
tired and sleepy he was, as he followed the man across a yard
with gardens on each side. At the far end of the yard stood a
dark, solid timber house.

"Yes, it's uncommonly awkward," said the sheriff as he
left. "But don't let it worry you too much, Selmer. Seriously, I
can't imagine on what ground they can base a charge against
you."

The jailer unlocked a tremendously strong door and let
Paul pass into the cell before him.

There was a little grated window high up; it was divided in
two and the upper pane stood open aslant. A clean taste in the
air and a distant murmur reminded one of the fiord outside.
"Would you like me to shut it—?"

The square little room had log walls painted a light colour.
There was a radiator and a plank bed, made up for sleeping,

and a desk with a fixed seat like a school desk. Down in one corner a white placard showed faintly.

"Well, you know, if there's anything you'd like sent out to you, you can have it," the jailer was chatty—"a nice chair and table, for instance. Detentions can have a lot in that way. Well, no, I'm afraid smoking's forbidden here," he said sympa- thetically, as Paul took out a cigarette and struck a match. "But you can get a quid off me, if you like—ah, I see, you don't chew—

"Well, now I hope you'll get a good sleep. There's one in the cell on the left here, he's been making an ugly row—case of reckless driving, we got him in last night, drunk as an owl— but now he's gone to sleep by the sound of him." Then the jailer departed and locked the door.

WHEN he was left alone he tried to say his evening prayers as usual. But he could not bring himself to touch upon the chaos into which he had been thrown by the events of the night. How *could* it all have happened—!

Word for word he repeated what he was in the habit of say- ing every evening. Perhaps he had not always paid so very much attention to what he was saying; it provided nevertheless a fixed formula for desires and moods. But when he said them now, the words seemed illumined with terrible significance. From the bottom of an abyss, a man's impotence to foresee what his own acts may lead to, it was miserable to pray for help, when he him- self had so great a share of guilt.

"Holy Mary, Mother of God, pray for us sinners, now and at the hour of our death. Amen."

"Sacred Heart of Jesus, who Thyself hast known the bitter- ness of death, have mercy on all who are to die this night."

"Jesus, who from the cross didst commend Thy Mother and Thy dearest friend to one another in their grief, be Thou a bond between the hearts of all those who tonight are stricken by a common sorrow. Teach them to console one another and be

442

Thyself their consolation."

—but how is *that* to come about, among us who are all scattered and sundered through being ourselves sundered by gulf after gulf? How can *I* pray for a man's soul which I myself have dispatched into the darkness—while he was in the act of killing her who has been a prey to both him and me?—And if the whole thing were repeated, I should do the same again, in Lucy's defence. Of course I should not have hesitated to use the revolver, if I had remembered I had it. After the event it is easy to pray God to have mercy on his soul—no, it is *not* easy; it is terrible to have to pray for a man one has wronged. Still worse when right and wrong are jumbled together—then it is a luxury to turn hard and implacable.—Certainly that man, Lövstö, has suffered wrong—even to being hated by his own son. Roy, yes—that is the worst. Are all the fiendish powers that we let loose to be allowed to fleer right in the face of a child who is growing up?

Lord Jesus, You have said: Suffer the little children to come unto me and forbid them not. Why do You not forbid *us*? You only say, *we* are not to hinder—and threaten us with the millstone about our neck.—

He had done nothing to *me*. *He* believed I was his wife's lover, that is obvious—he would have thought himself an idiot if he had had any doubt of it. And however he may have treated her and his children—it was she who once called him to her, married him and did not tell him what kind of traps she was inviting him to step into. But as for saying that she must take the consequences, that I must be excused from interfering, since she had left me out of it—I cannot wish I had done that, even now. Nor could it have been God's will that I should have made such an answer. I ought not to have said I loved her. But she had to be given a chance some time of telling me why she left me. And mere Christian charity is impossible where there has once been love.

Tried to carry it off and see what happened—that is what

443

I should have done, of course. Then I should have come to feel like a fool, and *that* is the truth. Go about like a fool for Christ's sake, as Jacob said—so I had a chance of doing that, but I declined it. For Björg's sake I could, for Ruth's sake too, but bah! that was only an ordinary happiness, and that I was never so keen on. But that she who really, really was my mistress should take me for a fool—no—

But this thought gave him at last a kind of worn-out rest.— However this may turn out, I shall try, my God, to take it handsomely, if I am now made a fool of—

Not till he had stretched himself between the blankets on the plank bed did he feel that he was pretty sore and stiff from the blows and kicks he had received. But this did not prevent his falling asleep almost at once.

He woke with a start—the sunshine filled the cell with a rescuing light, for he realized that he had been waked by the horror of a nightmare, and he was still trembling from it.

In spite of that he instinctively tried to recall what it was, and on closing his eyes one of the images of his dream came back, quite clearly:

He had seen something like a kitchen dresser, and on it lay a plucked goose. Its bare and ugly little head was purple, and blood had been dripping from the beak; the long, puckered neck was twisted and torn, with an ugly red hollow where it passed into the rounded breast, the skin of which was yellow and glossy and chequered. He seemed to be passing through the kitchen at Berven when he saw this goose lying there, and suddenly it meant, or it was, Lucy.—

For a moment it was as though he were again submerged in the horrors of the night. Then he took his hand from his face and turned towards the sunshine. No. Never in this world. Never in this world should anything make him ask if she had been worth his life—

Chapter Six

A BOUT FOUR THE NEXT AFTERNOON HIS LAWYER, HAUAN, came to see him. He still felt a certain nervous uneasiness, of course, when the jailer unlocked the door of the cell and locked it again so noisily, but no doubt he would get used to that.

"Well, this was an unpleasant piece of news to get the first thing in the morning." Arnt Hauan shook his hand with emphasis. "I needn't tell you how I feel about it."

"No, that's all right. Sit down, won't you?" The jailer had brought in a basket chair; Paul himself sat on the little school bench, moving some books from the desk on to the floor, so that Hauan might put down his case of papers.

Paul discovered all at once—he had really never paid much attention to it before, but it could be seen in Arnt Hauan too, that they were no longer young. He had a powerful, round head which was not flattened at the temples, reddish brown hair and complexion; but now his hair was getting thin and streaked with grey and his full face was scored with fine wrinkles. He had always been what one understands by a burly fellow, but now he had grown fairly fat—for which motoring was to blame, amongst other things.

"Well, the first thing I did was to go and have a talk with the sheriff. I was to give you a message from him: they don't think—the lady—is in any danger of her life. But she's been pretty badly knocked about. So there can't be any question of getting a statement from her for the present. In fact, Kastrud thought she ought to be taken to the Catholic hospital before she made her statement."

Paul said nothing.

"I may as well tell you how it is, Selmer. I've just seen the chief constable. Well—the charge against you will take the form of intentional homicide. It's that damned revolver you had on you."

"I see."

"You know that you can refuse to make a statement."

"But of course I shan't do that. It must clear the ground if they get my statement. Even if I am forced to admit what is the case, that when I took the revolver with me it was because I thought I might have use for it."

Hauan smacked the palm of his left hand with his glasses as he spoke:

"You understand—the preliminary inquiry will naturally include your relations with Fru Lövstö. Of course they have nothing to do with the realities of the case—for the present, when the question is whether a charge is to be brought against you or not. *If* you are charged, then, you know, it's another matter—before the assize court. But indirectly they may of course prejudice the inquiry in one direction or the other."

"Just so."

"And for that reason I dropped a hint about this to the chief constable, that in itself it was nothing exceptional on your part, if you have shown yourself generous to a lady with whom you were once very intimate—"

"Oh no, don't use such expressions, man!" Paul laughed nervously. "I was engaged to her, quite publicly, for three years—"

"Admitted. What I mean is that it ought to be brought out that you have always been willing to help people, where you could. Your family, Catholic institutions, your workmen at Haugen, at Berven too—"

"No, for God's sake, you really must keep all that out of

446

it," said Paul curtly. "This is *my* funeral, and don't let us drag in anything irrelevant."

"As you please. For the present at any rate. But you know, if this is to come before the court and I am to defend you, I may be forced to it. For you can see, can't you, Selmer—if it comes out that you, a man who for years has been contending with financial difficulties of his own, have made this lady a present of four thousand crowns in the course of one year—. You've even sold that famous Herrebö dish of yours—Skaare offered it to me last week. So you can guess the average man will hardly believe you gave Fru Lövstö all that for nothing—"

"No, I wasn't born yesterday!" Paul laughed. "I don't suppose you believed it either, did you, Arnt?"

"I didn't believe anything." Hauan turned a little redder. "That is to say, believed and believed. I'm willing to admit I didn't much like your hanging about her shop early and late. Especially late. You see, we really have had a certain respect for you—your old friends. You were man enough to live your own life, according to what you considered good morality, and not to care a damn for what folks said or thought or what was the usual thing. So I must say I didn't like the idea—that now perhaps you too had kicked over the traces—that perhaps you would even get mixed up in divorce proceedings and so on, just like any ordinary citizen—"

Paul smiled faintly and shook his head. He looked at his watch: "It's five o'clock we're to appear in court?"

"Yes, they'll send a car for us. All things considered, I can scarcely believe after all that they'll decide to bring a charge against you. But you know, Easter's upon us, and the examination will be a fairly long business, and a charge of this sort has to go right up to the attorney general—so you'll have to be prepared for being kept in custody a month in any case."

"I see."

The jailer rattled his keys and unlocked the cell; the car had arrived.

447

It seemed an eternity to Paul since he had been out in the open air—he stopped in the yard a moment and lit a cigarette:

"Is it Vilnes who's conducting the case, do you know?"

"Yes—do you know him?"

"He was a friend of my father's."

"The boy's statement is strongly in your favour," said Hauan as they took their seats in the car.

"The boy? They haven't taken statements from the children, have they? About what happened last night?"

"Yes, Sheriff Kastrud took them. This morning, before their mother was taken to the hospital. Yes, by the way, I was to tell you that his mother-in-law is taking in the children at Fosser meanwhile, so you needn't think about them just now."

"Ah, that's a good thing anyhow." Paul was silent a few moments. "When I think about those two youngsters of hers," he said hesitatingly, "I feel I was lucky not to be guilty of worse things than intentional homicide—"

"What do you mean?"

"You know, whosoever shall scandalize one of these little ones, etcetera. I presume you know the quotation."

Arnt Hauan paused before answering:

"Well, I dare say I'm not nearly so well up in the Bible as you are. But I do remember that it says something to the effect that whatever you have done to the least of my little ones, you have done to me—"

Paul shook his head: "I have done nothing for the poor things—not yet at any rate."

"That's as one may take it. But it wasn't them I was thinking of," said Hauan quietly. "I was thinking of Bubbe. Well, you must excuse my speaking of it. But when you begin *that* kind of thing—"

The car stopped outside the magistrate's court.

ONLY when they were driving back after the hearing did Paul summon up courage to say anything about his own family: "Do you know whether Björg has heard anything? It might be better if she came back tomorrow morning and went to Linlökka for the present—"

"Your brother and sister-in-law are going straight up with the car to fetch her this evening. Hans rang me up from Kragerö. —You know, it's possible he would be allowed to see you—as a doctor. You're a good deal swollen about the face, I see—it might not be amiss if a doctor had a look at you—"

"No need for that. I'd rather not." He couldn't have said why, but he positively disliked the idea of a visit from his brother. "Has there been anything about it in the papers, do you know?"

"Not with any names mentioned.—But in case of accidents I wrote a few words to Sunnie. So that she shan't be unreasonably scared if other people should write about it.—By the way, you won't forget that all communications between yourself and the outside world will be censored; I'm the only one who's allowed to see you. Well, of course—"

"Just so." They had arrived at the jail. "Well, good-bye, Arnt. And thanks for what you've done."

ARNT HAUAN came again on the morning of Good Friday to tell Paul the result of the post mortem. The direct cause of death was of course the fall downstairs—heart-failure. But dissection had disclosed luetic coronal sclerosis and aneurisma cordis, "if you know what that is." He had also been under the influence of alcoholic excess.

Paul made no remark.

Hauan's brows contracted: "You're looking poorly?"

"No, there's nothing wrong with me."

BUT he had a feeling that he had been in this cell, he did not know how long. And he did not care how long he might stay there.

It was a thing that was incapable of explanation: the very

449

certainty that he would never again feel his own ego as anything
real. He had been wiped out, and the only thing which really
had existence, in himself and in everything, was God.

It was not as it had been that morning in church, a tangible,
rapid and burning sweetness, like a fire that surrounded him.
This was not a feeling—or at any rate it was a feeling deep
down in the soul, where feeling had never penetrated before. It
was more like a seeing; all former things had vanished like a
daylight, a veil hiding the stars. But now it was as though he
had come through a long, black night—he lay motionless and
watched the white morning light grow and grow. God, he
thought, God. Every single beat of his heart said the same, God.

It was not by any means that he did not feel for and think
of all those near him—of Björg and the children, of Lucy and
her children, of the dead man. He thought of them all. Whether
the end of this was that he had to go through a trial and perhaps
be sentenced for homicide, or that the charge against him was
dropped and he was released, he would be a marked man in
people's eyes. And he would continue to be thin-skinned, on the
surface of his soul, as it were—perhaps more so than formerly;
for he no longer tried to deny it to himself; he had been trying
to deceive himself in pretending he was not sensitive. And now
he would never again be able to deceive himself in any case,
after what he had gone through.

But when everyday life returned, he would never again be
able to forget that the daylight does not merely reveal, it also
conceals. Below the surface in himself there would always be a
depth which no disturbances would reach. Fear and uneasiness
and indignation might chase each other on the surface. But love
was felt as something heavy which sank down and down—

However, all this was merely images—whether one pic-
tured to oneself the soul as a house with room within room and
an inmost chamber where God is, and the ego as having once
found its way in through that door and been recalled to life, and
as being changed from what it was, no matter how it may return

450

to its everyday life and live it again. Or whether one imagined oneself like a lake, with a surface ruffled by every wind and deep places where it is always calm. It was all images, and reality was what one knows one has experienced in such a way as to be convinced that this life is only a half-reality.

On the third day of Easter Father Auberive came to say Mass in his cell. The Frenchman came straight up, embraced him and kissed him first on one cheek and then on the other. With a vague, affectionate surprise Paul found that this was quite natural. And it was natural that he should make his confession, kneeling on the floor in the full light of the spring sun, before the priest who sat on the little school bench. There was no curtain around him and no grating between him and the young foreign monk with the thin dark face; the other's expression was mild and far-away, as though he were listening just as much to what he himself would say as to what he heard. Under the leather band of his watch on the left wrist was the scar left by a shell splinter.

The outer shrouds surrounding the sacraments were bent aside, as it were, like petals, and it was so natural that he should be nearer to the naked heart of the mysteries than he had ever been before. Perhaps he would never see them thus again; but he had seen them—

"I brought Jacob with me," said the priest, when they had both risen. "I thought perhaps you would rather not have to serve the Mass yourself—"

Jailer Olsen came in with a little kitchen table and placed it under the window. Jacob brought in a suitcase and helped to cover the table with the consecrated altar stone and the three liturgical linen cloths, two small candlesticks and a little crucifix. The improvised altar looked as bare and poor as any altar in vault or dungeon or cabin or hiding-place—a symbol of God's will to accept all that is most bitter as His share, for which all ecclesiastical magnificence is a thank-offering. Father

451

Auberive put on his Mass vestments one by one; the chasuble was the splendid white one with gold embroidery which Paul knew to have been made from his mother's wedding gown.

Jacob unpacked three pale pink roses: "These are from Fröken Alsaker," he whispered; "out of her own window-box, I was to tell you." He placed the glass of water with the roses in it on the window-ledge above the altar.

Paul followed the Mass as it proceeded; he was kneeling only two paces from the priest and his assistant. When he rose to his feet at the reading of the Gospel they were all so strangely close together:

"At that time: Jesus stood in the midst of his disciples and saith to them: Peace be to you. It is I: fear not—"

The canon of the Mass followed: in the garland of prayers which the priest repeated, he himself participated and was as it were extinguished—like the two little candles which burnt upon the altar, but whose light was swallowed up in the sunshine. And when the priest elevated the transformed Host, the morning sun shone through the crisp, snow-white veil of the bread.

WHEN Father Auberive and Jacob had risen and the table had been cleared out and he had once more the cell and solitude around him, the glass with Fröken Alsaker's roses still stood on the window-ledge. There they stood, and it seemed possible to imagine that they had a kind of consciousness and shared a knowledge of timeless marvels beyond time and matter.

NEXT day he was again summoned to appear in the magistrate's court, and Hauan came down to accompany him. This time a number of witnesses would be examined, said Hauan.

"There is something I must tell you," said Arnt Hauan as they drove. "The little boy, Johannes—he died yesterday morning. I know you were fond of him, so it is hard to have to tell you this, when you have so many other things."

452

Paul asked a few questions—wanted to know details and whether Hauan knew how Björg took it. It was worst for Björg —she must be distracted enough already at this time. He had written to her two or three times and had had some little notes in reply, but there had not been much in them. He had no idea how she was really taking it—that her husband was involved in an affair of this sort, and on account of another woman. Or how she felt about staying at his mother's just now. Evi and Hans were sweet to her, she wrote.

Johannes—he was no longer "poor little Bubbe." He must have died just as Father Auberive was saying Mass in his cell.

THEN he was sitting once more with Arnt Hauan in the same big grey room, with the same painted table in front of him, and there sat Vilnes, the magistrate, and the chief constable and all the same faces, no doubt, as he had seen at the first hearing.

His former statement was read out and the accused was asked whether he had anything to add or any observation to make.

"No, sir."

Old Fröken Fosser from the telephone exchange was brought in as the first witness. She explained at great length about the calls between Linlökka and Aamot's house. Yes, she had listened in sometimes—the fact was, she had known the Selmers ever since the sons were little boys, and she remembered Fru Lövstö very well in the days when her name was Fröken Arnesen and she used to visit at Linlökka as the accused's fiancée. She rather had the impression that Fru Lövstö had renewed her acquaintance with the whole family, not the accused in particular. It was generally Doctor Selmer she talked to, her boy was a patient of his. The deceased, Lövstö, had been out several times, trying to annoy his separated wife; Herr Aamot had rung up the sheriff once or twice, and once Selmer had had to see the lady home from the station. What was more, Aamot had said to Fröken Fosser one day when they met at the baker's, that if these disagreeable scenes with her husband were repeated, he would try to get rid of the lady; it was such a nuisance with that fellow.

Paul sat with a curious feeling of being a spectator of his own fate. So this was how it looked from the outside—the kind of story one reads about in the papers, a brief report: brutal husband tried to force himself on his separated wife, with threats. Huh! one thinks, why don't the police lay a fellow like that by the heels—poor woman. The inside of the affair was always a jumble of hatred and rancour and a kind of love, and there was the impossibility of people ever getting clear of one another. How the inside had appeared to the dead man, no human being would ever know. Hauan had told him that two or three friends of the deceased had given him an excellent character: a straight man, capable, fond of his wife and children, jealous, but then the wife had been very flighty in her younger days, and the husband had been wild because she wouldn't come back to him. It was true he had not been able to support his family financially the last few years, and for a time he hadn't let his wife know where he was living. But the witnesses had heard him say that while he had money he had certainly kept his wife like a princess, and she might very well remember that now. But she was looking for a pretext to get rid of him, because she had met one of her old lovers again, and now she was being kept by him. Yes, Lövstö had been a hard liver, and he had been fond of a drop; that was so. But he had been as good a man as anybody.—

Fröken Fosser explained that on the night of the tragedy Fru Lövstö had rung up the exchange about half-past twelve and asked to be put through to the sheriff. As she got no answer there, Fröken Fosser had told her that Kastrud himself was at the golden wedding at Fosser; would Fru Lövstö like to be put through to there? Fru Lövstö had replied: "No, it's so far away; I'd rather find out if there's anybody at home at Lin-lökka." It was three quarters of an hour later, in Fröken Fosser's opinion, that the accused had put his calls through to Doctor Lund and to Fosser.

Doctor Anna Heier, assistant to Doctor Lund, was the second witness. She looked like a little girl in her short pale green frock, with a golden, waved shingle, her rather ordinary girlish face masked by a pair of big spectacles with light tortoise-shell rims. Her manner was practical and direct—and Paul did not know how it was, but he was reminded of himself as a young man, new to business and enjoying himself in the part, as he showed linoleums and gave good advice about ventilation to Trondhjem couples setting up house. But he knew very well it was perhaps no more than a fancy, if he saw some resemblance to this in Doctor Anna Heier.—

She repeated in substance her evidence as to the state of things she found on arriving at Aamot's villa on the night of the tragedy. Fru Lövstö had been very severely injured by her husband's attempted strangling and had also suffered internal injuries in the abdomen; her assailant had knelt with one knee on her stomach. It must be characterized as a regular attempt to murder.

"Then your opinion is that if the accused had not intervened, the deceased would have taken the life of his wife?"

"There can scarcely be a doubt of that in my opinion. If the accused had come only a few minutes later, it would probably have been too late."

Then, with a sudden shock, Paul heard *her* name called, and the next moment the door opened. A Red Cross sister came in supporting Lucy; Doctor Heier walked on the other side of her.

Paul looked that way, as they helped her to a seat in a bent-wood chair with arms. She had a mass of violet veiling round her head and throat; within this he saw part of her face, yellowish white with two brown spots like abrasions on the cheek-bone right up under the left eye.

After that he sat looking down at his hands, which lay before him on the yellow table. He had an attack of palpitation, so violent that he felt ill and was unable to take in much of what

was going on around him—all he made out was that she had
herself applied to give evidence, and that she had already made
two statements. These were read out. Then the magistrate asked:

"You have expressed a wish to make some additions to the
statements you made to Sheriff Kastrud and Doctor Lund?"

"Well, that is, it's all correct what I said there, but there's
something else I'd like to say." Paul thought he did not recognize her voice. "I'd like to have it written down that it was always me that began it. Selmer has only rung me up once to ask
how my boy was and once to hear if I'd got a letter from him."
She paused as though to summon up her strength. "But all the
other times it was me; that was what I wanted to ask to have
written down. He's never been to see me either at the shop or
where I live, except when I'd sent for him and asked him to
come, because I didn't know what I was to do. He—well, and
his brother too, the doctor—they were the only friends I had
that I knew it was any good asking to do anything. And I
couldn't have any idea it was going to end in my getting him
into anything like this—"

Paul felt that now she was looking at him—he looked up
for an instant, and then he fainted in his seat.

THE golden yellow evening sunlight seemed to splash through
the huge budding chestnuts, and outside the little town the narrow strip of fiord lay gloriously blue, as Paul and Hauan got
out of the car.

"I can't imagine after this," said Hauan, "that the charge
against you will be sustained in any form. Naturally, there
might be some idea of grievous bodily harm resulting in death.
—But it seems to me very unlikely that any indictment will be
made out now."

Paul sat listening with half an ear. He remembered Lucy's
look all the time, and all the time it was as though he must faint
with the pain of it. She was going to die, of that he was quite
certain, and it had been like a severing of the last filaments of a

living tissue, when they looked at each other a while ago. Now there was nothing left in his life which could not be made new and different, he knew that; but it had been like a death, when the last tie broke which bound him to his own past.

Olsen the jailer was in for a moment that evening, just as he was going to bed. He evidently noticed that Paul was shame-faced over the scene he had made by fainting in court.

"Ho, that's nothing to worry about, that isn't. You see that every day, fainting in court, let me tell you. Defendants and witnesses and prisoners—bless your heart, they faint away and take fits and all sorts.—Why, I remember when I was a recruit —the boys had to be vaccinated, there was small-pox about that time—would you believe it, they toppled over one after the other all down the ranks, great big fellows. What do you think of that now!"

Paul laughed.

"You're a kind man, Olsen. You've done what you could to comfort me all the time!"

TEN days later he was informed that no charge would be brought against him and that the order for his detention was cancelled.

Julie Selmer drove down to fetch him.

A fine spring rain was falling fast when he came out into the yard; the smell of wet earth and growing grass and sea air was so good that it was quite incomprehensible that anything could be so good. In the gardens on both sides of the little prison yard the maples were bursting into leaf—the pale green clusters of flowers were still compressed, only half out of the reddish sheaths of the buds. And the celandine which grew along the stone wall—but he had always thought celandine such a pretty plant, with its big, strong green leaves and little, golden yellow flowers.

Julie Selmer laid her hands lightly on his shoulders, and they kissed each other on the cheek, rapidly and rather bash-fully.

"What a pleasant person he seems, that jailer."

"Yes, isn't he?"

"Will you drive or shall I?" asked his mother; they were standing by her little car and the rain drummed on its hood.

"Just as you like—unless you would prefer me to drive."

"No, no, get in," said his mother with a smile.

Paul sat watching the little wiper, which clicked and clicked and cleared a segment of the wind-screen of raindrops, and at his mother's hands on the wheel. The road was pretty bad in places; the little car jumped and muddy water splashed around them. Patches of it were being mended, so that they drove over road-metal that had just been laid. Light green fields and brown plough showed through the grey mist of rain.

Julie had a lot to say—told him how they all were at home. Paul did not say much. His mother told him nothing of how she had been during this time. Nor had she said anything about it in her letters.

They were nearing Linlökka; after some moments of silence Julie said suddenly:

"Do you remember that Easter, the year Sigmund was in the first class at school and I got him home—or rather, I *didn't* get him home, I got him to the hospital with a broken leg? Hans had been sewed up and put in plaster of Paris in the Christmas holidays, and you had had your arm in a sling ever since the ski-ing at Hegghullet? I've never cared to worry you by letting you see I was anxious about you. But heavens, what an appalling thing it seemed sometimes, that I'd collected three young males! One ought not to go in for bringing boys into the world, I often thought—they're either giving you scares all the time, or if they're not the kind you need get scared about, they're not worth having.—

"You understand, Paul, that I see very well you've done nothing all through but what you were bound to do. You couldn't get out of helping her—nor could you do anything but defend her, when she was attacked. Why do you smile when I

458

say that?"

"It's almost word for word what Father Auberive said to me. As you see, there *is* a bit of common ground after all, on which you and we can meet."

HE was standing in the hall at Linlökka, taking off his hat and coat; his mother went upstairs. Björg came stealing out; so small and woebegone she looked, in a black dress—oh yes, of course, she was in mourning for Johannes. She paused for a moment—then ran up to him, threw her arms round his neck, bent his face down to hers and kissed him, crying miserably:

"Oh, Paul—oh, it's terrible that you should have gone through all this! And you who've always been so good and kind—"

He laid his arm lightly about her shoulder—it was undeniably a relief that she took it like this. So long as it lasted, anyhow. He had dreaded the meeting with his wife a good deal.

"There, Puss—don't cry like that—" and he drew her with him into the drawing-room, where Hans and Evi were waiting at the tea-table.

459

Chapter Seven

Fru Lövstö had been transferred to Our Lady's hospital, and Hans Selmer, who was attending her, thought that if no unforeseen complications supervened she might well be up in the course of a week. Fröken Alsaker told Paul that she had been to visit her several times.—Marie Alsaker had received her chief, on his reappearance at the office, as though he had been away on a business trip, and everything she spoke of seemed a matter of course.

Paul thought, perhaps it was only due to the state of his own nerves that he had had that feeling on the day he saw Lucy again in court. But in his inmost heart the certainty remained. The invisible something that had passed between them, had been death.

But of course, his having felt that something died at that moment need not necessarily mean that she was to die.

It was not altogether easy to be back again.

Helge had excused himself from going out to Linlökka the day he came home: "I'm sure to see father in town tomorrow." Paul understood. So he and his son met in church next morning and said nothing to each other till they were coming out after Mass. Helge said: "Good-morning, father,"—and then he turned his face up to be kissed, as he had always done when he was smaller. Paul thought, I shall remember that expression in the boy's eyes as long as I live—precisely because he merely divined, certain that he was never to know, how much the child

460

had lived through in these weeks, without saying a word about it to anyone but his confessor, and scarcely to him either outside the confessional, if he knew Helge aright.

Then the Prioress herself came up, beaming with cordiality, and asked him to breakfast in the Institute. Paul fancied she was a trifle more cordial even than usual.—So he and Helge breakfasted together and talked about the school, and Helge asked when the new house would be ready—and he said something about Johannes's death and funeral too. "It was a very good thing Sunnie was where she is, while it happened," said her brother in passing. "It must have been easier for her to take it in the right way in those surroundings."

The letters he had had from her—he preserved them as precious little things. But that did not prevent his agreeing with his son—it was a very good thing Sunnie had been abroad at this time.

THE lower depths of his peace of mind were not disturbed by the sensitive shyness of which he was aware every time he met an acquaintance. What he usually experienced was a rather too demonstrative friendliness. But he did not meet very many. Only now did it dawn upon him how in the course of years he had become a stranger to all his old circle. He actually knew hardly anyone in Oslo now except a few intimate friends, and his co-religionists; the latter he certainly knew very well in one way and not at all in another.

He was inclined to wince too at the thought of the new house at Vindern—that just at this time he should be moving into a populous garden-city quarter. Certain of the papers had printed a good deal about the "drama of jealousy," as they called it; his name had been mentioned in some, but not in all. He could not say that he was insensible to this. But there were other things which he felt so much more strongly now, and felt continually—or was conscious of them, for it was not sentiment but a kind of perception of clear-mindedness. And for that he thanked God.

The fifth day he was in Oslo he went up to the hospital to visit Lucy. The Sister who showed him up was Norwegian, he could hear; she introduced herself as Sister Simona. She asked him to wait outside a moment while she announced the visit to Fru Lövstö: "her throat still looks rather ugly, so she would like to put something over it."

So he had to stand outside her door for a while, till Sister Simona threw it open and let him pass; then she shut the door behind her and he was alone with Lucy, who lay with the violet veil around her face in a white bed in a room where everything was white except herself and a black crucifix with a white plaster Corpus on the wall above the bed.

She had arranged the violet veil over her head as in the pictures of the Virgin Mary, but she held it gathered tightly under her chin with her yellow left hand, and her face within the veil was yellow and waxen; on the cheek-bone red scars of the abrasions could still be seen. Her eyes seemed twice as large as before and at the same time darker and clearer.

"You're getting on pretty well now, so Hans tells me?" he inquired, as he took a chair by the side of her bed.

"Yes, he says so. And I am doing pretty well, I think; but still I don't quite know. I can't explain how it is, Paul, but it's just as if I could feel it in me that I'm going to die after all."

He knew that she was right, but still he said: "You mustn't think like that—"

"I'm bound to think of it, you see, because I have to think of what's to become of my children. I'm not very sorry about it except when I think of them—especially when they've been here to see me. Do you think it's too much, Paul, if I ask you to keep an eye on them and help them, if you can?"

"No, Lucy." He had already thought of it. "You may be sure I shall do what I can for your children. It's partly my fault too if they're left alone in the world now. But just for that reason I would rather they didn't see me—for the present, at all

events; that man was their father after all.—Now there's a
friend of mine who is willing to take them into his house; he has
just been appointed manager of the Björkedalsfos power station and he will be glad to take Roy and Eva Marie with him
when he moves up there next month. Then you can go and fetch
them when you're well enough," he added rapidly, realizing that
he had spoken as if the contrary were certain.

"But if I don't get well, will he keep them?"

"I'm sure they will; they have no children of their own.
There's only this, Lucy, that they'll be under strong Catholic
influence; both he and his wife are very good Catholics. He's
a son of those Gotaas's, you remember, the people I lived with in
Schwensens-gate when we first got to know each other—"

"Oh, I see. Well, no, I haven't any objection to these Catholic ways any more. You're one. And so is Fröken Alsaker. And
one of the nuns here that came to see me—only fancy, she told
me she'd been with us for a trip in the Nordmark in old days.
She was here with your boy. What a nice, manly boy he is—I
thought it was such fun meeting him. And then one of their
priests has been here to see me a few times. Father Falk. And I
must say I thought he was a really nice, civil young man."

Paul couldn't help laughing. It was so comic to hear Father
Hotspur spoken of as a nice, civil young man.

"Do you think that's so strange? Well, but you know, I
haven't always been as I ought. And I'm afraid I've got quite
away from religion and that. For you know, I was brought up to
be very religious. But when they turned me out of my home the
way they did, though I hadn't done the least thing wrong—.
They had a place here in town, the Friends we belonged to; but
I knew very well that of course they'd have heard all that about
me, which wasn't even true, and so I never went to any meeting
there—"

Paul gave the hand that he was holding a little squeeze.
For that matter he had had the impression at the time that Lucy
probably regarded the God of her fathers as something like a

local divinity for Skiringssal.

"Well, but don't you think too," she asked timidly, "that I'd better try and think a little about God now—in case I should be going to die? Now that you've turned religious yourself, you must agree with me there?"

Paul sat looking down at the sallow face and the clear eyes which looked up into his. God—He judges none for what they do not know and understand. In a way he had never been so struck with her beauty as now, when there was only a remnant of it left, but her soul seemed to shine through it—a sort of vegetative soul which had been ravaged by good and evil without her having any clear knowledge of what was what—

"Those things that papa and the people at home were always talking about—the blood of the Lamb and all that, you know—why, Father Falk told me you believe in that too?"

"Yes, we do."

"Even the—more educated and intelligent among you?"

"All." He said quietly: "Last autumn, when I was in England, I confessed to a priest in Newcastle. He had been all through the war. He said to me, if death should come upon me suddenly, so that I had no time to prepare myself, I should only resign myself into God's hands and say: 'My God, when I think of Thine infinite perfection and of my own infinite imperfection, I am so sorrowful, so sorrowful, so sorrowful—' "

"Fancy, I think that was awfully nice," said Lucy, slightly stirred. "Yes, that was the impression I got too, from what Father Falk said.—But look here, if Roy and Eva Marie turn Catholic, they won't have such a strict time as I had when I was a child, will they? Not allowed to do a blessed thing?"

Paul laughed quietly:

"No. Eva Marie shall be taught to dance and Roy to play the piano, I can promise you that."

"Then you don't think it's sinful? But it seems to me the nuns here are kept so strictly. I say—what if your little girl should turn nun?"

"Sunnie was very fond of dancing. But she thought more of other things. If she is led to turn away from dancing and the like, she does so of her own choice."

Lucy gave a long sigh of relief, and Paul had a distinct feeling that a weight was taken off her—no doubt she had felt it her duty to say something to him about God and religion, since she lay here and was perhaps to die.—But now it was safely over.

"Paul, you must have had a terrible time over this," she whispered, and now her voice had quite a different sound, warmer and more natural.

"No, I hadn't." He smiled faintly, and again he squeezed her hand.

"You may be sure I thought about you!"

"Did you?"

"Yes—did you think about me? You weren't angry with me, were you?"

He shook his head: "No. I hope I thought nothing but well of you."

"I say." Her eyes wandered over the pale room which whitened all the light about them. "There's something I want to tell you." She took his hand and without looking at him laid it on her bosom and pressed it down, so that he felt a little hard object lying in the hollow of her breast. He guessed at once that it was an Agnus Dei or a medal which one of the Sisters had got her to wear.

"Do you remember one night when I was with you in Munkedams-vei? It was so frightfully cold that you had to get up in the middle of the night and go into the other room to light the stove. And then you found something amongst the coke which we thought so queer, because we couldn't make out how it had got there—two of those little sample bottles that had had eau de Cologne in them, and they were tied together with a bit of ribbon. So we each took one and were going to keep them for always. Do you remember that?"

Now that she spoke of it he seemed to remember something

465

of the sort. It was one of those things which seem utterly idiotic when you recall them next morning in broad daylight; he had an idea that he had thrown his little bottle into the stove.—Lucy went on:

"I've kept mine always. I tied a ribbon on to it and then I used always to wear it when I was really hopeless and thought there was never anything but trouble for me in this world—then I put it round my neck and thought of that time."

A moment after Sister Simona came in with the dinner tray, and Paul left.

HE rang up the hospital every day and asked how she was. One afternoon a few days later the answer was that Fru Lövstö was not so well, but he did not get the impression that it was specially serious. But next morning Hans came up to his office and told him that she had died an hour ago. The symptoms pointed to an affection of the brain. Whether this had any connection with the injuries she had received, it was impossible to say for certain, without holding a post mortem, but there was no occasion for that.

Hans sat there for a while, chiefly no doubt in order to satisfy himself that his brother took it calmly and was not going to do anything out of the way. But Paul was very calm, and when Hans Selmer had left he went up to the hospital to see the dead woman.

A DAY or two after Lucy's funeral Sister Simona came up to Paul outside the church. They talked for a few moments of Fru Lövstö's illness, and then the Sister gave him a little packet from her. Paul opened it; it was the little scent-bottle; a long light-blue silk ribbon was tied round it. He put it in his pocket for the time being.

That evening when he was up at the new house, trying to find a place in the little rooms for all the pieces of furniture that Björg refused to part with, he remembered the little bottle. He

took it out; the ribbon had become entangled in his rosary, and
he unravelled them and looked for a moment at Lucy's farewell
greeting. It smelt of the perfume she had used of late—"Œillet
blanc" was printed on the little shiny label that was stuck on
the bottle.

Why in the world had she hit upon *this*? he thought, with
a sad smile. Because after all it was true, naturally. It was as
true as anything in this world. Paul wound the ribbon round the
little bottle and stuffed it inside the white porcelain figure of
Our Lady of Lourdes which had been given him long ago by Fru
Gotaas and which he had carried with him ever since. Let her
keep it, as she has kept so many other secrets.

By the Seventeenth of May Paul and Björg were more or less
settled in the new house.

Paul had not seen a Seventeenth of May in Oslo since 1905,
he reflected—in 1906 he was at the Guards' camp. It was lovely
weather—he stood at the door of the veranda looking out while
waiting for Björg to get ready. Round about the bright little
villas were closely packed, with newly planted gardens bursting
into leaf; the morning sunshine had a grey glint from all the
broken slate roofs, and all the flags hung limp and still in the
still, summer-like air. Along all the little roads of the villa
quarter people were making for town, parents in their best
with bows of the national colours, little children in white with
little flags in their hands. The bigger children who were to walk
in the procession had gone in some time ago.

The telephone rang in the sitting-room.

"This is the Institute—is that you, Paul?" It was Sister
Marie-Halvard. "Now listen; Fru Lund's ill and we're in a regular fix—we can't get hold of anybody to play this afternoon,
when the children are to dance folk-dances. So we thought of
you. If you won't do it, we have only Sister Flavia and she's
never played the Norwegian dances before."

One of those thoughts which came so easily now—as insects

crawl over one's hand when one is lying in the grass—made him hesitate for a moment. Was it a kind of demonstration of friendliness that he was to be put in the foreground at the festival this afternoon?

"You know, if you can't get anybody else I'll come. But I don't even know what pieces you want played—"

"No, of course you'd have to come three-quarters of an hour before it begins, then you could have a look at the music. In the gymnasium—" So it was arranged.

DEAR goodness, yes, it was a fine sight—the closely-packed, endless stream of little red-blue-and-white flags gliding past, carried aloft by brightly-clad children, children in white, children in national costume. The sunlight flashed on the brass instruments, which looked as if they were carried along by the stream, and the notes of the patriotic songs throbbed rhythmically beneath the hurrahs of the youngsters. So thin and sharp the little voices were, when one could distinguish them separately, as they went past whisking their flags under the green foliage of the limes. But in front and in the rear all the children's voices were merged in one shrill roar.

Julie Selmer had put her arm through Paul's. The tears poured down without ceasing over her thin brown cheeks; she did not even trouble to wipe them away. Thank God, thought her son—at any rate she won't have to see what will be the end of the world that was hers.—

Clouds of dust already hung in the air like a yellow haze. As the procession passed up the low green slopes of the Palace hill between the thick black crowds it looked like a flickering stream of red flames. Behind the yellowish façade of the Palace fine-weather clouds welled up, edged with silver, in the clear blue sky. A wild cherry-tree up in the gardens stood out white and green among the other foliage; the cherry was just coming out. The leaves of the limes along Karl Johan were delicately transparent and shone like little flames in the sunshine.

"Do you know how far one would have to go to find snow now?" Paul suddenly asked Hans. "I feel I'd like to take a run on skis this evening." A memory of former Seventeenth of Mays had flashed across him, when he had walked up Bogstad-vei with his skis over his shoulder against the stream of holiday-clad folks who were making for town. There had been times when he could put on his skis at the gate of Frogner sæter and had the whole forest almost to himself, with a silvery crust covering all the broken ground, rotten ice on the tarns and here and there a little red flag to greet him, on some hut where people were staying—

"We're going to Sigmund's this evening, have you forgotten? I'm sure mother won't like it if you don't come—"

It was true. And they were to have an early dinner with Hans and Evi in their new flat in Kirke-vei. This rather hectic revival of family gatherings was—well, it was pleasant for Björg, who had so few other opportunities of meeting people now.

Besides, they could not tell how much longer they would have their mother with them.

Björg and Evi were waving and nodding spasmodically— on the other side of the street, along which the children's procession was still streaming past, stood Ruth and Jo Braastad-lykkjen in the front rank of the dense mass of people looking on. Ruth looked charming, in some ivory-white thing, younger than when he had last seen her, thought Paul.

Braastadlykkjen had picked up Wee Jo and the boy sat astride his father's shoulders. He was a fine youngster, golden brown all over—his ring of hair, his round little face and chubby bare arms and legs, and the velvet suit he had on. Paul was reminded of the latest child-psychology with all its twaddle about fear and repressions—one would think those people had never seen a child that is left alone by the grown-ups. Wee Jo looked in front of him with an unapproachably calm and rather cross expression like a self-sufficient and not too gracious little

469

idol. From time to time the father or the mother approached
the divinity with rites of adoration.

When the crowds closed in after the passage of the procession, the Braastadlykkjens came over to speak to the other family
group. They began to stroll back together in the throng. Ruth
walked in front with Björg and Evi; handsome and imposing
she looked between the two smaller, faded women. Julie Selmer
and Hans followed with Little Erik and Helge, and last came Jo
leading Wee Jo and talking to Paul about his recent work.

In the Great Square they got hold of two taxis. Braastadlykkjen insisted on their going out to look at his fountain which
had been set up in a square in the eastern quarter. So they drove
out through the decorated streets, where the street-cars carried
flags and pennons and the stream of people surged to and from
the centre of the city. The dust of the pavement was already
thick with chocolate-wrapping and a litter of coloured tissue
paper—here and there a serpentine flew over the crowd, caught
in the trolley-wires and fluttered its motley streamers overhead.

The square with the fountain was surrounded on three
sides by new blocks of flats—long, sober-looking façades of
orange-coloured stucco with big, square windows lying flush
with the wall. Along the pavement little spherically trimmed
trees had been planted. The whole arrangement was very neat;
one seemed to see just how it had looked in the architect's drawings only the other day.

"Do you recognize the motive?" Joe asked Paul with a
laugh.

It was a group of two young bulls butting at each other,
and under their feet the white jets of water foamed out and
splashed into the octagonal basin.

Certainly it was a fine work, and Jo had reason to be
pleased, and Ruth to be both pleased and proud.—Only Paul
was thinking of the moonlight and the wild landscape and the
elfish life there had been in the lingering movements of the
beasts as they closed with one another and gave way again, and

470

the short, coal-black shadow that played about the feet of them. The group was good—and the wildness of that night scene he had in mind was not a thing that could be carved in stone and set up in a square.

They did not get away without having been out to Bestum with the Braastadlykkjens afterwards—they had now settled at home for good and had found a pretty villa with a studio in the garden. Jo was very keen on showing the things he had done and the year-old little girl, Kari, "the best thing either of us has done."—Jo and Ruth seemed very happy together; Jo had degenerated into a real model husband, said Sigmund—with a little side-slip just now and then. So all was as well as it could be, and he had many fine things to show in the studio, and afterwards they all had to have egg-flip in the pergola—a loathsome article of diet, but it seemed to be the right thing on the Seventeenth of May. They sat there chatting very cosily, while loudspeakers and gramophones and distant music filled the air with sound under the fresh green of the trees, and Björg scolded to a rather irritating extent because Helge had spilt egg-flip on his white sailor suit.

It was too late for Paul to go on to dinner with Hans and Evi. He had to ask Jo to ring up a taxi. Helge said, then he would go back at once with his father.

"So you're going to join in the dancing, Helge?" said Paul as they drove into town. "That's something new for you?"

"There's none of the other boys that's taller than Therese Nilsen," said Helge indifferently. "And it looks so idiotic when the girls are taller than the fellows they dance with. So I came in just to make up."

THE school gymnasium was decked with flags and two Sisters and a caretaker were arranging the rows of chairs. Helge instantly volunteered to help. Paul sat down at the piano and began looking through the music, and then Sister Marie-Halvard came and gave him the programme.

"*Tosten og staven* comes first. Well, you see, the pro-gramme's not so original that you'll need very much prepara-tion."

Paul tried over the accompaniment to *Tosten og staven.*

"What made you think of asking *me,* by the way? Was it you?"

"No, it was our Mother. You know, you were such a bril-liant success with the music for 'Saint Cecilia' a few years ago. —You didn't mind our asking you, I hope?" she asked quickly. "You weren't going anywhere else? Helge said you were com-ing to the festival."

"Yes, that is what I intended—" He twisted this way and that on the piano-stool. "That is—to tell the truth I felt more inclined to take a long ski-run—a couple of days perhaps— alone, through the Nordmark. Or over in your country, Sister Marie-Randi!"

"But can't you do that? Take a couple of days off. There ought to be good going still on the shady slopes in the forest. And do you know—when there's snow on the north side and spring on the south, it's fine!"

He had slipped into saying Sister Marie-Randi instead of Marie-Halvard, and suddenly he noticed that they were on the familiar terms of old days.

"I suppose you never get out for any trips now, Sister Marie-Halvard?"

"Twice to Tryvandet with my class and once to Troldvand, that's the farthest I've been since I came home from France." She looked at him, and slowly the blush spread over her clear, freckled skin. In spite of the white head-band and the black veil she was all at once very like the Randi Alme of old days.

"You see, Paul, we haven't so very much time for dwelling on the past. But that's a small matter—that we haven't time. The great matter is, that we still have with us all there was of good in our old life, only that we possess it in a new way—all the past that is worth continuing to possess." She laughed softly.

"Even one's habits, good and bad—I don't mean simply that they continue to stick to one like a plague, a daily reminder of one's own imperfection. As for instance when I notice how difficult it is for me to be fond of those of my sisters whom I don't particularly like. But what I mean is that those things about us which are a part of ourselves and used to be our faults —we find that they are still a part of our being, but they're transformed into something else, which"—she made a gesture with her hands—"forms the outline of us. In such a way that we understand we shall continue to be ourselves for all eternity. As it says in the office for the dead: 'In my flesh I shall see God my Saviour. Whom I myself shall see, and my eyes shall behold; and not another.' " She changed her tone again, laughing but with a face as red as a berry. "As for instance—you know I was always a terrible one for preaching and jabbering. Now I have no time for that, nor am I allowed. But it has been turned inwards. Do you understand what I mean?"

Paul looked at her seriously:

"Yes. I understand what you mean. I believe."

She blushed again:

"So we may say, as your great-uncle St. Paul used to put it: 'Thy grace is sufficient for me.' "

A fleeting smile replied to hers:

"That too I have begun to understand. Now."

At that moment Sister Ilga came up, the little German Sister who was always laughing. She was laughing now: "Oh, Sister Marie-Halvard, you must come—" she whispered; some catastrophe or other had occurred in the boys' dressing-room.

Sister Marie-Halvard laughed and clapped her hands together—then she nodded to Paul and ran. Paul turned back to the music, looking for the next number on the programme.

A NOTE ON THE TYPE IN WHICH THIS BOOK IS SET

This book is composed on the Linotype in Bodoni, so-called after Giambattista Bodoni (1740–1813), son of a printer of Piedmont. After gaining experience and fame as superintendent of the Press of the Propaganda in Rome, Bodoni became in 1766 the head of the ducal printing house at Parma, which he soon made the foremost of its kind in Europe. His Manuale Tipografico, completed by his widow in 1818, contains 279 pages of specimens of types, including alphabets of about thirty foreign languages. His editions of Greek, Latin, Italian, and French classics, especially his Homer, are celebrated for their typography. In type-designing he was an innovator, making his new faces rounder, wider, and lighter, with greater openness and delicacy. His types were rather too rigidly perfect in detail, the thick lines contrasting sharply with the thin wiry lines. It was this feature, doubtless, that caused William Morris's condemnation of the Bodoni types as "swelteringly hideous." Bodoni Book, as reproduced by the Linotype Company, is a modern version based, not upon any one of Bodoni's fonts, but upon a composite conception of the Bodoni manner, designed to avoid the details stigmatized as bad by typographical experts and to secure the pleasing and effective results of which the Bodoni types are capable.

THE TITLE PAGE AND BINDING ARE AFTER DESIGNS BY W. A. DWIGGINS. THE BOOK WAS COMPOSED AND PRINTED BY VAIL-BALLOU PRESS, INC., BINGHAMTON, N. Y., AND BOUND BY H. WOLFF ESTATE, NEW YORK. THE PAPER WAS MADE BY S. D. WARREN CO., BOSTON.

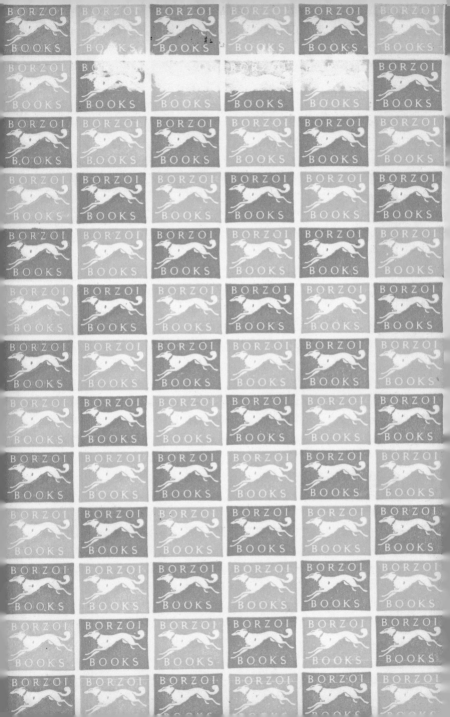